"A Tidal Wave of Encouragement"

"A Tidal Wave of Encouragement"

American Composers' Concerts in the Gilded Age

E. Douglas Bomberger

Westport, Connecticut
London

Library of Congress Cataloging-in-Publication Data

Bomberger, E. Douglas, 1958–
 "A tidal wave of encouragement": American composers' concerts in the Gilded Age / E. Douglas Bomberger.
  p. cm.
 Includes bibliographical references and index.
 ISBN 0-275-97446-4 (alk. paper)
  1. Concerts—United States—History—1865–1898. 2. Music—United States—19th century—History and criticism. 3. Nationalism in music. I. Title: American composers' concerts in the Gilded Age. II. Title.
 ML200.4 .B66   2002
 780′.78′7309034—dc21   2001034583

British Library Cataloguing in Publication Data is available.

Library of Congress Catalog Card Number: 2001034583
ISBN: 0-275-97446-4

First published in 2002

Praeger Publishers, 88 Post Road West, Westport, CT 06881
An imprint of Greenwood Publishing Group, Inc.
www.praeger.com

Printed in the United States of America

The paper used in this book complies with the
Permanent Paper Standard issued by the National
Information Standards Organization (Z39.48–1984).

10 9 8 7 6 5 4 3 2 1

Copyright Acknowledgments

The author and publisher gratefully acknowledge permission for use of the following:

Chapter 2, "The MTNA Concerts, 1884–1888: An Idea Whose Time Had Come," and Chapter 7, "The MTNA Concerts, 1889–1892: An Idea Whose Time Was Past," are modified versions of "When American Music Was King of MTNA," by E. Douglas Bomberger, in *American Music Teacher* 49/3 (December 1999/January 2000) and 49/4 (February/March 2000). With permission of the Music Teachers National Association, Inc.

To Joseph and Matthew, my all-American sons

Contents

Acknowledgments

This project developed over an extended period of time, and I am indebted to the persons who have helped me refine the ideas found in the following pages. My colleagues at the University of Hawai'i, Lesley A. Wright and Dale E. Hall, read and commented on portions of the manuscript as it evolved. Donald Reid Womack offered valuable advice from the composer's perspective. My parents, James and Doris Bomberger, also read the manuscript repeatedly. I was grateful for the opportunity to present preliminary papers on the Arens tour and the New York Manuscript Society at meetings of the Society for American Music and to publish abbreviated versions of the chapters on the Music Teachers' National Association (MTNA) concerts in *American Music Teacher*.

An archival study of this scope involved the assistance and cooperation of staff members at numerous libraries and archives. First and foremost were Wilma Wilkie of the Interlibrary Loan department of the University of Hawai'i libraries and Gregg Geary of the University of Hawai'i Music Library, who made countless resources available to me in Hawai'i. I am also grateful to the staff members of the Staatsbibliothek zu Berlin—preußischer Kulturbesitz, the Oesterreichische Nationalbibliothek and Gesellschaft der Musikfreunde in Vienna, the Sächsische Landesbibliothek in Dresden, the Herzogin Anna Amalia Bibliothek and Thüringisches Hauptstaatsarchiv in Weimar, the Universitätsbibliothek in Leipzig, the Bibliothek der Hansestadt Lübeck, the Staats- und Universitätsbibliothek in Hamburg, the Schlossmuseum in Sondershausen, the Bibliothèque nationale and Bibliothèque de l'Opéra in Paris, the Library of Congress in Washington, the Free Library of Philadelphia, the New York Public Library, the Boston Public Library, and the Newberry Library in Chicago for opening their collections to me. In particular, I wish to thank Dr. Ludwig

Müller of the Sächsische Landesbibliothek, Dr. Otto Biba of the Gesellschaft der Musikfreunde, and Wayne Shirley of the Library of Congress, who went well beyond their roles as librarians in generously sharing their musicological expertise.

In the preparation of the manuscript, Nina Duprey and the rest of the staff at Greenwood Press provided expert advice and assistance. If the printer's devil has worked his mischief, I accept full responsibility for any undiscovered errors.

Research for this book was aided materially by generous grants from the Research Relations Fund and Humanities Endowment Fund at the University of Hawai'i for travel to Germany and Austria in the summer of 1995, a grant from the Hung Wo and Elizabeth Lau Ching Foundation for travel to Paris in the summer of 1997, and a second grant from the Research Relations Fund for travel to New York and Washington in the summer of 1998. The university also granted a sabbatical leave in the fall of 2000 that enabled me to complete the manuscript.

Finally, I am indebted to my wife, Teresa, and sons, Joseph and Matthew, for their patience and support during the seven years necessary to complete this book. Their cheerful willingness to allow me to leave home for lengthy research trips and to give up the family computer indefinitely qualifies them as patrons of American music.

Abbreviations

ACCA	American Composers' Choral Association
IMTA	Illinois Music Teachers' Association
MMS	Manuscript Music Society (Philadelphia)
MSC	Manuscript Society of Chicago
MSNY	Manuscript Society of New York
MTA	Music Teachers' Association
MTNA	Music Teachers' National Association
NYMTA	New York Music Teachers' Association
OMTA	Ohio Music Teachers' Association
AAJ	*American Art Journal*
BET	*Boston Evening Transcript*
BMH	*Boston Musical Herald*
BMW	*Brainard's Musical World*
MC	*The Musical Courier*
NYT	*New York Times*

Introduction

A tidal wave of encouragement is sweeping over the land, and
will assuredly bear upon its crest some native talent capable of
and anxious to do honor to his profession and native land.
—Wilson G. Smith, 1888[1]

The history of American art music has been characterized by an ongoing struggle
for recognition. Owing to the unique evolution of musical life in the United
States, American composers of art music—except during portions of the twentieth century— have been marginalized by the society in which they lived. The
roots of this marginalization may be found in nineteenth-century America, when
there was a growing rift between two musical cultures: one promoting European
cultivated music and the other preferring (mostly American) vernacular music.
Neither of these cultures had a natural interest in art music by American composers, and, in fact, it could be argued that each viewed it with distrust. Proponents of popular music viewed American art music as pretentious and
"highfalutin," while advocates of classical music were busy promoting the masterworks of the European canon and secretly suspicious that the American variety
would not measure up to that lofty standard. American composers in the late
nineteenth century, then, faced not only the normal disappointments and strug-
gles that challenge any young composer but also a society that was predisposed
to ignore, trivialize, or deprecate their works.

In an effort to show support for the beleaguered American composer, the
Music Teachers' National Association (MTNA) presented a concert of American
piano works at its 1884 convention in Cleveland. The time was right for such
an effort, and for the next decade, American Composers' Concerts swept the nation in what Ohio composer Wilson G. Smith called "a tidal wave of encouragement." The tidal wave, or tsunami, as it is now called by oceanographers,
turned out to be an appropriate metaphor for the movement. This rare, but devastating, natural phenomenon typically begins with an undersea earthquake.
The resulting disturbance of the water generates a wave or waves that spread out

across the ocean as do the waves on a pond. These waves are amplified as they
cover thousands of miles of open ocean at speeds nearing 500 miles per hour.
When the waves finally reach a distant shore, their size and power are capable of
massive devastation. Wilson's use of the tsunami to symbolize the American
Composers' Concert movement was insightful, as it rose rapidly to unprecedented heights and then faded just as rapidly, leaving behind a changed landscape.

The American Composers' Concert movement aimed not only to make
audiences aware of the American art music that had already been composed but
also to create a climate hospitable to the development of a distinctive American
school of composition and the fostering of an American compositional genius if
and when one appeared. The movement eventually petered out in the 1890s, as
interest shifted from the promotion of American music to the inherent nature of
that music—a shift that took its inspiration from Antonín Dvořák's interest in
African American and Native American musics as source materials for art music.
The movement per se lost its momentum, but the idea of performing an entire
concert of American music has been revived periodically ever since.

The American Composers' Concert movement took place in an era of trade
protectionism in the United States and also coincided with a period of intense
missionary work by American Protestant denominations. The promoters of
these concerts borrowed practices and attitudes from both of these concurrent
trends in American society, a fact that had a significant impact on the development and eventual demise of the movement.

Historians have identified the period from 1886 to 1903 as the Missionary
Awakening, or Third Great Awakening. Like the previous awakenings of
American history, this one saw a renewed interest in spirituality accompanied by
major social upheavals. The special characteristic of the third awakening was
concern for the underprivileged of the United States and the unconverted of the
rest of the world. During the last two decades of the century, missionary activity expanded dramatically, as a small army of American Protestant missionaries
traveled to the most remote corners of the earth to win converts. At the same
time, social problems engendered by rapid industrialization and the unequal
distribution of wealth gave birth to a new strain of liberal Christianity dubbed
the "social gospel." Growing rapidly from 1880 to 1900, this new theological
perspective provided an alternative to what proponents viewed as the complacency of orthodox Christianity and shifted the emphasis of faith to a social activ-
ism that fed the poor and advocated improved working conditions. Proponents
of the social gospel took their missionary zeal to America's urban slums rather
than to foreign countries. Even outside the church, social reform was the order
of the day as youthful protesters fomented tens of thousands of strikes, and
muckraking journalists exposed the corruption of American industry and politics.

The American Composers' Concert movement likewise began as an effort to
help an underprivileged group that had been oppressed by unfair competition. In
the early years of the movement, the rhetoric of advocacy painted American
composers as helpless victims of a system that privileged foreign composers.
American concerts were presented as a means to right the injustices of previous
practice and lift the impoverished composers to a position of respectability. As

the movement proceeded, it became less believable to characterize American composers as "underprivileged," and, in fact, the correlation of American Composers' Concerts with trade protectionism became more typical.

The movement for the encouragement of American composers took place against the backdrop of a larger national debate over trade protectionism. Free trade had been an ideal espoused and protected by southern Democrats before the Civil War, when tariffs on imported goods were kept at historic lows despite the efforts of Northern Republicans to raise them. With the outbreak of the Civil War, the Republican Congress was able to increase tariffs as an emergency measure to raise funds to fight the war. During Reconstruction, tariffs remained generally high, contributing to the prosperity of manufacturers and creating a federal budget surplus by the 1880s. Critics of high tariffs claimed that the policy had reduced competition from foreign markets, thereby allowing American manufacturers to form monopolies and trusts to inflate prices; proponents who could no longer argue that the government needed to raise funds through tariffs claimed that protectionist policies helped keep wages high for American workers.

On December 5, 1887, Grover Cleveland, the first Democratic president of the postwar era, delivered a fiery message to Congress advocating a reduction in tariffs. In response to his call to arms, Roger Q. Mills, Democratic chairman of the House Ways and Means Committee, fashioned a bill instituting modest tariff reform that was introduced in the spring of 1888. The Mills bill focused the Congress and the nation on trade protectionism as never before, taking up 240 hours of congressional time, the longest debate of any bill in U.S. history to that time.[2] The bill was passed by the House of Representatives in a strict party vote on July 21 but subsequently weakened by Senate Republicans in the fall. By this time, though, the tariff issue was dominating the presidential election of 1888. Cleveland stood by his previous statement on tariff reduction and did little campaigning. Republican Benjamin Harrison and his supporters portrayed high tariffs as essential to maintaining American standards of living and stemming the onslaught of cheap labor from Europe. In a very close election in November, Harrison lost the popular vote but won the electoral vote.

The Republicans took their victory as a mandate for high tariffs, and new House Ways and Means chairman William McKinley pushed through a new tariff bill that raised tariffs significantly. The McKinley bill was viewed with outrage in Europe and was considered a blow to all but the wealthiest manufacturers in the United States. In the 1890 congressional elections the Republicans were decisively defeated, and two years later Harrison lost the presidency to his erstwhile rival Cleveland. As the nation slipped into a depression in the 1890s and attention shifted to the money issue, the Democrats were unable to repeal the high tariffs. The Republicans came back into power in 1894 and 1896, when they again succeeded in raising tariffs through the Dingley Act of 1897.

Joanne Reitano has argued convincingly that the "Great Debate" over trade protectionism was central to American politics in the late 1880s. The question of which industries should be protected from foreign competition and to what extent they should be supported was not merely academic but a matter of serious consideration by the public and press. Traditional economic policy had advocated protection of "infant industries," but the question of when an industry no longer needed protection was crucial in an era of rapid industrial growth. The American Composers' Concert movement was clearly an example of protecting an "infant industry," but the debate over it, like the debate over tariffs, revolved around the question of how long it was appropriate to continue such protection.

The story of this movement is an intriguing chapter in American musical history, in terms of both the large amount of music that resulted from these promotional efforts and the issues that it raised about attempting to mold public taste through protectionist measures. For the purposes of this study, I have chosen not to consider concerts devoted to the works of a single composer, for the simple reasons that these concerts have been common throughout the history of Western music and that they often involve issues of personal promotion that were less evident in the American Composers' Concert movement. The concerts to be discussed featured miscellaneous programs of the works of several composers who had only their American background in common. Typically, these concerts were billed as being restricted to works by "native or resident composers," to allow the inclusion not only of persons born on American soil but of those who had immigrated to the United States, no matter how recently.

This study is designed to provide both a detailed history of the movement and a consideration of the critical response to the idea of all-American concerts. The novelty of the idea in the mid-1880s resulted in such enthusiasm that few critics expressed any reservations whatsoever about the movement. By the late 1880s critics dealt with such musical patriotism more thoughtfully, raising questions and objections about the concerts and the music heard. Finally, by the 1890s the critical tide turned against the movement, forcing promoters into a defensive posture that eventually spelled the end of the movement.

Organized more or less chronologically, this book traces the most important concerts and concert series in separate chapters. The first chapter is devoted to the rare all-American concerts presented before 1884, the date when Calixa Lavallée's concert at the MTNA convention in Cleveland fired the imagination of the American musical world. The second chapter traces the rise of the MTNA through ever more impressive American concerts in its annual conventions from 1884 to 1888. Chapter 3 looks at the role of the *New York Tribune*'s chief music critic Henry Krehbiel in focusing the critical debate on nationalism in American music. The fourth chapter examines the Novelty Concerts presented by Frank Van der Stucken in New York, with special emphasis on the critical reaction to his festival of five American concerts in November 1887, a turning point in the maturation of the movement. Chapter 5 deals with the American concert at the Exposition universelle of 1889, analyzing the French critical reaction in light of European stereotypes about Americans. The sixth chapter describes the movement at its height, surveying the many organizations and persons who presented such concerts in the years around 1890. Chapter 7 returns to the MTNA, tracing the rapid decline of the organization from 1889 to 1894, by which time the appeal of American Composers' Concerts had worn off. Chapter 8 looks at the concerts presented by F. X. Arens in Germany and Austria during 1891 and 1892, a time when the concerts were out of fashion in the United States but could still evoke a range of opinion from German critics. The ninth chapter examines the role in the movement of composer Edward MacDowell, who was simultaneously the most famous American composer of art music and the most vocal opponent of American Composers' Concerts. Chapter 10 is devoted to the American concerts at the World's Columbian Exposition of 1893 in Chicago, an event marred by poor planning and mismanagement of the money set aside for concerts. Chapter 11 follows the Manuscript Society of New York from its auspicious founding in 1890 through the infighting around 1900 that eventually led to its decline and fall, with consideration of the other manuscript societies in Boston, Philadelphia, and Chicago. The final chapter, in the form of an epilogue, looks at Dvořák's American sojourn in light of the decade of American concerts that had preceded his arrival in 1892. Appendix 1 presents a list of the most prominent concerts of the movement. Appendix 2 lists the programs of the five concerts presented in New York by Frank Van der Stucken in November 1887. Appendix 3 provides the repertoire and a list of known reviews of the concerts in Europe, since these reviews are likely to be less accessible to American readers. Appendix 4 lists the works performed at public meetings of the Manuscript Society of New York from 1890 to 1901. The American Composers' Concert movement inspired thousands of articles, reviews, promotional releases, and other sources; the bibliography is therefore selective rather than exhaustive.

NOTES

1. Wilson G. Smith, "American Compositions in the Class and Concert Room," *The Etude* 6/8 (August 1888): 129.

2. Joanne Reitano, *The Tariff Question in the Gilded Age: The Great Debate of 1888* (University Park: Pennsylvania State University Press, 1994), p. 18.

Prelude: All-American Concerts before 1884

A prophet is not without honor, save in his own country, and in his own house.
                                              —Matthew 13:57

Before it strikes land, a tsunami is preceded by a lowering of water levels along the coast. For those who have never witnessed the force of this natural disaster, the unusual recession of water can create a deadly complacency. Minutes before the April 1, 1946, tsunami struck the Hawaiian Islands, Hilo Bay was inexplicably drained of water, leaving mudflats where there had always been ocean. Curious residents walked out to see fish flopping on the ground, only to be inundated moments later. One hundred fifty-nine people died that day, including sixteen schoolchildren and five of their teachers at the coastal town of Laupahoehoe, serving as an object lesson for Hawaiian children to the present day.[1] In a similar fashion, the American Composers' Concert movement was preceded by a low ebb of interest in concerts of American art music, making the following deluge seem even greater by comparison. Indeed, the movement was primarily precipitated by the indignation of those who believed that American composers were being unfairly ignored by performers and audiences. The heights to which the movement rose in the 1880s and 1890s were inversely proportional to the depths from which it had risen in the preceding decades.

When it comes to the art music of their countrymen, Americans have remarkably short memories. As each new generation takes up the cudgel in defense of American composers, they forget—or ignore—the efforts of previous generations. Much as Howard Hanson, Aaron Copland, and their compatriots saw themselves as pioneers in the promotion of American art music in the 1920s and 1930s, the promoters of American Composers' Concerts of the 1880s believed that they were the first to come up with this idea. In fact, American concerts had enjoyed a brief vogue before the Civil War but had been largely absent from the American scene ever since.

The decade of the 1850s saw a significant growth in art music in the United States, owing, in part, to an influx of German immigrants and the American tours of the Germania Orchestra, Jenny Lind, Sigismund Thalberg, and other European virtuosi. At the same time, local musicians like pianist William Mason and violinist Theodore Thomas raised the standards of performance for musical soloists and ensembles. New Orleans-born Louis Moreau Gottschalk (1829–1869) established an international reputation as a pianist and composer, bringing European attention to American music for the first time.

Composers William H. Fry (1813–1864) and George F. Bristow (1825–1898) were vocal advocates for American composers. Fry used his position as music critic for the *New York Tribune* to campaign for more recognition of American music, and he engaged in a heated war of letters with Richard Storrs Willis of the *Musical World and Times* in 1853–54 over critical response to new American works. He took issue with Storrs and John Sullivan Dwight over their preference for German music at a time when he believed that American composers were coming into their own.[2] Bristow likewise felt that American composers were neglected during this era. A conductor of various ensembles and a longtime member of the violin section of the New York Philharmonic, he resigned from the orchestra during the 1853–54 season to protest its lack of performances of American works. Many of his own compositions were on American subjects, including the opera *Rip Van Winkle* (1855), the cantata *The Pioneer, or Westward Ho!* (1872), and his Arcadian (1872) and Niagara (1893) Symphonies.

In this atmosphere of musical expansion and nationalistic awareness, a group of New York musicians led by Charles Jerome Hopkins (1836–1898) founded the American Music Association for the purpose of performing concerts devoted to the works of American composers. A letter of June 16, 1855, to the editor of the *Musical World*—signed, significantly, *Justitia*—outlined Hopkins' goals, which were remarkably similar to those that would be expressed by leaders of the American Composers' Concert movement thirty years later. The group sought to counter the perception that American composers had not produced anything of lasting worth by giving good performances of the best American works available. The definition of the word "American" was characteristically broad: "It has not been considered necessary to confine the privilege of membership to native Americans, but to allow foreigners to belong thereto, provided only their principles are Republican, and their aim be, in common with us, the production of native art." The fundamental idea behind the organization was the notion that American composers needed only a fair opportunity to have their works heard in order to win respect and acceptance. The letter concluded:

We think it will only be necessary for it to be generally known that there is now a chance for all young Americans who desire to distinguish themselves by musical composition to have their labors rewarded by a fair trial and impartial criticism, to secure the good will and cooperation of many individuals who otherwise would be disposed to throw a bucket of cold water upon the embryo idea of such a thing. But to all those who object to it on the ground that American music is not good music, it is unclassical, plagiaristic, or unfit to be compared with German productions, we would say, "Give it a fair trial." If Americans do not know how to compose now, it does not follow that they never *will* know how.[3]

Not for the last time in American history, the idealistic members of this group discovered that merely providing a "fair trial and impartial criticism" did not guarantee the acceptance of American art music. The society presented three concerts in the winter and spring of 1856, four concerts the following season, and three in its third season before disbanding. Though critics were generally supportive of the goals of the society, complaints about the concerts increased over the group's three-year history. Henry C. Watson of *Leslie's* objected after the second season to the selection process for new works. Theodore Hagen of the *New-York Musical Review and Gazette*, a critic who had recently arrived from Germany, where he had been a well-known writer on musical topics and contributor to the *Neue Zeitschrift für Musik*, repeatedly called for the organization to broaden its scope beyond purely American works. Willis was supportive of the organization but objected to the five-dollar fee required of each composer who submitted a manuscript.[4]

Despite the participation of Gottschalk, Fry, Bristow, and William Mason, the group could not be sustained beyond its third season. *Dwight's Journal of Music* credited the demise of the organization to the financial panic of 1857,[5] but the effort to give American composers a hearing required a significant amount of administration, and its failure may also have been due to the fact that most of the work fell on the shoulders of one man. As Willis noted after the second season: "'Jerome' is the President of the Society; or rather he is the Vice-President, Financier, all the Directors, Agent, and almost Door-keeper and Type-setter of the programmes—in short, he is the Society itself. He started it, keeps it in a state of active vitality, lives in it and for it; in a very close sense he is engaged to it, and one of these days, for aught we see to prevent, will marry it."[6] Though his pet project foundered after three seasons, Hopkins remained active in music until his death in 1898, becoming increasingly eccentric in old age. His letters to the editors of *The Musical Courier* provided amusement throughout the 1880s, as he repeatedly aired his individualistic opinions and touted his concerts and compositions.[7]

After the dissolution of the American Music Society, all-American concerts were a rarity. The society had proved that there was already sufficient music available in the late 1850s to sustain a concert series, but the perception persisted that American composers were in such a fledgling state that they had not yet produced an evening's worth of significant music. This notion became increasingly untenable in the 1860s and 1870s, as two young composers rose to prominence and established new career patterns for American musicians.

John Knowles Paine (1839–1906) was a native of Portland, Maine. He spent the years 1858–1861 in Berlin, studying organ and composition with Karl

August Haupt and others. Upon his return to the United States he settled in Boston, where he was appointed instructor of music at Harvard in 1862, eventually earning the honor of the first professorship in music at that tradition-bound institution in 1875. The appointment of a composer to an academic position and, indeed, the inclusion of a department of music in a university were new ideas in America at this time. Some of the members of the Harvard faculty felt that music had no place in an academic setting, being more appropriate for a conservatory. The high standards of Paine had much to do with changing that view, and by the turn of the twentieth century, nearly every major American university had a music department, led in many cases by a composer.

In part because of his prestigious position at Harvard, Paine enjoyed an unusual amount of success as a composer. His first and second symphonies were hailed as the equal of contemporary European works, and by the time of the American Composers' Concert movement, he was regarded as the senior statesman of American art music. He was perhaps the only composer of the era whose works were performed frequently before the advent of American Composers' Concerts. As such he was a model and an inspiration to his struggling younger colleagues.

Paine's compositional ideals were also influential. He believed that the best models for American composers of art music were the German masters from Haydn to his own day. He believed that the United States was essentially a European nation and that close connections to Europe were crucial for progress in art music. Recognizing the importance of European approval as a prelude to acceptance in the United States, he premiered his monumental Mass in D (1867) in Berlin, before a receptive audience that included members of the Prussian and British royal families. He made no apologies for composing in a cosmopolitan style rather than the nationalistic style of his contemporaries Gottschalk and Stephen Foster, urging his students to do likewise. His widely publicized views on the desirability of the cosmopolitan style were profoundly influential on his contemporaries, dominating the entire era of the American Composers' Concerts.

Dudley Buck (1839–1909) was also a composer and organist who studied in Germany, but, unlike Paine, he spent most of his career as a church musician rather than an academic. He was in Germany at approximately the same time as Paine, studying in Leipzig, Dresden, and Paris. He also returned to the United States during the Civil War, starting his professional career in his hometown of Hartford, Connecticut, moving on to Chicago and Boston, and eventually settling in Brooklyn in 1875. Except for a brief stint at the New England Conservatory in the early 1870s, he devoted his principal energies to composing, conducting, and organ playing.

As music director at the Church of the Holy Trinity in Brooklyn, one of the country's most prominent churches, he enjoyed a position of respect in sacred music circles. While there he published numerous organ works and sacred choral works. His chief contributions to art music, though, were in the genre of the secular cantata. In particular, *The Voyage of Columbus* (1885) and *The Light of Asia* (1886) were timed perfectly to capitalize on the popularity of American Composers' concerts. His rousing *Festival Overture on the Star-Spangled Banner* for orchestra (1879) was heard repeatedly during the era. Like Paine, he cultivated a style that was more cosmopolitan than nationalistic, recognizing that conservative American audiences felt most comfortable with the familiar sounds of European music.

If Paine and Buck achieved a modicum of success in postwar America, they were exceptions to the rule. In general, concerts of art music were dominated by European music, as conductors like Theodore Thomas pursued an agenda of introducing American audiences to the classic European repertoire. With no international copyright law in place, American publishers found it cheaper to pirate European works than to pay royalties to American composers. The American works that did find publishers were mostly light music or in the easily performable genres of songs, choral works, and piano compositions. Larger vocal works were occasionally published, but it was not until 1881 that the first American symphony (Paine's second) was published.

In this climate, the performance of an entire evening of American music was a rarity. The American centennial celebration of 1876 would seem to have presented an ideal opportunity for this sort of patriotic concert, but that was not the case. For the opening ceremonies in Philadelphia, Theodore Thomas commissioned works from both Paine and Buck, but these were overshadowed by the infamous *Centennial March* commissioned from Richard Wagner and performed on the same occasion.[8]

The following spring brought a pair of performances that were the best-publicized concerts of American art music before Lavallée's 1884 recital. Annette Essipoff (1851–1914), the brilliant Russian piano virtuosa, made her first tour of the United States in 1876–1877. Near the conclusion of her tour, she performed all-American recitals in New York (May 5) and Boston (May 12). In both cases she placed the American program prominently on Saturday evening after a week of mixed recitals, and she was reported to have dressed the stage with red, white, and blue decorations. The programs consisted entirely of short, brilliant compositions that showcased her virtuoso technique.[9] All those represented were living composers with the exception of Louis Moreau Gottschalk, and Essipoff took the opportunity to program several works by William H. Sherwood (1854–1911), a young pianist who had recently returned to Boston after studying in Germany.

Despite her best efforts to create auspicious events, the critics were not kind in their comments on the two recitals. The reviewer for the *New York Times* called the evening "a programme of minor compositions by American musicians," going on to state:

Gottschalk, Mills, Mason, Hoffman, and other composers were represented by light parlor pieces, none of which, however, afforded much testimony in favor of America's chances as a rival of Germany or Italy. Mme. Essipoff was not at her best, either, on the occasion we write of, and in the most effective because most characteristic works chosen for performance—that is to say, in Gottschalk's—she sacrificed both accent and expression to brilliant mechanism.[10]

The critic for the *Boston Evening Transcript* called the concert "precious time wasted," adding a characteristic jab at the inadequacies of American composers: "The main thing interesting about it was to observe how the artist's genius embellished and illuminated the composition in hand, which often suffered change into something rich and strange that the composer had but dimly conceived."[11] Thus, the critics disposed of the most prominent American concerts of the decade.

All-American concerts remained a novelty in the years following, even as the works of Paine, Buck, and other younger composers gained prominence in mixed concerts. The Wellesley College of Music was inaugurated on May 30, 1881, with a concert of American art music performed by William Sherwood and the Beethoven Quartette, earning a brief paragraph in the *Transcript*.[12] Adolph Liesegang's Chicago orchestra performed concerts of works by local composers on March 27, 1881, and August 5, 1884. Theodore Thomas tried another American concert in his 1882 summer series in Chicago, to a lukewarm response:

> That "a prophet is not without honor save in his own country" has ofttimes been verified. Music, American of the classic order, seldom enlists a large portion of a programme, but that presented for the delectation of the large audience assembled at the Exposition Building last evening bore the inspiring title, "American Composers' Night." Something new and strange, even though it be replete with the charm of originality, can hardly be expected to raise a conservative audience to a furor of applause. So it was that the programme last evening, while its many excellencies were evidently appreciated, aroused but little enthusiasm. . . . The number for the finish fell to Strauss and Wagner, American by popularity.[13]

But change was already in the air. Since 1877 the country's most widely read musical journal, *Brainard's Musical World*, had been profiling American musicians with monthly biographical sketches, calling attention to a growing body of native composers and performers.[14] A new journal founded in 1880, *The Musical Courier*, had been agitating for recognition for American composers in ever stronger terms. Its editor Otto Floersheim was himself a composer, and in the December 12, 1883, issue he published a proposal for an "American Composers' Society" with the purpose of performing and publishing American works.[15] Two weeks later an unsigned article decried "The Foreign Craze" in American music and drama.[16] This growing dissatisfaction over foreign domination of art music coincided with both the missionary movement and the trade protectionist movement, which were increasingly attracting attention in America. The stage was set for a new movement that would give preference to American composers and right the wrongs of the previous decades. All that was lacking was a catalyst.

NOTES

1. Walter C. Dudley and Min Lee, *Tsunami!*, second edition (Honolulu: University of Hawai'i Press, 1998), p. 42.

2. Betty E. Chmaj, "Fry versus Dwight: American Music's Debate over Nationality," *American Music* 3/1 (Spring 1985): 63–84.

3. The entire letter is reprinted in Vera Brodsky Lawrence, *Strong on Music: Reverberations, 1850–56* (Chicago and London: University of Chicago Press, 1995), pp. 749–50.

4. Vera Brodsky Lawrence, *Strong on Music: Repercussions, 1857–1862* (Chicago and London: University of Chicago Press, 1999), pp. 74–75, 204.

5. Trovator, "Musical Correspondence," *Dwight's Journal of Music* 16/16 (January 14, 1860): 333.

6. *Musical World* (June 6, 1857), quoted in Lawrence, *Repercussions*, 74, n. 9.

7. See also Nicolas Slonimsky, "The Flamboyant Pioneer," in *A Thing or Two about Music* (New York: Allen, Towne & Heath, 1948), pp. 250–56.

8. For further information on Wagner's role in this event, see Abram Loft, "Richard Wagner, Theodore Thomas, and the American Centennial," *Musical Quarterly* 37/2 (April 1951): 184–202. According to Lawrence W. Levine, *Highbrow/Lowbrow: The Emergence of Cultural Hierarchy in America* (Cambridge: Harvard University Press, 1988), p. 118, Thomas also included an American concert in his ill-fated series of orchestral concerts at the Edwin Forrest Estate.

9. The program of the New York recital (incorrectly dated as May 15, 1877) may be found in Mrs. Crosby Adams, "American Composition in 1877," *Music* 19/4 (February 1901): 432–33. The Boston program is listed in *Dwight's Journal of Music* 37/4 (May 26, 1877): 32. Dwight was unable to attend the recital and therefore did not include a review.

10. "Amusements," *NYT*, May 7, 1877, p. 5.

11. "Musical," *BET*, May 14, 1877, p. 1.

12. "Musical: Wellesley College of Music," *BET*, May 31, 1881, p. 1.

13. "Amusements: Thomas Concert." *Chicago Inter-Ocean*, August 3, 1882; clipping without page number in Frederic Grant Gleason scrapbook, I: 164–65, Special Collections, Newberry Library, Chicago.

14. For reprints of this complete series, see *Brainard's Biographies of American Musicians*, ed. E. Douglas Bomberger (Westport, CT: Greenwood Press, 1999).

15. Otto Floersheim, "An American Composers' Society," *MC* 7/24 (December 12, 1883): 343.

16. "The Foreign Craze," *MC* 7/26 (December 26, 1883): 375.

∽ 2 ∽

The MTNA Concerts, 1884–1888:
An Idea Whose Time Had Come

> The earnestness of purpose, the intensity of feeling and the unanimity of action which characterized the chief proceedings make it manifest that the association, as a representative body, has determined upon pursuing one principal and foremost object, and that is the development of American compositions and necessarily the encouragement of American and resident composers, and the zeal and impetuosity with which this object was pursued must have evinced to every careful observer that this has become a more interesting subject than the pedagogic topic which was formerly uppermost in the proceedings of this body.
>
> —*The Musical Courier*, 1886[1]

In March 1886, when the American Composers' Concert movement was in full swing, there was a discussion in the editorial pages of *The Musical Courier* over who had originated the movement. The "Personals" column of the March 3 issue gave credit to Frank Van der Stucken as "the first one who inaugurated in this country the present movement in favor of the production of worthy works by native and resident composers."[2] Wilson G. Smith of Cleveland responded with an extended letter defending the position that "to Mr. Calixa Lavallée, of Boston, belongs the honor of being the pioneer champion of the American muse."[3] The editors concurred with this view, adding, however, that Van der Stucken had done more since that time, especially in New York. The following week brought an even longer epistle from Smith Newell Penfield, who claimed credit for being president of the MTNA at the time of the first orchestral concert of American music, believing that this gave him precedence as the pioneer of the movement.[4] In the April 14 issue, the editors of *The Musical Courier* modestly reminded readers that they had advocated American music for years and therefore

deserved some of the credit for the movement as well.[5]   The controversy
amounted to much ado about nothing, but it demonstrates two important
things. First, American Composers' Concerts were sufficiently widespread in
early 1886 to be called a movement, and second, the movement enjoyed such
support that there were numerous persons eager to claim credit for having initiated it.

It is fitting that a movement to educate American audiences about American
art music began with an educational organization. The members of the Music
Teachers' National Association recognized a need in American society, made it
their primary mission for nearly a decade, and, in so doing, inspired a movement that transcended the activities of any single group. The short, but dazzling, flirtation with concert promotion by America's oldest association of music teachers divided the membership and nearly ruined the organization. The
story of the rise and fall of the American Composers' Concert movement is inex-
tricably entwined with that of the MTNA, and so it is with this group that we
must begin.

The MTNA had been formed in Delaware, Ohio, in December 1876. The
small group of music teachers who gathered there at the invitation of Theodore
Presser, instructor at the Female Seminary of that town and later founder of one
of America's leading music publishing houses, envisioned an organization that
would bring them together on a regular basis for mutual encouragement. The
word "national" in the title was perhaps a bit presumptuous, since the list of
sixty-two charter members included forty-seven from Ohio and only six from
outside the Midwest.[6] By the early 1880s, though, the membership had grown
to several hundred members and could make a legitimate claim to being a national organization.

The constitution adopted at Delaware included the following "Object":
"*First*: Mutual improvement by interchange of ideas. *Second*: To broaden the
culture of music among us. *Third*: To cultivate fraternal feelings."[7] As the
organization grew, its principal challenge was to balance these three goals of
intellectual interchange, musical cultivation, and social interaction. Beginning
with the organizational meeting in 1876, the first goal was given precedence
through paper presentations. These ranged from philosophical musings on the
meaning of music, to practical advice on teaching techniques, and they sometimes degenerated into endorsements of products or publications in which the
presenter had a financial interest. The second goal of musical cultivation entered
the organization's agenda when the first formal concert was given by the pianist
William H. Sherwood at the 1878 convention. The concerts were expanded in
later years to include vocal and chamber music, but the organization made a
commitment at the 1882 convention in Chicago not to pay members to give
concerts, even if they were well-known artists. The "fraternal" aspect of the association was for many members the leading attraction of the conventions since
it gave them the opportunity to reestablish their ties with fellow teachers from
other parts of the country.

At the 1883 convention in Providence, Rhode Island, the MTNA, now 312
members strong, flexed its muscles and took steps toward becoming an activist
organization. The group voted to support three agendas through its own efforts
and active lobbying of government. The first was the adoption of Uniform or

International Pitch (A=435) in an effort to standardize tuning practices in the United States. Even at this late date there was not a uniform standard of pitch, which caused havoc for professional and nonprofessional musical collaborations. The MTNA was in the forefront of the drive to adopt a universal standard at this time. The second goal was to lobby for an international copyright law that would put an end to pirated editions. Because U.S. law provided no copyright protection for foreign authors, American publishers were free to publish European works without royalties or permission. This situation resulted not only in significant losses for foreigners but also in a natural bias against American composers, whose works were actually more expensive to publish than those of Europeans. The efforts of Willard Burr Jr. of the MTNA, along with numerous other lobbyists, would eventually result in a complete revision of the U.S. copyright code in 1891. The third agenda embraced by the MTNA in 1883 was "Official recognition of the American Composer," a vague goal that was to be put to the test by a concert of American works at the following year's convention in Cleveland.[8]

The first American Composers' Concert at an MTNA convention was consequently presented on the morning of Thursday, July 3, 1884. The program was listed as follows in the MTNA's annual report:

Gavotte	Arthur Foote
Mazurka	Wilson G. Smith
Sarabande and Scherzo	Stephen A. Emery
Calixa Lavallée, pianist	

Adagio, from Quartette in C minor	J. H. Beck
Movement for stringed instruments	S. G. Pratt
Schubert Quartette	

Cradle Song	John Orth
Scherzo, op. 41	William Mason
Spring Idyll	J. K. Paine
Volktanz	Louis Maas
Calixa Lavallée, pianist	

Sunset	Dudley Buck
Ave Maria	Mme. Luisa Cappiani
Nettie M. Dunlap, soprano	

Regrets and Prelude	W. H. Sherwood
Vagabond Dance	F. Dewey
Scherzino	G. W. Chadwick
Calixa Lavallée, pianist	

Three movements from the piano trio in G minor	W. W. Gilchrist

1. Scherzo.
2. Adagio.
3. Finale, vivace

Richard Zeckwer, S. E. Jacobsohn, and Charles Heydler

Romance sans paroles—The Tempest (transcription)   Carlyle Petersilea
Feu follet   Emil Liebling
Gavotte   C. L. Capen

Calixa Lavallée, pianist[9]

After this mixed concert of short piano, vocal, and chamber works by eighteen different composers, the audience of teachers responded enthusiastically and demanded an encore of one of Lavallée's own compositions. He complied with a performance of his Etude in E minor.

Calixa Lavallée (1842–1891) was well suited to the role of pioneer, with a visionary sense of what American music might become and the zeal to put his ideas into practical projects. Unlike most of his American contemporaries, Lavallée was educated in France rather than Germany, studying with Marmontel, Bazin, and Boieldieu at the Conservatoire national in Paris. An obituary credited him with "just a tinge of the Gallic in his pronunciation and no little of the Gallic impetuosity in his temperament."[10] Upon his return to Québec, he was stymied in his efforts to start a conservatory and disappointed when the government commissioned a work for a state occasion but refused to cover all his expenses.[11] He subsequently moved to Boston, and there he established his reputation as a teacher, performer, and champion of American music, becoming "an American musician in all but the accident of birth."[12] In addition to his landmark MTNA concert, he performed a series of five American piano recitals in Boston during 1885 and 1886, served as president of the MTNA in 1886/1887, and represented the United States at the conference of the Society of Professional Musicians in England in January 1888. His health declined rapidly in the late 1880s, and he died on January 21, 1891, while the movement was still at its zenith.

Lavallée's 1884 concert was not spectacular either for the originality of the compositions or for the brilliance of the performers, but it was a rare event that was so right for its time and place that it started a movement. Over the next decade, the members of the MTNA and all those concerned about the inequities facing American composers looked to this recital as a seminal event. It was a turning point in the history of the MTNA, as plans were immediately pursued to continue this practice of American recitals. The official report of the convention contains the following resolutions:

WHEREAS, The progress of musical art-creation in America has not been commensurate with the progress of the other fine arts, nor with that of the other important branches of the musical profession; and,

WHEREAS, The prevailing attitude of the general public toward American musical works, the failure of Congress to pass an international copyright law and other influences, are serious impediments to the growth of such art-creation. Therefore be it

Resolved, That we as an organization hereby agree to encourage the creation of pure musical art in America, by giving each year a recital of representative American works, and in such other ways as may be consistent with other demands upon the Association. And be it further

Resolved, That we as individuals will endeavor as far as possible to use in our recitation rooms and for public concerts, such American works as will suit our purpose, with the same freedom as we do equally meritorious works of foreign nations.[13]

The reasons for this sudden interest in American music may be found not only in the MTNA itself, whose members were eager to support their fellow professionals on Lavallée's program, but in the confluence of several significant factors in the country as a whole. The period after the Centennial in 1876 was a time of growth in the United States, with a developing sense of the "American Spirit." As noted in the Introduction, this period was characterized, among other things, by trade protectionism: government policies designed to give an advantage to fledgling American businesses in their competition with foreign producers and importers. In a sense, the American Composers' Concert movement was a form of trade protection for American composers. The feeling both in and out of the MTNA was that American composers had been unjustly neglected and that the development of a school of composition would result from the proper encouragement. In the opinion of *The Musical Courier*:

Art life has reached that stage in this country where it begins to take on the character worth conservation and support. There are a number of composers here who understand the higher forms of composition and are capable of doing work which will compare favorably with foreign compositions, and there are many more who need only to feel that their work would find appreciation and sale to cause them to make use of their talents. It would be idle to argue that Americans have little or no talent for art creation. There is not a field which Americans have earnestly cultivated in which they have not distinguished themselves or surpassed all the older nations. There are American litterateurs who rank with any foreign contemporaries; there are scientists, sculptors, painters, actors, singers, pianists and organists who compare favorably with their transatlantic brethren, and why should not the talent for musical creation be as indigenous as all these other manifestations of the artistic germ? Why should we not have creative as well as interpretive musicians? Composers as well as sculptors, painters, actors, scientists and poets? That we have not had them has been due to a variety of causes, but chief among these has been and still is, the apathy and want of encouragement on the part of the whole musical and publishing fraternity. We have not fully outgrown that snobbish, toadyistic sentiment that foreign works of art are, as a matter of course, superior to the home-grown article.[14]

These protectionist attitudes coincided with the coming-of-age of a significant group of composers who had recently completed or were nearly finished with a rigorous course of European study. Among those who finished their studies in the late 1870s were George Whitefield Chadwick, Frank Van der Stucken, and William H. Sherwood. The early 1880s brought a concentration of talent seldom seen before or since in American musical history: Johann Heinrich Beck, Arthur Bird, Arthur Foote (the only one of the group not trained in Europe), Henry Holden Huss, Edgar Stillman Kelley, Edward MacDowell, Ethelbert Nevin, Horatio Parker, and Arthur Whiting. To this list could be added Paine, Buck, and Silas G. Pratt, who were somewhat older and more established by this time. These composers shared a familiarity with European repertoire and techniques as well as a strong cosmopolitan strain cultivated by years of study abroad. They were poised to provide the organizers of American Composers' Concerts with more than enough music for a decade of concerts.

After the successful concert and the resolutions adopted in Cleveland, the organizers of the 1885 convention in New York were eager to follow up with another concert of American music. The choice of this city was significant in the history of the organization, for it was the first time that the group had dared to meet in what was already acknowledged to be America's musical capital. The location offered maximum exposure for struggling composers, and over the course of the next year, composers sent so many works to the organization that they spilled over from the "official" American concert into the other concerts of the three-day convention.

The New York convention featured for the first time evening concerts with orchestra and chorus, a major step for the MTNA. The organizers announced in April that the Theodore Thomas orchestra had been engaged, but in the end they had to make do with a pickup orchestra instead.[15] The appreciative audience at the American concert on the evening of July 2 heard orchestral works by Buck, Frederic Grant Gleason, and Louis Maas; a piano concerto by Robert Goldbeck; choral works by Lavallée and Smith Newell Penfield; selections from the opera *Zenobia* by Pratt; a violin sonata by Paine; and piano works by Constantin Sternberg, Willard Burr Jr., and William Mason. The composers conducted their own orchestral and choral works, which resulted in ragged performances,[16] but this did not quell the enthusiasm of the audience for hearing the works of their countrymen performed under such auspicious circumstances.

The enthusiasm carried over into the business sessions as the members began planning for the following year's convention in Boston. Among the proposals that were not adopted was one by Lavallée to hear nothing but American works at that gathering. As absurd as it may sound, this notion was supported by Theodore Presser in his article for *The Etude*:

We expect the time is soon at hand when only the products of American composers will be heard at these meetings. We see no reason why at the next meeting original works only by living composers should [not] be given. Rubinstein, Liszt, Brahms, etc., might be prevailed on to write something for the Association, which could be made an important feature of these annual meetings. This would be far better than to be obliged to listen to pieces that have been familiar to us since childhood.[17]

The majority view was expressed in *The Musical Courier*:

Our energetic and radical friend, Mr. Lavallée, tried to carry through a proposition to instruct the Program Committee to admit none but American compositions to the program of next year's recitals and concerts. It is a good measure in politics and war, in times of danger from without, to put none but Americans on guard, but this effort to shut out the classics from the pianoforte recital was in flagrant violation of the golden rule of all such agitations as this in behalf of a native school of composition. If we are to hope for good and lasting results we must make haste slowly.[18]

In this heady atmosphere of musical patriotism, Albert Ross Parsons proposed changing the name of the organization to The American Society for the Promotion of Musical Art. This idea was discussed and referred to a committee on revising the constitution, where it seems to have died. Five years later, at the 1890 convention, the issue would resurface, but again a name change would prove to be difficult for the organization to assimilate.

Among the important changes made in New York was the election of a Board of Examiners to choose the American works to be performed. The large number of submissions for the 1885 convention had made a more rigorous selection process necessary, prompting the members to discuss a set of guidelines proposed by Burr to organize the submission and selection of American works. The three-person Board of Examiners was to select the works through a blind referee process by ranking works on a scale of one to ten and averaging the scores of the three examiners. The guidelines prohibited the selection of more than two compositions by a composer in a given year or the repetition of a work that had been heard at a previous year's concert. No composer could be heard at a convention if one of his works had been performed at the previous convention.[19] The complexity of the regulations and the limited time available in the business session did not allow for a thorough debate on the merits of the proposed regulations, which were tabled until the following year.

When the convention adjourned on Friday, July 3, the members left with the knowledge that major changes had taken place that would profoundly affect the organization's future. There was no doubt about the commitment of the membership to American composers, and the modest example of Lavallée's 1884 recital had resulted in a flurry of new ideas in 1885.

The next convention was held in Boston on June 30 and July 1 and 2, 1886. This convention featured not one but two grand festival concerts of American works with orchestra. Among the composers were familiar names like Paine, Chadwick, and Buck, as well some younger composers who had just completed their studies in Europe: Parker, Kelley, and Arthur Whiting. There were abstract works like the Louis Maas Piano Concerto and a suite by Arthur Bird as well as programmatic works like John A. Broekhoven's *Suite Creole* and Buck's "In Distant Andalusia" from *The Voyage of Columbus*. Vocal soloists, chorus, and orchestra were conducted by each composer in turn, again with mixed results. At this stage of the movement, though, the quality of the performances did not matter as much as the simple fact of hearing compositions by American composers. The Boston concerts proved beyond a doubt that there was a great deal of worthy American music waiting to be performed and that there were young composers who could be expected to write much more music in the years ahead. Presser went so far as to suggest that the composers in these programs were the equal of men of their age in Germany or other European countries: "True, we have not yet produced a Beethoven or a Wagner; but we can show as close an approximation to genius as can be found in Europe, and there is no reason to doubt the future of creative musical art in this country."[20]

The Boston meeting saw the election of Lavallée—the driving force behind the American Composers' Concert movement—as president of the MTNA, as well as the adoption of stringent guidelines on the selection of American works. Burr's original proposal had grown to a document of formidable length and complexity detailing every step of the selection process from submission, to judging, to acceptance.[21] Chadwick suggested that composers might feel "slightly humiliated" to submit their works to such a Byzantine process, adding, "I think possibly the works which are capable of being produced in this Association have got somewhat beyond the necessity of any such primary school pedagogism, and that this Association hardly needs so many bulwarks of defence against bad compositions as are provided for in this report."[22] After considerable discussion, most of which centered on the issue of submitting works already in print, the regulations were easily passed. A motion was also passed that extended future conventions from three to four days, making room for more concerts.

The electrifying changes that had come over the MTNA between 1884 and 1886 were summed up in *The Musical Courier* quotation at the head of this chapter. Most remarkable is that in such a short time the association had virtually abandoned the pedagogical emphasis that had been its purpose since its founding in 1876. This new direction for the MTNA had been developed in such a short time that its promoters had had little time to contemplate the potential pitfalls in such a radical course of action. The year that separated the 1886 convention in Boston from the 1887 convention in Indianapolis saw the emergence of a number of problems that did not immediately dampen the enthusiasm of the champions of American music but highlighted several weaknesses of the developing movement.

When the Boston convention was adjourned, the next meeting had been scheduled for Indianapolis, but the question of how to provide an orchestra had not been resolved. For the New York and Boston gatherings it had been possible to raise an orchestra and chorus of local musicians supported by donations from wealthy patrons in those cities. Though the commitment had been made to continue the tradition of grand orchestral concerts, there was no clear idea of where the orchestra would come from or how it would be financed. In the course of the winter these questions were answered. A group of Indianapolis residents subscribed to a guarantee fund, meaning that they were willing to make up any expenses not covered by ticket sales. Frank Van der Stucken, who for several years had been presenting orchestral concerts of new music (primarily European) in New York, was engaged to bring his orchestra to Indianapolis for the convention. Since Van der Stucken was the American conductor most closely associated with the performance of new music, the choice was seen as a brilliant one, even though the cost of transporting fifty-three men and their instruments nearly 1,000 miles to the conference had not been fully considered.

The announcement of the hiring of a New York orchestra brought a protest from the citizens of Indianapolis, who felt that their own local musicians were being neglected, despite the fact that a significant amount of the funding was coming from Indianapolis sources. Among those whose talents were not called upon for the MTNA convention was Carl Barus (1823–1908), who was famous throughout the Midwest for his work with German singing societies and who had been instrumental in the early musical development of both Cincinnati and Indianapolis.[23] Indianapolis journalists believed that with a man of his experience in residence, there was no reason to import an orchestra. The New York-based *Musical Courier* responded with a sarcastic article belittling the musicians and musical taste of the Hoosier capital, which did not smooth the ruffled feathers of those concerned.[24]

Even before the convention began, there was a brouhaha involving an American composer. Edgar Stillman Kelley of San Francisco had heard his incidental music to *Macbeth* at the previous year's convention at Boston but had not received the score and parts after the concert. This represented a substantial loss in an era when all parts had to be copied by hand. He accused the organization of "mismanagement" and demanded reimbursement if the program committee could not return the score. The settlement of this complaint, still unresolved in June 1888, was never aired in the press, but it highlighted the potential problems in soliciting and performing dozens of scores from around the country. A positive result was the appointment of an MTNA librarian who was charged with keeping track of all scores.[25]

In late spring the program committee announced an imposing list of works to be performed. There were to be two grand evening concerts of American orchestral works along with numerous other works by American composers during the daily sessions. Chadwick, Paine, Foote, and others were represented, and the first evening's concert was scheduled to end with Dudley Buck's *Festival Overture on The Star-Spangled Banner*. Shortly after the announcement of the program, a brief notice appeared in the *Boston Evening Transcript*, presumably written by its chief music critic, William F. Apthorp: "The American composer (by birth or adoption) is so numerous on the program of the meeting of the Music Teachers' National Association, at Indianapolis, that one has to hunt to find the names of Bach, Beethoven, Chopin, Schumann and some other foreigners, once famous in musical circles."[26]

This seemingly harmless jab touched off a chorus of indignation in the musical press. *The Musical Courier* called it "an ignoble slur" and combed the program to prove that Europeans were not underrepresented. *The Folio* of Boston lambasted the critic in an article headlined "The Opposition to American Composers." Clearly, the champions of American music were still testy about the former neglect of their repertoire and took this opportunity to challenge the patriotism of anyone who did not support the MTNA's efforts to promote American composers. Apthorp was not about to back down, however, as later that fall he explained his position regarding American Composers' Concerts in a review of one of William Sherwood's Boston recitals.[27] That review, which was an important turning point in the previously unbroken rise of the movement, is discussed in more detail in Chapter 4.

These problems were all set aside in anticipation of the convention in Indianapolis, which promised to be the most impressive to date. The American concerts on July 5 and 6, 1887, handsomely repaid the risks assumed by the organization in bringing an orchestra from New York. The Van der Stucken orchestra played well, although it was hampered by a weak male chorus from Indianapolis that assisted on the second evening in a performance of George E. Whiting's cantata *Henry of Navarre*. The compositions featured on the first evening had all been heard elsewhere previously. Foote's overture *In the Mountains* was among the most frequently performed American works of the period; Paine's "May-night Fantasy" from the Second ("Spring") Symphony was a long-standing favorite; and Van der Stucken's incidental music to *The Tempest* had been well received in Europe and in New York. The audience was extremely enthusiastic at the first concert, and that enthusiasm carried over to the second night's concert, which attracted a very large crowd.

An unusual feature of the second concert was the inclusion of a testimonial for Franz Liszt (who had died the previous summer), consisting of a speech, one of Liszt's songs, and his "Wanderer" Fantasy. The incongruity of including this set in the midst of an American concert puzzled many commentators. In general, the works of the second evening were not as strong as those of the first concert, but again the audience was supportive.

The fourth and final day of the convention brought a paper by Cleveland composer Wilson G. Smith urging further encouragement of American composers through increased use of their music as teaching material. Charles Landon of Claverack, New York, responded with a proposal that the MTNA compile lists of American works rated by a board of examiners, both as a guide to teachers and as pressure on publishers to print more American works. This discussion elicited a note of concern from *The Musical Courier*, and in commenting upon Landon's proposal, the writer articulated what would become the greatest objection to the movement within a few years:

The movement is one the success of which can only be endangered by hot-house cultivation. It must take its normal course if good is to result from it. No teacher or player would be true to his art if he permitted his patriotic feelings to get the better of his judgment in the choice of pieces for study or concert performances. The best ends of the movement can be subserved by extending encouragement to the American composers, such as they are receiving now in New York and Boston, and all talk of subordinating the magnificent piano literature which centuries of activity in the Old World have given us to the products of today is worse than idle. The American composer must win his way legitimately, and not through adventitious circumstances. He must grow naturally, patiently, slowly. The most that his true friends will claim for him is that he be given the opportunity, too long denied him, to try his wings when the spirit prompts him to soar. In the end he will fly best if he is compelled to measure his strength with the masters of the Old World. Too much coddling is more dangerous to a child than neglect.[28]

Later in the fall this opinion would be restated when a festival of five concerts of exclusively American music, presented by Van der Stucken in New York in November, prompted critics to suggest that it was time to "whistle down brakes" on the movement that was becoming a national fad. The organization that had started the trend showed no signs of slowing down, though, as newly elected president Max Leckner of Indianapolis began planning for the following year's meeting in Chicago, which would prove to be even more patriotic than those of previous years.

For the Chicago convention, the MTNA hired what was arguably America's best orchestra, led by Theodore Thomas. The involvement of this conductor was an important step in the MTNA's campaign to legitimate American art music. Thomas spent most of his career educating American audiences in the appreciation of classical music, and indeed he has been identified in a study by Lawrence Levine as a crucial factor in the "sacralization" of European classical music in America during this period.[29] Thomas made no apologies for his bias toward German music and earned a perhaps undeserved reputation as a conductor who did not like American music.[30] On the occasion of the 1888 MTNA convention in Chicago, he was willing to set aside any prejudices that he may have had against American music, undoubtedly swayed by the generous fee that his orchestra was offered.

The concerts took place in the cavernous Exposition Building on July 3, 4, and 5, 1888. Estimates put the crowds at between 6,000 and 10,000, with the largest audience on the final evening. W.S.B. Mathews, a Chicago writer and music teacher, noted that there was no reserved seating, and the acoustics were such that those sitting in the back of the building could not understand the words of the choral pieces.[31]   Other writers noted that the firecrackers, pistol shots, and yelling outside the building on July 4 further inhibited the pleasure of those inside the auditorium:

The violins wanted to create a favorable impression, so did the youngsters, and as a net result the product was far from soothing.   The castanets and cymbals held their ground bravely with momentary assistance from the brass instruments, but whenever it came to a square issue between the spluttering firecracker, manipulated by the youth of our land, and the fruit of genius, it was noticeable that the former's stock rose in the proportion that the latter's ebbed.[32]

The enthusiasm for American concerts continued unabated from previous years, despite the inauspicious acoustics in Chicago. Those inclined to be critical pointed out that the vocal soloists and the chorus were not on a par with the orchestra, thereby presenting the vocal works in a poor light.   It was also pointed out that owing to the restrictive selection process adopted by the MTNA, the concerts featured few works by the leading American composers and virtually nothing that was in print. Exceptions were Edward MacDowell's First Piano Concerto, op. 15, played by the brilliant pianist Teresa Carreño, and Chadwick's Second Symphony. Unfortunately, the latter work was placed at the end of an unusually long program on July 5, and many of the audience members left before the concert was over.

With the benefit of hindsight, it is possible to see the Chicago convention as the high point of the MTNA's campaign to promote American music.   From one piano recital of American works on a morning session of the 1884 convention, the MTNA had expanded to three festival concerts of American works with orchestra, chorus, and soloists in 1888.   With this expansion of the musical program had come a corresponding growth in the organization.   The MTNA membership for 1883 had been 312; by 1888 it had risen to 1,649, the highest level that it would reach in the nineteenth century.   The huge influx of new members with varying levels of commitment to the organization was not welcomed by all of the veterans, but it did help to pay the bills.[33]   The total expenditures for the 1883 convention had been $295.23, while the expenditures for 1888 totaled $5,673.37, of which the largest single item was the cost of hiring the orchestra.

The idealistic goals of the first advocates of American concerts had been exceeded in a stunning fashion.   Not only had these concerts become the principal feature of the MTNA conventions, but they were being presented by other groups all over the country.   Wilson G. Smith stated in a speech before the Ohio Music Teacher's Association, "A tidal wave of encouragement is sweeping over the land, and will assuredly bear upon its crest some native talent capable of and anxious to do honor to his profession and native land."[34]   The optimistic view that the movement would bring forth a truly great American composer was the main reason that the MTNA and other organizations were willing to put so much money and effort into these concerts.   As each year passed, the hope became stronger that the "American Wagner" would appear.

Amid this optimism there was one pessimistic voice. In his report before the 1888 convention, MTNA treasurer H. S. Perkins painted a different picture:

The financial question has within the past four years grown to be the most momentous and solicitous of any with which we have to deal. If we are not "beggars filled with blindness," yet we have begged for several years, and we have not been able to conceal the fact. We are compelled to call upon our generous friends annually in order to keep from insolvency, and then it has not been done. True, our expenses are heavy. We have taken upon us so much that unless relief shall come in some other way than that which has thus far been adopted, it does not require much foresight to prognosticate disaster.[35]

Perkins' prognostication would prove to be correct, and the resulting disaster was as rapid and unexpected as the meteoric rise that had preceded it. For the moment, though, the members of the MTNA could point with legitimate pride to evidence that their idea had inspired others throughout the country. Before continuing with the story of the MTNA's efforts, we turn to two of the most important of these—critic Henry E. Krehbiel and conductor Frank Van der Stucken.

NOTES

1. "M.T.N.A. Tenth Annual Meeting: Great Enthusiasm—Large Attendance—American Compositions." *MC* 13/1 (July 7, 1886): 2.

2. "Personals," *MC* 12/9 (March 3, 1886): 140.

3. Wilson G. Smith, "American Composers and Pioneers," *MC* 12/12 (March 24, 1886): 188.

4. S. N. Penfield, "Van der Stucken—Lavallée—Penfield," *MC* 12/13 (March 31, 1886): 205.

5. "In all the controversies that have lately been aroused as to activity in the movement in favor of American composers, THE MUSICAL COURIER modestly hopes not to be forgotten. We have all along insisted that we had plenty of material in this country worthy of public support, or at least a hearing. We prophesied that when once this hearing should be granted the novelties of foreign origin would not remain paramount, simply for their authors' names, over the works of resident composers of genuine merit. For years we have fought this battle and reiterated the statements to that effect until they were taken up by the press of the country, and until artists who were theretofore ignorant of the very fact that American composers of talent and merit were in existence first glanced at, then studied and at last brought out home productions of artistic value. Thus the movement, which is now rapidly extending all over the United States, was given its origin and received its impetus, and we take no little pride in the fact of the success of THE MUSICAL COURIER's policy, without wishing to detract aught from the merit of those who have actually carried out the idea." *MC* 12/15 (April 14, 1886): 237.

6. H. S. Perkins, *Historical Handbook of the Music Teachers' National Association, 1876–1893* (n.p., [1893]), p. 29.

7. Quoted in ibid., 31.

8. Ibid., 58.

9. *The Eighth Annual Meeting of the Music Teachers' National Association, Held at Cleveland, Ohio, July 2, 3 and 4, 1884, Official Report* (Chicago: O. L. Fox, [1884]), pp. 159–60.

10. "Calixa Lavallée," *MC* 22/4 (January 28, 1891): 75.

11. "Biographies of American Musicians Number Ninety: Calixa Lavallée," *BMW* 22/5 (May 1885): 167.

12. "Calixa Lavallée," *MC*, 75. This article goes on to note that he served two years in the Civil War and advocated the annexation of Canada to the United States.

13. *The Eighth Annual Meeting, 1884, Official Report*, p. 160.

14. "The Music Teachers," *MC* 8/24 (June 11, 1884): 379.

15. "Music Teachers' National Association," *MC* 10/17 (April 29, 1885): 261.

16. "M.T.N.A.: A Society for the Promotion of Musical Art," *The Etude* 3/8 (August 1885): 164; "M.T.N.A.: Ninth Annual Meeting of the Music Teachers' National Association," *MC* 11/2 (July 15, 1885): 18–19.

17. "M.T.N.A.: A Society for the Promotion of Musical Art," 164.

18. "M.T.N.A.: Ninth Annual Meeting," 18.

19. *Music Teachers' National Association, Ninth Annual Meeting, at New York, 1885. Official Report* (Music Teachers' National Association, 1885), pp. 141–42.

20. "M.T.N.A.," *The Etude* 4/7 (July 1886): 158.

21. These regulations may be found in the *Official Report, Music Teachers' National Association, Tenth Annual Meeting at Boston, 1886* (Music Teachers' National Association, 1886), pp. 229–31; and "M.T.N.A.: Preliminary Report of the Program Committee," *MC* 13/14 (October 6, 1886): 211.

22. *Official Report, Tenth Annual Meeting*, p. 231.

23. See "Carl Barus," in *Brainard's Biographies of American Musicians*, ed. E. Douglas Bomberger (Westport, CT and London: Greenwood Press, 1999), pp. 24–26.

24. "The M.T.N.A. at Indianapolis," *MC* 14/18 (May 4, 1887): 288-89; see also "Indianapolis Musicians and Journalists," *MC* 14/22 (June 1, 1887): 352-53.

25. "Mr. Kelley's Complaint," *MC* 14/12 (March 23, 1887): 190; Edgar Stillman Kelley, "The Lost or Stolen Macbeth Score," *AAJ* 46/24 (April 2, 1887): 377; "Mr. Kelley's Letter on the M.T.N.A.," *MC* 17/1 (July 4, 1888): 7. S. B. Whitney's proposal at the 1887 convention for the appointment of a librarian was referred to committee; the duties of the librarian were described in the revised bylaws adopted at the 1888 convention.

26. Quoted in "An Ignoble Slur," *MC* 14/24 (June 15, 1887): 384; and "The Opposition to American Composers," *The Folio* 31/7 (July 1887): 273.

27. "Mr. Sherwood's Concerts," *BET*, November 9, 1887, p. 1.

28. "M.T.N.A. Eleventh Annual Meeting of the Music Teachers' National Association," *MC* 15/3 (July 20, 1887): 36.

29. Lawrence W. Levine, "The Sacralization of Culture," in *Highbrow/Lowbrow: The Emergence of Cultural Hierarchy in America* (Cambridge: Harvard University Press, 1988), pp. 85-168.

30. See, for instance, the anonymous letter to the editor of the *New York Tribune*, April 17, 1876, p. 4, cited in Abram Loft, "Richard Wagner, Theodore Thomas, and the American Centennial," *Musical Quarterly* 37/2 (April 1951): 186; and "A Few Remarks to American Orchestral Conductors," *AAJ* 46/2 (October 30, 1886): 20.

31. W.S.B. Mathews, "M.T.N.A.," *The American Musician* 10/3 (July 21, 1888): 61.

32. "Thomas' Concert," *Daily Inter-Ocean*, July 5, 1888, p. 4; see also "M.T.N.A. Twelfth Annual Meeting of the Music Teachers' National Association," *MC* 17/2 (July 11, 1888): 351.

33. See for instance "M.T.N.A.: Money the Only Restriction," *MC* 16/23 (June 6, 1888): 386-87; Buckeye, "Hot Shot and Shell Fired into the M.T.N.A.," *AAJ* 49/9 (June 16, 1888): 130-31.

34. Wilson G. Smith, "American Compositions in the Class and Concert Room," *The Etude* 6/8 (August 1888): 129.

35. "The Treasurer's Report," in *Official Report of the Twelfth Annual Meeting of the Music Teachers' National Association, Chicago, Illinois* (Music Teachers' National Association, 1888): 177.

∽ 3 ∽

Henry E. Krehbiel, Critic

Many persons speak about music in an extravagantly sentimental manner; many more affect not to be able to speak about it at all. Which of these two affectations is the less objectionable I do not know; but this I do know, neither is amiable, and neither reflects credit on the civilization of which this century makes frequent boasts.

—Henry Krehbiel, 1890[1]

The newspaper now fills the place in the musician's economy which a century ago was filled in Europe by the courts and nobility. Its support, indirect as well as direct, replaces the patronage which erstwhile came from these powerful ones.

—Henry Krehbiel, 1896[2]

Dubbed the Dean of American Critics, Henry Edward Krehbiel (1854–1923) was among the most feared and respected reviewers of the golden age of music criticism in America. The role played by the *New York Tribune*'s chief critic was crucial in the development of the American Composers' Concert movement: far from merely critiquing the performances that he was assigned to cover, Krehbiel took a proactive role in supporting the cause of American music, both in his probing and insightful concert reviews and in a range of other writings and lectures. In the case of the American Composers' Concert movement, his early support was crucial to its growth, while his later doubts contributed to its decline.

Krehbiel came to music criticism by an unorthodox path. Unlike the majority of his peers, he had neither a college degree nor formal training in music. As a child in Cincinnati he took private lessons in violin and music theory, but his postsecondary education was limited to a brief period of studying law. Coming up through the ranks in the newspaper business, first with the *Cincin-*

nati Gazette and later with the *New York Tribune*, he taught himself music to prepare for his work as chief music critic of the latter paper from 1884 to his death. His reviews were noted for direct, incisive prose and for his interest in new music. He was instrumental in the acceptance of works by Tchaikovsky, Brahms, Wagner, and Dvořák early in his career, though he balked at the music of Schoenberg and Stravinsky in old age.

For five years beginning with the 1885/1886 season, Krehbiel published an annual *Review of the New York Musical Season*, containing repertoire lists for hundreds of concerts and excerpts from his *New York Tribune* reviews of the most important events. Each volume included a retrospective essay on the season as well, allowing him to expound his views on trends in American concert and operatic life. In the introduction to his review of the 1885/1886 season he explored the idea of an American school of composers:

It is exceedingly common whenever the question of American music is under discussion to have the objection urged that there is nothing in the national characteristics of the American people to justify the belief that we will ever produce music which will show distinctive traits, that we will ever develop what is called a "school." I do not hold it to be essential to the existence of an American school of music that it should have a flavor which shall distinguish it from all the music produced elsewhere. It will be enough if we bring it to pass that the productions of native composers in the field of music shall receive the same respect and attention as the productions of native composers in the field of literature do. The objections of a want of national style might be urged against American prose writers with the same force as against musical composers, yet no one is foolish enough to do it. Every student of literature knows that in the progress of time, without change in the national character of a people, there are great changes in their literary productions. This phenomenon is so marked that we divide the history of literature into eras, and no one would be likely to confound a writer of Chaucer's time with one of Elizabeth's, or one of Queen Anne's with one of today. The body of successful writers in each of these periods make up a literary style or "school," and each of these schools was distinct from the others; yet there was no essential change in the national character of Englishmen. How these special literatures are brought about is an exceedingly interesting question, and in the answer, I believe, will be found the explanation of how a school of composers is going to arise in this country who will be recognized as typically American.[3]

Continuing with his analogy to literature, Krehbiel cited the British literary critic Walter Bagehot, whose view of the development of national styles involved one author whose style appealed to those around him and who was consequently imitated by others. The others may have had more talent and originality than the first, but they owed the foundation of the national style to the initial writer. Krehbiel illustrated this concept by pointing to the national schools of the European countries, which in each case sprang from the work of one or two composers. Further, he noted that imitation was essential to the process: "Since the rise of instrumental music all of the European 'schools,' without exception, have been the fruit of imitation."[4] To the objection that the United States was too young and diverse to have a recognizable national character, he replied that the school of composition could start even before this character coalesced. Only two things were necessary: a strong example for composers to follow and public encouragement of their efforts. His essay ended with an optimistic call for cooperation:

If composition on good lines be encouraged; if our best musicians put the claims of art above the claims of self; if conductors and managers but open their eyes to the merits of home productions; if the public be made to recognize the fact that a foreign label is not necessarily a proof of excellence or a native label of inferiority, it will not be long before the musician will arise who will compel the attention of the world, and furnish the example whose imitation will speedily develop an American "school" of composition.[5]

As the movement matured, Krehbiel continued to offer support tempered with warnings against impatience or overenthusiasm. His view was that the evolution of a national school was unpredictable and could take a long time, necessitating audiences and critics to continue to hear what composers had to offer while maintaining the same standards of critical judgment that they applied to other new music. In a thoughtful essay on American composition in his review of the 1887/1888 season, he again urged moderation. On the one hand, he noted, "There was no want of encouragement to American composers, of native or European birth, in the season. In fact, there were times when it seemed as if the promoters of the 'American movement' would be obliged to 'whistle down brakes' for the good of the cause."[6] On the other hand, he decried the view that America was too young to have a national character, discussing the fusion of different cultures into one nation and the emergence of certain distinctive American types in the western prairies. He argued at great length that many of Europe's best-known composers were themselves cosmopolitan rather than nationalist in style. The conclusion of his essay expressed his fundamental view of American art music: "We are not hoping for an American school in a day or even in a decade. But some day the strong, successful writer will come and the school will quickly follow."[7]

Krehbiel was responsible for the oft-quoted remark about the "coddling" of the American composer, a statement that makes sense only in its original context in a review of the inaugural concert of the Manuscript Society of New York on December 10, 1890:

If there were not a corrective in the methods of the two organizations which have sprung into exceedingly active life within a year, for the purpose of giving a hearing to the American composer, one would be tempted to say that that individual, after long suffering neglect, now seems to be in imminent danger of being coddled to death. It is something to excite special wonder that New York should boast an American Composers' Choral Association and a Manuscript Club, and that both these organizations should successfully appeal to the public for support in their effort to acquaint that public with the products of native composers. It is the kind of a reaction from which benefits flow, and the fact that their existence is due primarily to the musicians themselves is calculated to excite all the greater admiration for them. But the presence of the two societies is not merely a sign of reaction from the long neglect; it is also the flowering and fruit of such unselfish labors as those of Mr. Van der Stucken a few years ago, and of the Music Teachers' National Association, which used to spend all its energies in vapid talk, but of late years devotes the best of them to giving concerts of American music.[8]

When the *New York Tribune* celebrated its fiftieth anniversary in 1891, Krehbiel was instrumental in arranging an American Composers' Concert under the direction of Walter Damrosch at the Metropolitan Opera House on April 10. In this instance, as in the quotation in the first paragraph of this chapter, the newspaper literally played the role of patron.

An avid reader of foreign newspapers, Krehbiel pointed out that the glowing reviews sent back from Germany by F. X. Arens in 1892 did not tell the whole story of the critical reaction to his tour, a point that was subsequently used by the *Boston Musical Herald* to cudgel the conductor upon his return to the United States.

During the 1890s, Krehbiel's interest turned to the study of American folk music and the music of other cultures. He delivered a paper titled "Folk Song in America" at the World's Columbian Exposition in 1893 and published studies of Native American music and African American music, notably, *Afro-American Folksongs: A Study in Racial and National Music* (1914), which analyzed 500 spirituals. In light of his interest in these areas, it is not surprising that he welcomed the innovations of Antonín Dvořák during the latter's tenure at the National Conservatory of Music in New York from 1892 to1895. Krehbiel's close contact with the composer allowed him to write a detailed and perceptive analysis of the symphony "From the New World" at the time of its premiere.[9]

Though his own interests tended toward folk musics in his later years, Krehbiel never forgot his early zeal for American Composers' Concerts. A retrospective published in 1906 reminded readers that American composers had been agitating for performance of their works since the 1840s, traced the history of the American Composers' Concert movement, and provided an extensive list of works by American-born composers that had been heard at these concerts. By this time he admitted that the earlier neglect of American music had not been entirely because of prejudice on the part of conductors, maintaining his position against blind patriotism:

The memory of the writer of these notes covers a full generation of American musical activity. During this time *The Tribune* has consistently championed the cause of American music, though not always approving or lauding the efforts made in the name of that cause. *The Tribune* has always thought and said that American composers had more to fear from coddling than from indifference, and there are few among the New York composers of today who cannot remember the time when there was so active an effort to let American composers be heard that it was felt on all hands to be a wise [illegible] when the friends of the American movement themselves whistled down brakes, lest they lose the good opinion they were holding of the value of American music.[10]

More than any contemporary critic, Krehbiel took an active interest in the music of American composers, supporting their efforts to be heard and writing fair and thoughtful reviews of their works. Though some of the composers suffered from his astute ear and unflinching prose, they could not have asked for a better advocate for their cause.

NOTES

1. H. E. Krehbiel, "How to Listen to Wagner's Music: A Suggestion," *Harper's New Monthly Magazine* 80/478 (March 1890): 530.

2. Henry E. Krehbiel, *How to Listen to Music* (New York: Scribners, 1896), cited in Mark N. Grant, *Maestros of the Pen: A History of Classical Music Criticism in America* (Boston: Northeastern University Press, 1998), p. 58.

3. H. E. Krehbiel, *Review of the New York Musical Season, 1885–1886* (New York and London: Novello, Ewer, 1886), pp. xix–xx.

4. Ibid., xx.

5. Ibid., xxi.

6. H. E. Krehbiel, *Review of the New York Musical Season, 1887–1888* (New York and London: Novello, Ewer, 1888), p. 171.

7. Ibid., 174.

8. [Henry E. Krehbiel], "The Manuscript Society," *New York Daily Tribune*, December 12, 1890, p. 7.

9. This analysis is reprinted and discussed in Michael Beckerman, "Henry Krehbiel, Antonín Dvořák, and the Symphony 'From the New World,'" *Notes* 49/2 (December 1992): 447-73.

10. H.E.K., "On the Performance of American Compositions," *New York Daily Tribune*, April 15, 1906, sec. V, p. 4.

∞ 4 ∞

Frank Van der Stucken's Novelty Concerts

> What we need in this country is a little more union and co-
> operation on the part of the composers themselves and a few more
> Van der Stuckens, an unbiased and able judgment by the press,
> and then the great public will, as always, soon follow suit.
> —*The Musical Courier*, 1885[1]

The American Composers' Concert movement began with the MTNA, which made these concerts central to its mission in the second half of the 1880s. It was not long, though, before the idea caught on outside this organization, first in Chicago, Boston, and New York and later in smaller cities and towns throughout the country. Chicago saw several pops concerts of local composers in the early 1880s and a pair of song recitals devoted to Chicago composers at the beginning of 1885. In Boston the initial manifestation of the movement was in piano recitals, as Lavallée gave a series of American concerts in spring 1885 and again in spring 1886, followed in 1886 by Carlyle Petersilea and in 1887 by William Sherwood. In New York the movement first branched out to orchestral music with the Novelty Concerts of Frank Van der Stucken. The conductor's bold strategy to present American orchestral works during the height of the New York concert season represented a significant step beyond the summer conventions of the MTNA and the relatively less risky piano recitals in Boston. Though Van der Stucken's venture did not prove to be remunerative for the conductor, he succeeded in drawing attention to the movement and inspiring a level of critical sophistication that had previously been lacking.

Arguably the finest American-born conductor before Bernstein, Frank Van der Stucken (1858–1929) played a crucial role in the American Composers' Concert movement. Born to a Belgian father and a German mother in the German community of Fredericksburg, Texas, he was taken to Belgium as a child. There he received his early training in music with Peter Benoit. He later pursued advanced studies with Carl Reinecke in Leipzig, where he was befriended by Edvard Grieg. After traveling extensively throughout Europe, he was engaged as conductor of the Breslau municipal theater from 1881 to 1882. Like many young composers, he paid homage to Franz Liszt in Weimar, but unlike most of his compatriots, he was given the privilege of presenting a concert of his own works with the Weimar court orchestra and chorus in 1883.

Van der Stucken became known for his sharp ear, musical intelligence, and strong leadership. At the same time, he was notorious for his brusque manner and fits of temper in rehearsal, as illustrated by an incident from later in his career:

Apropos of singing masters, Frank Van der Stucken ought to be a good one, if he teaches all other branches of vocalism as well as he imparts the trill. On a certain occasion he was leading the orchestra in accompaniment to a well-known soprano. Suddenly he stopped and glaring at the soloist, said: "You made a simple turn on that note, but the composer desires a trill. Let us begin again." The selection was started over, but as before the soloist avoided the trill indicated and substituted the easier ornamentation. Van der Stucken was furious. He pointed his baton at the offender. "Why don't you trill?" he shouted. "I can't," was the helpless reply. "You can't? You must. Damn you, trill." One look at the enraged face of the conductor was sufficient; the lady trilled.[2]

Van der Stucken returned to the United States in 1884, replacing Leopold Damrosch as conductor of the Arion Society of New York. Like Damrosch before him, he used the conductorship of the Arion Society as a springboard for other musical activities in New York. The ambitious conductor initiated a series of Novelty Concerts with four performances during the 1884/1885 season, his first as conductor of the Arion Society. This society not only gave the newcomer contacts in New York but also provided the financial support for what would otherwise have been an unprofitable venture.[3] Though the powerful German singing club provided the financial guarantee, there is no evidence that its members influenced his repertoire choices. In addition to a healthy dose of German music, including Brahms' Symphony No. 3, Raff's overture "Ein feste Burg" Overture, and Wagner's "Siegfrieds Rheinfahrt," the first three Novelty Concerts featured a diverse group of compositions from Europe and the United States. Included in this first season's concerts were new works by Grieg, Chabrier, Dvořák, Tchaikovsky, Sgambati, Godard, Massenet, and Van der Stucken's former teacher Benoit.[4] The concerts were performed at Chickering Hall, on the corner of Fifth Avenue and Eighteenth Street.

The significance of Van der Stucken's series was not lost on New York's critics, who bemoaned the lack of new music to be heard elsewhere in the city. The reviewer for the *Times* stated that "when it is taken into consideration, furthermore, that in the series of concerts now closing more new things have been rendered than are usually interpreted in a hundred Philharmonics, their importance can scarcely be overrated."[5] The critic for the *Sun* called him "a snapper-up of unconsidered trifles," adding that, "he has, as we have said before, made a niche for himself, and he fills it most usefully and satisfactorily. He is the right man in the right place. We need just at the present time, when creative genius is beginning to blossom in America, a judicious and energetic person to bring out and give voice to its efforts."[6]

The fourth and final concert of the first season was an evening devoted exclusively to American works on March 31, 1885. Over the years there had been performances of individual orchestral works by American composers (Van der Stucken had included several in his earlier concerts), but this was the first time that critics could recall an entire concert by native composers. In contrast to the other three Novelty Concerts, the American program featured a mixture of new works and compositions that had been heard before in New York:

Prelude to *Oedipus Tyrannus*	John Knowles Paine
Concerto in A minor (second and third movements)	Edward Alexander MacDowell
Overture to Scott's *Marmion*	Dudley Buck
"Once as I told in glee" from *The Tale of the Viking*	George E. Whiting
Interlude from *Vlasda* Singers' Festival Procession	Frank Van der Stucken
American Legend, op. 101, for violin and orchestra	Ellsworth C. Phelps
Symphonic Poem to La Motte-Fouqué's *Undine*, op. 14	G. T. Strong

The interest was strong among the city's music critics: extensive reviews appeared in several of the New York papers, and the reviewer for the *Times* attended and wrote about both the public rehearsal on the afternoon of March 30 and the performance itself. The auspicious occasion called forth more than the usual share of general observations, on everything from the significance of Van der Stucken's concert series to the present state and future possibilities of American music.

The press was unanimous in praising the conductor for the contribution that he had made to New York concert life through his series of four concerts. The reviewer for the *Post* expressed the critical consensus when he stated, "Mr. Van der Stucken's novelty concerts have been among the most interesting musical events in the city this winter. Some of the compositions produced, it is true, will never be chosen to occupy a permanent place in our concert repertory; but even these had a claim to at least one hearing."[7] Henry Krehbiel pointed out that a composer needs the mediation of an interpreter in order to make his works known and that the expense of orchestral concerts in particular was a serious impediment to young composers and, by extension, to the development of a national school of composition in the United States. For this reason, he continued, "No project that is now before our people offers so fair a prospect for the advancement of music in the United States as this."[8]

The New York correspondent of the *Boston Evening Transcript* echoed this praise for Van der Stucken and his efforts, adding a reproach for the members of New York's high society:

Mr. Van der Stucken's concerts have not paid expenses. He gives his own services. And to whom does he look to make up the deficiency? To the prominent Americans of the city, who are continually asking why there is no American school of music? By no means. He is backed by the Arion society, by the great German brewers, George Ehret, Jacob Ruppert, D. Yüngling, and by a half-dozen other wealthy Germans. Hence it appears that American composers as a body are securing their first hearing through the liberality of Germans. This is rather a humiliating fact. Conservatism and tradition in New York, as well as, I believe, in Boston, have stood in the way of the proper recognition of American composers.[9]

From unanimous support for the idea of the concert, the critics moved on to discussion of the individual numbers on the program. With the exception of Krehbiel, none of the critics could resist identifying the works that they considered best and worst, giving the concert the flavor of a talent show. All of them cited Phelps' *American Legend* as the weakest piece on the program; noting its opus number, the critic for the *Post* stated that "it was fortunate that Mr. Van der Stucken gave his concert at a date late enough to avoid the 100 works by the same author which preceded it."[10] Most critics labeled Paine's prelude, which had been heard in New York before, the strongest piece. Taking exception to this majority view were the critics for *The Musical Courier* and the *Sun*, who gave the prize to Templeton Strong's symphonic poem.

Ranking of the pieces in such a manner seems to reflect the underlying attitude that these composers were not ready to be taken seriously as artists but were critiqued as one might a student or a child who is still learning. This seems to be why Paine, as the oldest and best established member of the group, was favored by most critics. Strong was given points for originality, which weighed relatively higher than technical proficiency in the minds of the two critics cited earlier. Phelps was seen as simultaneously unoriginal (despite the title, the critics heard no discernible "American" elements) and technically inept. What the critics seem not to have realized was that this composer was actually ten years older than Paine.

In keeping with the view of these composers as beginners, the critics repeatedly noted the influences that they heard in the works. Most cited the influence of the New German school, with the critics for the *Times*, the *Post*, the *Transcript*, and *The Musical Courier* mentioning Liszt and Wagner by name. The critic for the *Herald* betrayed his aesthetic orientation by decrying the amount of program music heard in the concert. In his view, "It is easier to take a story ready made and develop a few of its emotions in music according to rule than to create without reference to a result already before the composer. The one act is almost mechanical, the other belongs only to genius."[11] This game of hunting for influences would continue to plague the American Composers' Concert movement in the years ahead, effectively relegating the composers to student

status. The *Times* reviewer, though obviously attempting to be indulgent, characterized the millstone that was placed around the neck of American art music
when he stated, "American composers, however, may be permitted to copy for a
while; later on it is fair to suppose that, having acquired a mastery of form, they
will be free to create."[12]

The one critic who did not adopt a patronizing tone in his review was
Krehbiel. His review began with a long preface outlining why he took the concert so seriously. In Krehbiel's view, nationalism had been the most important
ingredient of art music in Europe for the past half century. By providing a forum
in which American composers could be heard, Van der Stucken was doing more
than anyone else in the country to promote nationalism in the United States.
Regardless of the characteristics of the music itself—and Krehbiel would elabo-
rate on his views on this subject in the years ahead—the very fact that the concert was presented merited the highest critical regard. Krehbiel saw Van der
Stucken's enterprise in this way:

It is not surprising that there was apparent a strong disposition on the part of many
of those who give direction to comment on musical subjects to regard such a concert
in the light of an experiment from which scarcely anything else than a momentary
gratification of curiosity was to be expected. But it was equally evident that Mr. Van
der Stucken, the projector and conductor of the concert, took a different view of the
matter, for the result attained gave plainest proof that he considered the music quite
as deserving of careful study and preparation as the most ambitious of his earlier
schemes.[13]

Somewhat detached from the rest of the critical response was a curious paragraph from the German-language belletristic journal *N.Y. Figaro*. In a brief notice, the reviewer refused to comment on the music played or whether the concert
had "succeeded." He welcomed the event as an indication of a new direction in
New York's concert life that would help to alleviate the difficulty that young
composers experienced in finding performance opportunities for their works.
The critic ended with a sentence that proved to be a harbinger of the journal's
reaction to future concerts: "Should nonetheless the Novelty Concerts be for the
present a depository for all sorts of useless musical patchwork—it will not be
long before the wheat is separated from the chaff."[14]

Over the next two years, Van der Stucken remained busy with the Arion
Society and the Novelty Concerts, in which he performed American works
alongside European works without devoting an entire concert to them. The
American Composers' Concert movement was growing, meanwhile, inspired by
the MTNA conventions in New York (July 1885) and Boston (June/July 1886).
As enthusiasm for the concerts grew, Van der Stucken again became the focus of
attention. The year 1887 found him involved in a series of American concerts
that culminated in his festival of five American concerts in November 1887—in
many ways the high-water mark of the movement.

Crucial to the growth of the movement was the support of Krehbiel. As
noted in Chapter 3, he did not limit his comments to reviews of all-American
concerts but took the initiative to make his views known through essays in the
New York Tribune and his *Review of the New York Musical Season*. In the
October 17, 1886, issue of the *New York Tribune*, he again made the case for

American music, but this time with a specific project to propose. Several weeks before this, English writer Francis Hueffer had written in the *Musical World* of London that he was completely ignorant of the state of American music, prompting Krehbiel to suggest that Van der Stucken present American Composers' Concerts in London.[15] The London critics responded favorably, and Van der Stucken began planning for a concert in England the following spring. Over the next six months, the idea was mentioned repeatedly, although the project seems to have been quietly dropped sometime in the spring. Van der Stucken did travel to Europe, but it was to perform several of his own works with the Berlin Philharmonic in June 1887.[16]

Immediately after his return from Europe, Van der Stucken conducted the orchestra at the highly successful MTNA convention in Indianapolis, further bolstering his position as the foremost conductor of American Composers' Concerts. Meanwhile, he was planning for his most ambitious project yet, and in September he was able to announce a festival of five American concerts to be performed in November. Originally projected as a festival on five consecutive nights, the schedule was modified to avoid conflicts with Metropolitan Opera performances.[17] These concerts would include three evenings devoted to orchestral and choral-orchestral works, one evening of organ, piano, and choral works, and one evening of chamber music spread out over two weeks.[18] The goal, as he stated in a prospectus released a week before the concerts began, was to broaden his previous efforts:

Of necessity, however, he (the projector and conductor), has heretofore been restricted in the choice of "forms." To escape this restriction, to quicken the interest of Americans in the creations of their compatriots and to extend to composers that encouragement which flows from public performance and discussion, he has planned a set of concerts to follow each other in quick succession which shall present the achievements of native American composers in all the phases from a symphony to a song.[19]

The programs, listed in Appendix 2, encompassed a prodigious amount of music from thirty-two different composers. Major orchestral works on the first program were Paine's Spring Symphony, Henry Holden Huss's *Rhapsody* for pianoforte and orchestra, MacDowell's symphonic poem *Hamlet*, and Harry Rowe Shelley's *Dance of the Egyptian Maidens*. The second concert brought Arthur Foote's overture *In the Mountains*, Arthur Whiting's Piano Concerto in D minor, and shorter pieces by Arthur Bird, Silas G. Pratt, and Edgar Stillman Kelley. The final concert featured Strong's Symphony No. 1 and Ernest Guiraud's "Carnival" from the Suite in F. Large choral/orchestral works were the *Pastoral* by L. A. Russell (first concert), Dudley Buck's cantata *The Voyage of Columbus* (second concert), and Horatio Parker's cantata *King Trojan* (final concert). There were individual arias by George Whiting and Frederic Grant Gleason, choral works by Samuel P. Warren and W. W. Gilchrist, chamber music by Chadwick, Paine, and Beck, organ works by Buck and Eugene Thayer, and a sampling of art songs by Van der Stucken, Chadwick, Willard Burr, Jr., Hermann Rietzel, Edgar H. Sherwood, and Foote, along with short piano pieces by William Mason, Edward B. Perry, William Sherwood, Kelley, Edmund S. Mattoon, F. Dewey, Wilson G. Smith, and William H. Dayas. No composer had more than two works in the concerts, though the symphonies by Strong and Paine and the cantatas by Buck and Parker certainly commanded more attention than the songs and short piano pieces of their lesser-known contemporaries. In addition to the orchestra assembled for the occasion, the concerts drew on the talents of the Schubert Vocal Society of Newark, the Apollo Club of Brooklyn, the choir of St. Stephen's Church, and numerous professional soloists. Pianist William H. Sherwood played in two of the concerts (November 19 and 22) despite the fact that he had just concluded his own series of three piano recitals—including American Composers' Concerts on November 8 and 15—in Boston.

The audience for the concerts varied significantly. According to several reviewers, the chamber music concert on November 22 attracted noticeably fewer auditors, while the final concert of large orchestral and choral works on November 24 drew the best crowd.[20] The reviewer for the *Sun* noted that the concert on November 19, consisting of solo songs, solo organ works, and choral compositions, attracted a different audience from what he was accustomed to seeing:

The third concert of Mr. Van der Stucken's patriotic series was given in Chickering Hall last evening before an audience that had more of the personal friend element and less of the musical appreciation in it than has been the case with the others. Undeserved encores were given, and the effect of good, artistic work was marred in the old time way by love scenes in the parquet, fashion comments in the orchestra, and general gossip upstairs. This is an unusual fault in a Chickering Hall audience, and for that reason deserves to be recorded.[21]

The audience may have been fickle, but the city's critics turned out in force. As a group they recognized that this festival was an auspicious event, and several of them—notably Krehbiel of the *Tribune*, W. J. Henderson of the *Times*, and William M. Thoms of the *American Art Journal*—doggedly attended every performance. Again the press was virtually unanimous in praising the idea of American concerts. The critics commented at length on the prejudice against American art music and hailed the festival as an important step toward righting that wrong. Krehbiel began his first review with a preliminary statement on the worthiness of Van der Stucken's endeavor and the significance of the American Composers' Concert movement in general. For the first time he characterized the movement with the word "reform," stating that as with any reform movement it was necessary to work "energetically and unwearyingly" but also to be patient for tangible results.[22] Both he and Henderson stated that American composers deserved the opportunity to be heard but that they needed the freedom to develop at their own speed. Henderson opined, "The advocacy of a protective policy in music would be foolish, but the unwillingness to permit native compositions to see the light is not patriotic, to say the least. Once performed they must stand or fall on their merits, for the American public is ruthlessly cosmopolitan in taste and has no sentimental forbearance for homely work by homekeeping wits."[23] Krehbiel seconded Henderson's assertion by stating that it would be injurious to the cause if "critical judgment will surrender any of its privileges or functions in the presence of the laudable effort to encourage a National spirit."[24]

The statements by these two prominent reviewers highlight the paradoxical situation that the critics had created for themselves. On the one hand, they advocated the idea of American concerts as a means of encouraging the development of an American school of composition. On the other hand, they refused to suspend critical judgment of the works that they heard. They were repeatedly forced to admit that the music that they were hearing had been chosen for patriotic rather than purely artistic reasons, meaning that they supported the *idea* of the concerts but not necessarily the music that was played. This forced them to look to the future with hope while—despite Krehbiel's assertion to the contrary—being indulgent about the present state of American art music. With this framework in mind, we can turn to the critical assessment of the compositions themselves.

In an advance over the 1885 Novelty Concert, most of the reviewers did not place the compositions in rank order, giving the 1887 festival less of the flavor of a talent show. The exception was the reviewer for the *New York Times* (presumably Henderson), who gave his readers a box score at the end of his first review: "Thus in Mr. Van der Stucken's first concert out of six compositions three were good—a very respectable average, if we are to estimate success by numbers."[25] In a curious twist on the practice of ranking, Henderson ranked the concerts themselves, stating that the second was better than the first and that the third was not as interesting as the previous two.

Reaction to the Paine symphony and violin sonata showed a substantial divergence of opinion on the works of this senior statesman of American art music. The *Sun,* the *Post*, and *Freund's Music and Drama* called the symphony the most important work played, with the *Sun* devoting approximately three-fourths of its review of the first concert to this work alone. This reviewer saw it as uniquely appropriate that Paine was chosen to open the first program because of his stature as "the one masterly composer of this country." He went on to describe the blend of intellectuality and melodic beauty in the piece, calling it a particularly fine balance between the formal and the romantic. He also stated, "In the light of the Paine symphony the other works on the programme seemed unhappily trivial."[26]

This view was not shared by all, and, in fact, the reviewer for *The Musical Courier* stated that the work was disappointing in light of the composer's reputation, since "it is particularly weak in point of invention and not very interesting as regards thematic treatment."[27] As a weekly paper, the *Courier* had the opportunity of commenting on the *Sun*'s review in the editorial page of the same issue: "As ludicrous as the over-praise bestowed on Mr. Paine's work [by the *Sun*] is, it is yet not so sickening as the few lines given to Mr. Huss's 'Rhapsody.'"[28] This journal continued its diatribe against Paine in the following week's issue, calling the violin sonata "labored and dry."[29]

Other reviewers approached Paine's work more diplomatically, giving cautious praise or simply stating that the work had been heard previously in New York. In descriptions of the composer and his symphony, the words "scholar" and "scholarly" appear frequently, with the subtle implication that scholarship limits creativity in a composer. James Huneker was more blunt than most in stating, "John K. Paine's Spring Symphony in A minor-major showed the learned professor throughout, but was not very fruitful as regards themes."[30]

Ironically, this discrepancy of opinion was exactly what American composers needed. Those reviewers who had heard the work before were able to comment more intelligently than if the work had been heard for the first time. The differences of opinion caused critics and audience alike to analyze the work more thoughtfully, except in those cases in which a reviewer's mind was already made up through previous exposure. The reviewer of the *Sun* made a strong case for repeated hearings of American works in his comments on Paine's symphony:

At first hearing the scholarly rather than the inspirational features of the symphony are noticeable; for no musician of this generation, at home or abroad, attaches more importance to thematic development than does Paine, and the skill with which the leading themes are treated successively in the different instruments, are interwoven with each other, transformed and expanded with ever varying effect, is the standing admiration of every student of theory. But those who have heard the symphony several times know that it is also a masterpiece of melodic beauty, and that in no bar is tunefulness sacrificed to intellectual treatment.[31]

Two days later, the reviewer for the *Evening Post* made a similar comment on hearing Paine's symphonic poem *The Tempest* at a Theodore Thomas concert: "Prof. Paine's symphonic poem has been highly commended in this column on previous occasions, and it now remains to add the highest of all compliments— that one likes it better and better at every repetition. . . . The dramatic power displayed in the piece arouses curiosity as to how Prof. Paine is getting on with his opera."[32] Surely no composer could ask for more than this—enough repetitions of his pieces that they became familiar and aroused curiosity about his next work. After living most of his life in an era when American art music was seldom heard and less often given a fair critical hearing, the forty-eight-year-old Paine must have felt grateful indeed to Van der Stucken and others who were programming his works so frequently.

For the young composers on the programs, the festival was even more important. Parker, Huss, and Arthur Whiting had just completed their European studies two years earlier and were still struggling for recognition. MacDowell, Strong, and Bird were young American composers living in Germany and eager for exposure in the United States. For Foote, the performance of his overture represented an important repeat performance of a work completed a little over a year earlier. As residents of the "West," Kelley (San Francisco), Smith (Cleveland), and Beck (Cleveland) had limited access to New York audiences.

For these little-known composers, the reception depended in large part on the strength of the performers. While the orchestra was consistently reliable in its readings, there was a noticeable range of competence among the pianists. Sherwood, the leading American virtuoso of his time, played most of the works for piano solo with dazzling technique and expression. His performance was undoubtedly strengthened by the fact that he had performed the same works on his own Boston recitals earlier in the month. Huss and Arthur Whiting chose to play the solo parts to their own compositions, which may not have been a wise decision. Most reviewers commented that Huss was more competent as a composer than as a pianist, while those who had heard Sherwood play the solo part in the same piece at the previous summer's MTNA convention were doubly disappointed by the comparison.[33] The reaction to Whiting's pianism was also the result of comparison with the prevailing style of playing:

At this time, when power and force are valued so highly in the interpretation of piano music, it was curious to note the effect that Mr. Whiting's playing had upon the public. He has little power, but plays with spirit and exquisite taste, executing most daintily, yet with abandon, the greatest technical difficulties. At first the feeling was one of disappointment, but as the delicate shades of color became apparent to the audience and they saw his virtuosity, the opinion changed to admiration, and at the close of the Concerto the applause was as much for [the] skill of the pianist as for the musical value of his work.[34]

In their opinions of the compositions played over the course of the five concerts, the critics were again divided. The one exception to this diversity of reception was the Beck sextet, which received universal praise. This musician was repeatedly cited during the American Composers' Concert era as an underrated composer whose works were not published or heard as often as they deserved. Nearly all the reviewers felt that the sextet overshadowed the other works in the fourth concert in originality and melodic interest. Krehbiel and the critic of *Freund's Music and Drama* both called it "the gem of the evening," while the reviewer for *The Musical Courier* labeled it "one of the most powerful and original works presented at these concerts."[35]

Strong's symphony dominated the discussion of the final concert of the series. Reaction was generally positive, and the pinnacle of hyperbole was achieved by *The Musical Courier* with the comment, "The work, which is fanciful in the extreme, is, on the whole, the most interesting that has yet been begotten by American musical brains."[36] This work also elicited comment on the sources of Strong's stylistic inspiration, and, as usual, Krehbiel had the most perceptive comments on this issue:

It is to be expected that young composers will fall into the habit of copying the manner of the masters whom they admire before they develop an individual style of their own, but it would help them greatly if they would cultivate the lofty virtue of self-criticism until they were able after completion to prune their scores of every quotation direct or indirect which they are able to detect after a work has been long enough out of mind to make calm examination possible. For Mr. Strong's talent we have heretofore expressed much admiration. We believe that he will be a credit to the art of his native land, but before then he must become more original in his manner of expressing his musical thoughts. Nothing is more contemptible in musical criticism than the common penchant for hunting down reminiscences, but sometimes it becomes necessary to direct attention to borrowed ideas, and it can benefit the American movement if the men who stand for it now should be held to a strict accountability in the matter of meum and tuum.[37]

This statement at first seems to be in contradiction to Krehbiel's statements of the previous year regarding the importance of imitation in the establishment of national schools. In this case, though, he seems to be referring not so much to stylistic imitation as to literal reminiscences from the scores of other composers. Though not a composer himself, Krehbiel astutely recognized that the compositional process involves both an initial setting down of ideas and a subsequent revision and modification of those ideas. It was in the second step that he believed a composer should be able to recognize inappropriate borrowings, and this was the shortcoming that he critiqued in his statements on Strong's symphony. The phrase "self-criticism" appeared also in Krehbiel's review of the fourth concert, but in this case it was used as a compliment:

Mr. Chadwick's quartet was modest in respect to length, but this fact brought into prominence a quality in the composer which deserves commendation. It suggested the possession by the composer of the art of self-criticism, which was not conspicuous in the compositions brought forward in the preceding concerts. Mr. Chadwick, in this quartet at least, stops talking when he has nothing more to say. The quartet is not burdened with "remplissage." It is straightforward, even in its confession of indebtedness to its model (in the second movement), the posthumous quartet in D minor by Schubert. This second movement is a theme in D minor with variations. The theme, slightly reminiscent of Schubert's, is a fine, broad melody, and two of the variations, the first and third, are excellently conceived and admirably carried out.[38]

Krehbiel was not the only critic confronted with questions of originality and musical influence. The question of how far American composers had gone toward creating a distinctive school of composition—which seemed to be the most interesting for those commenting on the series—forced them to examine the works by comparing them to current European trends. The consensus, based largely on the proportion of program music in the concerts, was that the young Americans were most influenced by the New German school of Liszt and Wagner and by the eclectic works of Joachim Raff. Simply looking at the programs showed also a paucity of French influence, the Guiraud "Carnival" being the only piece not in the sphere of German influence. The recognition of progressive German influence on the Americans led naturally to the question of whether it was possible for a composer to be strongly influenced in this way and still have something original to say. Many of the critics concluded that this influence precluded originality, an assumption that made their job easier but would eventually create an untenable situation for composers who did not wish to discard completely the qualities and techniques that they admired. Though few critics went so far as *Freund's Music and Drama*, which stated that "not one of [the composers represented on the first concert] can boast of inventive genius and of striking and original ideas,"[39] the tone of the critical response to the series can be summed up in the words of the reviewer for the *Herald*: "Mr. Van der Stucken and his orchestra, who deserve much credit for their work in these concerts, may not have revealed much that is original or promising, but certainly have awakened considerable interest, and have given noteworthy encouragement."[40]

Amid the widespread support for Van der Stucken's festival and the American Composers' Concert movement in general there were two detractors. The first appears to have been a radical view, while the second came from a serious and respected critic. A rarity in 1887, these criticisms would eventually become dominant as the movement began to wane in the 1890s.

The *N.Y. Figaro* had been cautiously supportive of the 1885 concert by the new director of the Arion Society. By 1887 it was sharply critical of the American concerts. The reviewer stated that the most significant achievement of the

November 15 concert was to furnish proof that "an actual characteristic school of American music does not yet exist at the present time."[41] He went on to give his opinions of the music performed:

The general impression made by the compositions performed in Chickering Hall on Tuesday evening can be summarized in a few words. American musicians have studied the works of German composers of the Classic and especially the Romantic schools with loving earnestness and admirable conscientiousness. They have succeeded, in some cases at least, to make themselves masters of form, but that is all. Of any original, affecting thoughts, of freshness and abundance of feeling, there is no trace; the joyful, invigorating spirit that speaks to us from a German composition is completely absent. It is all patchwork, but not art work.[42]

The reviewer closed with a jab that would be echoed frequently by German reviewers at the concerts of F. X. Arens in 1891–1892: the conducting of the German-speaking director was the best part of the concert.

The position of this journal became clear over the next several years, culminating in an 1890 article attacking Jeannette Thurber's efforts to found a national conservatory of music. The author of this article, like the reviewer of Van der Stucken's concerts, expressed disdain for American music and musicians, taking umbrage at American attempts to free themselves from German influence. In an extreme example of racism, the article detailed the temperamental and physiological reasons that Anglo-Saxons in both England and America could never be good musicians and why attempts to support American music were detrimental to German-Americans. The article concluded with a summary that demonstrates the extreme views of the editorialist and explains the tone of the concert reviews from 1885 and 1887:

If one observes, in the light of all these conditions, the efforts of native music supporters to create an independent American art music, the question suggests itself whether this whole battle is not a battle against windmills. It would be possible that with time the German immigrants and the members of other musical nations could impart at least to *American* Anglo-Saxons enough of their musical gifts to produce an American art music. But perhaps Anglo-Saxon dullness would keep even this from coming into being. The Anglo-Saxons are, and will probably remain, an unmusical race.[43]

It is not clear whether this view reflected the opinions of a significant number of German-Americans or came from the radical fringe. In either case, arguing against American music on racial grounds never became an important tactic for opponents of the movement. The other detractor, though, came from much closer to home and struck at the very essence of the movement—concerts devoted exclusively to American music. William Apthorp, critic of the *Boston Evening Transcript*, commented on Sherwood's American Composers' Concert on November 8, 1887, in terms that could easily have been used to discuss Van der Stucken's series, which started a week later in New York:

We have more than once taken occasion to express our want of faith in the policy of giving whole concerts of music by American composers, and yesterday afternoon brought fresh confirmation of our views on this head. Far be it from us to doubt for a moment the propriety of bringing native works to public performance, of letting the musical public hear for themselves what American composers can do, and are doing. It is only the policy of presenting such works in large batches, of giving concerts of nothing but American compositions, that seems to us unwise, and even injurious to the effect the works produce upon an audience. Even setting aside the supposable or actual musical value of the compositions thus given *en masse*, the very fact that by far the greater part of them will, almost by necessity, be new to the audience militates against their being enjoyed, and no proper appreciation of a good work is possible without a modicum of musical enjoyment. A programme made up almost entirely of new music, no matter how good the music may be, is a terrible thing to face; it is an inordinate strain upon the listener's attention, and, before the concert is half over, his musical perceptive faculty has become so worn out that he has little power of discrimination left, and good and bad sound pretty much alike. No sense of patriotism can long nerve up the ear against actual boredom, and we are much mistaken if many a well-disposed listener, yesterday afternoon, did not heartily wish the American Composer (with a capital C) to the deuce before the concert was over. Now, we take it to be no part of Mr. Sherwood's object to make any one, even for a moment, wish the American composer to the deuce; but we see no feasible way of avoiding this unpleasant result, save by giving American music in less Gargantuan doses.[44]

Apthorp exposed the fundamental flaw of these concerts in this review, and eventually his views would be widely shared, even by committed advocates of American music. His critique of concerts of exclusively new music, along with questions about Americans' abilities to create a distinctive musical style (albeit not so radical as those of the *Figaro* editorialist), would in time be the most potent arguments against the movement, but in 1887 these voices of opposition went largely unnoticed, for the American Composers' Concert movement was at its height. Credit for this belonged to Van der Stucken, whose recent efforts had given American composers an unprecedented number of opportunities. When one considers the situation just three years before, the reversal in fortune for this formerly beleaguered group was remarkable. Van der Stucken had more work to do on behalf of American music, though, and he would take the major step of exposing the works of American composers to European critics during the Exposition Universelle of 1889.

NOTES

1. Editorial comment on Van der Stucken's Novelty Concert, *MC* 10/13 (April 1, 1885): 194.

2. Clipping from *MC*, July 10, 1912, New York Public Library clipping file.

3. Several music critics pointed out that the concerts did not pay for themselves, while Frederic Archer attributed the financial support for the concerts to "the generosity of the Arion Society." Frederic Archer, "The Novelty Concerts," *The Keynote* 6/8 (April 11, 1885): 4.

4. A complete list of the new works of the first season may be found in "The Third Novelty Concert," *MC* 10/5 (February 4, 1885): 70 and in J. Travis Quigg, "Van der Stucken," *American Music Journal* 1/24 (December 1, 1885): 1.

5. "Novelty Concerts," *NYT*, March 31, 1885, p. 5.

6. "Mr. Van der Stucken's Fourth Novelty Concert," *New York Sun*, April 1, 1885, p. 3.

7. "An American Concert," *New York Evening Post*, April 1, 1885, p. 3.

8. "A Concert of American Music," *New York Daily Tribune*, April 1, 1885, p. 4.

9. E.W.M., "American Composers: What Mr. Van der Stucken Is Doing in Their Behalf," *BET*, April 3, 1885, p. 8.

10. "An American Concert," p. 3.

11. "Novelty Concert," *The New York Herald*, March 31, 1885, p. 4.

12. "Novelty Concerts," *NYT*, April 1, 1885, p. 5.

13. "A Concert," p. 4.

14. "Mögen immerhin die Novelty-Concerte zunächst eine Ablagerungsstätte sein für mancherlei unbrauchbares musikalisches Flickwerk—es wird so gar lange nicht währen, bis auch hier die Spreu sich vom Weizen gesondert hat!," *N.Y. Figaro* 5/14 (April 5, 1885): 7.

15. H.E.K., "American Music," *New York Daily Tribune*, October 17, 1886, p. 5.

16. *The Musical Courier* followed the development and eventual collapse of the London plan with periodic updates: *MC* 13/17 (October 27, 1886): 258; 13/24 (December 15, 1886): 373; 13/25 (December 22, 1886): 386; 13/26 (December 29, 1886): 402; 14/11 (March 16, 1887): 173; 14/24 (June 15, 1887): 386. See also *AAJ* 46/12 (January 8, 1887): 179.

17. "The American Concerts," *AAJ* 48/3 (November 5, 1887): 36. In a letter of September 1 to Frederic Grant Gleason, Van der Stucken listed November 15, 16, 17, 18, and 19 as the dates of his festival. He also asked the composer not to communicate with the press until after his official announcement. Undated letter (envelope postmarked September 1, 1887), Frederic Grant Gleason Collection, Newberry Library, Chicago.

18. "An American Festival," *MC* 15/10 (September 7, 1887): 147.

19. Quoted in "Chickering Hall. The First American Concert," *Freund's Music and Drama* 9/3 (November 19, 1887): 4, and "Van der Stucken on His Efforts in Behalf of American Composers," *AAJ* 48/2 (October 29, 1887): 19.

20. The November 22 audience was estimated at fewer than 800 in [William M. Thoms], "Fourth American Concert," *AAJ* 48/6 (November 26, 1887): 85.

21. "Another 'American' Concert," *New York Sun*, November 20, 1887, p. 2.

22. [Henry E. Krehbiel], "First American Concert," *New York Daily Tribune*, November 16, 1887, p. 4.

23. [W. J. Henderson], "Music by Americans," *NYT*, November 16, 1887, p. 5.

24. [Krehbiel], "First American Concert," p. 4.

25. [Henderson], "Music by Americans," p. 5.

26. "Mr. Van der Stucken's American Concerts," *New York Sun*, November 16, 1887, p. 2.

27. "The American Concerts," *MC* 15/21 (November 23, 1887): 339.

28. Editorial comment, *MC* 15/21 (November 23, 1887): 338.

29. "The American Concerts," *MC* 15/22 (November 30, 1887): 355.

30. J[ames] H[uneker], "News of the Month," *The Etude* 5/12 (December 1887): 185.

31. "Mr. Van der Stucken's American Concerts," p. 2.

32. "Yesterday's Concerts," *Evening Post*, November 18, 1887, p. 5.

33. See, for instance, [William M. Thoms], "First Night with American Composers," *AAJ* 48/5 (November 19, 1887): 68.

34. [William M. Thoms], "Second American Concert," *AAJ* 48/6 (November 26, 1887): 84.

35. "The American Concerts," *MC* (November 30, 1887): 355.

36 Ibid.

37. [Henry Krehbiel], "The Last American Concert," *New York Daily Tribune*, November 25, 1887, p. 5.

38. [Henry Krehbiel], "American Chamber Music," *New York Daily Tribune*, November 23, 1887, p. 4.

39. "Chickering Hall," 4.

40. "The Last American Concert," *New York Herald*, November 25, 1887, p. 10.

41. "Eine eigentliche, charakteristische Schule amerikanischer Musik bis heute noch nicht existirt." "Van der Stucken-Koncert," *N.Y. Figaro* 7/47 (November 20, 1887): 4.

42 Ibid.

43. "Wenn man unter Berücksichtigung all dieser Verhältnisse die Bestrebungen hiesiger Musikfreunde, eine selbstständige amerikanische Tonkunst zu schaffen, beobachtet, so liegt die Frage nahe, ob dieser ganze Kampf nicht ein Kampf mit Windmühlen ist. Es wäre möglich, dass der eingewanderte Deutsche und die Angehörigen anderer musikalischer Nationen wenigstens dem *amerikanischen* Angelsachsen mit der Zeit von ihren musikalischen Gaben genügend zutheilen, um daraus eine amerikanische Tonkunst zu gewinnen. Aber vielleicht lässt die angelsächsische Nüchternheit auch diese nicht aufkommen. Die Angelsachsen sind, und bleiben wahrscheinlich, eine unmusikalische Rasse." "Amerikanische Musik und Sänger," *N.Y. Figaro* 10/27 (5 July 1890): 8.

44. [William Apthorp], "Mr. Sherwood's Concerts," *BET*, November 9, 1887, p. 1.

∞ 5 ∞

The Exposition Universelle of 1889: American Music on a World Stage

The American genius seems to tend toward a different ideal than
that of the arts. It is by way of science that it must reach the sum-
mits.

—Auguste Boisard, 1889[1]

Presenting American music in Europe had been a goal for the organizers of
American Composers' Concerts almost from the beginning of the movement. A
trio of amateurish concerts organized by Louis Melbourne had been ridiculed in
London in 1885,[2] while Van der Stucken's scheme to present concerts there in
1887 had fallen through, apparently because of lack of interest. The opportunity
to present a sampling of American works to European audiences finally came
during the Exposition Universelle of 1889, when Van der Stucken conducted a
high-profile concert in Paris. The gala concert was an important showcase for
the art music of the United States, but the critical reception ranged from conde-
scending to hostile. The harsh assessment of the American concert was not entirely due to the music itself but also to French attitudes about Americans and
their culture. This initial foray into Europe offers a chance to examine the European critical response in detail, a response that is particularly revealing of perceptions regarding high and low culture in the United States.

The Exposition Universelle of 1889, held in Paris from May to November, is remembered as a multicultural event. Europeans were exposed as never before to cultures from Africa, Asia, and South America, with profound results. Claude Debussy's subsequent interest in the music of the Javanese gamelan is well documented, and contemporary reports highlighted the ethnomusicological aspects of the exposition.[3] The concerts of Western music also focused on national styles, with a series of orchestral and choral concerts featuring the music of Russia, Finland, Norway, Spain, and the United States.

The musical offerings at the exposition were so rich and varied that the French critic Victorin Joncières wrote that there was too much music. He pointed out that an exhibit of 5,000 paintings could be assimilated gradually, whereas a series of concerts demanded a different level of attention.[4] The concerts must have been doubly enervating, since visitors were constantly assaulted with music even on the exposition grounds. There were four kiosks set up at the corners of the exposition grounds on the Champs de Mars, where four different bands played simultaneously. Because of the proximity of the kiosks, visitors had the experience later immortalized by Charles Ives of hearing two bands playing different pieces at the same time.[5] Native music was played in many of the pavilions devoted to different cultures, with the Annamite theater attracting the most comment. There was even a competition of "musiques pittoresques," in which gypsies and other folk musicians vied with each other for prizes.[6] Outside the exposition grounds there were café musicians and street musicians, making it virtually impossible to escape the bombardment of music. Small wonder that Gabriel Baume wrote of a "musical orgy."[7]

The concerts of art music took place in the cavernous auditorium of the Palais du Trocadéro, directly across the Seine from the exposition grounds and the newly constructed Eiffel Tower. They were held in the afternoons because "the administration would hear nothing of serious concerts after dinner."[8] While some of the national concerts showcased performers from the featured country itself, the American concert was performed by French orchestral musicians, with an American conductor and several American soloists. Van der Stucken was apparently invited sometime in May to conduct the July 12 concert, forcing him to act quickly in choosing repertoire and soloists. One of his first invitations went to Edward MacDowell, the rising young American pianist and composer who had lived in Europe from 1876 to 1888. The composer had settled in Boston in 1888 and had not been back to Europe since. The invitation was tendered in person to MacDowell's mother in New York, and a subsequent letter from his father to MacDowell on May 23, 1889, gives some clues as to Van der Stucken's plans and the financial risks involved: "If you would go, he would want you to start about the end of June, to be one week in Paris, and all he could offer would be your actual expenses of travel there and back and hotel expenses for the week. If he made any profit over & above the expenses he would share percentage with you which can not be counted on."[9]

MacDowell decided to accept Van der Stucken's proposal, for it offered both an excellent professional opportunity and a chance to spend the summer with friends in Europe. The other soloists on the program were violinist Willis Nowell, who played Henry Holden Huss' *Romanze et Polonaise* for violin and orchestra, and two American vocal students of Mathilde Marchesi, to whom we return later.

According to Otto Floersheim of *The Musical Courier*, Van der Stucken was allowed to use the auditorium free of charge. The orchestra was that of the Opéra Comique, one of the best in Paris. They had a total of five rehearsals, during which Floersheim reported that they were put through the wringer: "Also did they take Mr. Van der Stucken's not always very complimentary remarks and his frequent criticisms with the utmost good nature and followed all of his instructions in the most careful and minute manner."[10]

Van der Stucken's program featured the most successful of recent American art music in a variety of formats and styles. The major works were five large orchestral compositions: MacDowell's Second Piano Concerto, op. 23, Paine's Prelude to *Oedipus Tyrannus*, op. 35, Chadwick's dramatic overture *Melpomene*, Arthur Foote's overture *In the Mountains*, op. 14, and Van der Stucken's own orchestral suite *The Tempest*, op. 8. MacDowell had premiered his concerto in New York in March, followed by another performance in Boston the following month. By reprising the concerto in Paris with MacDowell as soloist, Van der Stucken not only featured the latest work by the composer who many felt was America's "man of the future" but also featured one of the best pianists in the country. Paine was the senior member of the "Second New England School," whose *Oedipus Tyrannus* (1881) has been compared to Mendelssohn's *Antigone* and *Oedipus in Kolonos*. As noted in previous chapters, Paine made no apologies for following German models throughout his career, believing that they provided the best example for composers in a nation that did not have a long tradition of orchestral composition. Chadwick's *Melpomene* (1887) had been extremely well received in the United States. In the years ahead, frequent performances on both sides of the Atlantic would make it Chadwick's best-known work. Its unmistakable allusions to Wagner and their implications for an American composer are discussed in chapter 8. Arthur Foote's *In the Mountains* (1886) had already been played twice by the Boston Symphony Orchestra under Wilhelm Gericke and twice by Van der Stucken on previous American Composers' Concerts. It would later be heard in Van der Stucken's Washington concert in March 1890 and in concerts in Berlin and Dresden in 1891. The conductor's orchestral suite, *The Tempest*, had been written during his sojourn in Breslau and changed from *Der Sturm* to *La Tempête*, depending on where it was being performed.

In addition to these principal works, the concert included six art songs and three shorter orchestral works: Huss's *Romanze et Polonaise*, Arthur Bird's sparkling *Carnival Scene*, op. 5, and Dudley Buck's *Festival Overture on the Star-Spangled Banner*, which concluded the program. None of the works received its premiere in Paris, as the conductor opted for a program of "chestnuts" from the recent American repertoire. To the French critics, though, all the works were unfamiliar. Compounding the difficulty noted by William Apthorp in 1887 of remaining attentive during an entire program of new music was the length of this particular concert. Like F. X. Arens several years later, Van der Stucken apparently wanted to include as much music as possible on such an auspicious occasion.

The program was subject to change until a few days before the concert, as indicated by this postcard from MacDowell to Margaret Ruthven Lang in Boston:

10 July Paris
Dear Miss Lang,

I showed your songs to to [*sic*] van der Stucken who says he will put <u>Ojala</u> on his programme. I expect to accompany it myself and hope it will bring down the house. Concert is day after tomorrow. All Well. Kind regards to all.

E. A. MacDowell[11]

Lang (1867–1972) was the daughter of Benjamin Johnson Lang (1837–1909), the prominent Boston conductor. She had recently returned from a year of study in Munich, and the Paris performance of her song was an important milestone for the young composer.[12]

An unusual feature of this concert was the installation of an Edison phonograph in the balcony of the auditorium to record the entire performance. The machine must have been quite large, for several of the French critics commented on the imposing sight of the machine and on its symbolic significance in the concert setting. The recording was subsequently returned to the United States, though this was before the days of commercial distribution of phonograph records.[13]

The concert was eagerly anticipated by the American community in Paris. An anonymous letter to the editor of the Paris edition of the *New York Herald* spoke in glowing terms of Miss Sylvania, one of the featured singers, and reminded readers of the upcoming concert. The letter closed with a sentiment that was shared by many Americans: "Let us wish all our prime donne success, and let us hope that the American composers will at last give us what we should have, and have long been wishing for—a distinctively American school of music."[14] Thanks to the cosmopolitan nature of the compositions on Van der Stucken's program, this was the one thing that audiences would *not* hear in Paris.

In the days and weeks before the concert, Van der Stucken was busy not only rehearsing but also promoting the event. A press release, which went out shortly before the concert, was printed in whole or in part by many of the Parisian dailies:

M. Frank Van der Stucken, the director and conductor of the grand American concert that will take place at the Trocadéro this Thursday, deserves the recognition of musical France for the large part that he has given to French composers in his concerts in the United States. It is through him that the majority of the orchestral works of Massenet, Delibes, Lalo, Saint-Saëns, Chabrier, Godard, Lacôme, Widor, and others have been presented for the first time to the American public. At the time of the inauguration of the statue of liberty presented to the United States by France, M. Van der Stucken was chosen by the French colony of New York to conduct the festive concert given at the academy of music in honor of the French representatives, among whom were found MM. Spuller, de Lesseps, Bartholdi, etc. We therefore invite the French public to come applaud the works of the composers of the United States of America, which M. Van der Stucken will perform under their orders, Thursday 12

July, in the grande salle des fêtes of the Trocadéro. Nothing has been spared to give a grand character to this solemnity. M. Carnot [president of France] has promised to attend and the minister of the United States has reserved his box. In addition, in order to honor the president of the republic, the American section has promised to send to the Trocadéro on that day, as an honor guard, the soldiers whom everyone has admired in this section.[15]

This press release was the subject of bemusement and indignation on the part of several French critics. A. Landely began his review in *L'Art musical* by commenting on the publicity:

M. Frank Van der Stucken . . . let us know by a short notice that he deserved the recognition of France by reason of the efforts he has attempted for the vulgarization of our music. As unconscious Americanism it is rather fine. . . . Banging a big drum with the president of the republic and the minister of the United States and, finding these insufficient advertisement, reinforcing them with *admired soldiers* is the limit. Oh Paris, what is becoming of you![16]

In fact, the president of France did not attend, but his wife's presence was noted in the report of the concert that appeared in *Le Petit Journal*, also reprinted verbatim in other newspapers.[17] The soldiers that raised Landely's hackles were also not there, although the concert was reportedly attended by 3,000 persons, including many of France's most prominent musicians. The result was an event described by Floersheim in ecstatic terms:

The performance therefore was, as I said before, one worthy of the occasion and the American composers represented by the program have every reason to feel flattered and grateful to Mr. Van der Stucken for the pains he took, the risks he incurred, financial and otherwise, and for the success he achieved for them; for the concert was an artistic success of the most pronounced kind and created a most favorable impression as regards our native born musical creators among the French portion of the audience present, while the Americans were elated beyond description, and altogether the audience of about three thousand persons was one of the most enthusiastic and at the same time one of the most musical that can well be imagined. Among the musicians of note whom I noticed were Massenet, Lalo, Joncières, Dubois, Lacôme, Chabrier, Messager, Jonas, Danbé, Vianesi and Bruneau. Gounod and Saint-Saëns would undoubtedly also have honored themselves and the concert giver with their presence if they had not been absent from Paris.[18]

Floersheim went on to summarize the French critical reaction for his American readers thus:

Among the other distinguished people there were . . . all the most prominent music critics of Paris, notably Charles Darcours, Weber, Victor Wilder, Kerst and others. All of these have shown in their criticisms the same kind, but rather more expectant than positively praising, disposition which the French art critics have evinced toward the modern American school of painting: they are most friendly and sympathetic, but hardly very enthusiastic.[19]

If an American reader had only Floersheim's notice in *The Musical Courier* as evidence, he could have been forgiven for assuming that the Paris concert was an unqualified success. Indeed, the other reviews that were read at home also exhibited the "friendly and sympathetic" tone mentioned by the author.   A mildly encouraging review by Charles Darcours was reprinted in translation in the *American Musician*,[20] another lukewarm review appeared in the *New York Times*,[21] and Julien Tiersot's book of collected musical reviews from the exposition (featuring a lukewarm review of the American concert) was read in the United States.[22] As a consequence, Americans believed that the French critical response, while not enthusiastic, was at least encouraging. A more extensive survey of contemporary periodicals reveals a different story.

At the beginning of 1889, the *Annuaire de la presse française* listed no fewer than 1,811 periodicals of all sorts published in Paris. Most of these, of course, had nothing to do with music, but among them were close to 100 daily newspapers, fifteen music journals, twenty-two theater journals, fifty-six literary journals, and twenty-six journals dedicated to the fine arts.[23] Thanks to the rich collections of the Bibliothèque nationale, the Conservatoire, and the Opéra, the present study is based on all the extant newspapers and journals known to have had musical or theatrical reviewers on staff, along with the most likely music, theater, and literary journals, for a total of well over 100 journals and newspapers.[24] Appendix 3 lists the reviews published in these sources, which proved to be more extensive than Americans realized at the time and also less "friendly and sympathetic" than Floersheim led his readers to believe. The reactions of the French press were indicative of deeply ingrained continental stereotypes about Americans, and while they revisited some of the themes addressed by American critics at previous American Composers' Concerts, they also raised new issues for the movement.

The first surprise is the relatively small number of reviews that were published in French papers. Of the twenty notices listed in Appendix 3, three are from American papers, and the "review" in *Le Petit Journal*, is so short that it is stretching the definition of the term to include it. The remaining sixteen reviews were published in six daily newspapers (fewer than one in ten Paris dailies printed a review of this concert), eight journals devoted to music or drama, and three literary journals (the article by Darcours appeared in both a daily paper and a dramatic review).

There are several significant names among the reviewers. Alfred Bruneau (1857–1934) had won the Grand Prix de Rome in 1881 and had premiered his first opera, *Kérim*, in 1887. He went on to a long and distinguished career as a composer and music critic. Louis Gallet (1835–1898), critic of *La Nouvelle Revue* from 1879 to his death, wrote libretti for operas by Bizet, Massenet, Saint-Saëns, and others. Saint-Saëns, who had recommended him to the editors of *La Nouvelle Revue*, said of Gallet, "He is not a musician in the sense that he has not studied music, but he is a musician at heart, which is worth more."[25] Adolphe Jullien (1845–1932) was a prominent critic for many years, during which time he earned the epithet "Porc-epic malintentionné" (ill-disposed porcupine) for his ardent defense of Berlioz, Schumann, Brahms, and Wagner as well as for his attacks on Franck, Gounod, and Saint-Saëns.[26] Victor Wilder (1835–1892) provided reviews for many papers, none more important than the literary daily *Gil Blas*. Johannès Weber provided thoughtful reviews from 1861 to 1895 for *Le Temps*, a paper of unimpeachable moral authority that was

"serious to the point of boredom."[27]   Darcours, Tiersot, Edmond Stoullig, and
Julien Torchet were also respected critics.

These writers, while providing a useful cross-section, represent only a fraction of the critical establishment. This small representation may be partially
explained by fact that the concert fell two days before the Centennial celebration
of the French republic. It was also due, however, to the nature of French music
criticism at the end of the nineteenth century. The Parisian critics and the public to which they catered at this time were much more interested in theater than
in concerts. Many papers ran a weekly or biweekly column (*feuilleton*) of theatrical reviews without devoting a column to music. In those papers that did publish musical reviews, the majority of the space was devoted to opera. Though
this concert was of major significance to Americans, it was perhaps not viewed
as an important event by some of the Parisian critics.[28] It also seems that some
critics attended the American concert but chose not to write about it.   The
American Register, a weekly paper dedicated to the interests of the American
community in Paris, listed Van der Stucken's address in Paris and announced
his concert but did not review or even mention the concert after it had taken
place.[29] Floersheim noted in his review for *The Musical Courier* that he had
seen the influential critics Joncières of *La Liberté* and [Léon] Kerst of *Le Petit
Journal* in attendance at the Trocadéro, but neither critic mentioned the concert,
either in his regular column or in a separate article. This may have been a polite
way to avoid echoing Camille Benoît, who appended the following note to his
"Chronique Parisienne" in *Le Guide musical*: "P.S.—The American and Span-
ish concerts did not teach us much that was new and were only interesting from
the point of view of execution."[30] It is impossible to know how many music
critics were among the estimated audience of 3,000, but it is clear that some of
those in attendance chose not to review the concert or chose to pass over it in a
sentence.

The two most positive reviews have one thing in common—they were both
written by composers. Floersheim was an aspiring composer whose works had
been performed at the MTNA conventions, and he may have hoped that kind
words on the exposition concert would cause Van der Stucken to look favorably
at programming his works in the future. His review for *The Musical Courier*
was clearly written in close consultation with the conductor, as it detailed all his
preparations and described the rehearsals. Floersheim repeatedly stressed the
positive reaction with glowing prose such as the passage quoted previously.
The other positive review came from Bruneau, who was more inclined than his
fellow French critics to be indulgent toward the young American composers:
"The majority of the composers heard on this concert are at the beginning of
their careers. For this reason alone, we owe them, it seems to me, a fraternal
sympathy, and they merit our applause."[31] He went on to state that it was perfectly natural that they would be somewhat lacking in originality and mastery of
the orchestra but that their works held much promise for the future. He concluded with a statement that reflected perhaps more of the composer's than the
critic's view: "For my part, I am anxious to point out this courageous attempt
at art, for it proves again the immense power of contemporary music, which, in
spite of everything, rises, grows, and triumphs everywhere in a radiance of deliv-
erance, hope, work, and faith."[32] Bruneau expressed his gratitude for Van der

Stucken's efforts on behalf of contemporary French composers and may have hoped for future consideration from the American conductor.

Though not as effusive as Floersheim or Bruneau, Wilder praised the Americans without the condescension found in many of the other reviews:

> The program of this concert . . . carried ten names; they are all practically unknown to us, because—it is necessary to repeat unceasingly—our vainglorious indifference leaves us in the most crass ignorance about what is produced beyond our borders. The compositions that M. Van der Stucken allowed us to hear are nevertheless not such as one could coldly disdain. If the personality is still lacking, they at least attest that, on the other side of the Atlantic just as on ours, people are pursuing serious musical studies. There is a vigorous and resolute effort that merits attention and who knows? if, some day, the grain of genius falls by chance in the head of a Yankee composer, we will see a renewal, in the realm of art, of the miracles of which Edison's works have been the brilliant manifestation in the realm of science.[33]

These three supportive articles were exceptions to the general rule, as the others ranged from qualified support to outright hostility. The French critics who disliked the concert descended to a level of animosity seldom encountered in the polite world of art music. One of the most vicious reviews was written by a critic named Brument-Colleville in *Le Monde musical*. He stated frankly what others only hinted at—his preconceptions about Americans and their artistic abilities:

> I was very curious to see how the country which has given the world such super-stupendous [*surabracadabrantes*] inventions as the telephone, suspenders, washing machines, and rich uncles would manage from an artistic point of view. I went to the Trocadéro—why should I hide it?—with defiance and a stupid prejudice, devoid in any case of a spirit that strains to be impartial. Well, for once, my defiance was not disappointed, and I spent there, in that *désert trocadéreux*, two of the worst hours I have ever spent—musically speaking, of course.[34]

Close examination of the reviews shows that this writer was not the only one who went to the concert with prejudices. The critical reaction yields insight not only into what the critics heard but into what they *expected* to hear. While the critics did not all agree on the merits of individual pieces, certain themes recur consistently.

At this period in French history, American singers were enjoying disproportionate success on the operatic stage, so it is not surprising to learn that the performance of the two vocal soloists was very well received. Both of them used stage names for this performance, but Floersheim identifies them as Mrs. Starkweather of Boston and Miss Walters of Philadelphia. The latter was a young soprano whose voice and appearance were particularly pleasing to the audience and critics. Though both were students, it is easy to understand why the critics were able to listen to them with appreciative ears. For several decades, American singers had been going to Paris to study with famous voice teachers, then going on to dazzling careers in opera. By 1889 American opera stars were to be heard throughout Europe, having earned a reputation as diligent and intelligent performers. In this context, it was natural for the French to praise two of Mar-

chesi's most promising American students, even if they were less receptive to
the repertoire that they sang.

The other two American soloists did not fare so well. Floersheim suggested that violinist Willis Nowell was "evidently laboring somewhat under the
excitement due to the importance of the moment,"[35] while the French critics
were not so kind. "Flamen," noting the presence of Massenet in the audience,
stated that the famous composer and teacher must have felt that he was back in
the conservatory listening to one of the weaker violin students. Brument-
Colleville stated, "He has neither attack, nor precision, nor virtuosity, but he
has, I must confess, something that is half of a violinist . . . an incommensura-
ble head of hair."[36] MacDowell received faint praise from the critics, although in
this case the critiques were mainly of the composition rather than the playing.
Wilder had read that MacDowell was one of America's most significant rising
composers, but he "found the virtuoso well above the composer."[37] Though
none of the critics mentioned it, they may have recalled that a decade earlier,
MacDowell had studied for two years at state expense in the Conservatoire national, earned a first prize in piano, and then promptly defected to Germany.[38]

Turning to the music, there was much disagreement over the merits of individual compositions. None of the critics wrote a long review of the concert (all
but three of the French reviews were under 600 words), so it is not surprising
that their comments on individual works were neither extensive nor insightful.
Also not surprisingly, two critics could have completely opposite opinions
about the same piece after only one hearing, resulting in mixed reviews for
nearly all the compositions.

The most positive response was to Van der Stucken's *La Tempête*. Over
half the critics singled out this work for special mention, with several citing it as
the best piece on the program. Most critics heard in the work a genuine individuality, aided no doubt by the composer's added control as conductor. The
exception to this view was aired by Auguste Boisard, who called the work labo-
rious and derivative in such strong terms that one is led to wonder if he was
expecting a bribe that he did not receive.[39] Chadwick's *Melpomene* was the
other major composition that was generally well liked. Brument-Colleville,
whose review is a model of vitriolic prose, found this work and a Chadwick
song to be the only redeeming points of the afternoon. Wilder also found the
Chadwick and the Paine to be the most impressive works on the program. Not
surprisingly, though, other critics had very different opinions. Weber felt that
Beethoven had already done all that could be done in a dramatic overture, while
Gallet wrote that the work was not at all in good taste. The Huss composition
was not treated kindly, while reaction to the Bird and Foote works varied
widely. Among the songs, those of Van der Stucken and Lang fared best.

Much more enlightening than the superficial comments on individual pieces
were the overall impressions of the critics regarding the state of American art
music. A phrase that appears often is "not yet," as demonstrated by the following excerpts:

Difficult as it is to admit it, American composers are not yet sufficiently gifted with
the "sacred fire" to make a concert containing only their works entertaining. (*New
York Herald*)[40]

This music does not yet have a character of its own; sometimes it draws inspiration from Germany, sometimes from Italy or France; one can say that it is conscientiously and solidly written, but it is cold. (André Blois, *Art et Critique*)[41]

American music is not yet born; it is still searching. In the country of Edison, all discoveries are possible, and as everything there goes at great speed, we may expect, one of these days, to see the music of the New World arise, fully formed, dazzling, and original to enchant us at the first note. Meanwhile, it has not found itself. (Darcours, *Le Figaro*)[42]

Variations on this theme are found in many of the other reviews. The essence of the idea is that American music was in a preliminary stage of evolution, with better results likely to follow. In a century whose byword was "progress," discussing musical works in evolutionary terms was accepted without question. This Darwinian model of development permeates the thinking of nearly all the writers, with some dismissing the music as worthless because it has not evolved sufficiently and others lauding the efforts of these "juvenile" composers as the foundation for future development. In all cases, though, the idea serves to belittle the composers represented. This view of American music in a preliminary state of development was based on the critics' perception of the concept of originality, and the point to which the reviewers returned most often was that of European influence on the American works. The assessment of Torchet is typical:

It is the first time, I believe, that we have been allowed to hear music written exclusively by American composers. From the specimens shown to us last week—they must be a select few—it follows that up to now there does not exist in America a compositional school, properly speaking. These works, very purely written, I recognize, lack originality: like the race that produced them, they are formed of a melange of German, English, and French elements. One senses by turns the influence of Mendelssohn and Schumann, of Saint-Saëns and Massenet, all of which is marred by a dryness and a stiffness that evidently come from Great Britain.[43]

This basic idea is encountered repeatedly, even with culinary images, as in Brument-Colleville's summary: "There is everything in this music, a filet of Mendelssohn with a salmi of Schumann, some hors-d'oeuvres from here, from there, from Wagner or from Brahms, not a few nebulosities and for dessert, boredom and monotony."[44]

    These themes are echoed repeatedly, which will not surprise those familiar with the music. All of the composers represented on the program wrote in the cosmopolitan style of late nineteenth-century art music, which was everywhere under the powerful influence of Germany. The more astute critics recognized the primary importance of German orchestral models, especially the works of Mendelssohn, on the American works. This was a source of satisfaction for anti-Wagnerites like Delphin Balleyguier: "We feared that young America, so determined to be always and in everything at the fore, would have embraced with passion the tendencies of the Wagnerian school. None of that at all. Over there they belong to Mendelssohn and Weber; that is the style that dominates their works, and likewise the instrumental groupings."[45]

While the German influence should have been obvious, it is more surprising to note that some critics seem to have been uncertain as to exactly what they were hearing. More than one critic suggested that the American compositions were equally indebted to French and German music, while Gallet stated that the works were pastiches of French style. Part of this may have been due to the "crass ignorance" of which Wilder accused French audiences in the passage cited earlier, along with a lack of awareness of the extent of German influence on the works of their own countrymen. Tiersot seems to have changed his mind about the works after further reflection—the original article that he published in *Le Ménestrel* cited only the influence of the "German Neo-Classical School" of Mendelssohn, Brahms, and Raff, but the version of the essay that was included in his book on the exposition included an added sentence identifying the influence of Gounod, Massenet, and Ambroise Thomas.

The conclusion that most of the critics drew from this European influence was that the Americans lacked originality. Balleyguier, one of the more diplomatic of the critics, wrote that while one could have wished for more personality, there were at least no "unwholesome eccentricities."[46] Several of the critics were much harsher:

In summary, it is the personality that seems to be missing in the American composers. They are adapters more than creators, and the majority of their adaptations are to the honor of our French school, to which they contribute in spreading the taste and augmenting the influence of our country. (Gallet, *La Nouvelle Revue*)[47]

. . . a desperate monotony that left in the spirit of the hearer a spectral vision of a poor composer, or supposedly such, fanning the flames to make the ideas and notes come out. The notes come . . . but the ideas . . . !!! (Brument-Colleville)[48]

Was the music of these American composers really that bad? The answer to this question depends primarily on the criteria applied in judging the works. To understand why the French critics were so negative, we must examine the composers and their works in the context of late nineteenth-century European music, particularly the problem of musical nationalism.

The French critics returned repeatedly to an issue that had been debated in the United States since the beginning of the movement—the question of whether the American national character was sufficiently well defined to produce a national school of composition. As had been the case in America, this issue could be debated in abstract terms with no reference to actual compositions. Alphonse Duvernoy began his review with a blunt statement that essentially ruled out the possibility of American music: "The Americans are a people too young and formed of elements too diverse to possess a well-defined musical school at this time. Originality in art, or more precisely, artistic nationality, is only found in older nations where the races have long been blended into a homogeneous whole."[49] Clearly, there was a logical flaw in Duvernoy's statement, since he was arguing from his conclusion rather than from the evidence at hand, but his view was shared by other critics. Jullien stated that the American compositions represented the first stages of national development, while Wilder believed that "the musical art of Americans is like their nationality, an amalgam of races in which the fusion is not sufficiently complete to constitute an irreducible type."[50]

With this idea, the critics struck a sore spot of the American Composers' Concert movement. The stated purpose of the movement was to stimulate development of a distinctive school of American composition by encouraging American composers. This encouragement, however, could not guarantee that composers would create a unique style or even that they would share the same aesthetic ideals. After five years of American Composers' Concerts, there was no evidence that the United States was any closer to developing a national style. At this time in history, the failure to make progress toward an identifiable national style was viewed as a serious shortcoming in the political and aesthetic climate of Europe.

In the late nineteenth century, nationalism of all sorts was a primary philosophical and political ideal. In music, the ideal is reflected by dozens of composers from "minor" countries who attempted to reflect the qualities of their own ethnic group with music that contained some unique element of their culture. While this produced compositions that were inspiring to oppressed peoples in Bohemia and other enclaves of Europe, the final result was a ghettoization of art music, with composers from such diverse areas as Norway, Russia, Spain, and England lumped together under the umbrella of "nationalism." This was the inspiration for the series of concerts at the Trocadéro, and it conditioned the expectations of critics and audiences when listening to any music from a country other than Germany or Austria.

Carl Dahlhaus noted in *Nineteenth-Century Music* that identifying national characteristics in art music is problematic for two reasons. First, the typical markers for "folklorism" are almost universal, as Grieg, Balakirev, Bizet, and others use the same set of technical devices to denote nationalistic elements in their respective countries: pentatonicism, the Dorian sixth and Mixolydian seventh, the raised second and augmented fourth, nonfunctional chromatic coloration, and bass drones, ostinatos, and pedal points as central axes.[51] Second, the techniques for denoting folkloristic nationalism are indistinguishable from those denoting exoticism, making the context essential for understanding the composer's intentions. Dahlhaus notes that nineteenth-century listeners were largely ignorant of these similarities but that the fact of inserting an element audibly different from the European norm mattered more than the actual ethnic origin of the gesture.[52]

At the root of the nationalist mentality was the idea that every country or ethnic group has a distinct character that must be expressed before its art music reaches maturity.[53] Perhaps the best illustration of this quest is the work of the "Mighty Handful" in Russia, who rejected many of the traditional rules of Western music in order to create an art music based on distinctive Russian elements. Even these composers, however, were open to criticism for their attempts at developing a national style. Weber used his review of the American concert as an occasion to critique the Russians, showing that nationalism as a critical construct can serve as a double-edged sword: "Today the composers of [the United States] at least have the advantage over the Russians of not seeking to acquire originality through 'pulling it by the hair,' a process that never succeeds. They will in time form a symphonic school; for now they are only at the beginning."[54]

It will be recalled that Krehbiel had addressed this issue pointedly in his *Review of the New York Musical Season* for 1885–1886. In his view, it was foolish to wait for universal agreement on the issue of national character before promoting American music. He believed that the process of creating a national school could begin while the American population was still in flux because of immigration. He had argued convincingly against the idea that only older nations can produce a legitimate body of art music, but his opinions were not widely shared. The most damning indictment of the composers heard in the Trocadéro came from an American author in a review for the *New York Times*: "What we still lack almost entirely is abandonment to any sense of spontaneous coloration or originality. We are neither German nor French, and unfortunately, not American."[55]

Ironically, the cosmopolitan aspect of American culture was the one thing that neither the American nor the French critics wished to hear. Whereas Debussy's early style could be based quite naturally on Massenet, Strauss could draw heavily on the inspiration of Wagner, and even Smetana could employ healthy doses of Liszt, any hints of European influence in the American works were viewed as signs of lack of originality. Torchet seems to have recognized this dilemma in his assessment of the reaction: "The performance was relatively cold, despite the exuberant efforts of the expatriate colony to provoke enthusiasm. It seems to me that the public did not prove to be completely fair in these manifestations; they were wrong to demand an original school from composers who do not boast of having one, and they should have listened without preoccupations of this sort."[56]

In the context of the Exposition Universelle of 1889, the expectation for nationalism was taken a step further because of the exotic musics of Asia and Africa. These cultures provided something titillatingly different for a Paris that was already experiencing a fin-de-siècle ennui and overcultivation. To the French critics of 1889, the sophisticated and highly polished art music of the American composers was too similar to their own. Conditioned by the expectation for exotic nationalism, they found little to appreciate in music that sounded so close to home.

Was this cool reception the result of proverbial anti-American attitudes in France? Hardly. French audiences in 1889 were fascinated by Americans, so long as they met their expectations of what Americans should be. This point is brought home forcefully by the reaction to another American who performed in Paris during the eventful summer of 1889—the king of the Wild West showmen, "Buffalo Bill" Cody (1846–1917).

Buffalo Bill and his troupe went to Paris in the spring after a record-breaking season in England, setting up camp at Neuilly-sur-Seine, just northwest of the city. Today the area is covered with office and apartment buildings, but it is still evident that the area is very flat. In 1889 Neuilly was a large plain with plenty of room to rope and ride. The French public was enthralled by the Buffalo Bill show, which played two performances daily for the entire summer. The arena was packed with dignitaries and commoners alike. Along with thrilling scenes from the Wild West, Parisians had their first taste of a new snack that would prove enduringly popular—popcorn.

The critics were equally enthralled with the show. Jules Guillemot, theatrical critic for the *Messager de Paris*—a paper that did not review the Van der Stucken concert—called the Buffalo Bill show "one of the most original shows occasioned by the Centennial."[57] The allure of this piece of New World exoticism is summed up by an article in *La République illustrée* (which also did not review the American concert):

I sincerely admire these men of the Far West, pioneers of American civilization, who in their continual forward march have assured their compatriots of the tranquil possession of land watered with their blood. Fenimore Cooper and Gustave Aymard themselves remained far from reality in attempting to make us understand through their novels the rough existence, the harsh labors, the cleverness and heroism of these cowboys who have come to us from America for the Exposition.[58]

The significance of the Buffalo Bill show goes beyond its popularity as entertainment, for the show also purported to represent truthfully the events involved in taming the West. In a recent study of the Buffalo Bill legacy, Sarah J. Blackstone has noted that this was essentially a falsehood. The cowboys and Indians who performed in the show were persons who had actually participated in the winning of the West, but the show's portrayal of these events was anything but realistic. Blackstone concludes:

The show was full-blown propaganda—glorifying the process of the winning of the American West and declaring to the world that America had won a resounding victory in its efforts to subdue the wilderness. The back-breaking, bloody, and often fatal task of taming the frontier was romanticized and glorified by Cody through his Wild West until the truth was so totally mixed with the myth as to be indistinguishable. The image that Americans have of themselves and the image that Europeans have of Americans is closely tied to both the reality and the myth of the American West.[59]

This image of Americans was the central message of the show, which was a resounding success in Paris. Though some of the French press expressed disdain for the show and the culture that it reflected,[60] most were caught up in the enthusiasm of the public. In particular, a recently discovered essay by the popular French satirist and observer of Parisian life Henri Lavedan sheds light on the extent of the adulation of Buffalo Bill and some possible reasons for it. The essay, entitled "Adieux à Buffalo," was published on November 15, 1889 and expressed his regret at seeing the performer go.[61]

Lavedan began his essay by describing the arrival of the company by train the previous spring. Lavedan noted that Cody traveled with an immense retinue of cowboys, Indians, and livestock—150 horses and scores of live buffalo—as well lavish sets, costumes, and props for the extravaganza.[62] The author was most impressed with the cowboys, though, as their weather-beaten faces fired his imagination of places far away:

For several seconds I believed myself transported to the country where they search for gold with a pistol in the fist. I recalled the typical sign in a little café concert over there . . . "Don't shoot the pianist, he's doing the best he can!" And then, as soon as I returned from my hallucination, I had a profound regret not to know at all these happy countries where one chats with the revolver, where one eats, where one loves, where one sleeps with the finger on the trigger and where a simple hello is said with six shots.[63]

For this author, the American West represented violence, which simultaneously attracted and repelled him.[64] The musical reference in this passage is significant, for it seems to contrast music with the "real" nature of America.

Lavedan went on to relate that he attended the Buffalo Bill show many times, "never without pleasure, like all the Parisians of the entire universe."[65] He summed up his feelings about the show and the culture that it represented with a fanciful episode that again contains a musical reference:

One evening, when I had slipped out of the show and wandered alone, a little before closing, through the grounds of the camp, I was struck by a strange low noise. It was something sweet, shrill, and melodious, I knew not what uncertain, veiled, yet vibrant music; one would have said the chords of the zither, perceived more than heard, through a wall, in the silence of the night, in a hotel room abroad. I discovered that the sound came from a tent not far from where I found myself. I approached on tiptoe, and by the opening, I saw a great cowboy, lazy giant, sprawled on his cot. Legs apart, eyes closed, comfortably smoking a long cigar of forty centimeters, he strummed nonchalantly with his right hand a sort of guitar of ebony, resting on his chest. The incoherent and suave melody no doubt accompanied his dream, lulling it among the blue tobacco smoke, while he forgot about life for a moment, lying in his little house of canvas. Certainly it roused in his head and in his heart a bit of country, a bit of family, a bit of woman, a bit of the past; they call that (even for a cowboy) playing to the angels.[66]

This romantic portrayal of cowboy life is full of evocative and symbolic details (e.g., the unusually long cigar), but for our purposes, the cowboy's "uncertain, veiled, yet vibrant music" is particularly striking. This image of American music could hardly be further from the tradition of European art music, and it is perhaps just this remote quality that made it attractive to Lavedan. The appeal of this music was not its polished or professional sound but rather its power to reinforce the author's perception of cowboy life. How ironic that none of the composers on the Van der Stucken program received as good a musical review as this unsuspecting cowboy in his tent. Clearly, the French critics preferred to consign lower culture to the United States while reserving high culture for Europe. This dichotomy between "low" and "high" art is the subject of Lavedan's concluding paragraph:

Today the cowboy with the guitar must be packing his scanty valise with satisfaction. After having seen other countries in quantity, he will return to see his own, which is always the best. After all, everything seems to indicate that he is content. But you, are you content, my colonel? They tell me no. Yes, they tell me you leave with a bit of chagrin. Here is what you say, it seems: "I made a million, that's good, but I have not been received by the aristocracy as I expected, and it is that especially which gives me real pain." If I understand, my colonel, you find that the nobility has been cold to you; the Jockey stayed away, and the Faubourg did not give what you expected. What do you want? Climb on your big horse, run your fine hand through your hair, and console yourself that, after all, you are not absolutely wrong. The presumptions, like your regrets, are not excessive, and when you lament not having convinced the leading names of France to take a tour of your grounds in a mail-coach,[67] I say to myself that you are logical, and that the number of dukes and duchesses who have scorned you has risen, not so long ago, in plenty of other carriages![68]

Lavedan's essay underscores the stereotypes that Europeans held about America. The New World was seen as the home of coarse, violent people whose simple charm and unself-consciousness made them the ideal purveyors of low culture. Lavedan understands Cody's desire for recognition by the European nobility but chides him gently with the reminder that he has a nobility of his own. Likewise, Parisians fell in love with a show that glorified the murder of Native Americans and the slaughter of endangered animals, but they could not as easily accept a performance of American concert music. The idea of Americans writing orchestral works, especially orchestral works that were closely related to the European tradition, defied preconceptions of what Americans should be. In a metaphorical sense, the Parisian critics could not resist shooting the piano player, even though he was doing the best that he could.

The other event that sheds light on French perceptions of the United States was the visit of Thomas Edison to the exposition. The famous inventor arrived with a group of American engineers to tour the exhibits and was treated with deference wherever he went. The French author Victor Fournel described him in epic terms:

Nothing is more audaciously provocative than this American, imbued with cold resolve, with the consuming activity of the trappers and pioneers of the new world, who wrestles hand to hand with elemental forces like the mythic heroes with monsters, guardians of coveted treasure; who for twenty years has gripped without respite this Proteus of sudden transformations, striving to seize it completely and tear out its secret. Edison seems to have taken for his scientific watchword the Yankee slogan: *Go ahead.* At the Institut Pasteur, when he was presented with the register where illustrious visitors enter their names, he signed: Edison, *inventor.* It is no doubt the first time a man has signed this title as his professional token.[69]

Edison, like Cody, is elevated in this passage to the status of a hero and compared to the mythic heroes of the past. Fournel casts Edison as a fighter, highlighting his brashness and impatience. These qualities again reflect the pioneer spirit, a spirit that Europeans viewed as prosaic and practical rather than poetic. As noted earlier, Edison's presence was felt at the Trocadéro concert through his phonograph. Boisard commented on the significance of this machine:

Was not moreover one of the most curious things about this performance the extraordinary and colossal phonograph aimed in the direction of the performers, to record every number of the program in its gigantic auditory tube? It is already very fine to have invented that, and one could maintain that this apparatus is worth much more than symphonies. Independent America, our big sister, should therefore console herself for again having to give precedence to us in artistic matters. In return, we salute with admiration and enthusiasm her practical genius in these marvelous inventions of M. Edison.[70]

The great irony of the events of 1889 is that the Wild West show, which was basically a falsehood, was taken at face value, while the music played at the

Trocadéro, which represented a sincere expression of its composers' aesthetic ideals, was decried as derivative and hence insincere. The problem with Frank Van der Stucken's concert was not that the music was badly written or poorly performed but rather that it did not fit the French perception of the United States. As the descriptions of Cody and Edison demonstrate, the American spirit was viewed as brash, pragmatic, and unsuited to artistic expression, while the music of Van der Stucken and his compatriots did not fit this model. This expectation of finding the "cultural essence" of the United States in its art music was at the heart of the negative reaction to the Trocadéro concert.

In terms of educating the French audience about American music, Van der Stucken's concert at the Exposition Universelle was a failure. Though the performance represented a milestone for Americans in terms of European exposure, the critical response shows clearly that the French did not understand what these composers were saying. In their expectation that the music would somehow reveal a nationalistic essence of the United States, they overlooked the most obvious aspect of the country and its music at this time—cosmopolitanism. In the context of late Romanticism in general and the Exposition Universelle of 1889 in particular, cosmopolitan was the one thing that American musicians were not permitted to be. It would be a year and a half before American Composers' Concerts were again presented in Europe, this time by Arens in Germany and Austria. The stolid German critics proved to be less cavalier than the French about dismissing American art music; they would revisit the issues of cosmopolitanism and nationalism in new and perceptive ways.

NOTES

1. A[uguste] Boisard, "Chronique musicale," *Le Monde illustré* 33/1686 (July 20, 1889): 43. Unless otherwise noted, all translations are by the author.

2. See "An American Concert," *London Times*, January 24, 1885, p. 5; "American Concerts," *London Times*, January 28, 1885, p. 5; "An American Concert," *London Times*, March 10, 1885, p. 10; "An American Concert," *London Times*, June 12, 1885, p. 13.

3. See, for instance, Julien Tiersot, *Musiques pittoresques: promenades musicales à l'Exposition de 1889* (Paris: Fischbacher, 1889) and M. Benedictus, *Les musiques bizarres à l'Exposition* (Paris: Hartmann, 1889). See also Jean-Paul Montaignier, "Julien Tiersot: Ethnomusicologie à l'Exposition Universelle de 1889," *International Review of the Aesthetics and Sociology of Music* 21/1 (June 1990): 91–100.

4. Victorin Joncières, "Revue musicale," *La Liberté*, November 11, 1889, p. 1.

5. Henry-Abel Simon, "La Musique et les musiques à l'Exposition," *Le Monde orphéonique* 7/197 (September 10, 1889): 1.

6. For an amusing account of this competition, held on July 4 in the Trocadéro, see Fernand Bourgeat, "Le Concours des musiques pittoresques," *L'Entracte* 58/189 (July 7, 1889): 2.

7. Gabriel Baume, "Orgie musicale," *L'Autorité*, July 10, 1889, p. 2.

8. Simon, "La Musique," 1.

9. Letter, [Thomas F. MacDowell] to Edward A. MacDowell, May 23, 1889, Library of Congress, Music Division. Quoted in Margery Morgan Lowens, "The New York Years of Edward MacDowell" (Ph.D. dissertation, University of Michigan, 1971; UMI 71-23,812), pp. 49–50.

10. Otto Floersheim, "The American Concert at the Trocadero, Paris," *MC* 19/5 (July 31, 1889): 107–8.

11. Lang family scrapbooks, 1887–1904, Boston Public Library.

12. For further information on Lang's European study and her early career, see E. Douglas Bomberger, "European Training for American Musicians: Three Women's Experiences," in *Proceedings of the Beach Conference at The University of New Hampshire on 28 October 1998*, ed. Adrienne Fried Block and William E. Ross (forthcoming).

13. To date, I have not found an answer to the logical question of whether this recording still exists today.

14. An American Amateur, "American Music," *New York Herald* (Paris edition), July 11, 1889, p. 3.

15. As quoted in "Grand concert américain du palais du Trocadéro," *Tintamarre* (July 14, 1889): 6. This was not the only paper to print the announcement after the concert was over.

16. A. Landely, "Concert américain," *L'Art musical* 28/13 (July 15, 1889): 100.

17. Jean de la Tour, "L'Exposition: Chronique du Champs de Mars," *Le Petit Journal*, July 14, 1889, p. 1.

18. Floersheim, "The American Concert," 107.

19. Ibid., 107–8.

20. There are three versions of this article: Charles Darcours, "Notes de musique à l'Exposition," *Le Figaro*, July 17, 1889, p. 6; "La Musique à l'Exposition," *La Revue théatrale illustrée* 21/15 (1889): 3; "Van der Stucken in Paris," *American Musician* 14/5 (August 3, 1889): 7.

21. L. K., "American Music in Paris," *NYT*, July 28, 1889, p. 9.

22. Tiersot, *Musiques pittoresques: promenades musicales a l'Exposition de 1889*. The review of the American concert was a slightly altered version of the original review, which appeared in *Le Ménestrel* 55/29 (July 21, 1889): 227–29.

23. Émile Mermet, *Annuaire de la presse française* (Paris: Mermet, 1889): lxiv. The volatile nature of the French press during this period is indicated by the fact that Mermet lists 660 new journals for the year 1888.

24. The Paris critics were listed annually in Mermet and in Édouard Noel and Edmond Stoullig, *Les Annales du théatre et de la musique* (Paris: Charpentier, annual from 1875 to 1916).

25. Quoted in Christian Goubault, *La Critique musicale dans la presse française de 1870 à 1914* (Geneva and Paris: Slatkine, 1984), pp. 52–53.

26. Ibid., 30.

27. Ibid., 30–31.

28. Commenting on how a composer like Bruneau could find time to be a music critic, Arthur Hervey observed, "The profession of musical critic in Paris is in some respects different to what it is in London. One *feuilleton* a week, besides an account of any new opera, is the most that is expected from a French critic. This is indeed more than most French newspapers provide—a short account of the usual Sunday concerts and a notice of the *première* of any new opera being generally considered sufficient. ... The Paris critic has therefore a fairly easy time of it in comparison with his English colleague. The numberless small concerts which are the plague of the London critic exist in Paris as well, but they are wisely left unmentioned." (Arthur Hervey, *Alfred Bruneau* [London: John Lane, 1907], p. 77)

29. *The American Register* 25/1,109 (July 6, 1889) includes the address on p. 1 and the announcement in the "Music and the Drama" column on p. 6.

30. Balthasar Claes [Camille Benoît], "Chronique Parisienne," *Le Guide musical* 35/29, 30 (July 21, 28, 1889): 189.

31. Alfred Bruneau, "Musique," *La Revue indépendante* 12/34 (August 1889): 209.

32. Ibid., 209–10.

33. Victor Wilder, "La Musique américaine au Trocadéro," *Gil Blas*, July 16, 1889, p. 3.

34. Brument-Colleville, "Le Concert américain au Trocadéro et les concerts espagnols au Vaudeville," *Le Monde musical* 1/6 (July 30, 1889): 7. This article was reprinted in translation in *The Sonneck Society for American Music Bulletin* 24/1 (Spring 1998): 10.

35. Floersheim, "The American Concert," 108.

36. Brument-Colleville, "Le Concert américain," 8.

37. Wilder, "La Musique américaine," 3.

38. The issue of foreign students receiving free instruction at the Conservatoire was discussed extensively during the summer of 1889. See, for instance, "Les Étrangers au Conservatoire," *Le Petit Journal*, July 23, 1889, p. 3.

39. Boisard, "Chronique musicale," 43.

40. "American Music: Audition at the Trocadéro of Works by United States Composers," *New York Herald* (Paris edition), July 13, 1889, p. 1.

41. Andre Blois, "Concert américain," *Art et Critique* 1/8 (July 20, 1889): 121.

42. Charles [Réty] Darcours, "Note de musique: À l'Exposition," *Le Figaro*, 17 July 1889, p. 6; reprinted as "La Musique à l'Exposition," *La Revue théâtrale illustrée* 21/15 (1889): 3; translated as "Van der Stucken in Paris," *American Musician* 14/5 (August 3, 1889): 7.

43. Julien Torchet, "Concert de musique américaine au Trocadéro," *Le Monde artiste* 29/29 (July 21, 1889): 449.

44. Brument-Colleville, "Le Concert américain," 7.

45. Delphin Balleyguier, "La Musique à l'Exposition: Concert américain," *Le Progrès artistique* 12/582 (July 20, 1889): 1.

46. Ibid., 1.

47. Louis Gallet, "Chronique du théatre: Musique," *La Nouvelle Revue* 11/59 (August 15, 1889): 821.

48. Brument-Colleville, "Le Concert américain," 7. The crotchety tone of this reviewer has already been noted. It is perhaps instructive to read his assessment of all the international concerts: "I would not hesitate to give the first prize to Russia, the second to Norway, the third to Italy, the fourth to America, which hardly exists, and the last to Spain, which does not exist at all." Brument-Colleville, "Les Concerts norwegiens au Trocadéro et vues d'ensemble sur les concerts internationaux," *Le Monde musical* 1/7 (August 15, 1889): 6.

49. Alphonse Duvernoy, "Revue musicale," *La République française*, July 29, 1889, p. 3.

50. Wilder, "La Musique américaine," 3.

51. Carl Dahlhaus, *Nineteenth-Century Music*, trans. J. Bradford Robinson (Wiesbaden, 1980; English edition Berkeley, Los Angeles, and London: University of California Press, 1989), pp. 305–6.

52. Ibid., 306.

53. This argument is stated succinctly in Oscar G. Sonneck, "National Tone-Speech versus Volapük—Which?," trans. Theodore Baker, in *Suum Cuique: Essays in Music* (New York, 1916; reprint Freeport, NY: Books for Libraries Press, 1969), pp. 25–34.

54. J[ohannès] Weber, "Critique musicale," *Le Temps*, July 15–16, 1889, supplement p. 1.

55. L. K., "American Music in Paris," p. 9.

56. Torchet, "Concert de musique américaine," 449.

57. Jules Guillemot, "Chronique Théâtrale," *Messager de Paris*, July 15, 1889, p. 10.

58. A. R., "Buffalo-Bill," *La République illustrée* 9/472 (July 27, 1889): 467; see also the illustrations of the show on pages 477 and 504. This journal also did not review the Van der Stucken concert.

59. Sarah J. Blackstone, *Buckskins, Bullets, and Business: A History of Buffalo Bill's Wild West* (Westport, CT: Greenwood, 1986), p. 1.

60. Albert Boime, "The Chocolate Venus, 'Tainted' Pork, the Wine Blight, and the Tariff: Franco-American Stew at the Fair," in *Paris 1889: American Artists at the Universal Exposition* by Annette Blaugrund (Philadelphia: Pennsylvania Academy of the Fine Arts, 1989), pp. 85–86.

61. Henri Lavedan, "Adieux à Buffalo," *La Revue illustrée* 8/95 (November 15, 1889): 319–20.

62. The logistics of traveling with this enormous collection of people, livestock, and equipment are discussed in "Getting the Show on the Road," Chapter 2 of Blackstone, *Buckskins, Bullets, and Business*, 37–52.

63. Lavedan, "Adieux à Buffalo," 319-20.

64. This perception of the United States is still alive over a century later. In a recent article on Franco-American relations, the French author opines, "I believe that one understands nothing about the United States unless one integrates the fact that violence is a founding element here. It is part of the history, the climate, and the culture of this country. Think, for instance of the liberty that exists for the buying and selling of individual firearms." [Jean Kaspar] "Faut-il haïr l'Amérique?" *Passages* 82 (April 1997): 21.

65. Lavedan, "Adieux à Buffalo," 320.

66. Ibid., 320.

67. In one of the segments of the Buffalo Bill show, audience members were invited to ride in a mail coach, which was then "attacked" by Indians.

68. Lavedan, "Adieux à Buffalo," 320. The precise meaning of Lavedan's final sentence is unclear, but it may be a topical political reference. The author uses the archaic term *berline* for the second reference to carriages. This may have been intended as a pun on the city of Berlin, a reflection both of growing political tension between Germany and the United States and of lingering animosity in France over the Franco-Prussian War (je me dis que tu es logique et que le nombre de ducs et de duchesses qui t'ont méprisé sont montés, il n'y a pas encore si longtemps, dans de biens autres berlines!).

69. Victor Fournel, "Les Oeuvres et les hommes," *Le Correspondant* 61 (September 25, 1889): 1160.

70. Boisard, "Chronique musicale," 4.

∽ **6** ∽

Interlude: Flood Tide

The American composer . . . after long suffering neglect, now seems
to be in imminent danger of being coddled to death.
                                  —Henry Krehbiel, 1890[1]

At its height, a tsunami is one of the most devastating forces in nature. The
rapid rise in the ocean level sweeps the waters of the sea over the coast with such
speed and force that nothing can stop the onslaught of water. Seawalls and other
man-made barriers are powerless to hold it back, and the speed of the advance
makes it impossible to outrun. A horrifying photograph of the 1946 tsunami
shows terror-stricken men running down the streets of Hilo with a wall of water
behind them.[2] It would certainly be hyperbole to suggest that the American
Composers' Concert movement exerted that sort of devastating power on nineteenth-century American music, but in the sense that its momentum proved to
be unstoppable at its height, the metaphor is remarkably apt.

Van der Stucken's American festival of 1887 had brought the critical debate
surrounding American Composers' Concerts to a crucial juncture. Though recognizing the important work that these concerts had achieved in bringing more
attention to neglected American works, Krehbiel and other critics began to have
doubts about the efficacy of segregating American music in this way. Their admonition to "whistle down brakes" went unheeded, though, as the movement
spread to middle America.

The American Composers' Concert was recognized as a festive and patriotic
way to celebrate an auspicious event, especially since the press followed such
concerts with interest. On March 26, 1890, Jeannette Thurber sponsored an all-
American concert in Washington, D.C., to publicize her National Conservatory

of Music. The event ostensibly signaled the opening of a branch in the nation's capital that would eventually supersede the one in New York, but critics doubted whether this would actually take place. They proved to be correct, as the conservatory never relocated to Washington. Instead, the event served the function of lobbying, for Thurber was in the midst of appealing to the U.S. Congress for a congressional charter for her conservatory. The guest list for the concert and the gala reception read like a who's who of American politics, as the rich and powerful were treated to a lavish party. Van der Stucken was engaged to plan and conduct the concert. He evidently decided to take the easiest way out by repeating nearly all the numbers from the previous summer's concert at the Paris Exposition. The event succeeded in its principal objective, as a year later Congress granted the National Conservatory the only charter ever awarded to a school of music.

The following year, the *New York Tribune* used another American Composers' Concert to celebrate its fiftieth anniversary on April 10, 1891. It seems likely that despite his growing misgivings about such events, the concert was the brainchild of the *Tribune*'s distinguished critic Henry Krehbiel. The concert was performed at the Metropolitan Opera House, with Walter Damrosch and his New York Symphony hired to provide the music for the occasion. The *American Art Journal* commented on the appropriateness of the concert for the occasion: "It was eminently fitting that the great daily founded by Horace Greeley and perpetuated by Whitelaw Reid should place itself in the advance guard on this memorable occasion, and thus set its seal of approval on the movement for the emancipation of the American composer."[3]

American Composers' Concerts were used not only for important celebrations, though. In fact, it is remarkable how widespread these events became in the late 1880s and early 1890s. Professionals and amateurs, soloists and ensembles, urban groups and rural groups—all seemed to recognize the potential of these concerts. Some tried them once and never came back, while others established long-running series of such events, helping to make them a vital part of American concert life.

As the state music teachers' associations grew in power during the late 1880s, they appropriated many of the ideas and practices of the MTNA. By 1889 there were fifteen state Music Teachers' Associations (MTAs), with more founded in the years following.[4] The state organizations allowed local teachers to exercise more influence than they could in the MTNA, and since the conventions were held in each state, it was also less expensive for teachers to travel to their state convention than to the national convention. The American Composers' Concert exerted a strong appeal for the state MTAs, because it allowed the organizations to limit the repertoire even further to composers from their own state.

Ever since the 1876 organizational meeting of the MTNA in Delaware, Ohio, the Ohio contingent had been crucial to the national association. The first American Composers' Concert in the MTNA had taken place in Cleveland in 1884, which would also be the site of the last convention to feature American Composers' Concerts in 1892. When the organization returned to the idea for one convention in 1899, the site was Cincinnati. Thus, it was natural for the powerful Ohio Music Teachers' Association (OMTA) to embrace the idea at its state conclaves, which typically took place a week before the national convention. The first OMTA concert to receive national publicity was at the 1887 convention in Columbus, the week before the Indianapolis convention of the MTNA. This concert featured Ohio composers exclusively. The same was true of the following year's convention, also held in Columbus. In 1889, the year of the disappointing MTNA convention in Philadelphia, the OMTA featured two concerts on June 27 in Cleveland's Case Hall. The morning program was devoted to Ohio composers, while the afternoon featured a recital of American works played by Lavallée. In subsequent years, the OMTA concerts featured many compositions by composers from Ohio and the rest of the United States without segregating them into special concerts.

The other state with a large and influential group of composers was Illinois. Like its sister organization in Ohio, the Illinois Music Teachers' Association began presenting concerts of Illinois composers with its 1887 convention. This organization stuck with the idea more tenaciously than the Ohio group, however, as Illinois Composers' Concerts remained a central part of their program through the mid-1890s. The Illinois teachers were not zealously restrictive in repertoire selection, as indicated by the 1889 concert at Peoria. Billed as an "Illinois Composers' Night," the concert began with a piece by Flotow and included a Beethoven concerto played by eleven-year-old pianist Gussie Cottlow of Shelbyville.[5]

New York, Pennsylvania, Rhode Island, and Iowa presented American Composers' Concerts that were noted in the national press, and it is likely that other state MTAs did as well. Because the state conventions met in different cities each year and usually were not well publicized, it has not been possible to verify the extent of this trend among all the state associations, but it is safe to speculate that the high-profile concerts in Ohio and Illinois represent only a fraction of the total.

The educational appeal of all-American concerts went beyond the state and national teachers' organizations. For members who were inspired by what they heard at the conventions, it was natural to take the idea back home to their students. This idea seems to have taken hold during the 1887/1888 academic year, as American Composers' Concerts were featured by W. L. Blumenschein in Dayton, Ohio, J. J. Hahn at the Detroit Conservatory of Music, and Theodor Salmon at the Pittsburgh Female College. During the following year the Detroit Conservatory presented a series of American Composers Concerts.[6] Perhaps in recognition of the responsibility implied by its name, the American Conservatory of Music in Chicago instituted a series of annual concerts devoted to American composers in 1889. The school remained committed to the idea and in 1893 presented its fifth annual American Composers' Concert.[7]

As these concerts became popular with teachers, it became necessary for publishers to supply more music at a variety of levels by American composers. Choosing American repertoire for students was made easier by Willard Burr Jr., who compiled lists of works graded by level of difficulty. Though his original idea was to create a survey of all available educational music by American composers, the resulting pamphlet, published by Theodore Presser, featured only works available from that publisher.[8]

In the 1890s American conservatories developed their composition programs to the point that it became possible to adopt a practice that had been used in European conservatories for decades—the composition concert. At the end of Dvořák's first year as director of the National Conservatory, he conducted two such concerts in New York. The concert in Madison Square Garden on March 30, 1893, featured the winning compositions from the nationwide competition sponsored by the conservatory. In May he presented a more modest recital of the works of his own composition students. Though still a rarity, this sort of concert was presented by other composition teachers as well, notably Frederic Grant Gleason and Adolf Weidig.

The notion of a competition offering cash prizes to American composers originated before the American Composers' Concert movement. In 1879 the Cincinnati Music Festival Association under the direction of Theodore Thomas offered $1,000 and a performance at the May Festival of 1880 for the best choral/orchestral work by a native-born American composer. Thomas was accused of favoritism when a work by his friend Dudley Buck was chosen over one by George Whiting of the Cincinnati College of Music by a vote of three to two. As chair of the selection committee, he had been obliged to cast the tiebreaking vote and was criticized in the press for his dealings in the competition.[9] A second contest, in which William Wallace Gilchrist's *Forty-Sixth Psalm* was awarded first prize, was held in 1882. According to Ezra Schabas, the hassles involved with the selection process as well as the poor reviews of the work's performance "finally soured Thomas on competitions."[10] The composition contest enjoyed a vogue during the heyday of American Composers' Concerts, as organizations found it increasingly difficult to find new works.

The range of composition contests reflects the breadth of the fad for American Composers' Concerts. The National Conservatory prizes were certainly the most prestigious of these competitions, offering very large cash awards and the opportunity of "discovery" by Dvořák. In the first competition (1893), Henry Schoenefeld, one of the few composers to incorporate African American themes in orchestral compositions before the arrival of Dvořák in the United States, earned the first prize in the symphonic category for his *Rural Symphony*. Chadwick won the second competition in 1894 with his Third Symphony. A third competition, with less generous cash prizes, was announced for the following year, but it is not clear whether these prizes were ever awarded.[11] Among the state MTAs, Rhode Island offered a prize for the best anthem by a Rhode Island composer in 1888, while Iowa offered two $25.00 prizes for the best vocal and instrumental submissions in 1892. The Apollo Club of Chicago offered prizes of $100.00 and $50.00 in the 1884/1885 season, and the Musurgia Society of New York offered prizes of the same amounts in the following year. The American Composers' Choral Association, which is discussed at greater length in the chapter on manuscript societies, offered two gold medals valued at $50.00 and $100.00 for original choral compositions.[12] The *Ladies' Home Journal* ran a widely publicized composition contest in 1892.[13] The Mansfield (Ohio) May Festival Association offered a $50.00 prize for a choral work by an American composer to be performed at its 1893 Festival.[14] To promote its "Liszt organ," the Mason & Hamlin Company sponsored a competition for the best American solo and duo compositions for that unique instrument.[15] The composition prize was sometimes used to gather repertoire for American Composers' Concerts, but more often it was simply another way of promoting American music. In 1896 the Polish pianist Ignacy Paderewski placed $10,000 in trust to fund triennial prizes for American composers. His rationale for doing so reflects his generosity and gratitude for the warm welcome that he had received in America: "I do not intend to thank the American people for all they have done for me, because my gratitude to your noble Nation is and will be beyond expression. But I desire to extend a friendly hand towards my American brother-musicians; towards those who, less fortunate than myself, are struggling for recognition or encouragement."[16]

The idea of an evening devoted to American music was initially promoted by professional musicians like Lavallée and Van der Stucken. It was not long, though, before it spread to amateur choral societies. These groups, which often featured a professional conductor but volunteer singers, found the format a welcome change from their usual repertoire of European works. In Boston, B. J. Lang led the Apollo Club in an American Composers' Concert on April 29 and May 4, 1885. At the other end of the country, David Loring of San Francisco led his group of musicians in a similar concert on May 18, 1887. The following years saw American Composers' Concerts in cities from coast to coast, including Cincinnati, Minneapolis, Chicago, and Lincoln, Nebraska. The conductors covered the spectrum of experience, from Mrs. P. V. M. Raymond, who led the Lincoln Oratorio Society in a December 9, 1892, performance, to Thomas' protégé Arthur Mees, who conducted American Composers' Concerts at the Orpheus Club of New York, the Mendelssohn Union of Orange, New Jersey, and the Schubert Club of Albany, New York within a one-month span in early 1891.

The concerts eventually spread to the numerous small, informal music clubs found in every city of the United States. Organizations like the Amateur Musical Club of Chicago, the Morning Musical Club of Fort Wayne, Indiana, and the Ladies' Thursday Musicale of Minneapolis consisted of amateurs who gathered on a regular basis to perform for each other. Essentially social clubs, many of them nonetheless featured attractive printed programs and invited distinguished performers in addition to their own members. The list in Appendix 1 features a few such concerts that were reported in the national press, but these are obviously only a small percentage of the concerts presented by such groups during an era when music clubs were at the height of their popularity.

In the midst of this heady atmosphere, American composers who had formerly felt neglected began to flex their muscles. Nowhere is this better illustrated than in the events surrounding the premiere of Dudley Buck's cantata *The Light of Asia* in 1887. This large-scale choral work was published before it was performed, a phenomenon that would have been unheard of just a few years previously. The Washington Choral Society began rehearsing the work with the intention of performing it in February 1887, which would have been the premiere. Unfortunately, Washington did not have a professional orchestra at that time, and since the society could not afford to hire an out-of-town group, it wrote to inform Buck that it would perform the work with organ accompaniment instead. His letter of reply was subsequently published in the *Washington Post* and the musical press:

My Dear Sir—I heartily appreciate the compliment which the Choral Society of Washington proposes to pay me, but I am forced to be ungracious and say that I should very deeply deprecate any such performance. I do not exaggerate in the least when I say that I had rather that the "Light of Asia" should never be publicly given than that it should be given without an orchestra. The nature of the subject, the whole Oriental coloring, makes the orchestral accompaniment of this work a vital thing. No matter how relatively interesting the voice parts might prove, they do not make it, nor does the orchestra, but the union of the two. I would not be thought vain in saying that I know of comparatively few works of a choral nature which would so utterly lose their true significance as would the "Light of Asia," if given without a good orchestra. Not only is it actually impossible to properly play the accompaniments upon an organ, but, in case of such attempt, a new and foreign tone would be added, bitterly misrepresenting me as its composer. I sincerely trust that your society may reconsider and postpone until they can do me simple justice. In conclusion I must say, my dear sir, that I have rarely been called upon to write a letter so disagreeable to myself as this. I more than appreciate the enterprise shown by an organization willing to take up a large American work, but I also wish to bide my time for proper representation. Deeply regretting the necessity of writing you thus, I remain, very truly yours, Dudley Buck.[17]

The secretary of the society responded with a letter detailing the difficulties that faced his group and reiterating his desire to perform the work in spite of local conditions. Buck responded with a second letter that spelled out his principles in the matter:

At this time in our musical history the first public performance of a large American work is of more than merely local significance. I am now speaking not of my work only, but of the American cause, of the hopes of the future and for younger men. By not giving a work its adequate and proper rendering at the outset, you hinder, not advance, the progress of American musical art. Had my work already been given in its completeness, had it been judged by a fairly adequate performance, for what it is, not for what it is not, I should, in your case, simply confine myself to an expression of regret, partially consoled by the compliment the Washington Choral Society propose to give me. As it is, I owe it to myself to protest against such a first performance.[18]

According to the *Washington Post*, the group then attempted to secure a larger theater and hire an orchestra from Boston or New York. A satisfactory date could not be found, and when the publisher could not make the orchestral parts available either, the group reverted to its original plan and performed the cantata with organ accompaniment on May 6, 1887.[19] The first complete performance of the work with orchestra was presented by the Newark Harmonic Society on May 31, 1888; it was also performed at Novello's Oratorio Concerts in London in 1889.

The controversy was widely discussed in the musical press, with the majority of writers supporting the composer.[20] On principle, his point that a performance without orchestra would not represent him or his work fully was valid, and it revived the issue that had given rise to the American Composers' Concert movement in the first place: music more than any of the arts needs to be performed in order to be appreciated, placing the composer at the mercy of his performers in a way that the painter or novelist never is. The controversy reaffirmed the vital importance of the movement to the advancement of American music and was used by *The Musical Courier* to applaud the decision of the MTNA to bring the Van der Stucken orchestra to Indianapolis that summer rather than use less-experienced local musicians.[21]

Principles aside, though, there is something vaguely surreal about a composer's going to such lengths to prevent the performance of his latest work. Buck had endured decades of neglect at the hands of performers, but in 1887 American music was on such a roll that he could afford to be particular about how and when his works were heard. His sense of self-importance had been boosted by the events of recent years, allowing him to stand boldly on principle rather than humbly accepting whatever came his way. Despite his assertions of gratitude for "the compliment which the Choral Society of Washington proposes to pay me," one can't help feeling that the composer was, in the words of Krehbiel, in imminent danger of being coddled to death.

The old adage "a rising tide lifts all boats" proved to be true of the American Composers' Concert movement, as the rush to present all-American programs resulted in the performance of a quantity of mediocre music. A careful survey of hundreds of these programs reveals that many of the concerts featured forgotten works by local composers or the pretentious effusions of inept writers buoyed by the fad. Critics and audience members struggled to assess the creations of S. G. Pratt, Caryl Florio, P. C. Lutkin, and a myriad of other composers on the basis of a single hearing. The flood of concerts encouraged persons with little skill or training to try their hand at composing while it allowed less assertive composers like Johann H. Beck to be overlooked in the wave of new music. To their detriment, good composers like Chadwick, Foote, and even MacDowell came to be associated with this excess, and their reputations suffered as a result.

The breadth of the American Composers' Concert movement in the late 1880s and early 1890s makes it impossible to identify all such concerts that took place. It is clear from contemporary journals and the personal papers of musicians, though, that all-American concerts were ubiquitous during this era. No performer could avoid them, no composer failed to benefit from them, and no concertgoer could help feeling assaulted by them. This saturation of American concert life finally turned the tide and caused American concerts to lose their popularity. Appropriately, the first signs of their weakening appeal came where they had begun in 1884—at the MTNA conventions.

NOTES

1. *New York Tribune*, December 12, 1890; quoted in Sumner Salter, "Early Encouragements to American Composers," *The Musical Quarterly* 18/1 (January 1932): 88.

2. Walter C. Dudley and Min Lee, *Tsunami!*, 2nd edition (Honolulu: University of Hawai'i Press, 1998), p. 20.

3. "The 'Tribune' and the American Composer," *AAJ* 57/1 (April 18, 1891): 4.

4. "Music Teachers' Associations," *The Etude* 7/6 (June 1889): 84. This article includes the names and addresses of the presidents of the state MTAs in Alabama, California, Colorado, Illinois, Indiana, Iowa, Kansas, Kentucky, Michigan, Minnesota, New York, Ohio, Rhode Island, and Texas. The organizational meeting for the

72 "A Tidal Wave of Encouragement"

Pennsylvania MTA is detailed in "Pennsylvania State Music Teachers' Association," *The Etude* 7/8 (August 1889): 113.

5. A copy of this program is preserved in the Frederic Grant Gleason scrapbooks, Special Collections, Newberry Library, Chicago, v. 8, p. 230.

6. "The third of the American composers' series of concerts was given at the Detroit Conservatory of Music, J. J. Hahn, director. The composer was Arthur Foote, and the selections included his Trio in C minor." *The Etude* 7/7 (April 1889): 53.

7. Programs of the first and fifth concerts are preserved in the Frederic Grant Gleason scrapbooks, Special Collections, Newberry Library, Chicago, v. 8, p. 161 and v. 10, p. 441. The others were reviewed in the Chicago press.

8. Willard Burr Jr., *A Catalogue of American Music, Comprising Carefully Selected Lists of the Best Vocal and Piano-forte Compositions by American Composers, Giving Key, Grade, Compass and Price* (Philadelphia: Theodore Presser, 1888).

9. Ezra Schabas, *Theodore Thomas: America's Conductor and Builder of Orchestras, 1835–1905* (Urbana and Chicago: University of Illinois Press, 1989), pp. 95–96.

10. Ibid., 118.

11. *NYT*, December 23, 1894, p. 10.

12. "Prizes for Composers," *Freund's Music and Drama* 16/11 (July 11, 1891): 5.

13. See the advertisement in *The Etude* 10/8 (August 1892): 162.

14. "Here and There," *The Musical Visitor* 21/11 (November 1892): 306–7.

15. "To American Composers," *Freund's Music and Drama* 15/7 (December 13, 1890): 6. The winners were announced in "American Composers Encouraged," *Freund's Music and Drama* 16/10 (July 4, 1891): 5.

16. Quoted in "Editorial Bric-a-Brac," *Music* 10/1 (May 1896): 80–81.

17. "Letters from Dudley Buck: Why He Objected to the Staging of 'The Light of Asia' in Washington," *Washington Post*, May 1, 1887, p. 3; reprinted in "Buck's 'Light of Asia,'" *MC* 14/19 (May 11, 1887): 305.

18. "Letters from Dudley Buck," 3.

19. The performance was reviewed in "Amusements," *Washington Post*, May 7, 1887, p. 2. This reviewer commented on the inadequacies of a performance without orchestra but opined that even with proper accompaniment the work would not be a masterpiece: "But after reaching a point where the listener feels that the composer and author are working on the same high plane, the music again descends, and the final numbers are disappointing, the climax being especially so. It is hardly likely that a presentation, even under more favorable circumstances than last night, would remove the impression of unevenness in the work."

20. See especially "Dudley Buck and his 'Light of Asia,'" *Brooklyn Daily Eagle*, May 8, 1887.

21. "Dudley Buck's Position," *MC* 14/19 (May 11, 1887): 304.

∽ 7 ∽

The MTNA Concerts, 1889–1892:
An Idea Whose Time Was Past

> On the whole the national association still lacks a *raison d'etre*.
> It is one of those institutions which once having had we cannot
> do without; yet the best use of which we do not quite under-
> stand.
>   —W. S. B. Mathews, 1892[1]

The idea of presenting concerts containing music only by American composers
started with a single piano recital during the 1884 convention, but by the 1888
convention in Chicago it had become the principal focus of the MTNA. There
were three festival concerts that year with orchestra, chorus, and soloists attracting crowds of 6,000 to 10,000. Since 1883 the membership of the organization
had more than quintupled, but its annual expenditures (led by the cost of hiring
the orchestra) had increased nearly twentyfold.

The MTNA had become a national leader in music as the idea of American
Composers' Concerts spread throughout the country. The list of concerts in
Appendix 1 shows the range of orchestras, choral groups, and soloists from San
Francisco to Boston that were presenting similar concerts. Though a few critics
felt that the movement had gotten out of hand, most believed that the American
composer was finally being treated fairly after years of neglect. The organization
that had initiated the trend was not about to relinquish its leadership role, as the

leaders looked for ways to build on the successes of Indianapolis and Chicago in the years ahead.

As the 1889 convention in Philadelphia approached, the MTNA was confronted with a problem that had been growing for several years—competition from state associations. The national organization had grown so large that since the mid-1880s a number of states had formed their own associations and were holding state conventions in June, right before the national convention in July. In Ohio, New York, and several other large states, the conventions rivaled those of the national organization in musical interest and in the prominence of the speakers. Several of the state groups, notably the Ohio Music Teachers' Association, believed that they were not adequately represented in the national body.[2] The 1889 convention was the first time that attendance at the national meeting was demonstrably lower because of these state organizations. The problem forced the MTNA to act quickly in affiliating the various state organizations and encouraging their members to attend both conferences.

Noticeably lower attendance at the Philadelphia conference made the event less festive than in previous years. Adding to this was a much lower quality in the orchestral performances. Though there were two orchestral/choral concerts advertised as containing "American and miscellaneous" works, the first evening did not contain even one American work. On the second evening, critics agreed that the performances were so inept that it was impossible to gain an accurate impression of the new works presented. This excerpt from *The Musical Courier* reflects the critical consensus:

Mr. Charles Abercrombie, the Chicago tenor, is responsible for the murdering of Johann H. Beck's "Moorish Serenade," and it must be confessed the orchestra aid[ed] and abetted him in his efforts. The composition is full of color and piquant rhythms, and like all of Beck's work shows the thinker and all round musician. E. C. Phelps' "Elegie" followed and Brandeis' "Danse Heroique," both of which were badly played. The same may be said of Henry Holden Huss' motet, a particularly noticeable composition, but about which it is obviously unfair to criticize, as the soloist, chorus and orchestra were not on the most amicable terms either as regards pitch or tempo. Enough: the task of criticism is always an unpleasant one. Philadelphia again, as heretofore, revealed her thoroughly unmusical temperament by declining to patronize these concerts. The officers of the association labored hard and earnestly to make the affair a success, but fate and Philadelphia were against them.[3]

As in past years, the organization relied on donations to cover the enormous cost of hiring orchestra and soloists. A new issue came to the fore in Philadelphia, though, that called attention to the means employed by the MTNA to raise funds. It was revealed that much of the money came from manufacturers, particularly piano companies, who, in turn, expected publicity at the convention. A group of Philadelphia piano makers protested that they had contributed to the expenses but that their instruments had not been used in the concerts. It was subsequently revealed that they had not contributed as much as some powerful New York companies and therefore had not been featured. There was much comment on the advisability of allowing the convention to be "auctioned off to the highest bidder."[4]

The scandal over support from piano manufacturers once again provoked discussion on a long-term solution to the problem of funding the American concerts. In his opening address to the convention, President W. F. Heath of Fort Wayne recommended the establishment of a permanent fund for the support of the orchestral and choral concerts. A committee was promptly formed, and before the Philadelphia convention was adjourned, a thirteen-point proposal outlining an "Orchestral and Choral Concert Fund" was adopted by the MTNA. The gist of this proposal was that members would solicit contributions with the goal of raising $100,000. Any member who contributed $25.00 or more would be granted life membership in the organization. The interest from this fund would be used to support concerts from year to year, with the stipulation that the principal would never be used and that if the organization were ever dissolved, the funds would be returned to the original contributors.[5]

Over the course of the next year, contributions were solicited in a variety of ways, including public concerts.[6] The results were not so favorable as the committee had hoped, though, since by the time of the 1890 convention in Detroit the total amount of the fund was only $563.56, a figure that would grow to $869.16 by the time the final report of the treasurer was published. The treasurer, William H. Dana, also pointed out that the committee had been too hasty in offering life memberships for $25.00 when the annual dues were $2.00:

As a matter of business, there is one feature of our Orchestral Fund that is, to me, very peculiar. On the payment of $25, you are promised that you will have no further membership fees to pay. The result is that, if we go on in this way, we will deduct eight per cent of it each year, and I wish we might have stricken out that feature of it. It is nothing more nor less than borrowing that amount and paying eight per cent interest for it. If we could look upon this $25 subscription as something given by you it would be better. I know of a good many people who would like to loan money at that rate, and I could get you a large amount of it within twenty-four hours.[7]

A recurring theme in the deliberations of the organization in these years was the notion that music teachers do not make good businessmen. In this case it seems to have been true.

After the disappointments of the Philadelphia convention, the organizers were determined to make the next year's convention in Detroit a memorable one, and this determination would result in the most festive concerts of the movement and also the most expensive convention of the century. This convention also witnessed a heated argument over procedure that would have serious ramifications in the years ahead. The movement that had begun in Cleveland six years earlier was destined to go out with a bang in Detroit.

Remembering the triumphs of the Chicago convention two years earlier, the executive committee again engaged the Theodore Thomas orchestra, despite the fact that his fee had risen substantially. The financial report for 1888 lists the combined cost of orchestra and accompanist at $1,842.40, with no statement on the exact fee paid to the orchestra.[8] The financial report for the 1890 convention shows that Thomas and his orchestra received $4,500.00. A new twist was that Thomas gave an extra concert of European compositions on his own initiative, of which the MTNA received a percentage of the proceeds. Even with this additional income, the costs were higher than in previous years, with the total operating budget for the year coming in at just under $10,000.

If the 1888 Chicago convention was the high point of the nineteenth century in terms of attendance, the 1890 Detroit convention was the high point in terms of American concerts. The conference brought a feast (or perhaps an orgy) of American music, performed by one of the best orchestras in the country. The MTNA program committee evidently wanted to get its money's worth out of the Thomas orchestra, presenting three festival concerts of American choral and orchestral works at the Detroit Rink. The first concert featured MacDowell's Second Concerto in D minor with the composer as soloist, Paine's symphonic poem *An Island Fantasy*, and Foote's Second Suite for orchestra, op. 21, along with choral works by H. S. Cutler, Adolph M. Foerster, and Hugh A. Clarke. The second concert brought orchestral works by Louis Maas, Henry Schoenefeld, Arthur Bird, and S. G. Pratt as well as choral works by Max Vogrich and Frederic H. Pease. The audience at the final evening's concert heard works by Frederic Grant Gleason, Chadwick, Arthur Whiting, Carl Busch, Beck, and (in a performance by the brilliant pianist Fannie Bloomfield-Zeisler) the Chopin Concerto in F minor. This Fourth of July concert, and with it the convention, concluded with a rendition of "The Star-Spangled Banner."

If the orchestral concerts were not sufficient to sate the appetite of American music lovers, they could attend chamber concerts of American music, a piano recital of mostly American works, and a vocal recital of art songs by American and European composers. The paper presentations were shorter in 1890, and the executive committee planned wisely to allow more breaks for socializing during the convention. At the business meeting on July 3, the association voted to adopt the title that had been proposed in 1885 but never formally adopted: The American Society for the Promotion of Musical Art. This name would be used on all society publications for the next year and then quietly dropped.

The quality of the performances, the size of the audiences, and the enthusiasm of the members were all in direct contrast to the depressing conference in Philadelphia the year before. By the end of the conference the mood was upbeat, and it might have been considered an ideal event but for one disagreeable incident during the last day's business session that would return to haunt the MTNA in years ahead.

In the flush of enthusiasm from their successful concerts of American music, the leaders of the MTNA were eager to showcase their specialty in a more auspicious forum—the World's Columbian Exposition scheduled for 1893 in Chicago. Despite general agreement that this was a project worth pursuing, there was dissension over the procedures to be followed. The resulting argument was so vigorous and so uncharacteristic of the organization that it is worth reprinting in this colorful description from the *American Art Journal*:

There the matter of analyzing the association's position anent a Festival during the World's Fair came up. The vice-presidents reported a complete line of action for an International Congress of Musicians at Chicago in 1893, to be given under the auspices of the M.T.N.A. The following commission and officers for the proposed congress were nominated: Dr. Ziegfeld of Chicago, president ... [a long list of names followed, in which the officers of the MTNA were prominently represented].

These names were very imposing, the project seemed most delightful, and the association had puckered its lips to make it a fact when S. G. Pratt, a gentleman with a clear head and a lot of self-control, arose and began to expatiate upon the importance of the project in hand. There were cries of "question," and the chair, holding that the project had long since been determined to be most desirable, declared the gentleman out of order. But Mr. Pratt didn't want to sit down; he kept right on talking, and in a moment the association's first symphony in temper was exhibited.

"Sit down. Keep quiet!" howled Mr. Pratt's unwilling auditors, but the demonstration did not move him.

A little man with a red face and much fervor yelled: "He tried that dodge in the committee, and he can't come it here!"

"But I maintain," came the stentorian tones of Mr. Pratt, "that I have a–"

Pandemonium again drowned the objector. E. M. Bowman, who is large, bland and imperturbable, walked down the aisle and asked for enlightenment. He wanted to know why Mr. Pratt was not granted an audience. The chair said Mr. Pratt did not discuss the question before the house. Mr. Heath, of Fort Wayne, again moved the plan of the vice-presidents be accepted. Mr. Pratt shouted in the din that he had an amendment to offer. The chair recognized Mr. Pratt, who walked down the aisle to the orchestra pit with some manuscript in hand. He began to read about the gigantic importance of a World's Festival. The chair again stopped him, cautioning him to present the amendment. This was an incentive for the opposition, who renewed cries of "question."

"Mr. Chairman!"

In the carnival of discords a woman's treble was heard. A pretty brunette, looking very cool in a blue and white challie and a white straw hat, stood on tip-toes in the rear of the parquet, calling vigorously.

The excited members in front, who couldn't talk fast enough, paid no heed to the latest participant in the debate, but howled right on. The president nearly demolished his gavel.

"There's a lady trying to talk," he yelled.

The uproar subsided, and the perspiring combatants turned about in surprise. "I wanted to motion," said the young woman, with evident embarrassment, "that Mr. Pratt be heard."

"Just give me five minutes!" cried Mr. Pratt.

He started his paper anew, but his voice was engulfed in protests.

"This is gag law!" shouted Edmund Myer, of New York, excitedly, springing to his feet and shaking a fist at the speaker.

"Yes, let this gentleman be heard," dryly supplemented Mr. Heath, who led the faction opposing Mr. Pratt.

Constantin Sternberg moved that Mr. Pratt be given five minutes in which to make known his objection. This granted, Mr. Pratt criticized the system of organizing the commission. He wanted a commission nominated which would meet at Chicago in September, elect its own officers and perfect its own organization. He thought the secretary and treasurer, as nominated, were better qualified for other branches of work in the proposed festival. There would be $100,000 to handle, and he wanted a banker, not a music teacher, to handle it. "This will be called a measure for private benefit, and the odium will fall upon the M.T.N.A."

This raised another protest, and the chair called Mr. Pratt to order. The Heath faction was wild, and right in the midst of all this confusion Mr. Pratt was asking for more time.

"Give him more rope!" cried a Heathite.

However, Mr. Pratt was authorized to continue, and when he had done Mr. Heath amended the amendment of Mr. Pratt by a motion to accept the plan of the vice-presidents, with the exception of the nominations of secretary and treasurer. This motion was carried 42 to 12, and Mr. Pratt left the theatre. Then Mr. Perkins was elected secretary and Mr. Heath treasurer, as per original plan. President Parsons dashed his 'kerchief about his face, heaved a sigh, and adjourned the association sine die.[9]

The person who had caused this "symphony in temper" was one of the more colorful characters involved with the American Composers' Concert movement. Silas Gamaliel Pratt (1846–1916) began his career as a composer almost by default, having ruined both his voice and his arm through too much singing and piano playing as a youth.[10] Once embarked on a compositional career, he gained a reputation for his grandiose ideas and audacious publicity stunts. Rupert Hughes opined, "If Pratt had been born in old Egypt, he would have found his chief diversion in the building of pyramids, so undismayed is he by the size of a task,"[11] while Louis C. Elson summed up his career thus:

There never was a better example of the irrepressible Yankee in music than Mr. Pratt at this time. A hundred schemes seemed to form in his mind simultaneously. Large musical events and great musical compositions, many of them intensely patriotic and even of the "spread-eagle" order, were planned. . . . When the bombast is eliminated from some of his "patriotic" works, there is a residue of good technique and worthy music, and in the less magniloquent works Mr. Pratt is often very effective. . . . Had this composer been less ambitious, he would have achieved more; yet he has won his triumphs, and stands as an example of American energy and pluck.[12]

Pratt's propensity for self-promotion earned him enemies, though. Among the many examples that might be cited is his opera *Zenobia*, produced in Chicago in 1882. Because the promotional campaign had been so overzealous, critics were not inclined to be forgiving of its weaknesses, and a work that might otherwise have achieved a modest success was instead a spectacular failure. Among other outlandish claims, the advance publicity had labeled Pratt "the American Wagner." When word of this reached Franz Liszt in Weimar, he responded, "Pratt, the 'American Wagner'; then why not say 'Wagner, the German Pratt'?"[13]

In the case of the business meeting at the 1890 convention in Detroit, Pratt's reputation as a huckster seems to have been partially responsible for the violent reaction of his opponents, which kept them from considering his ideas carefully. The assumption of both parties was that the World's Fair Commission would give a large sum of money—the arbitrary figure of $100,000 was mentioned repeatedly—to the MTNA to be used by the association for the presentation of grand festival concerts of American music in the manner of the convention concerts. The argument centered on who should have control of the program and who should be in charge of the large amount of money to be placed at their disposal. The slate prepared by the MTNA included a number of the association's current executive officers, including persons from various parts of the country. Pratt believed that the large amount of money involved made the tasks of secretary and treasurer too daunting for anyone but a banker, and he further urged that the committee be centered in Chicago. Since he was himself a resident of Chicago, his ideas appeared to be self-serving. Further, his objections to Heath as treasurer and Perkins as secretary were taken to be personal attacks, and as soon as he left the room, these two were voted back on the MTNA's committee. When the 1890 convention ended, the organization was divided on the issue of the 1893 exposition, and these rifts would not be healed for years to come.

In the end, this "symphony in temper" turned out to be much ado about nothing. The World's Fair commission did indeed set aside a large sum of money for concerts at the exposition—$175,000—but the MTNA had no part in spending it. The music secretary for the fair, George H. Wilson of Boston, stated that the music bureau "would not give official recognition to any musical organization." To those who believed that the MTNA was the nation's musical leader, this lack of recognition was galling:

This would signify that the great representative National Organization of American Musicians and Musical Educators, the organization that has evolved the American composer and American compositions, the association that for many years has struggled and has succeeded in its efforts to create a solidarity of musical forces in this country is to be placed on a level with the Vocal Club of Podunk and the Male Quartet of the Quinsigamond Athletic Club, and not be officially recognized in the musical factors constituting the "world's fair" events.[14]

At the 1892 MTNA convention in Cleveland, the organization was presented with a proposal by Florenz Ziegfeld to stage six concerts of American music during the Chicago Exposition. The board of vice presidents rejected this proposal, according to Chicago writer W. S. B. Mathews, because it was thought "unbecoming" to appear in Chicago at the same time as the exposition and because the percentage of receipts offered by Ziegfeld (10 percent) was too small.[15] The MTNA voted to meet next in Utica, New York, in 1894, leaving the possibility of an event in Chicago in the hands of a committee.

The workings of the organization during this time period were inconsistent, as decisions seem to have been motivated in many cases by self-interest. After the jostling for position in 1890 and after the 1892 resolution not to meet in Chicago, the MTNA did, in fact, convene in Chicago on July 4 and 5, 1893. The meeting, which was not announced until mid-June, consisted of reminiscences by each of the living past presidents on the conventions that they had chaired, along with four papers and a display of Indian headdresses. There was nothing of the festive character associated with recent MTNA conventions, and the atmosphere seems to have been very somber. No doubt the officers recognized that their bickering and refusal to work together had resulted in the squandering of a potentially great opportunity.[16]

The halfhearted showing by the MTNA during the Chicago exposition reflects the general decline of the organization and its national conventions during the 1890s. After the successful convention at Detroit in 1890, the association decided to postpone the next meeting until 1892 in Minneapolis so as to appease the growing state organizations by allowing them to hold conventions in alternate years. During the two years separating these two conventions the Minneapolis committee was plagued with bad luck. First, two of the three members of the executive committee, Carl Lachmund and Walter Petzet, left Minneapolis to live in New York. Before they were replaced, the Republican Party announced its intention to hold its convention in Minneapolis during the summer of 1892. Rather than compete with this major event, the MTNA moved its convention to Cleveland at the last moment.[17]

Because of the change of venue, organizers were unable to raise the necessary funds for an orchestra. Orchestral concerts had been an important part of the conventions since the 1885 meeting in New York, and the Cleveland meeting suffered by comparison. Despite the lack of an orchestra, there were three concerts devoted to chamber music and art songs by American composers along with numerous individual American works scattered throughout the four-day convention. *The Musical Courier* saw fit to poke fun at the American composers in one of its articles on the convention:

At the Cleveland meeting sixteen compositions of one American composer were produced. These were evidence that as a prolific specimen the American composer will not be sneezed at, but it suggests that the members of the program committees of the National and the various State associations should hereafter limit the number of compositions of their own to be played or sung at the meetings they arrange to no higher a number than sixteen for any one composer for any one meeting. Sixteen is a readily divisible factor, and it is now the banner number, and to surpass it by playing or singing at one of the next conventions or meetings seventeen or twenty-three American compositions of each of the members of the program committee might result in an injustice toward foreign composers . . .[18]

Cleveland composer Wilson G. Smith took the bait and pointed out in a letter to the editor that there had actually been only twelve of his compositions—all short pieces and songs—on the program. He added that as chairman of the program committee he had felt ambivalent about the performance of so many of his own works but that his musical colleagues had urged him to proceed with the compositions chosen.[19] His humble apology did little to allay the impression that the organization was once again becoming insular. The program committee had ignored the strict guidelines adopted in 1886, which expressly forbade the performance of more than one work by a single composer, the performance of works by the same composer at consecutive conventions, and the performance of works by members of the program committee.

The organization still clung to its goal of promoting American music, which was the focus of J. B. Hahn's presidential address on the opening day of the convention. He was able to point with pride not only to the concerts of the MTNA but to the inspiration that these concerts had given to other organizations throughout the country. Looking back on Lavallée's concert at the 1884 convention, he stated, "In the eight short intervening years last past more has been accomplished to promote the culture and growth of American music than in all preceding time combined, and the American composer of today is a potent factor in American musical affairs."[20]

Ironically, the idea that had seemed so fresh and exciting eight years before was rapidly becoming passé. In a telling editorial published two weeks after the convention, *The Musical Courier*, a journal that had always supported the MTNA in the past, suggested that the American composer no longer needed special treatment. The writer stated that the Cleveland programs had seemed "unnaturally forced" now that American music was not the novelty that it had once been and concluded with a statement that reflected a growing nationwide disenchantment with the MTNA's pet project:

It is time to put the American composer just where he belongs and permit him to stand or fall on his merits as a composer uninfluenced by small-minded patriotism that overlooks glaring errors of musical form and frequently despises the accepted laws of counterpoint and harmony. The American composer has demonstrated his capacity of absorption, and many of the greatest musical thoughts, as well as a few of the most diminutive musical ideas, have been heartily and even boldly adopted and adapted by him. His fame is fixed. Let him abide by it without demanding a distinctive program. A program of American compositions has become an anomaly; no such a thing now exists.[21]

As quickly as it had come, the MTNA's moment in the sun was gone. The anticlimactic Chicago meeting of 1893 has already been described, and the next biennial convention in 1894 was even more of a disappointment. After making great promises of support for a festive convention in Utica, New York, executive committee chairman Louis Lombard resigned, forcing a last-minute change of venue to nearby Saratoga Springs. This convention was very poorly attended, in part because of a pamphlet circulated by the executive committee before the meeting under the title *Shall the MTNA Disband or Reorganize?*[22]

In a desperate attempt to hold on to the members who were deserting the organization en masse, the advance publicity for the 1894 convention emphasized the social aspect of the convention: "A 'social interlude' and 'social postlude' will be among the new and interesting features of every session of the regular four days' meeting, and the pleasures and benefits of fraternization will be promoted in every way possible, which will surpass any previous meeting of the association. A large Committee on Goodfellowship, comprising many of the oldest and best known members of the association, will have this matter in charge."[23] After years of emphasizing either the paper presentations or the concerts, this elevation of social interaction to primary importance was a pathetic sign of the loss of credibility of the organization. *The Musical Courier* snidely remarked, "The only thing that was not a failure was the weather, and it is lucky that the association had no power over the elements or the air would have been as blue as the association."[24]

There was no American concert in 1894, though American works were sprinkled liberally throughout the concerts of piano, vocal, and chamber music. Curiously, there were not enough members present at the sessions to form a quorum until the last day. President E. M. Bowman refused reelection, even though the following year's convention was scheduled for his hometown of St. Louis—the dubious honor went instead to A. A. Stanley of the University of Michigan. The 1894 meeting produced no significant policy changes, but *The Etude* noted that, "it was generally considered wise to in the future omit the festival and orchestra features of past meetings, and confine the work to educational lines."[25]

The association returned to the idea of all-American concerts just once more, in the 1899 convention at Cincinnati. Though less than a decade had elapsed since the heyday of these concerts in the MTNA conventions, the leadership seems to have forgotten its former accomplishments. The advance publicity did not mention previous American Composers' Concerts but stated: "The concert programs speak for themselves. Never before in the history of the M.T.N.A. has the American composer been placed before his fellow musicians in such an advantageous position."[26] For the only time in its history, the concerts were true to Lavallée's radical suggestion: members heard three concerts by Frank Van der Stucken's Cincinnati Symphony, three organ recitals, and two chamber concerts, all containing nothing but American works. The response could have been predicted, as reviewer J. A. Homan summarized the prevailing view in the United States at this time: "The twenty-first convention of the M.T.N.A. is a record of the past. Its distinguishing feature was the presentation of exclusively American compositions at the concerts. Much was given that was good, bad and indifferent. No particular excellence can ever be attached to a composition on the mere ground that it is American. Musical art must stand on universal, not national foundations. To appreciate it, as it ought to be, its productions ought to be placed in juxtaposition with the best that is offered by the world."[27]

The budget and membership figures in the following table illustrate the rapid decline of the organization:

Convention Date and Site		Membership	Expenses
1883	Providence, RI	312	$295.23
1884	Cleveland, OH	575	(budget figures not available)
1885	New York, NY	760	1,178.00
1886	Boston, MA	952	2,216.71
			(not including orchestra)
1887	Indianapolis, IN	722	3,283.81
1888	Chicago, IL	1,649	5,673.37
1889	Philadelphia, PA	706	4,932.00
1890	Detroit, MI	1,101	9,620.59
1892	Cleveland, OH	532	2,355.50
1894	Saratoga Springs, NY	124	1,762.34

The bad luck associated with the 1892 and 1894 conventions was partly to blame, as was the failure to act decisively with regard to the Chicago exposition of 1893. More than this, however, was the sense that the MTNA had been poorly managed during the years of the American Composers' Concerts. Secretary H. S. Perkins offered blunt words in his 1893 history of the MTNA:

This grand "festival" idea, blow of trumpets and "go-you-one-better" each year is what has brought the Association to the verge of bankruptcy and ruin. Such blind recklessness is more than liable to result in failure. It is not unlike throwing dice or feeling for the drawing paste-board, in three-card-monte. While it smacks loudly of enthusiasm and hurrah, and *promises* great things beyond precedent, yet it proves the inefficiency of men to act as leaders, and that the affairs are not managed upon sound, business principles. Men who engage in business will count the cost before plunging into expenses; also figure upon the probable income. . . . [T]oo much money has been expended to employ an orchestra, and in this connection, it is pertinent to ask: "Has it paid to invest so much money for the special purpose of giving a few American works, thereby depleting the treasury and keeping the Association in beggary?" . . . We have struggled hard to encourage the American composers—

including those who have had no sympathy with us; those who would not contribute a dollar or an hour to help on the cause, not unless it was to attend the performance of one of their own works. Was the M.T.N.A. organized to perform the compositions of Americans or to encourage the American composers, *per se*, regardless of
cost; to pet a few authors of orchestral works while they sit in their easy chairs and
look down and sneer upon the plebeians who have toiled day and night and done
the drudgery which has caused their exaltation? Let the Constitution speak.[28]

What had started a decade earlier as an inspiring and patriotic idea had ended in
cynicism about American composers. Why did it fail, and why did the MTNA
nearly fail with it? The answers lie in the organizational history of the association, the popularity of the idea, and the nature of American composers and their
music during the period.

When the MTNA began its grand campaign for American music, the officers
were driven by idealism rather than pragmatism. Between 1884 and 1894 they
repeatedly showed that their enthusiasm for American music was not tempered
by careful financial planning. Presenting the concerts was enormously expensive, and the planners needed to rely on generous patrons, most of whom came
from the city in which the convention took place. This was easy to manage in
New York (1885) and Boston (1886), when the movement was still a novelty
and the conventions were held in cities where both musicians and patrons were
plentiful. The Indianapolis and Chicago conventions stretched the goodwill of
their respective cities, while the Philadelphia fiasco was largely the result of inadequate sponsorship. The Detroit convention was an artistic triumph but the
most expensive convention of the century, draining the organization's treasury
and making it difficult to continue on such a scale. Perhaps the most telling
sign of the decline of support for the idea was the failure of the association to
raise even $1,000 for the Orchestral and Choral Concert Fund, despite the attrac-
tive inducement of life memberships.

During the years of the American Composers' Concerts, the MTNA followed the curious practice of electing its presidents at the convention, allowing
each person who paid the convention fee an equal vote. This resulted in the
election of local favorites, meaning that a series of presidents was charged with
planning conventions in distant cities: Lavallée was elected president in his
hometown of Boston but planned the convention in Indianapolis; Max Leckner
was elected president in his hometown of Indianapolis but planned the convention in Chicago, and so on. Each president relied on a local committee to do
the actual work, and in years when the committee was not as capable, the conventions suffered. Mathews astutely pointed out, though, that even the best
leadership cannot be held completely responsible for the success or failure of a
convention: "In any case, so far as experience teaches, a national or a state association is an entirely new problem every year. Success one year is like a good
crop; it is the good luck of the farmer who prepared the ground, sowed the seed
and tended the growing crop; nature played the main part of the game, but the
farmer did his share of the work."[29]

The MTNA's efforts to promote American concerts also suffered because of
their own success. Lavallée's concert in Cleveland was a novelty, and the idea
was so attractive that it immediately caught on across the country. While the
MTNA rode a wave of success in the 1880s it had numerous imitators. By the

1890s American audiences had heard so many all-American concerts that it was difficult to raise the necessary support for the MTNA's annual extravaganzas, despite the fact that the organization had originated the idea and had been a leader throughout the trend. Like all fads, this one had a limited life span and eventually died of its own excesses. The "infant industry" that had seemed so worthy of special treatment a decade before was now ready to stand on its own feet.

Without the unifying goal of American Composers' Concerts, the MTNA entered a period of stagnation. As Mathews wrote in August 1892, "On the whole the national association still lacks a *raison d'etre*. It is one of those institutions which once having had we cannot do without; yet the best use of which we do not quite understand."[30] It limped along with small membership figures and modest annual gatherings throughout the 1890s, accompanied by much hand-wringing over what was to be done with the formerly vibrant association.[31] When it was reinvigorated in the early twentieth century, the organization was once again committed to its original purpose—education.

To a cynic, the MTNA's brief flirtation with American concerts may look like the misguided work of a group of fanatics who forgot their primary purpose and subsequently paid a steep price. In one sense, though, the organization did a valuable service to American musical life. The MTNA initiated and carried through a bold venture that was the first real acknowledgment of the potential of American composers. Their efforts inspired others to present similar concerts, turning their original brainstorm into a national movement. Though the organization fell on hard times following the Detroit convention in 1890, the movement it had initiated was by no means over. Among those who had contributed compositions to the MTNA convention programs was a German immigrant by the name of Franz Xavier Arens, whose ambition went far beyond his modest position as a conductor and teacher in Cleveland. His concerts of American orchestral works in Germany and Austria in 1891 and 1892 would be the most impressive and the most controversial of the American Composers' Concert movement.

NOTES

1. [W. S. B. Mathews], "Cleveland Meeting of the M.T.N.A.," *Music* 2/4 (August 1892): 413.

2. See, for instance, Johannes Wolfram, "Ohio Music Teachers' Association versus National Music Teachers' Association," *MC* 13/3 (July 21, 1886): 38; Anton Strelezki, "M.T.N.A. State Associations," *MC* 16/22 (May 30, 1888): 373.

3. "M.T.N.A. Thirteenth Annual Meeting," *MC* 19/2 (July 10, 1889): 47.

4. "Art and the Piano Trade: The Danger Confronting the Music Teachers' National Association," *The American Musician* 14/1 (July 6, 1889): 12.

5. The entire proposal was printed in *Official Report: Music Teachers' National Association Thirteenth Annual Meeting at Philadelphia, Pa., July 2–5, 1889* (MTNA, 1890), pp. 141–43.

6. See "M.T.N.A.: The First Benefit Concert," *Freund's Music and Drama* 13/20 (March 15, 1890): 14; "M.T.N.A. Orchestral Fund," *MC* 20/21 (May 14, 1890): 450–51; Chas. W. Landon, "An Appeal to the Musical People of America in Behalf of the Music Teachers' National Association Orchestral and Choral Concert Fund," *The Etude* 8/4 (April 1890): 54.

7. *Official Report: Music Teachers' National Association Fourteenth Annual Meeting at Detroit, Mich.., July 1, 2, 3 & 4, 1890* (MTNA, 1891), pp. 172–73.

8. This figure was given in the official report of the 1888 convention. The accounting practices of the MTNA are open to suspicion, since the budget figures kept shifting. The initial announcement at the business session of the convention had stated ambiguously, "Milward Adams, for rehearsals, Theodore Thomas, $900." Amy Fay, Thomas' future sister-in-law, wrote to *The Musical Courier* that, in fact, "Mr. Thomas gave his services to the association, and the above mentioned sum was paid over to the members of the orchestra for rehearsals" ("A Communication from Miss Fay," *MC* 17/5 [August 1, 1888]: 86). Whatever the actual sum may have been, it is clear that Thomas and his orchestra did much better in 1890 than in 1888.

9. "Pandemonium at the Music Teachers' National Convention. Discord Caused by the Proposed '93 Congress in Chicago," *AAJ* 55/13 (July 12, 1890): 224–25. For the official view of this scene, with the full text of Pratt's speech, see *Official Report, 1890*, 183–93.

10. "Biographies of American Musicians, Number Twenty-Four: S. G. Pratt," *BMW* 16 (1879): 146; reprinted in *Brainard's Biographies of American Musicians*, ed. E. Douglas Bomberger (Westport, CT, and London: Greenwood, 1999), p. 229.

11. Rupert Hughes, *American Composers* (Boston: Page, 1900), p. 235.

12. Louis C. Elson, *The History of American Music* (New York: Macmillan, 1904), pp. 200–201.

13. *Living with Liszt, from the Diary of Carl Lachmund, an American Pupil of Liszt, 1882–1884*, edited, annotated, and introduced by Alan Walker, Franz Liszt Studies Series No. 4 (Stuyvesant, NY: Pendragon Press, 1995), p. 236.

14. "The Cleveland Meeting. Important Results," *MC* 25/2 (July 13, 1892): 5.

15. W. S. B. Mathews, "Music Teachers' National Association," *The Musical Record* 367 (August 1892): 12.

16. The reminiscences of the past presidents were reprinted in *The Secretary's Official Report of the Special Meeting of the Music Teachers' National Association, Held at the Art Institute in Chicago, July 4th, 5th and 6th, 1893* (n.p., [1893]).

17. J. B. Hahn, "President's Address," *Official Report of the Music Teachers' National Association Fifteenth Meeting at Cleveland, Ohio* (MTNA, 1892), p. 15.

18. "The American Composer," *MC* 25/3 (July 20, 1892): 5.

19. "Those Sixteen Compositions," *MC* 25/4 (July 27, 1892): 7.

20. Hahn, "President's Address," 15.

21. "The American Composer," 5.

22. "Preface," *Music Teachers' National Association (The Society for the Promotion of Musical Art): Proceedings of the Sixteenth Meeting, held at Saratoga Springs, N.Y., Tuesday, Wednesday, Thursday and Friday, July 3, 4, 5 and 6, 1894* (n.p., [1894]), n.p.

23. "M.T.N.A.," *The Etude* 12/6 (June 1894): 132.

24. "M.T.N.A.: Sixteenth Meeting Held at Saratoga, N.Y., July 2–4, 1894," *MC* 29/2 (July 11, 1894): 16.

25. "Meeting of the M.T.N.A. at Saratoga," *The Etude* 12/8 (August 1894): 168.

26. "M.T.N.A. Cincinnati, June 21 to 23, 1899: A Word about the Programs," *MC* national edition (May 10–17, 1899): n.p.

27. J. A. Homan, "M.T.N.A., Twenty-first Annual Convention in Cincinnati," *MC* 38/25 (June 28, 1899): 29.

28. H. S. Perkins, *Historical Handbook of the Music Teachers' National Association, 1876–1893* (n.p. [1893]), 81, 83. W. S. B. Mathews believed that the concerts had not been at the root of the MTNA's financial problems and came up with

different figures from those cited in the annual reports: "Editorial Bric-a-Brac," *Music* 18/4 (August 1900): 385.

29. Mathews, "Editorial Bric-a-Brac," 380.

30. [Mathews], "Cleveland Meeting of the M. T. N. A.," 413.

31. See, for instance, W.S.B.M., "Future of the M.T.N.A.," *Music* (1894): 447; H. S. Perkins, "Future of the M.T.N.A.," *Music* (1894): 37; "Future of the M.T.N.A.," *Music* (1894): 337–48; Amy Fay, "M.T.N.A.," *MC* 33/7 (August 12, 1896): 21; "Mr. Greene's Novel Plan for the M.T.N.A.," *Music* 10/5 (September 1896): 502–7; W.S.B.M., "Editorial Bric-a-Brac," 375–91.

⤠ **8** ⤡

The Arens Tour of 1891–1892: Propaganda, Parochialism, and All-American Concerts

A concert of singular interest will take place on 6 April in the Berlin Konzerthaus. Under the auspices of the resident American ambassador W. W. Phelps and with the assistance of distinguished soloists and the Meyder Orchestra, the German-American Mr. Arens will conduct major works of his countrymen Van der Stucken, Beck, Bird, Foote, [and] Boise. Mr. Arens will present a similar concert in the Dresden Gewerbehaus. As the young generation of American composers is almost entirely unknown in Germany, those in musical circles look forward to the above-mentioned concert with the greatest interest.[1]

—*Neue Zeitschrift für Musik*, April 1, 1891

The interest in these concerts was indeed great—enough so that F. X. Arens presented concerts of American orchestral music in major German cities for the next year and a half, culminating his tour with a performance at the Vienna International Music and Theater Exhibition in July 1892. In the course of this tour, European audiences heard over twenty major works by America's leading composers, and the concerts were reviewed by over fifty of the principal music critics of the German-speaking nations. Though not the first performance of American music in Europe, it was the first time that a broad cross-section of the Central European critical establishment was exposed to a representative sampling of American art music. Ironically, the Arens tour came at a point in the American Composers' Concert movement when such concerts had become so commonplace that they were no longer a cause for universal acclaim in the United States. As a result, Arens' efforts were scrutinized by his colleagues at home and eventually became the target of a controversy in the summer of 1892.

The Arens tour evoked some of the most extensive and thoughtful reviews of the movement while also drawing some of the harshest criticism.

If Lavallée and Van der Stucken were men who found themselves in the right place at the right time, Franz Xavier Arens had the misfortune to arrive on the scene too late. An enigmatic figure in American music, Arens seems to have had the vision of Lavallée and the conducting skills of Van der Stucken but lacked the connections to achieve a similar level of respect for his efforts. Nonetheless, his name recurs often in the history of American Composers' Concerts.

Born in Neef, Rhineland, on October 28, 1856, Arens was brought to America by his parents at the age of eleven, part of the massive German migration that has been the subject of much study on both sides of the Atlantic.[2] Southwest Germany and the Rhineland were the regions that had suffered most from Germany's failure to keep pace with the Industrial Revolution, and these regions produced the largest proportion of the German immigrants.[3] Over 3 million Germans emigrated to the United States during the nineteenth century, and by the time of the 1900 census, 27 percent of all Americans had at least one parent born in Germany.[4] The Arens family, though coming after the initial flood of Germans in the 1850s, was among the many who settled in the Midwest, and they joined the large number of Germans in Ohio, taking up residence in or near Cleveland. Already in 1860, over one-fourth of the combined population of Cleveland, Cincinnati, and Dayton had been born in Germany.[5] Arens was therefore part of a large and sometimes maligned group of "German-Americans."

The young Franz received his first musical training from his father, Clemens Arens, and later studied with John Singenberger at the Normal College in St. Francis, Wisconsin. After his studies there he moved to Buffalo, New York, where he taught music at Canisius College and served as organist and choir director at St. Michael's Church.[6] Like many of his American contemporaries, though, he did not feel that his musical training would be complete without a course of study in Germany, and in the fall of 1881 he enrolled in Josef Rheinberger's counterpoint class at the Königliche Musikschule in Munich. He studied there for two years, adding Rheinberger's organ class to his curriculum in the second year. His two years in Munich coincided with the beginning of Rheinberger's fame as a teacher of American composers. Among his fellow students during the first year was Charles Carter, a former classmate of George Whitefield Chadwick and later a prominent member of the Pittsburgh musical community. During Arens' second year he had the opportunity to meet a class of incoming students that included Horatio Parker, Henry Holden Huss, and Howard Parkhurst. Present in Munich but not yet enrolled as an official student at the Musikschule was Arthur Battelle Whiting.[7] During the 1883/1884 school year he studied organ with Paul Janssen and composition with Franz Wüllner at the Königliches Conservatorium in Dresden. His progress there was so rapid that after one year he was awarded a "Preiszeugnis," one of only six so honored out of a student body of 734. His commendation read: "Herr Franz Arens from Detroit [sic] North America, enrolled on 1 September 1883, from the composition class of the artistic director and the organ class of organist Janssen, by reason of his diligence and of his rapid progress and capable accomplishments in composition, of his good accomplishments as organist and as conductor and of his excellent attitude."[8]

At the age of twenty-seven, Arens returned to America to begin his professional life in earnest. From 1884 or 1885 until 1888, he conducted the Cleveland Philharmonic Society and the Cleveland Gesangverein. While in Cleveland he had his first major success as a composer when his *Symphonic Fantasie* was performed at the 1887 MTNA convention in Indianapolis. James Huneker commented on the work in terms that would be echoed by European critics several years later: "The Orchestral novelty was a Symphonic Fantasie, by F. X. Arens, of Cleveland, an ardent disciple of the new school, who has lots of ideas, knows how to clothe them with the proper orchestral garb, but has much to learn in moderation and self control. The work, however, as a whole, impresses one as the production of a gifted and poetic mind."[9]

By 1890 he was once again in Europe, this time studying voice in Berlin with Julius Hey, the eminent vocal instructor and disciple of Wagner. His studies allowed him to secure a position as instructor of voice at the Schwantzer Conservatory in Berlin, where he taught from October 1891 to May 1892.[10] During this second visit to Europe Arens, now in his mid-thirties, presented at least nine concerts of American music.

Arens had an uncanny ability to use publicity throughout his career. During his concert tour, there were numerous reviews from German critics, the best of which were reprinted in American periodicals shortly after. Because this chapter is primarily concerned with the critical reception to the Arens concerts, a different citation method is used: Appendix 3 shows the itinerary of the Arens tour with repertoire and a list of known reviews for each concert. To facilitate citation, each review has been given a siglum designating the city and the chronological order in which the reviews appeared in print; since Arens performed in Berlin and Dresden twice, the reviews for these two cities are numbered sequentially through both seasons. These sigla are used for references to individual reviews.

Arens began his series in April 1891 with two concerts in familiar territory: in Berlin, where he was living at the time, and in Dresden, where he had studied at the conservatory. The Berlin concert took place in the Konzerthaus. This hall, in its twenty-fifth year of operation, presented daily concerts at inexpensive prices for eight months each year. The performances in this hall were *Tischkonzerte* (table concerts), meaning that refreshments were served, and— except during symphony concerts—smoking was allowed. The orchestra, under the direction of Carl Meyder, was at least reasonably competent, and contemporary reports indicate that the audiences were attentive.[11]   The Dresden concert took place at the Gewerbehaus, a setting similar to the Berlin Konzerthaus, whose orchestra was led by August Trenkler (1836–1910).

A letter from the composer O. B. Boise to the *American Art Journal* indicates that the first concert did not go as well as the subsequent concerts. Boise characterized the Meyder Orchestra as "poor" and noted that the soloists were not adequate for the performance of his own *Romeo and Juliet* suite, despite Arens' "extraordinary ability as a drill master."[12]   The composer also gave the first report of critical bias, which he attributed to a somewhat comical circumstance:

The critics were invited, but when they arrived there were no seats for them. Starting with this annoyance, and evidently thinking the American school would resort to aboriginal themes and methods, they listened with distorted ears. Some of them speak respectfully of the whole enterprise, and praise what they fancied. Others evinced a disagreeable animus, but the audience, which was made up more or less of musicians, showed their approval. The great mistake was in leading critics to expect a new style—like the Hungarian or Scandinavian.[13]

In both Berlin and Dresden, Arens relied heavily on American expatriates for his audience. Several of the Berlin reviewers (B1, B6, B9) commented on the fact that the audience consisted primarily of Americans, with Karl Homann of the *Tägliche Rundschau* going so far as to call it a "Familienfest" (B6). In Dresden the advance notice of the concert, presumably written or at least approved by Arens, read: "The Trenkler *Gewerbehaus Orchestra* will present an *American Composers' Evening* today. . . . Both in musical circles and in the numerous English and American families that live here, one may look forward to the concert with interest, if only to be able to note the influence exercised on the American composers by the German music that is held in such high esteem by all Americans."[14] While this strategy resulted in large and enthusiastic crowds at both concerts, the conductor may have regretted the wording of the Dresden publicity notice, for all of the reviews of this concert emphasized both the American audience and the German influence on the American compositions performed. The review in the *Neue Zeitschrift für Musik* (D4) was not really a review at all but consisted simply of the previously cited publicity notice with verbs changed to the past tense.

The two concerts were only five days apart, and Arens was thus required to put the program together with a minimum of rehearsals. The critic for the *Dresdner Nachrichten* commented in both 1891 and 1892 on the excellent results achieved with limited rehearsal time, and as the concert series progressed, admiration for Arens as a conductor grew continuously. For the 1891 concerts in Berlin and Dresden, he used nearly identical programs, deleting two numbers from the first program and adding one for the second. In both cases he was limited in repertoire choices because of slow mail from the United States. Johann Beck's *Symphonic Scherzo* was performed in Dresden, but the score arrived too late to be included on the Berlin program. Henry Holden Huss' *Polonaise* also arrived too late for performance in Berlin. Arens had programmed several art songs for each concert, which had to be dropped at the last moment because of the illness of his soloists, Agnes Passekel in Berlin and Edith Walker in Dresden.[15]

A week after the Dresden concert, Arens presented a third concert at the Concerthaus Ludwig in Hamburg with the Laube Orchestra. In a letter to *The Musical Courier* he called this hall "the finest hall devoted to popular concerts I have ever seen, built in strict Italian Renaissance and possessed of very fine acoustic properties."[16] His report of an enthusiastic reception by the Hamburg public is supported by a notice in the *Hamburgischer Correspondent* (H1). After these three concerts with popular orchestras, Arens set his sights on more prestigious organizations. A projected concert at London's Crystal Palace in May fell through, but he was able to perform at the renowned Loh concerts in

Sondershausen on July 5. The court orchestra there was excellent, and again Arens received plaudits for his conducting (S1).

Encouraged by the success of his four concerts, Arens retired to the island of Frauenchiemsee in Bavaria to rest and set about planning a much more ambitious series for the 1892 season. A letter to MacDowell, dated August 12, 1891, reveals his plans and the means by which he hoped to fulfill them:

Dear sir:

I expect to repeat my concert on a grand scale next season and would ask you, what you would like to have performed in way of overtures, suites, solos for violin, cello, or voice with orchestral accompaniment, besides your Piano Concertos, which I will produce as often as possible. In case of the latter, will you please ask Breitkopf and Haertel to place score and parts at my disposal. (I suppose you know, that there is not a cent of money for me in the undertaking, but to the contrary, quite an expenditure of both time and money.) Should you wish other published works performed, you will please ask the resp. publisher to do the same. I expect to concertize in Berlin, Hamburg, Dresden, Leipsic, Weimar, Sondershausen and possibly at Cologne, Munich, Paris and London, so you see it would be worth the while for your publishers to acquiesce.[17] Now to another matter in connection with the above: In order to carry out above plans effectively, i.e. with fine orchestras, good soloists, sufficient number of orchestral players, it has been proposed by my American friends of Berlin to raise a guarantee fund of some 2–3000 Mk. The few wealthy Americans [in Berlin] will do all in their power but the rest must come from America. My request would therefore be to the effect, that you interest your musical friends and acquaintances in this laudable undertaking. Hon. W. W. Phelps, U.S. Minister at Berlin, will be glad to receive subscriptions. The Berlin concert (at the Philharmonic, if sufficient funds) will be under the auspices of Hon. Phelps and Lady. The names of patrons will be published and strict acct. of expenditures will be furnished to each at the close of season. As remarked above, I neither ask nor expect any remuneration for my time and labor, every cent therefore will go towards producing American Comp. in the best of manner. Hoping to hear of you per return of mail,

I subscribe
Yours Very Sincerely,
F X Arens[18]

MacDowell's answer to this letter has not been found, although he stated in a letter to *The Musical Courier* of the following summer that he attempted to dissuade Arens from going ahead with the concerts.[19] Despite this assertion, it seems that the score that Arens used to conduct MacDowell's Suite was on loan from the composer.[20] In general, Arens' efforts were rewarded handsomely, as the repertoire for the second season was much more varied and included works by the foremost American composers, among them Chadwick, MacDowell, and Paine. Raising funds does not seem to have been so easy—*The Musical Courier* gave progress reports on the success of the conductor's fundraising efforts, but in the end the Berlin concert was not performed at the Philharmonic, and only about half of the proposed concerts for the second season actually took place.[21]

On January 30, Arens presented the first concert of his 1892 series, again in the Berlin Konzerthaus with the Meyder orchestra. Curiously, this concert, which had presumably been planned more carefully than any other, was the low point of the tour. The audience was small, and in contrast to the previous year's Berlin concert, the American contingent was poorly represented (B10, B11, B12, B15). Also disappointing was the critical response. A number of papers that had carried reviews of the first Berlin concert ignored the second, including two music periodicals, the *Neue Berliner Musik-Zeitung* and the *Allgemeine Musik-Zeitung*. The editor of the latter journal, Otto Lessmann, had written a sniping review of the first concert (B9), so Arens was fortunate that he chose to miss the second. Those reviewers who did attend the 1892 concert commented on the extreme length of the program: "Two overtures, two symphonic works of four movements each, five songs, all more or less in the same style, eventually fatigue even the most well-disposed listeners, among whom I have every right to count myself; I had to forgo the final two numbers (two songs and an overture), which were to begin at a quarter to ten.—My other colleagues had already left much earlier" (Heinrich Ehrlich, B10). It is perhaps indicative of the hectic Berlin concert life of this period that in both Berlin concerts, a substantial number of the critics admitted to arriving late, leaving early, or both (B1, B4, B5, B8, B9, B10, B12, B13). As we shall soon see, however, this did not stop them from generalizing about the state of American music. The Prussian capital was rapidly becoming the musical leader of German-speaking Europe, making the importance of a Berlin concert—and the opinions of the Berlin critics—very significant indeed: "One must concertize in Berlin, because of its reputation and for the critiques, through which the 'provinces' allow themselves to be bribed; here every budding virtuoso is willing to receive a baptism by fire [Feuertaufe], and here is where the concert agents, the 'managers' and the critical Areopagus are found."[22] Arens survived the Berlin "Feuertaufe," but the "critical Areopagus" provided nothing worthwhile for his promotional material.

After taking a month to regroup, Arens presented concerts in Dresden (March 19), Weimar (March 23), and Leipzig (April 9). These concerts were very well received, and it was during this three-week period that Arens achieved his greatest successes. The critic of the *Dresdner Journal* noted that while the previous year's concert had consisted of lighter music, the 1892 concert contained much more serious works. The Dresden concert was also noteworthy because of the musical luminaries present in the audience. Several reviewers (D6, D8, D9) commented on the attendance of Anton Rubinstein, and Arens stated that he came to the green room after the concert, where they spoke for half an hour.[23] Before long, rumors had even reached America:

The Chicago *Evening Post* says: "A friend in Dresden has written a letter to Henry Schoenefeld, of this city, in which the writer states that Rubinstein was an interested auditor at one of the latest American Composers' Concerts, given under the direction of F. X. Arens. Rubinstein clapped his hands after the performance of Schoenefeld's suite and loudly ejaculated: 'Now, that I like.' Of course, under the circumstances, Mr. Schoenefeld is immensely tickled over the news."[24]

More important in the long run, though, was Jean-Louis Nicodé, a composer and teacher at the conservatory who was so impressed with the Dresden concert that he wrote on Arens' behalf to Franz Wüllner, a member of the commission that was engaged in selecting concerts for the International Musical and Theatrical Exhibition in Vienna.[25]

In terms of critical response, the concert in Weimar was the high point of the tour. This concert was played by a very good orchestra, the Weimar Hofkapelle, assisted by students from the Weimar Musikschule. The reviewer for the *Weimarische Zeitung* commented,

Even though the language of the music is an international one and clear echoes of the compositional and instrumental techniques of German masters were unmistakable, the compositions performed offered so much that was singular and musically interesting that the audience, among whom furthermore were all of Weimar's musical authorities, grew more enthralled with each piece and was inspired to break out in repeated applause. (W2)

All four of the reviews of this concert were full of enthusiastic praise for Arens, his concert series, and the American works that he had played. Two of them were written by Alexander Wilhelm Gottschalg, the Weimar court organist and Liszt protégé. He wrote a brief, but laudatory, review for the *English and American Register* in Berlin (W4) and a longer review in *Der Chorgesang* (W3). The latter is in the form of an open letter to Leo Kofler, a German musician resident in New York, that commends the concert series and the state of American music in general.

The Leipzig concert was, in a sense, another "Feuertaufe," because of the musical traditions of that city. Here Arens played in the Altes Gewandhaus with the orchestra of the 134th Infantry Regiment, augmented by eight American string players studying at the Leipzig Conservatory (L10). This concert received the most attention from the musical press, with two substantial reviews by different critics in the *Neue Zeitschrift für Musik* (L5, L7) as well as reviews in the *Musikalisches Wochenblatt* (L6), *Neue Musikzeitung* (L8), *Leipziger Musikzeitung* (L9), and *Der Chorgesang* (L10) and a brief mention by the Leipzig correspondent of the London *Monthly Musical Record* (L11). The Leipzig concert also evinced some of the longest and most thoughtful signed reviews (L1, L3, L7).

While Arens was enjoying success in Germany, plans were under way for the exhibition in Vienna. This event was a major international showcase for publishers and instrument manufacturers. In addition to current products, the exhibition was to feature historical exhibits of scores and antique instruments. A temporary theater was being constructed on the Prater for concerts to be performed throughout the exhibition, which was to last from May to September 1892. In January auditions had been announced for an exhibition orchestra to perform all concerts,[26] and by early March the planning commission was able to announce a schedule of two popular concerts per week and "eine Reihe von Concerten unter Leitung der berühmtesten Componisten und Dirigenten der Gegenwart"[27] (a series of concerts under the direction of the most famous composers and conductors of the present). By the time the exhibition opened in May, the list of conductors in this latter series had been announced, with Arens scheduled to present a concert of American orchestral works after the fashion of his previous concerts.[28]

The Vienna concert took place on July 5, 1892.[29] According to all accounts, the orchestra played magnificently, and Arens was at his best, eliciting much comment by performing the long program entirely from memory (V8, V9, V10, V15, V16). *The Musical Courier* reported on the event in glowing terms:

At the conclusion of the first part, members of the music committee on behalf of the official commission went on the platform and personally handed Mr. Arens a huge laurel wreath amid the tumultuous plaudits of both audience and orchestra. On the streamers attached to the wreath (which Mr. Arens brought with him [to America] as a souvenir) this inscription is printed in large golden letters: "Dem ausgezeichneten Dirigenten Herr F. X. Arens, Die Commission der Internationalen Ausstellung für Musik und Theaterwesen, Wien 1892" (To the distinguished conductor, Mr. F. X. Arens, from the Commission of the International Musical and Theatrical Exhibition, Vienna, 1892).[30]

With this final triumph, Arens sailed for New York, having been in Europe for two years and having introduced American orchestral works in many of the major musical centers. The tour had been successful by nearly every standard, especially in light of the fact that such a tour had never been attempted before. In addition to the scores of the works that he had performed to such acclaim, he brought with him excerpts from a large number of reviews, which would soon become the subject of heated debate.

American readers had received periodic updates on the tour in the pages of *The Musical Courier* and the *American Art Journal*, but to Arens and those who supported his idea of performing American music in Germany, the following notice in the December 1891 issue of the *Boston Musical Herald* must have come as a surprise:

It is impossible for us to commend the enterprise of Mr. F. X. Arens in giving American concerts in Europe. We must go further than this and say that special propaganda of the kind which in his mistaken ardor Mr. Arens is furthering is hurtful to the ultimate position in art of music written by Americans, and ought not to be encouraged. We regret giving Mr. Arens pain but it is a question of much more moment than the happy issue of a set of concerts in Berlin.[31]

The *Boston Musical Herald* was a small journal with a limited circulation, edited by George H. Wilson (1854–1908). If every good story needs a villain, Wilson is as close as one can get in describing a movement based on encouragement, support, and optimism. Among all the high-minded idealists and well-meaning buffoons, he stands out as a man whose greed, incompetence, and maliciousness did serious damage to the American Composers' Concert movement and several of the people involved in it.

Wilson was born in Lawrence, Massachusetts, and went to Boston as a boy to study piano and organ. He sang in the 1872 Peace Jubilee as a teenager and was also a member of the Apollo Club, the Handel and Haydn Society, and other groups in Boston.[32] In the 1880s he became known as a musical journalist, initially as music critic for the *Boston Traveller*. Whether because this position did not pay well or because he wished for more influence, he added other responsibilities in the years ahead. Beginning in 1884, Wilson published an annual retrospective of the musical season titled *The Boston Musical Yearbook*. This consisted of listings of concerts given during the previous season, with special attention to the Boston Symphony Orchestra. From the fourth volume, devoted to the 1886/1887 season, it was retitled *The Musical Year-Book of the United States*, though it was still mainly concerned with Boston, and the coverage of the rest of the country was spotty. The yearbook, which eventually reached volume 10, was similar to Henry Krehbiel's *Review of the New York Musical Season*, but without the in-depth reviews or comprehensive coverage of concerts.[33] Wilson made perhaps his most important contribution to Boston musical life when he inaugurated the practice of writing program notes for the Boston Symphony Orchestra shortly after the arrival of conductor Wilhelm Gericke in 1884. The notes written by Wilson were modest in length and not terribly insightful, but they established a precedent that would later be carried to great heights by William F. Apthorp.[34]

In 1891 Wilson bought the *Boston Musical Herald*, which had been founded by Eben Tourjée in 1880 as the house organ of the New England Conservatory of Music. He assembled an impressive list of associate editors, including the prominent New York critics Krehbiel, Finck, and Henderson. One of his first actions after acquiring the journal in November was to make his controversial statement regarding the Arens tour in the December issue. The resulting controversy gained a great deal of publicity for his newest editorial venture. This paragraph would hardly have been noticed had it not become the subject of comment in other journals later in the year. Wilson's opinion was aired two months before the start of the second season of concerts, but nothing more was written until the summer of 1892, when it blossomed into a war of letters to rival the famous musical disputes of Paris. The *Boston Musical Herald* stuck obstinately to its position and was eventually joined by the *New York Tribune* in decrying Arens and his concerts. *The Musical Courier* and the *American Art Journal* came to the conductor's defense. As the war of letters heated up, it brought the question of journalistic criticism into sharp focus, since all participants relied heavily on the evidence of reviews from Germany to support their opinions.

Known as *Watson's Art Journal* from 1867 to 1875, the *American Art Journal* had been published in New York since 1864.[35] Its editor since 1875 had been William M. Thoms (1852–1913), known especially for "advocating a recognition of American composers."[36] He relied heavily on concert reviews in reporting on the Arens tour in May and June 1892.

Responding to these positive reviews of the Arens tour, the *Boston Musical Herald* expanded on its position in the July issue. The article began with the statement that its opposition to Arens was not personal but was rather on purely philosophical grounds, namely, that the American school of composition was still too immature to be thrust onto the European stage and should instead "take its chances along with French and Russian or any other music, and bide its time."[37] Wilson then proceeded to contradict his initial assertion by making some damaging comments about Arens personally, stating that the concerts were being performed "through the medium of an insufficient orchestra and under the direction of a conductor who is not acknowledged a conductor in his own country." The author went on to say that "of course Mr. Arens can secure bushels of good notices commending his scheme; press notices in the majority of cases are at the call of any good-mannered fellow the world over." Immediately following this statement he brought up the negative critiques in Berlin and quoted a brief notice from the *Monthly Musical Record* (London) that had castigated the Leipzig concert (L11).

The *American Art Journal* responded to this second article with more quotations: the July 9 issue contained excerpts of testimonial letters from Arens' voice teacher Hey and Wilhelm Blanck, the director of the conservatory where he had been teaching. It also presented excerpts from two of the Leipzig reviews (L3, L7).[38] This journal chose to avoid mudslinging throughout the process, never once mentioning the negative comments in other journals but simply reprinting positive excerpts from German reviews.

The Musical Courier, one of America's most successful and long-lived music journals, was not so reticent about name-calling. In fact, part of its appeal was the irreverent tone that characterized its pages. According to W.S.B. Mathews:

The Musical Courier affords a great variety of interesting matter, and the treatment is light and brilliant rather than earnest and dignified. It is the tone of the club man after dinner, rather than of the enthusiast at his desk. Accordingly, it has a large following of what might be called the "worldly element" in music. It fills a place, and it would not be impossible to remove from its columns everything against which gentlemanly taste would rebel without in the act depriving it of the source of its real power.[39]

A motivation for the editors of *The Musical Courier* in supporting Arens may have been the fact that during his two years in Germany, he had served as Berlin correspondent for this periodical. On July 20 they referred for the first time to the "attack" on Arens by the *Boston Musical Herald*,[40] and for the next several issues their criticism of this journal became increasingly heated.

The *New York Tribune* jumped into the fray on July 24, publishing an even stronger denunciation of the Arens tour that included negative quotations from V6 and V7. Although unsigned, the article must have been written or at least approved by Krehbiel, chief music critic of the *Tribune*, who was also a contributing editor to the *Boston Musical Herald*. He prided himself on keeping abreast of European newspapers, and in this case his desire to set the record straight on the European critical response seems to have outweighed any lingering patriotic sentiments for his American compatriots. Arens was evidently offended by Krehbiel's editorial, referring facetiously to Krehbiel in a private letter to MacDowell after the whole episode was over as "that arch-friend of the Am. Composer."[41] The *Tribune* article became a centerpiece for both sides, as both *The Musical Courier* and the *Boston Musical Herald* reprinted it in the following weeks. The *Courier* reprinted the *Tribune* article on July 27 in order to refute its claims, taking issue with both antagonists over the use of reviews.[42] In response to the *Tribune*'s quotation of negative reviews from Vienna and the *Herald*'s earlier comment about press notices in general, the author wrote:

Now in all fairness the "Tribune," which musically is fond of riding a high ethical horse, should give its readers the other side of the picture. Mr. Arens has favorable criticisms from critical authority quite as exalted as those quoted by the "Tribune." Does the "Tribune" know this or does it believe, to use Mr. Wilson's words in the magazine edited by the secretary of the Columbian Exposition Music Bureau, that "any good fellow can get a favorable press notice?" This sentence conjures up appalling visions of all the good fellows in Mr. Wilson's category (we are among them ourselves).[43]

Three days later, the *American Art Journal* published another article in praise of Arens, this time reporting that he had returned to America and stopped at the office "to express his appreciation of our support of his efforts on behalf of the American composer while abroad."[44] His presence in New York further exacerbated the antagonistic debate.

The August issue of the *Boston Musical Herald* reprinted the *New York Tribune* article as vindication of its own position.[45] This forced a detailed response from *The Musical Courier*, in a lengthy article entitled "The Boston 'Musical Herald' and Mr. Arens" that appeared on August 3. This time, the editors addressed each of the criticisms against Arens in turn. They listed the orchestras with which Arens had played in order to refute the charge of "insufficient performances," cited the unanimous German assessment of Arens as a first-rate conductor to show that his lack of reputation in America was not relevant,[46] and detailed the selection process of the Vienna International Exhibition to show that Arens had not obtained the appointment under false pretenses. Most importantly, they addressed the issue of critical reaction directly:

The article in question contains a sweeping assertion to the effect that Mr. Arens secured bushels of favorable criticisms because he is a good mannered fellow. While this would almost place Mr. Arens on a level with the chevalier d'industrie of suave manners and brilliant accomplishments who at regular intervals infests these shores, it also means a direct insult to the music critics the world over. It furthermore strikes a severe blow at the "Musical Herald" itself, for if bushels of favorable criticisms are at the call of any good mannered fellow the world over, how are the readers of the "Herald" to know whether its favorable comments on artists are due to good manners or to real artistic merit? We are afraid that whatever Mr. Wilson's susceptibility to good manners may be, his associate editors, Messrs. [Louis] Elson, Philip Hale, Krehbiel, [W. J.] Henderson and [Benjamin] Cutter, will seriously object to any insinuations of this nature. THE MUSICAL COURIER for one wishes to enter an emphatic protest against the wholesale slur hurled at the entire guild of music critics the world over. That a journal of the standing of the Boston "Musical Herald" should thus denounce musical journalism is more than we can comprehend.[47]

This article also included quotations from Arens himself on his concerts, on the criticism by Wilson and the *New York Tribune*, on the state of American music, and on its reception in Europe. Three days later the *American Art Journal* reprinted more excerpts from European reviews (L4, L6, L10, W3, W4).[48] In order to end the argument conclusively, the August 10 issue of *The Musical Courier* featured a photograph of Arens on the front cover, a detailed biography, and no less than twenty excerpts from different reviews.[49]

This issue also contained an open letter from Edward MacDowell address-, ing several of the central points. First, he condemned the *Tribune* and the *Boston Musical Herald* for printing and endorsing negative criticisms of works that they had previously praised: "Do our own critics (of whom I personally have always been rather proud) confess that they are inferior to the foreign 'authorities' quoted? If they do not, why then reprint a set of obviously incorrect and worthless criticisms, and by calling their authors 'authorities,' or agreeing with them, thus directly contradict what they themselves have said of the same works?"[50] He went on to state that he was opposed to the concerts from the start but that since they were given, it was only fair to acknowledge the positive reviews that far outweighed the negative ones. The letter, although it mentioned in passing his opposition to the Arens tour, is primarily an indictment of the *Tribune* and *Boston Musical Herald* for unfair editorial practices.

The war of letters finally subsided with the September issue of the *Boston Musical Herald*, in which the entire first page was devoted to the dispute over Arens and his tour. While not completely retracting his earlier statements, Wilson modified them to show that he had rethought his position, particularly in regard to the skills and motives of Arens himself. The one position on which he remained adamant, though, was the issue of criticism. As a parting shot, he reiterated his former stance:

My reference to the ease with which press notices commending persons and schemes can be secured is no idle statement. . . . I do not consider press notices and signed articles to be synonymous terms, and while I am very glad indeed to be informed concerning the signed articles in the *Musikalisches Wochenblatt* and the *Leipsiger Tagblatt* commending Mr. Arens, I am still of the opinion that a "good mannered fellow" can get good notices "in the majority of cases."[51]

The whole dispute revolved around the issue of reviews and press notices. Both sides quoted extensively from sources known to them, most of which had been supplied by Arens himself. What none of the combatants could have known, though, was the breadth of the actual critical response. The present study draws on over twice as many reviews as the ones cited by contemporary American writers. More importantly, few of the reviews are so simplistic as to be entirely positive or entirely negative. Most examine the works in depth, some with astonishing insight and others with exasperating parochialism. The original reviews hold the key to the significance of Franz Xavier Arens and his European concert tour.

The Arens tour coincided with a flourishing of journalism in Europe. In the final decades of the century, the number and quality of daily newspapers in the German language exploded, while their prices gradually fell, allowing circulation to rise to unprecedented levels. During the 1890s there was a fierce rivalry among the three principal publishers in Berlin, which made this city "the home of an entertaining and lucrative newspaper industry for several decades."[52] Vienna during this period has been called "a magnet for the talented in German-language journalism."[53] Ironically, a contemporary writer bemoaned the fact that Vienna had only thirteen daily papers, as opposed to the 90-100 published in Paris.[54] Vienna's press, however, was quite varied in emphasis and political viewpoint, running the gamut from political papers of various orientations to literary and fashion journals. Vienna's critical establishment was second to none at this time, and as Appendix 3 clearly demonstrates, the critics turned out in force for the concerts of the International Exhibition.

Music journals were also numerous during this time, as shown by Imogen Fellinger's list of music periodicals in the *New Grove Dictionary*. According to this list, there were twenty-eight music periodicals founded in Germany during the 1850s, forty-eight during the 1860s, forty-nine during the 1870s, sixty-five during the 1880s, and eighty-eight during the 1890s.[55] Many of these journals were short-lived, while others were narrow or specialized in their coverage; nevertheless, there were enough reviews of the Arens concerts in the musical press to counterbalance the reviews in general newspapers and periodicals.

In his history of music criticism, Max Graf characterized German-language music criticism of this period as predominantly serious and ponderous rather than witty and elegant:

Certainly in no other country were musical questions treated so earnestly and so thoroughly as they were in Germany. The idea of music as entertainment was unfamiliar to the German mind. As a consequence, musical criticism in Germany had dignity and weight, and music critics were responsible for an important part of Germany's public and cultural life. The critics were almost a species of town councillor, members of the magistracy, public officials of municipal life.[56]

This seriousness is reflected in the critical reception of the Arens tour. Many of the reviews are substantial essays, running to thousands of words in length. The majority of the critics, no matter what their preconceptions about American music, pondered the music carefully and wrote thoughtful, often thoroughly detailed reviews. As a group, these reviews offer a remarkable view of German perceptions of American music.

Among the scores of reviews of the Arens tour there is a diversity of opinion on nearly every topic. In some cases the critics who reviewed a given concert were more or less in agreement, especially in the smaller cities like Weimar and Dresden, where it is tempting to assume that they consulted each other before writing their reviews. In Berlin and Vienna the situation was just the opposite, as critics disagreed strongly over the success of the concerts or the value of individual works. There are even cases when two critics disagreed over the size of the audience and its reception of the concert.[57]

The one topic on which there was unanimous agreement was Arens' skill as a conductor. Even the most negative of the critics had nothing bad to say about his conducting, and, in fact, most expressed admiration for his skill. Gottschalg called him "einer der besten uns bekannten Dirigenten" (one of the best directors known to us) and quoted an orchestra member who credited Arens with achieving in two rehearsals what a less intelligent and gutsy (schneidig) leader would have needed four weeks to do (W3). In Vienna, he was called an "eminenter Dirigent" (eminent conductor) (V6) and a "souveräner Meister" (sovereign master) (V15), and he was credited with "Heldenthaten" (heroic deeds) (V11) in preparing this performance. The admiration for his work centers on two aspects of his conducting: his ability to teach new music quickly and his musical sensitivity.

In each case, the limits on Arens' budget forced him to produce the concerts with only two or three rehearsals. Even though the orchestras were experienced and the musical language of the works was basically familiar, this circumstance required efficient effort on the part of the conductor. He knew the scores so well that, as noted previously, he could conduct the final concert in Vienna entirely from memory, a feat that was not common in the 1890s. This intimate knowledge of the scores was coupled with a disciplined rehearsal technique described by a reviewer of the Leipzig concert:

Herr Arens as composer but most especially as conductor possesses an admirable talent. With an orchestra of about sixty men that was completely strange to him he got on so well that in only three rehearsals, fourteen movements that were absolutely unfamiliar here were favorably performed. Already in the first rehearsal, in fact in a few minutes, the players sensed that a master of his art stood before them. Energetically—one might say electrifyingly—he gathered his forces around him and spurred each one to do his very best. Light and shadow, ppp and fff, sweetness, fire, magic: he governed all passions and feelings. (L10)

His disciplined approach to rehearsals earned the respect of the players, but his sensitivity earned the respect of critics and audiences. His model, as he confided to MacDowell, was Felix Weingartner, whom he called "the finest and most eclectic of all well known conductors, Nikisch not excepted."[58] Arens' bold and expressive movements impressed both audience and critics, several of whom referred to his "virtuosity" as a conductor (D8, V11). Arens seems to have used his body less to keep time than to communicate expression, a style of conducting that would not become the norm until the twentieth century. At the same time, though, Hans Paumgartner noted that he never allowed expressiveness and rhythmic elasticity to inhibit the overall rhythmic solidity (V8). One of the most astute observations about his conducting was made by Alfred Michaelis, who called it "subject-appropriate, that is quiet and restrained or fiery and exciting according to the development of the work."[59] This view of Arens as a conductor is echoed in the comments of Albert Kauders, which effectively sum up the views of critics throughout the tour:

Regarding the conducting performance of Herr *Arens*—he conducted the entire program from memory—there was unanimous praise. With an orchestra unfamiliar to him he worked out all these difficult works in their smallest details after minimal rehearsals. Herr Arens is clearly filled with a splendid enthusiasm for the cause he champions; however he also knows how to communicate his enthusiasm to the orchestra, haranguing and electrifying the players to their best performances. Light and shadow, energy and sweetness adhere slavishly to the tip of his baton. Herr Arens earned his laurel wreath honestly, and—to tell the truth—of all the new acquaintances that he imparted to us, his (as conductor) was our favorite. (V9)

These opinions are shared so widely that there can be no doubt about Arens' ability to perform the works of his compatriots as well as they could be performed, effectively ruling out inadequate performances as a factor affecting the critical response. As Michaelis put it, "the American composers have in fact found in Herr Arens the right man, who is specially equipped to help them obtain wider dissemination of their art" (L9). The way that he approached the wider dissemination of American music, though, had an important effect on the critical reception of that music.

By performing all-American concerts, Arens created the interest necessary to earn him the right, as an unknown conductor, to perform in Germany's major cities. At the same time, an all-American concert created a critical atmosphere that he may not have sought intentionally. As demonstrated in the previous discussion of the American reaction to the Arens tour, the value of all-American concerts was not universally acknowledged in the United States. MacDowell, who was America's most vocal opponent of this type of concert, summed up his beliefs in a letter written the previous year: "As it is now, whenever an exclusively American concert is given, the players, public and press seem to feel obliged to adopt an entirely different standard of criticism from the one accepted for miscellaneous concerts—Some people would run down an American concert before hearing the music—and others would praise it (also before hearing it)."[60]

This observation proved to be true in Europe as well. In some cases—most notably with the Weimar critics—those who wrote about the concerts were inclined to praise the concert series and the "progress" of American music despite calling attention to any number of weaknesses in the individual works. At the other end of the spectrum were critics who seemed to be distrustful of the whole enterprise even before hearing the music, calling into question the motives behind the concerts:

The Americans are great in invention and possess innumerable patents; but they are also truly not small in publicity. Since we do not travel to America to hear the works of the composers who live there, America sent its capable director F. X. Arens to Europe to perform the tone poems of his countrymen in our concert halls. (V13)

Herr Arens has been set up as a pioneer to clear the ground for the reception of overseas sound products and to prepare for the import of American musical merchandise. With that he certainly still has a long way to go. (V17)

Herr Arens proved himself to be a prudent conductor, to whom his countrymen can be very grateful for this propaganda for their works. (H1)

Felix von Wartenegg took these arguments to their logical conclusion by suggesting in the *Neue Zeitschrift für Musik* that Americans had grown tired of seeing the money spent on art and music go to foreigners and had therefore cooked up a scheme to extract money from Europeans instead (V18). Though not universal, these attitudes colored many of the reviews. Indeed, MacDowell went so far as to suggest that the negative reviews from European critics "evidently derived their animus from the unfortunate title of the concerts in question."[61]

A second problem inherent in the format of the concerts was that an all-American concert invited critiques of the state of American music in general. As a preface to his remarks on the individual pieces in the first Berlin concert, Homann commented on the difficulty of assessing American music on the basis of what he had heard: "Each composer was given a hearing with only one work apiece, or even just a portion of one work, and therefore it would be risky to pass judgment on the individuality or the overall character of the individual men on the basis of what we heard" (B6). This sensible observation was a solitary voice, however. Among the scores of reviewers who wrote about these concerts,

Homann is the only one to acknowledge that it might not be possible to generalize about American music based on the individual pieces heard. Instead, all but the briefest of press notices begin or end with summations of the concert, passing judgment on all the pieces heard and, either overtly or implicitly, on American music in general.

Most reviewers admitted total ignorance about American music before these concerts, although several of the Berlin critics knew of the works of Bird, who had lived in that city for the past five years, and many were familiar with the concertos and shorter piano works of MacDowell. Max Graf was the only critic who mentioned having read Ritter's history of music in America, although he noted that this book was more concerned with the performance and fostering of music than with American composers (V14). Despite this acknowledged ignorance, an entire evening of American music seems to have served as an invitation to generalize about Americans and their music that few of the reviewers could resist.

In making generalizations about American music, the reviewers often drew upon stereotypes or preconceptions of the United States. It is noteworthy that despite the millions of Germans who had crossed the Atlantic since 1848, German views of America in the late nineteenth century were highly unrealistic. Hans W. Gatzke writes:

When they told their families back home about the United States, . . . German-Americans rarely painted a realistic picture but instead presented stereotyped descriptions, either of a heaven-on-earth land of boundless opportunities (Land der unbegrenzten Möglichkeiten) or of an uncultured, artificial, heartless, and mechanistic society, bent merely on chasing the dollar. Both stereotypes have survived into our own day and have not contributed to better American-German understanding.[62]

These stereotypes were used by reviewers in two ways. Either they cited them as support (or justification) for their negative views on the music, or they presented them as a foil against which a positive impression of the music was contrasted. The latter view, by far the most typical, is illustrated by a review of the Weimar concert:

Until now we have only been accustomed to musicians, singers, conductors, generally speaking all who called themselves stage performers and longed for laurels and tinkling gold, who swam over to the promising Dorado, the Land of Dollars; not, however, to the importation of these artistic products to us. Consequently the opinion has gradually been built up among us, that the residents of the "New World," especially in the musical realm, were not yet much more than half barbarians, among whom the Gospel of Art as good as never worked its creative power. On that score we should now have had our misconceptions corrected on Wednesday evening, as a number of sensitive musical poems were performed, that surprised as much through the originality of their conception as the virtuoso orchestration. (W1)

On the negative side, America was characterized as "Dollarland" (V7, V17) and a country of practical, not artistic, invention (B13, L3, V1, V9, V13). Josef Stolzing began his critique of the Vienna concert by citing Nikolaus Lenau's assessment of America in 1833 as proof of the "prosaic emptiness" (poesielose Nüchternheit) that he heard in the 1892 performance:

The nature itself is cold. The conformation of the mountains, the hollows of the valleys, all is uniform and unfanciful. No true songbirds, all is just chirping and unmelodious whispering. Even the people have no voice for song. I was often in musical company where young women let their singing be heard. Their tone was in truth to be compared with that which one creates if one runs a wet finger on the rim of a glass filled with water, a peculiar shriek that comes closest to that of a seagull. (V16)[63]

The central issue for all the critics is neatly summed up by yet another stereotype of Americans. As noted in the Introduction, Germany and the United States were involved in a trade dispute that had resulted from the adoption by the U. S. Congress of the so-called McKinley bill, a sweeping set of trade reforms that imposed extremely high tariffs on foreign goods, most notably, German products. Germans felt victimized by the bill, and not all Americans were convinced of its benefit to U.S. trade. References to the McKinley bill found their way into several of the reviews (B3, B13, V6, V12, V17) as an expression of what many of the reviewers perceived to be the most obvious aspect of the American works: "The compositions make it clear that the McKinley bill does not apply to the import of foreign artistic production. A quantity of German material is contained in the works, which give themselves away as much through the earnestness of ideas, purity of expression, and solidity of technique as through the particular step toward Mendelssohn, Schumann, and Wagner."[64]

This review highlights the fundamental misunderstanding that plagued the Arens tour and, indeed, American art music generally in the late nineteenth century. The tour, like the American Composers' Concert movement in general, was an example of what Barbara Zuck has called "conceptual" Americanism, defined as activities that promote music written by Americans. The German critics expected to hear "compositional" Americanism: musical works that incorporate native elements.[65] The two concepts are not necessarily compatible, and in the case of Arens, his fervent support for American music was the result not of an interest in art music based on native materials but rather of a desire to provide a forum for art music written by Americans.[66]

A glance at the repertoire performed by Arens at the nine concerts shows that the works chosen are highly dependent on German models. Of the twenty composers featured, only one, Arthur Foote, had not studied music in Germany. The conductor performed scores that were sent to him by the composers, who clearly submitted works that were not far from German traditions. In addition, Arens exercised a certain amount of discretion in programming each concert, favoring works that would have a familiar sound to German ears.

This sound was not lost on the sharp ears of the critics, nearly all of whom commented on the striking similarity of the American works to contemporary European compositions. Again there were two attitudes toward this phenomenon. The critics were more or less evenly divided in their interpretation of this issue, with a significant number of critics viewing the "appropriation" of European materials as a sign of lack of originality that in some cases bordered on plagiarism and with an equally sizable group of critics praising the Americans for basing their works on the best possible models rather than inventing a totally new musical language.

Those who decried American use of European techniques were most likely to be very specific about the influences that they heard and to claim these influences as uniquely German rather than broadly European. A case in point is B. Horwitz's assessment of the conductor's own work:

With his symphonic fantasy, Herr Arens has thrown himself into the arms of Richard Wagner. An assortment of ideas stemming from Rienzi, Tannhäuser, and Lohengrin pass by the ears of the listeners. Great is the variety of orchestral effects that are used. The author has taken more than one idea in regard to timbral effects from the scores of the Bayreuth Master, which he seems to have studied carefully. (B8)

Those who viewed the influence in a positive light were less nationalistic in their views, choosing instead to stress the cosmopolitan nature of European art music in the late nineteenth century: "Art knows no restricted, local parochialism: its domain is cosmopolitan. In the realm of musical art the watchword reads 'pleasing sound,' from whichever nation it originates and resounds. In the land of the *rolling dollar* and the *smartest businessman*, a true and genuine striving for art is asserting itself."[67]

These two fundamental viewpoints are expressed in a variety of subtle variations, depending on the individual critic and work. An examination of four compositions that were considered by Germans and Americans alike to be the most successful works on the tour illustrates the range of the European critical opinion on the issue of musical influence. John Knowles Paine's "Spring" Symphony is a work with strong ties to the conservative branch of German Romanticism; George Whitefield Chadwick's Dramatic Overture *Melpomene* makes obvious references to the works of Wagner; Edward MacDowell's *Suite für großes Orchester*, op. 42 is a work in the European tradition that was nonetheless heard as a highly original composition; and Henry Schönefeld's *Marcio Fantastico* is the only clear example of "compositional" Americanism in the concerts.

Paine's Second Symphony, subtitled "Im Frühling," was the earliest work on any of the programs, though it was a little over a decade old in 1892. Its character is perhaps best reflected by the response of John Sullivan Dwight, America's staunchest advocate of German musical culture, to its 1880 premiere in Boston—he was so excited by the new work that he stood on his seat, repeatedly opening and shutting his umbrella to demonstrate his enthusiasm.[68] His review of the new work expressed his feelings in more objective terms:

We cannot but regard this "Spring" Symphony as a remarkable, a noble work, by far the happiest and ripest product, thus far, of Prof. Paine's great learning and inventive faculty, and marking the highest point yet reached in these early stages of American creative art in music. It is worthy to hold a place among the works of masters, and will reward many hearings wherever the symphonic art can find appreciative audience.[69]

The symphony did, indeed, earn many hearings in Boston in the decades following its premiere. The full score was published by Arthur P. Schmidt of Boston in 1880 and released simultaneously by August Cranz of Hamburg and C. A. Spina of Vienna, making it the first American orchestral work ever to appear in print.[70] It was discussed in depth by A. J. Goodrich in his 1889 text-book, *Complete Musical Analysis*. Although the work fell out of fashion after World War I, it has been recorded twice in recent years, confirming its position as a major American work.[71] Like the rest of Paine's output, the symphony reflects his debt to the German Romantic tradition. Throughout his fruitful career as teacher and composer, Paine stressed his belief that American art music should draw on the best models of the European tradition rather than attempt to create a radically different musical style. In keeping with this ideal, he had studied for three years in Berlin and developed a disciplined style firmly rooted in the music of Beethoven and his successors. His view of originality did not encompass a rejection of past stylistic trends but rather aimed to build upon them. In this regard, the symphony is one of his most successful compositions. Its structure and harmonic language are firmly rooted in German Romanticism, but the assurance with which he handles his materials places it far above his earlier works. While his first symphony is clearly dependent on Beethoven's fifth symphony, the second symphony shows more individuality. With this work, Paine incorporates a wider variety of influences and confidently places his own stamp on the work. John C. Schmidt characterizes it thus: "A happy result of two differing influences on Paine, this symphony seems to reflect both the traditional standards of Beethoven as the supreme symphonic composer and the exciting experiments in form, melody, and harmonic materials by such later masters as Mendelssohn, Schumann, Berlioz, possibly the young Brahms, Bruckner, and even Liszt and Wagner."[72]

The German critics also recognized the Paine symphony as an important work, although they did not hear it as a product of the new school of composition. In their attempts to pin down Paine's influences, they tended toward the conservative branch of German Romanticism. The critics identified most frequently the influence of Mendelssohn (B11, L1, V4, V7, V8, V14), followed by Beethoven (D8, L3, W3), Schumann (V6, V8, V14), Gade (L1), and Spohr (V6). This assessment may be due, in part, to the format in which the work was presented. Arens played the entire work only once, in Berlin. On subsequent occasions he performed excerpts consisting of two or three movements. This undermined the "almost Wagnerian manner"[73] in which Paine develops his principal motives throughout the four-movement work. Even in an uncut performance, the subtle connections between movements would have been difficult to identify on one hearing. Paine's reiteration of the themes of earlier movements in the finale is characteristic of the era that Carl Dahlhaus has labeled "The Second Age of the Symphony," when works like the Franck D-minor Symphony (1888) and the Dvořák Symphony "From the New World" (1893) achieved a similar cyclic effect by recalling themes from earlier movements.

The programmatic nature of the work was certainly not enough to associate it with the New German School. The symphony is subtitled "Spring" (Im Frühling), but this designation refers more to a general evocation of mood than to specific programmatic content. The original score and performances did not feature programmatic titles, which first appeared in the Goodrich analysis of 1889. Schmidt speculates that Paine downplayed the programmatic element to avoid offending conservative critics,[74] although Dwight's review indicates that he at least knew the programs of the first two movements. For the 1892 concerts, Arens printed the titles of the movements:

I. Departure of Winter—Awakening of Nature (Winters Abschied—Erwachen der Natur)
II. May-night Fantasy (Mainacht-Fantasie)
III. A Romance of Springtime (Romanze)
IV. The Glory of Nature (Die Herrlichkeit der Natur)

The titles were not enough to offset the impression among the critics that Paine was essentially a conservative composer, for none of them accused him—as they did Chadwick and others—of being a scion of the New German School.

In regard to the program, two of the Dresden critics took issue with Paine's depiction of spring (D6, D8). In the words of the critic of the *Dresdner Anzeiger*:

How differently the American portrays spring as opposed to the German! The printed titles of the individual movements are indeed approximately the same: Winter's Departure, Awakening of Nature, May Night (presented here as a scherzo), the Glory of Nature. Upon hearing such music, we Germans miss the picture of blooming, buzzing, and budding; we would wax poetic, sing, dream, and revel. Not so the American—he seems hardly to know and hastily skips over the deeper nature of spring. (D6)

This reaction was a result of Arens' decision to perform a shortened version of the symphony. In his review of the 1880 premiere, Dwight had noted an unusual seriousness in the portrayal of spring, but significantly, he spoke of it in reference to the adagio movement, which was omitted from the Dresden performance.[75] The different conception of spring did not detract seriously from the positive impression of the work, though, for another Dresden critic went on to state: "The above-mentioned symphony, the most outstanding work of the evening, is nevertheless so skillfully worked out and so effectively constructed, so rich in thrilling details, that the European art world should not look away from such appearances of overseas origin" (D8).

Two of the Berlin critics (B11, B12) and one of the Weimar critics (W1) commented that the work was too long. At fifty minutes, the work is, indeed, monumental in scope, and it is only surprising that more did not call attention to this fact. At the Boston premiere in 1880, nearly all the critics but Dwight criticized its length, which was out of proportion to the length of contemporary European works.[76] It is possible that by 1892 the length did not seem so unusual in the context of recent German works. Those who did find fault with the length were concerned with the difficulty of sustaining the unity of the piece over such vast expanses of time: "Indeed the spatial expansion generally goes well beyond the acceptable dimensions, and then even the most successful effects do not ultimately banish the relaxation; fanciful invention and an excellent ability and knowledge cannot be denied the composer" (B12).

In light of this criticism, it is not surprising that the movements praised most consistently throughout the season were the shortest: the second-movement scherzo and the finale. Arens reacted to this criticism by programming selected movements in succeeding concerts, each time pairing the scherzo with the finale (Weimar), the first movement (Leipzig and Vienna), or both (Dresden). The long adagio third movement was not heard again after the Berlin concert.

Throughout the 1892 season, critics repeatedly praised Paine's technique. In particular, they seem to have been impressed by his control of form. The overall shape of the various movements was cited often, as was the handling of motives. The orchestration was praised as well, and, in all, the impression was that Paine was a master of the techniques of nineteenth-century symphonic writing. In the analysis of Bernhard Vogel, though, who wrote two of the most negative reviews on the tour, this technical mastery was turned against the composer: "In some details of his tone paintings we encounter many [things] truly and sincerely observed and also warmly felt; the joy in solid musicmaking lures him into alarming pomposity, which in the lack of any inventive originality whatsoever is doubly evident."[77]

This assessment reflects the subjective nature of the issue. It is easy to speak in concrete terms about technique, but much more difficult to objectify the presence or absence of creativity. Paradoxically, the most important criterion of artistic creation is the hardest to analyze. Time and again the critics repeated the same judgment of the American composers—excellent technique but no originality. Richard Heuberger compared the Americans to persons at a dinner party who regaled their fellow guests with tales of Africa and the Arctic but left them with the impression that their detailed descriptions were taken from books rather than firsthand experience. As to *why* he felt this way, Heuberger could not fully explain:

The American composers, whose works Herr conductor F. X. Arens performed in most excellent fashion for us the day before yesterday, are particularly well-trained, high-minded artists, in whom actually nothing is missing except the chief thing: individuality [and] original talent. To discuss this deficiency frankly is even easier, since we are prepared to acknowledge without reservation the many merits of construction: consummate form, the greatest skill in the handling of the orchestra, etc. (V6).

The issue of what constitutes originality is particularly vexing in the case of Paine, since the critics were nearly unanimous in recognizing European influences but silent on the aspects of the "Spring" Symphony that allowed them to do so. In Paine's case, the impression of influence was largely subjective. That was much less the case with the next composition.

If Paine made no apology for working in the mainstream of European compositional practice, Chadwick was less inclined to emulate his predecessors. Even as a student at the Leipzig Conservatory in the late 1870s, he took pride in using an American folk tune in his first string quartet and scored his biggest success with an overture on the American tale *Rip Van Winkle*. With one exception, it would be difficult to accuse Chadwick of neglecting American themes. In light of Arens' propensity for programming works of obvious German influence, it should not be surprising that the one exception is the composition featured in the Arens concerts—the dramatic overture *Melpomene* (1887).

This work, dedicated to Wilhelm Gericke, was the composer's most successful orchestral composition, appearing on concert programs around the world and receiving numerous hearings in Boston under the direction of its dedicatee. It was a particular favorite of Van der Stucken, who played it at an Arion Society concert in New York, at the Exposition Universelle in Paris, and at the Lincoln Hall concert in Washington, D.C., in 1890. Victor Fell Yellin has noted the irony of its popularity and discussed the unusual place that it occupies in the composer's oeuvre:

Of all Chadwick's orchestral music it is the least representative of his "American" or personal style. More than any other piece, *Melpomene* raises the question of the validity of a musical Americanism index that some have seemingly used to rank the worthiness of American composers of this period. . . . In *Melpomene* he dares to concern himself with the theme of tragedy. He presents himself not as a provincial craftsman turning out souvenirs for the sophisticated but as a member of a larger, Western culture. He is not limited by artificially imposed restrictions on the artistic expression of his subject matter just because he is working on this side of the water. His musical romanticism is just as firsthand and his sentiment just as genuine as that of his European contemporaries. Chadwick feels himself just as entitled to inherit the mantel [*sic*] of Beethoven and Wagner as any German composer.[78]

Not all of the German critics were prepared to concede that Chadwick was entitled to "inherit the mantle," however. Because of a very obvious reference to one German work, the reception was sharply divided, with some critics calling it the best work on the program and others deriding it as the worst. The question of influence is taken to another level with this work, for while the Paine symphony was based on the broad outlines of German symphonic tradition, the Chadwick overture makes unmistakable reference to a familiar work at the smallest level of detail. The critics did not agree on the significance of this reference or on Chadwick's right to use it.

Melpomene opens with a twenty-six-measure introduction marked "Lento e dolente" that sets the stage for the "Allegro agitato" that follows. In the initial measures of the introduction, Chadwick makes clear reference to the opening of the Prelude to *Tristan und Isolde*. Like its famous predecessor, it begins with three phrases, each of which features the distinctive sonority of the English horn, a melodic shape that outlines a rising sixth, and the "Tristan" chord itself. Also like the Wagner work, each successive phrase is on a higher pitch level, and the third reaches an emotional and dynamic climax. Because it is prominent and specific, the reference is more obvious than in Paine's symphony, where critics were sure there was German influence but were uncertain as to its exact nature.

Seven reviews (including the two by Vogel) cited the influence of Wagner on this work (B11, B12, L1, L6, L8, V7, V9), with four of those noting also the specific similarity to *Tristan und Isolde* (B11, L1, L8, V9). One critic heard the influence of Liszt (W3), and another classified the work as a product of the New German School (D8). Four others characterized *all* the American works as indebted to Wagner (W4, V5, V10, V17), while one lone critic heard echoes in *Melpomene* of Henri Litolff's *Robespierre Overture*, a famous example of program music taken to excess (L5). What distinguishes the reaction to *Mel-pomene* is the vehemence of the opinions expressed:

Opening the evening was a dramatic overture, "Melpomene," by G. W. Chadwick, a work with serious intentions[79] that flirts strongly with Wagner. For example at the very beginning it comes palpably close to Tristan, only unfortunately just missing Wagner's genius; nonetheless it must be admitted that despite the trifling significance of the ideas, the overture still develops dramatic life, and from this point of view the composer doubtless is not without talent. (B12)

In Vienna, the reaction varied wildly, as critics who sat in the same hall and heard the same performance could claim that the work made "an insignificant impression" (einen unbedeutenden Eindruck) (Albert Kauders, V9) or that it was "an impressively intensifying work with true dramatic life, [which] must be counted among the best compositions in this genre" (ein sich imposant steigerndes Werk von echt dramatischem Leben, zu den besten Compositionen dieser Gattung gezählt werden muß) (Hans Puchstein, V15).

   These radically differing viewpoints seem to revolve around the reaction to the *Tristan* reference. Those critics who pointed out the connection invariably used it in a negative way, to chastise Chadwick for a lack of creativity. Those who liked the work did not mention the *Tristan* connection or else mentioned a general affinity with Wagner. The difference seems to lie in the opinions about Chadwick's intentions and what they signify.

   Because of the widespread familiarity of Wagner's work in 1892 and because of Chadwick's prominent use of the material in the opening, it is unreasonable to assume that only three listeners heard the connection. Those three were apparently the ones who were so deeply offended that they wished to call attention to it. On the other hand, they may have been the only ones willing to guess at Chadwick's intentions in using the allusion, while the others chose not to address such a problematic issue in the forum of a review.

   The use of the allusion forces speculation on Chadwick's motives. One can eliminate the possibility that the composer did not recognize the similarity of the opening gesture of his work to the *Tristan und Isolde* prelude. Not only was he writing during the heyday of Wagnerism in Europe and America, but he himself had been attracted to the works of Wagner since his student days. Even if he had unconsciously cited it in his initial draft, the connection would have been obvious as he reworked the piece. The notion that he quoted the work because of "infatuation" with Wagner is also untenable. While imitation may be the sincerest form of flattery, this allusion could be said to border on plagiarism. The more commonly held view of the German critics that the allusion showed a lack of originality is also implausible. If a composer were so bereft of ideas that he needed to appropriate thematic materials from other composers, it is unlikely that he would turn to the opening motive of one of the most famous pieces of the century.

   Presuming, then, that Chadwick was fully cognizant of the similarity of his opening to the *Tristan* prelude and that he expected intelligent listeners to hear that similarity, it seems clear that he intended to invoke a particular mood through allusion to the earlier work. The *Tristan* chord was so distinctive that it carried powerful connotative value. Even such an opponent of Wagner as

Claude Debussy used this to advantage in his orchestral scores, as did countless other European composers in the decades after Wagner's death.[80] In Chadwick's case, he uses an allusion to the best-known representation of tragedy in the modern musical repertoire to set the stage for a musical representation of the Classical Muse of Tragedy. In this the European critics agreed that he was successful. Among those who reported on the work in positive terms, nearly all cited the drama of the work and its evocation of tragedy as the principal strengths.

There is another possible interpretation of the *Tristan* allusion. Recent scholarly discussion on musical influence has pointed out the tremendous weight of the past that composers felt during an age that was more historically aware than any previous era and simultaneously more obsessed with the notion of originality. The resulting "anxiety of influence" stymied the great composers of the late nineteenth century and forced them to come to terms with the influence of their creative predecessors. One response to this imperative was to deliberately quote or allude to a specific work by a previous composer and then to "misread" or misrepresent the original composer's intentions. It could be argued that in the succeeding Allegro, Chadwick effectively confronts and undermines the mood of the original quotation, thereby asserting his own artistic individuality.[81]

A final point must be made about the critical reaction to this piece. Although most critics liked the work, there were more detractors than for either the Paine symphony or the MacDowell suite. The reason seems to lie in the connection to Wagner. With Paine and MacDowell the references are to the general tradition of German music, which was so prevalent that it could easily be considered a cosmopolitan style. With Wagner the issues were different because his works could be heard as more specifically German than cosmopolitan. It is no coincidence that the most vocal opponent of this piece, Vogel, was a committed Wagnerite.

The critical reception of the MacDowell suite was mentioned specifically by Arens himself. After the concert tour and the resulting controversy in America were over, and Arens had settled in his new home in Indianapolis, he wrote to MacDowell in response to his letter to *The Musical Courier*:

Now whatever views you may hold in regard to the influence on a young composer to have his works performed in a country where up to date such a thing as a musical score written by an American had been considered an impossibility, you for one did not suffer through these performances, for at every concert your suite was enthusiastically recd and just as enthusiastically criticised. . . . You are now known in Europe as one of the composers of the day, American or otherwise, while in some of the cities visited, your name had never been mentioned, and in others only as a piano composer. Of course, you ultimately would have found your way, but not until someone else had taken you up (as Mdme Carreño had done with your piano works) Vide Wagner's friends.[82]

The reviews support this assessment, as critics repeatedly identified MacDowell's *Suite für grosses Orchester*, op. 42 the most interesting (B11, B16, V3, V13), most important (B10, V11), and most pleasing (B16, V5) work of the concert series. The reviewer for the *Musikalisches Wochenblatt* called it "poetically sensitive, highly interesting music that would enrich any concert program" (L6). Typical of the glowing praise inspired by the suite is this statement by Robert Hirschfeld of *Die Presse* in Vienna: "MacDowell possesses a very sound sense of form, he controls the modern means of orchestral expression with virtuosity and makes them subservient to his aesthetic sense of nature, which is vividly concerned with both the tranquil floating and the restless outpouring of nature's power" (V4).

MacDowell was praised most often for his orchestration, which is, indeed, varied and colorful. Especially in the final movement, "Waldgeister" (Forest spirits), MacDowell shows himself to be a master of orchestral color. This movement was most often singled out for praise in the reviews, although the first movement, "In einem verwunschenen Wald" (In a haunted forest) was also cited as being inspired. The third of the four movements, "Lied der Hirtin" (The shepherdess' song), was practically the only Adagio featured on a concert tour filled with brilliant showpieces and was therefore praised for its soulful melodies.

Unlike the majority of the composers represented, MacDowell was credited with a high degree of originality by the critics. Many of them noted European influences, especially Wagner (L9, L10, W1, V6, V8, V16) and Berlioz (D7, D8, V1), but this was not viewed as a flaw in the way it was by some of the critics of Paine and Chadwick. Paumgartner expressed the sentiment of many of the reviewers in his analysis:

A quality—and it is not one of the smallest—is possessed by MacDowell: he is interesting. Further, one can hear so much Wagner in the MacDowell suite without being allowed to blame him for plagiarism because of it. A composer who wishes to depict and illustrate like MacDowell and announces his work to be a picturesque, characteristic piece of music through the prescribed representations of the individual movements of the suite will not immediately find new colors in the [paint] can. . . . If we observe only his own talent and command of artistic resources (and MacDowell possesses both), we can still be satisfied. Poetic feeling, which happily and colorfully gives expression to the music, is present throughout. (V8)

MacDowell was the best-known composer on the programs, and this may have predisposed the critics to his music, but their comments indicate that they also heard a level of inspiration and technical skill absent in the other works. As Max Graf wrote, "With him one has the feeling, this man knows what he wants, wants what he knows, and can also do what he wants."[83] Because of this assessment, the critics were, with a few exceptions, complimentary of his talent and originality. The suite was the most successful piece on the tour because the critics were willing to excuse his European influences in deference to his talent and originality.

The "Marcio-fantastico" by Henry Schoenefeld (1857–1936) is in every way an anomaly among the works performed on the Arens tour. It portrays a scene from "Southern Negro Life" with themes patterned after AfricanAmerican music. Its instrumentation is extremely unusual—string orchestra supplemented by tambourine, triangle, and tam-tam. Although it bears some formal similarities to European music, the sound is so unusual that it stands out from the rest of the works on the concerts.

Schoenefeld was born in Milwaukee, Wisconsin, and after four years of study in Leipzig and Weimar he settled in Chicago in 1879 as conductor of the Germania Männerchor. His compositions did not achieve the same level of fame as those of Paine, Chadwick, or MacDowell, and, in fact, most of his orchestral pieces were never published. His work is distinguished by an ongoing interest in Native American and African American thematic materials, which figure prominently in all his major works. His "Rural" Symphony won the $500 prize awarded by the National Conservatory in 1892, earning him the praise of Antonin Dvořák. In 1899 he won the prize offered by Henri Marteau for a sonata for violin and piano. The *Suite characteristique*, from which the "Marcio fantastico" is drawn, was published jointly by Clayton F. Summy of Chicago and C. A. Klemm of Leipzig in 1893, an indication of the attention that it had attracted during the second season of the Arens tour.[84]

Schoenefeld's interest in American themes and the composition of the suite predated Dvořák's famous call to American composers to turn to their native music, and despite the European acclamation, Schoenefeld's work is uniquely American. In a not-so-subtle jab at Dvořák, Rupert Hughes stated, "Schoenefeld's negroes do not speak Bohemian."[85] On the Arens tour, many of the reviewers found it difficult to comment intelligently on the piece, since it was so far removed from their normal frame of reference.

Of the four movements of the suite, the second, labeled "Marcia fantastica" on the Arens programs and "Marcio fantastico" in the printed score, is the most unusual. The movement depicts a celebration of African Americans with two sprightly themes, the first in A minor and the second in A major. The transition from the first to the second themes is syncopated in the style of minstrel songs of the period. The mood of celebration is broken suddenly by a "maestoso sostenuto" interlude that represents the passing of a funeral procession, after which the mood and thematic materials of the first part return. The final measures of the piece incorporate the funeral theme, the syncopated transitional material, and the A-major theme into a dazzling coda. The syncopation and predominantly pentatonic flavor of the second theme lend an exotic character to the short piece.

The work was performed in only four concerts—at Dresden, Leipzig, Weimar, and Vienna—but the reviewers of these concerts devoted a disproportionate amount of space to the short piece. Several commentators noted that it received the most applause (D10, V3, V14, V18), and two counted it among the best works performed (V2, V3). On the other hand, the work was so unusual that it was called "grotesque" (L3, L6, V17), "bizarre" (L3, V7, V16), and even "brutal" (V8). Vogel, whose negative perceptions of the Leipzig concert have been noted already, suggested that "one enjoys that sort of realism much more when one hears it from a distance, perhaps a half hour from the orchestra" (L1). The majority, though, were of the opinion of J. Schucht of the *Neue Zeitschrift für Musik*, who wrote that he would have liked to hear it repeated (L5).

Most significant is the fact that only one reviewer noted any European influence on the work—a Dresden critic stated that it had "Berliozsche Orchesterbrillanz" (Berliozian orchestral brilliance) and French tendencies (D6). Indeed, the word "original" is used to describe this piece more than any other in the tour's repertoire (D6, D10, L7, L10, W2, W3, V17, V18), as is the word "interesting" (W1, W3, V3, V11, V13). Typical of the positive comments are those of Ferdinand Pfohl: "This piece is burlesque, grotesque, and strongly naturalistic, but captivating as a lively portrayal of southern Negro life with its peculiar dances, to which a funeral procession that interrupts the noisy slave celebration for several minutes produces a wonderful, fantastic contrast" (L3). As noted earlier, the piece was so unusual that words like "grotesque" and "bizarre" were used not infrequently. For those who admired the work, this was actually a positive factor: "Henry Schönefeld's 'Marcia Fantastica' produced a great effect. This picture from the Negro life of the south is distinguished through lively shaping and unusually clever exploitation of unfamiliar musical elements. The picturesque effects often clash roughly with each other, without damaging each other in the least, and the whole picture is frankly fascinating" (V12).

The very elements that were hailed as fresh and original by most critics, though, were viewed as too exotic to be taken seriously by some. One of the Weimar critics wrote, "The whole still gives more the impression of an ingenious pastime than of a serious promotion of art" (W1). In Vienna, two critics (V2, V4) questioned the authenticity of the thematic materials, in effect suggesting that Schoenefeld's exoticism was not exotic enough: "This tone picture by the impressionist Schönefeld did not especially please us. The Negro melodies may be authentic, but even the 'authentic' Negro airs originate mostly in more or less skillful whites, whose [phonograph] cylinders the gracious black boys are also gladly in the habit of carrying" (V4).

The critical response to these four pieces shows that Arens placed the American composers in a "damned if you do, and damned if you don't" situation. Paine and Chadwick were recognized as talented composers, but their works could easily be dismissed on the grounds that their obvious European influences must indicate lack of originality. Schoenefeld's work was recognized as highly original but could be dismissed because it was too exotic to be taken seriously as an artwork. Only MacDowell was seen as simultaneously original and part of the stream of Western music history. The critics were quick to point out, though, that there was nothing distinctively American about his music, and they did not need to point out that he had spent most of his creative life in Germany.

A second and more troubling observation is that despite the firmness of their convictions on American lack of originality, the German critics could not describe precisely what was missing, other than to state that there is nothing uniquely American about the works. Their comments provide no insight on the exact nature of musical influence and its effect on a composer's originality, except to reinforce its subjective quality. In this one area of musical criticism, it seems that a critic is free to state an opinion without tangible proof.

The issue of originality, a highly subjective concept at best, was therefore used repeatedly to undermine the significance of the music. American ingenuity was already a cliché in the late nineteenth century, and, in the most cynical terms, the concert tour provided Europeans with an opportunity to claim superiority in at least one area of endeavor. As one Berlin critic stated, "The expression *self-made man*, of which the Americans are so proud, cannot be applied to these composers."[86] Kauders summarized many of the issues raised by the tour in a passage notable for its insight as well as its mixed metaphors:

From American music, no one would have imagined something singular in the national sense; one knows that the prevailing cosmopolitanism on the other side of the big water allows no national individuality. A characteristic national coloring would be drawn only from the musical expressions of the redskins and the negroes; strangely enough, of all the composers performed in the concert of Herr Arens, only a single one (Henry Schönefeld in "Marcia fantastica") reached into this territory. In other ways, though, one expected surprises. The Americans are a people of invention, of original heads. Wealth of invention and originality would then be the most precious virtues of a contemporary composer, the more precious the more seldom they actually appear. Unfortunately, however, the American inventive spirit also remains unproductive in the area of musical art. All of the composers who were performed for us drove the mills of their symphonies, suites, and overtures either with streams of Wagnerian passion or with breezes of Schumannesque sentiment, and the grain that is thereby ground is the same that has been stored for decades on the threshing floors of our Neo-Romantics. [Upon hearing] this musical import from America, I had to think unintentionally of certain Bordeaux wines, picked and pressed from vines in the regions of Tirol or Dalmatia. As new additions, the vintages appear only with so many stars. Thus it is in our case—the star-spangled banner, in whose shadow the recently heard musical works were produced, is the only mark distinguishing them from the productions of modern Germany. (V9)

In the final analysis, the American concerts of 1891/1892 produced mixed results. Europeans heard more American music than ever before, and many of the critics gave thoughtful responses to compositions that they heard. In contrast to the French reaction to Van der Stucken's Paris concert, the German critics took their responsibilities more seriously, analyzing the works in detail and (except in some cases) attempting to remain impartial. Arens felt that MacDowell's reputation was boosted, and the publication of Schoenefeld's *Suite charactéristique* in 1893 indicates that this piece enjoyed at least a momentary popularity. Certainly, Arens' reputation as a conductor was increased, although it did not result in a high-profile position for him. The tour also provoked discussion on both sides of the Atlantic about the issue of all-American concerts, which were beginning to fade in the United States by this time. While many Americans welcomed the publicity generated by the Arens tour, the consensus of opinion in the United States seems to have begun to shift in MacDowell's direction. The eminent critic Heinrich Ehrlich commented astutely on the phenomenon of all-American concerts after the second Berlin concert:

Another question is whether a long concert program should be comprised exclusively of works by Americans and whether the repetition of such a program in different cities is consistent with the desired results, that is whether it will in fact raise *the general interest in American composers*? The concert on Saturday offered many that, performed as single pieces between other non-American compositions, would undoubtedly have made a stronger impression; in conjunction with so many nearly similar works, the impression of the others was weakened. (B10)

In terms of European impressions of American music, the tour had little lasting effect. While individual works on the tour were praised, there is no evidence that European conductors adopted them into their repertoires. And while numerous critics expressed surprise at the level of accomplishment demonstrated by the concerts, the overall impression served to reinforce two basic assumptions that have continued to plague nineteenth-century American art music to this day.

The first is the perception that American art music was essentially cosmopolitan, an idea that the composers featured on the concerts would not have disputed. What is surprising, however, is the strength of this impression among the German critics. Nearly all of them noted the presence of European influence, and many of them made it the centerpiece of their critiques. The impression was apparently so strong that it overshadowed everything else that was heard. Numerous critics conceded that the music that they heard was well constructed and in many cases quite moving, but the connection to German traditions was so evident that this was viewed as the unifying factor.

The second impression was not stated as overtly as the first but is nonetheless an underlying assumption for many of the writers. For the land that had produced the telephone, the phonograph, and the incandescent light, music composed in a cosmopolitan style, no matter how competent, was simply not good enough. Never mind if the Americans were the equal of many contemporary European composers—a New World demanded new music. This imperative was strengthened by the format of the concerts. By presenting a concert consisting entirely of American works, Arens created the expectation that these works would somehow be different from contemporary European works. By this standard, even eminently gifted composers like Chadwick, Paine, and MacDowell could not fail to disappoint. Vogel, admittedly one of the most negative critics of the tour, presented his view of American music based on what he had heard in the Leipzig concert: "For the time being, America clearly does not yet have the calling to play first violin in the world orchestra; will it later, when a powerful creative genius arises? I daresay only a new century will give the old as well as the new world an answer" (L8).

The new century did bring several powerful American creative geniuses who reshaped both popular and art music. But for the time being, the advocates of American art music were still looking for a messiah. As each year went by and that messiah did not appear, patience for American Composers' Concerts grew thinner. Ironically, the one person who might have had a legitimate claim to this title—Edward MacDowell—would soon become the movement's most vocal opponent.

NOTES

1. "Vermischtes," *Neue Zeitschrift für Musik* 87/13 (April 1, 1891): 153. Unless otherwise noted, all translations are by the author.

2. See, for instance, Peter Marschalck, *Deutsche Überseewanderung im 19. Jahrhundert: Ein Beitrag zur soziologischen Theorie der Bevölkerung* (Stuttgart: Ernst Klett, 1973); Frederick C. Luebke, *Germans in the New World: Essays in the History of Immigration* (Urbana and Chicago: University of Illinois Press, 1990); Bruce Levine, *The Spirit of 1848: German Immigrants, Labor Conflict, and the Coming of the Civil War* (Urbana and Chicago: University of Illinois Press, 1992).

3. Levine, *The Spirit of 1848*, 15–34.

4. Hans W. Gatzke, *Germany and the United States: A "Special Relationship"?* (Cambridge: Harvard University Press, 1980), p. 31.

5. Secretary of the Interior, *Statistics of the United States in 1860* (Washington, DC: Government Printing Office, 1866), pp. lvii-lviii; cited in Levine, *The Spirit of 1848*, 59.

6. Louis C. Elson, *The History of American Music* (New York and London: Macmillan, 1904), p. 71.

7. Detailed information on the course of study pursued by Arens may be found in the *Jahresbericht der Königliche Musikschule in München*, vols. 8 and 9 (Munich: Wolf, 1882, 1883) and Rheinberger's manuscript *Inspektionsbücher*, housed in the Josef Rheinberger-Archiv, Vaduz, Liechtenstein.

8. *Achter Bericht des Königlichen Conservatorium für Musik* (Dresden: Georg Tamme, 1884), p. 50. "Herr Franz Arens aus Detroit [*sic*] (Nord-Amerika), eingetreten am 1. September 1883, aus der Compositionsclasse des artistischen Directors und der Orgelclasse des Herrn Organist Janssen, wegen seines Fleisses und seiner raschen Fortschritte und tüchtigen Leistungen in der Composition, seiner guten Leistungen als Orgelspieler und als Dirigent und seiner trefflichen Gesammthaltung."

9. James Huneker, "M.T.N.A.," *The Etude* 5/8 (August 1887): 106.

10. By 1895 there were 112 conservatories and music schools of all sorts in Berlin (Heinrich Ehrlich, "Das Musikerproletariat und die Konservatorien," in *Modernes Musikleben* [Berlin: Allgemeiner Verein für deutsche Literatur, 1895], p. 83). Since British and American students were strongly represented in these schools, English-speaking teachers were in great demand. Other prominent Americans who taught in Berlin were Otis Bardwell Boise (1888–1901) and Edgar Stillman Kelley (1902–1910). Arens' success as a teacher was confirmed by testimonial letters from Hey and from Wilhelm Blanck, director of the Schwantzer Conservatory, reprinted in "F. X. Arens Will Settle in America," *AAJ* 59/13 (July 9, 1892): 331.

11. Paul von Schönthan, "Musikleben in Berlin," *Neue Musik-Zeitung* 12/4 (1891): 41–42; Adolf Glaser, "Populäre Konzerte in Berlin," *Neue Musik-Zeitung* 12/7 (1891): 75.

12. O. B. Boise, "The American Composers' Concert in Berlin," *AAJ* 57/3 (May 2, 1891): 37. Further indications of trouble within this orchestra surfaced just a few weeks later when the musicians' union censured Meyder for unfair labor practices. See H. Vogelgesang, "Zum Vertrag K. Meyder, Kapellmeister im Konzerthaus zu Berlin," *Deutsche Musikzeitung* 22/17 (April 25, 1891): 189–90.

13. Boise, "American Composers' Concert," 37.

14. *Dresdner Nachrichten* 101 (April 11, 1891): 3. "Die Trenkler'sche *Gewerbehauskapelle* veranstaltet heute einen *Amerikanischen Komponisten-Abend*. . . . Sowohl in Fachkreisen, wie in den hier wohnenden zahlreichen englischen und amerikanischen Familien dürfte man dem Concert mit Interesse entgegensehen, schon aus dem Grunde, um dem Einflusse folgen zu können, den die von allen Amerikanern hochgehaltene deutsche Musik auf die amerikanischen Komponisten auszuüben gewußt hat."

15. F. X. Arens, "The American Composer in Germany. Berlin, April 15, 1891," *MC* 22/17 (April 29, 1891): 412.

16. F. X. Arens, "The American Composer Abroad. Berlin, April 26, 1891," *MC* 22/19 (May 13, 1891): 489.

17. Breitkopf and Härtel were apparently not prepared to "acquiesce," for Arens did not play the piano concertos in any of the season's concerts. The *Suite für grosses Orchester*, op. 42, published by Arthur P. Schmidt in 1891, was the only MacDowell work featured on the 1892 concerts.

18. Letter, F. X. Arens to E. A. MacDowell, August 12, 1891, MacDowell Collection, Music Division, Library of Congress. There is a virtually identical letter to Frederic Grant Gleason preserved in the Gleason Collection, Newberry Library, Chi-

cago. Gleason was much more responsive than MacDowell, as Arens benefited from a number of contributions from Gleason and other Chicago friends, as well as a sizable article lauding his efforts: "Helping American Composers," *Chicago Evening Post*, September 25, 1891.

19. "A Letter from E. A. M'Dowell," *MC* 25/6 (August 10, 1892): 6. MacDowell's antipathy to all-American concerts has been thoroughly documented in Margery Morgan Lowens, "The New York Years of Edward MacDowell" (Ph.D. dissertation, University of Michigan, 1971; UMI 71-23,812), pp. 102–6, and is the subject of Chapter 9.

20. After returning to the United States, Arens took a position in Indianapolis, where he programmed MacDowell's *Suite* for the 1893 May Festival. He wrote to MacDowell to ask "for the kind loan of the score, as I want to brush up my memory somewhat in regard to some details" (undated letter beginning, "My dear MacDowell. . ." MacDowell Collection, Music Division, Library of Congress). A subsequent letter accompanying the returned score proves that MacDowell acceded to this request. The implication is that he had also used a borrowed copy for the European concerts rather than purchasing his own.

21. Lists of contributors to date with amounts donated may be found in the following issues of *MC*: 23/25 (December 16, 1891): 705; 24/3 (January 20, 1892): 5; 24/8 (February 24, 1892): 5.

22. Schönthan, "Musikleben in Berlin," 41. "Man muß in Berlin konzertiert haben, des Renommées wegen und der Kritiken zuliebe, durch die sich 'die Provinz' bestechen läßt; hier will jeder angehende Virtuose die Feuertaufe empfangen, hier befindet sich der Konzertagenten und 'Manager' und der kritische Areopag."

23. F. X. Arens, "Music and Musicians in Dresden," *MC* 24/19 (May 11, 1892): 12.

24. *AAJ* 59/9 (July 16, 1892): 353.

25. "The Boston 'Musical Herald' and Mr. Arens," *MC* 25/5 (August 3, 1892): 7.

26. "Vermischtes," *Neue Zeitschrift für Musik* 88/2 (January 13, 1892): 20–21.

27. *Neue Zeitschrift für Musik* 88/9 (March 2, 1892): 105.

28. Felix v. Wartenegg, "Die Wiener internationale Ausstellung für Musik und Theaterwesen," *Neue Zeitschrift für Musik* 88/21 (May 25, 1892): 239.

29. For this concert, an "ausführliches Programm-Buch . . . nach englischer Sitte" (V10) (detailed program book after the English custom) was prepared, with biographies of the composers and extensive comments on the works played, complete with musical examples. I am grateful to Dr. Richard Hoffman for locating a copy of this program as well as the less extensive program of the Leipzig concert among the Arthur Foote scrapbooks in the Boston Public Library.

30. "The Boston 'Musical Herald' and Mr. Arens," 7.

31. *BMH* 13/2 (December 1891): 17.

32. This information on his early years was provided to Philo Adams Otis by Wilson's widow in 1917: Philo Adams Otis, *The Chicago Symphony Orchestra: Its Organization, Growth, and Development, 1891–1924* (Chicago: Clayton F. Summy, 1924), p. 73.

33. The final volume included detailed coverage of the World's Columbian Exposition of 1893. The entire run of this yearbook is available on microfilm from Chadwyck-Healey.

34. For further information on Wilson's program notes, see M. A. DeWolfe Howe, *The Boston Symphony Orchestra: An Historical Sketch* (Boston and New York: Houghton Mifflin, 1914), pp. 138–39.

35. William J. Weichlein, *A Check-list of American Music Periodicals, 1850–1900* (Detroit: Information Coordinators, 1970), p. 79.

36. W.S.B. Mathews, associate editor, *A Hundred Years of Music in America: An Account of Musical Effort in America* (Chicago, 1889; reprint New York: AMS Press, 1970), p. 382.

37. *BMH* 13/9 (July 1892): 147.

38. *AAJ* 59/13 (July 9, 1892): 331.

39. M., "Musical Journalism and Journalists," *Music* 2/3 (July 1892): 240.

40. *MC* 25/3 (July 20, 1892): 16.

41. Undated letter, F. X. Arens to E. A. MacDowell, MacDowell Collection, Library of Congress, Music Division, 2v.

42. "Mr. Arens' Work," *MC* 25/4 (July 27, 1892): 5.

43. Ibid., 5.

44. "F. X. Arens Returns to American Shores," *AAJ* 59/16 (July 30, 1892): 393.

45. *BMH* 13/10 (August 1892): 156–57.

46. "Musical conditions in the United States are peculiarly unfavorable to the young American conductor; no matter how great his abilities may be, it is for the time being utterly impossible for a young man from the West to gradually rise to the position of conductor of the Boston Symphony Orchestra or of the New York Philharmonic Society, since Europeans only are intrusted with those positions. Unless, however, the unanimous verdict of the European press be one huge preconcerted lie . . . he evidently seems possessed of quite extraordinary gifts as orchestral leader" ("The Boston 'Musical Herald' and Mr. Arens," 6).

47. Ibid., 6.

48. "Foreign Tributes to F. X. Arens," *AAJ* 59/17 (August 6, 1892): 412.

49. "F. X. Arens," *MC* 25/6 (August 10, 1892): 7–8.

50. "A Letter from E. A. M'Dowell," 6.

51. "A Chronicle," *BMH* 13/11 (September 1892): 169–70.

52. Anthony Smith, *The Newspaper: An International History* (London: Thames and Hudson, 1979), p. 119.

53. Ibid., 118.

54. Ernst Victor Zenker, "Die Wiener Presse," in *Wiener Almanach: Jahrbuch für Literatur, Kunst und öffentliches Leben 1893*, ed. Heinrich Bohrmann and Jacques Jaeger (Vienna: Moser, 1893), p. 325.

55. Imogen Fellinger, "Periodicals," *The New Grove Dictionary of Music and Musicians*, ed. Stanley Sadie (London and New York: Macmillan, 1980), 14: 471–75.

56. Max Graf, *Composer and Critic: Two Hundred Years of Musical Criticism* (New York: Norton, 1946), p. 270.

57. The reviewer for the *Wiener Sonn- und Montags-Zeitung* wrote, "Accordingly, the applause of the not-so-large audience never went beyond the bounds of politeness" (V13). Other reviewers, however, described a large crowd (V3, V18) and enthusiastic applause (V1, V2, V3, V4, V5, V7, V10, V16, V18). In this case the weight of numbers suggests that the latter assessment of the concert was more accurate.

58. Undated letter, Arens to MacDowell, p. 1v. In the same letter, Arens related an anecdote about Weingartner: "It is he, on whose acct. Bülow resigned his post with the Philharmonic saying: 'Ich bin ja doch nur der Biergärtner.' Great, isn't it!"

59. "Fachgemäß, d. h. je nach dem Verlaufe des Werkes ruhig und decent, oder auch feurig und anregend" (L9).

60. Letter, E. A. MacDowell to Frederick Grant Gleason, April 10, 1891, Gleason Collection, Newberry Library, Chicago.

61. "A Letter from E. A. M'Dowell," 6.

62. Gatzke, *Germany and the United States*, 32.

63. In citing this passage to support his negative view of the concert, Stolzing neglects to point out that Lenau's American visit was a low point in the life of an unusually depressed and disturbed poet.

64. "Die Kompositionen ließen erkennen, daß die Mac Kinley-Bill nicht auch auf den Import fremdländischer Geistesprodukte sich erstrekt. Eine Menge deutschen Stoffes ist in den Arbeiten enthalten, der ebenso durch den Ernst der Gedanken, geläuterte Empfindung, und Gediegenheit der Technik, als in dem speziellen Zuschritt nach Mendelssohn, Schumann, und Wagner sich Verräth" (B13).

65. Barbara Zuck, "Americanism as a Concept in Music History," in *A History of Musical Americanism* (Ann Arbor, MI: UMI Research Press, 1980), p. 8. Victor Fell Yellin suggests the terms "musical Americanism" and "musical americanisms" in place of Zuck's "conceptual" and "compositional" Americanism (book review, *American Music* 1/1 [Spring 1983]: 70–76).

66. This brings us back to the definition of "American." The issue was widely discussed during this period because of the enormous number of immigrants, and it was not lost on the European commentators either: "Now of course it is not stated to what extent the gentlemen Chadwick, DeKoven, Nevin, Paine, MacDowell, Smith, Arens, and Boise are only Americans by birth, or whether they live on the other side of the ocean or received their training there, or how after all they justify their claim as particularly American composers. In the music one hears nothing characteristic whatsoever, and so the undertaking appears to be purely a formality, with no significance" (B12).

67. "Die Kunst kennt keine beschränkte locale Kirchturmspolitik: ihr Wirkungskreis ist weltbürgerlich. Im Reiche der Tonkunst lautet die Parole: 'Wohlklang,' gleichviel von welcher Nation er stammt und tönt. Im Lande des *roling* [sic] *dollar* und der *smartest businessman* macht sich ein wahres, echtes Kunststreben geltend" (L7).

68. Richard Aldrich, "John Knowles Paine," in *Dictionary of American Biography*, ed. Dumas Malone (New York: Scribner, 1934), 14: 151–53.

69. [John Sullivan Dwight], "Mr. J. K. Paine's New Symphony," *Dwight's Journal of Music* 40/1016 (March 27, 1880): 54.

70. John C. Schmidt, *The Life and Works of John Knowles Paine* (Ann Arbor, MI: UMI Research Press, 1980), p. 130.

71. The recordings are by the New York Philharmonic, Zubin Mehta conducting (New World 350-2) and the Royal Philharmonic Orchestra, Karl Kroeger conducting an abridged version (Musical Heritage Society MIA-103).

72. Schmidt, *Life and Works of John Knowles Paine*, 347.

73. Steven Ledbetter, liner notes to the New World recording cited in note 71, p. 5.

74. Schmidt, *Life and Works of John Knowles Paine*, 347–48.

75. Dwight, "Mr. J. K. Paine's New Symphony." 53.

76. Schmidt, *Life and Works of John Knowles Paine*, 136.

77. "In einzelnen seiner Tonmalereien begegnet uns manches treu und wahr Beobachtete und auch wärmer Nachempfundene; die Freude an solidem Musiciren verleitet ihn zu beängstigenden Breitspurigkeiten, die bei dem Mangel irgend welcher erfinderischen Ursprünglichkeit doppelt fühlbar werden" (L1). Vogel (1847–1898), a critic and piano teacher in Leipzig, was himself a composer of symphonic poems and other works, as well as a prolific writer, particularly on musicians associated with the New German School.

78. Victor Fell Yellin, *Chadwick: Yankee Composer* (Washington, D.C., and London: Smithsonian Institution Press, 1990), p. 155.

79. The phrase "ein ernst gemeintes Werk" might be considered a compliment in the context of Max Graf's comments earlier about the significance of "seriousness" in German music. On the other hand, the phrase is suspiciously close to a German proverb: "Das Gegenteil von 'gut' ist 'gut gemeint'" (The opposite of "good" is "well-intentioned").

80. The French composer's use of the Tristan chord is chronicled in Carolyn Abbate, "*Tristan* in the Composition of *Pelléas*," *Nineteenth-Century Music* 5 (1981): 117–41.

81. This interpretive method is explained and illustrated through analyses of five nineteenth-century orchestral works in Mark Evan Bonds, *After Beethoven: Imperatives of Originality in the Symphony* (Cambridge and London: Harvard University Press, 1996).

82. Undated letter, Arens to "My dear sir," MacDowell Collection, Library of Congress, Music Division.

83. "Bei ihm sagt die Empfindung: Dieser Mann weiss, was er will, will, was er weiss, und kann auch, was er will" (V14).

84. According to copyright records in the Library of Congress, the work was entered as No. 11,152Y on March 2, 1893.

85. Rupert Hughes, *American Composers*, revised edition (Boston: Page, 1914), p. 131.

86. "Die Bezeichnung *self-made man*, auf die die Amerikaner so stolz sind, läßt sich auf diese Komponisten nicht anwenden" (B14).

∞ 9 ∞

Edward A. MacDowell,
Reluctant Hero

True, we have not yet produced a Beethoven or a Wagner; but we can show as close an approximation to genius as can be found in Europe, and there is no reason to doubt the future of creative musical art in this country.

—Theodore Presser, 1886[1]

One of the principal aims of the American Composers' Concert movement was to create a hospitable environment for a great American composer of art music who would prove, in Wilson G. Smith's famous dictum, "capable of and anxious to do honor to his profession and native land."[2] What the leaders of the movement did not count on was that the most likely candidate for the title of "the American Wagner" would be violently opposed to the idea of all-American concerts and would do everything that he could not only to keep his own music from being performed in them but to discourage their proliferation. MacDowell's biographers have thoroughly chronicled his antipathy to all-American concerts, citing his numerous public statements on the subject from the 1890s and 1900s.[3] An examination of the composer's relation to the American Composers' Concert movement, though, shows that his ideas developed over time and that he did not always oppose such concerts. The hardening of his opposition mirrored both his growing fame and the loss of prestige of the movement.

Edward Alexander MacDowell was born in New York on December 18, 1860. Like many talented musicians of his era, he had the opportunity to study in Europe. Unlike the majority of his compatriots, though, he stayed for over a decade and did not return to the United States until after he was well on the way to a successful career as a composer and pianist in Germany. He first studied at the Paris Conservatory from 1876 to 1878 and then moved to Germany, citing his disenchantment with French taste. He studied piano and composition at the newly opened Hoch Conservatory in Frankfurt until 1880, continuing his composition lessons with Joachim Raff until the latter's death in the summer of 1882. For the next six years, MacDowell pursued opportunities for performance, composition, and teaching from his home base in Wiesbaden. Within a number of years he had succeeded in establishing a reputation as the best-known American composer in Germany. His scores were published by German publishing houses, and he was simultaneously gaining a reputation in the United States through performances by Teresa Carreño and others.

MacDowell was finally enticed to return to the United States by the Boston conductor B. J. Lang. The composer's wife, Marian, later recalled that during a visit to Wiesbaden in the summer of 1888,

[Lang] rubbed it in so hard and so vividly that it was MacDowell's duty to come back to his own country and not become an American foreigner of which there were too many. . . . Reluctantly we refused . . . although we were on the very edge of using up the little we had. Mr. Lang . . . was so insistent as to its being his duty that finally MacDowell yielded. He had had a great success in those early years in Germany; he was recognized immediately as a composer, had endless concert engagements for he was a fine pianist, and we could have struggled along there and really made a fairly good place for ourselves, but he was made by Mr. Lang to feel that he ought to go back home.[4]

The composer moved to Boston a few months later, in the fall of 1888, leaving behind his house and many of his possessions but hoping to maintain his European contacts. The process of finding students proved to be slow, but he immediately pursued performing opportunities as a pianist and promoted his compositions to American publishers and conductors. Within a few years, his reputation as America's most prominent composer of art music had been solidified.

Already in the mid-1880s, while MacDowell was still living in Europe, his works had appeared in American Composers' Concerts. Van der Stucken programmed the second and third movements of the Piano Concerto No. 1 on his Novelty Concert of March 31, 1885. At the first concert of his American festival of 1887, Van der Stucken played the symphonic poem *Hamlet*. Teresa Carreño also played his Piano Concerto No. 1 with the Thomas orchestra in the July 5, 1888, concert at the Chicago MTNA Convention. Ironically, MacDowell was known as a composer of large works at this point in his career, and the piano miniatures for which he was later remembered—and which would have added luster to the programs of Lavallée, Sherwood, and other pianists—had not yet been written.

As a performer, MacDowell willingly participated in American concerts during his early years in Boston. The first such opportunity was presented by Van der Stucken, who invited him to perform his Piano Concerto No. 2 on the program at the Paris Exposition of 1889. This concert gave MacDowell and his wife the opportunity to revisit Europe a year after their departure, which was surely an added incentive to participate. The French critics, as noted in Chapter 5, were not kind to MacDowell as composer or pianist. A year later, he again performed the concerto with the Thomas orchestra at the first American concert of the Detroit convention of the MTNA on July 2, 1890. During the same convention, two of his piano works and a song were performed on all-American concerts by other performers.

As Margery Lowens has pointed out, MacDowell's opposition to American Composers' Concerts seems to have hardened during the winter of 1890–1891. In light of the poor reviews that he received from the French critics in 1889, it is significant that his first recorded statement on the issue, in an April 10, 1891, letter to Frederic Grant Gleason, stresses the critical response to such concerts: "As it is now, whenever an exclusively American concert is given, the players, public and press seem to feel obliged to adopt an entirely different standard of criticism from the one accepted for miscellaneous concerts. Some people would run down an American concert before hearing the music—and others would praise it (also before hearing it)."[5] By the beginning of the 1891–1892 concert season, he had decided not to participate in such concerts, but he now faced a new dilemma—it was difficult to stop others from performing those of his works that were already in print. During the summer of 1891 he was notified that the Worcester Music Festival intended to program his recently published *Suite für grosses Orchester*, op. 42, on an American Composers' Concert on September 24. He objected strenuously but could not prevent the performance of his work, since the performance parts were available for purchase. In the end, he chose not to attend the performance, which was the premiere of this major work.[6]

At the same time that he was attempting to dissuade the Worcester group from performing his suite (August 1891), he received a request from F. X. Arens for help with his second season of European concerts. As detailed in Chapter 8, MacDowell's Suite was among the successes of that tour, and Arens felt that he had helped the composer's European reputation significantly through his performances. In the heat of the debate over the Arens tour, MacDowell seems to have regretted his association with the conductor and disavowed any support for his efforts in *The Musical Courier* letter cited previously.

Following these two negative experiences, MacDowell never again swerved in his opposition to American Composers' Concerts. He was therefore cast in the role of maverick, fighting a quixotic battle against the concerts that became a small, but persistent, part of the American musical scene even after the movement initiated by the MTNA was finished. Over the years he became increasingly strident in his public and private statements on such concerts, responding in anger whenever he discovered that his works were included in the program of an American concert.

An exchange of letters with Augustus A. Stanley of the University of Michigan in 1899 illustrates MacDowell's attitude. Stanley wrote to him on March 26, 1899, requesting a photograph for use in an upcoming program in which one of his works was scheduled to be played. In MacDowell's draft book he struggled over the wording of the following letter:

My dear sir,

I cannot send you the photograph you desire as I do not possess one—I regret to hear that an "American concert" is projected. My ~~views somewhat pronounced views on publicized repeatedly pi~~ views on the subject of their pernicious influence on American Art have been too often published to need re-iteration however, and I will not trouble you with them. By the withdrawal of my $2^{\underline{0}}$ suite from the programme though, you would be enabled to give at least a couple of works by some struggling young American to whom such a chance ~~would~~ might mean encouragement and material help. If there is any possible good in giving "American concerts" it may lie there. I regret having to so decidedly disagree with you, but at least you will admit I am frank.

> Believe me yours sincerely,
> Edward MacDowell
> (not "Alexander" MacD.)[7]

That the composer was torn between principle and his desire to maintain professional collegiality (not to mention a desire to have his works performed) is reflected by the much warmer tone of another letter written shortly after:

My dear Professor Stanley—

I was delighted to receive your letter. Certainly I shall be glad to have you give anything of mine. You know that once a thing is published the comp. has pract. no control over it. Therefore I wish to thank you specially for having so kindly offered to accede to my personal wishes in the matter. I thoroughly appreciate the courtesy and only fear that the bluntness of my letter may have offended you or made me seem petulant. This was certainly far from my thoughts. The concerts you are to give will, I am sure bear fruit and be of great help to our Art. It only needs a few sturdy examples to procure for American works a dignified position which can never be attained by means of Am. Concts.[8]

The first letter to Stanley noted that MacDowell's views were widely known, and indeed, his public statements on the subject were aired repeatedly throughout the 1890s. The most direct public statement of his views was contained in an 1899 letter to Mrs. Edward F. Uhl, president of the Federated Music Clubs, that was read at the organization's national meeting and circulated widely in the press. At the heart of his convictions was the principle of moderation—no concert should consist entirely of American works, but neither should concerts be given without at least one:

An "American" concert is, in my eyes, an abomination, for the simple reason that it is unfair to the American. Such a concert offers no standard of judgment, owing to our want of familiarity with the works presented. Then, if our work is preferred to another, it only does harm to the weaker work, without helping the stronger one to any fixed value. Added to this, an American concert is a direct bid for leniency on the part of the public, which, I need hardly say, is immediately recognized by it. American music must and will take its position in the world of art by comparison with the only standard we know—that of the work of the world's great masters, and not by that of other works equally unknown to the world. In other words, we crave comparison with the best in art, not only the best in America. If our musical societies would agree never to give concerts composed exclusively of American works, but, on the other hand, would make it a rule never to give a concert without at least one American composition on the programme, I am sure that the result would justify my position in the matter.[9]

This statement was printed and commented upon in the same issues of *Musical America* and *The Musical Courier* that announced MacDowell's election as president of the Manuscript Society of New York, a group that had dedicated itself to American Composers' Concerts since 1889. The choice of a president who opposed their fundamental aims was a desperate attempt to gain prestige for their now-foundering society. His subsequent attempts to reshape the organization over the objections of a majority of its members would prove to be his most potent blow to the American Composers' Concert movement.

NOTES

1. "M.T.N.A." *The Etude* 4/7 (July 1886): 158.

2. Wilson G. Smith, "American Compositions in the Class and Concert Room," *The Etude* 6/8 (August 1888): 129.

3. See especially Margery Morgan Lowens, "The New York Years of Edward MacDowell" (Ph.D. dissertation, University of Michigan, 1971; UMI 71–23,812), pp. 102ff; and Alan H. Levy, *Edward MacDowell: An American Master* (Lanham, MD, and London: Scarecrow, 1998), pp. 108ff.

4. Typescript, Marian MacDowell, Notebook No. I, pp. 62–63, Library of Congress, Music Division; as quoted in Lowens, "The New York Years," 41–42.

5. Letter, E. A. MacDowell to Frederic Grant Gleason, April 10, 1891, Newberry Library, Special Collections.

6. The MacDowell suite received fairly good reviews, and fellow composer George Whitefield Chadwick wrote in glowing terms of the premiere (Undated letter, G. W. Chadwick to E. A. MacDowell, Library of Congress, Music Division, MacDowell Collection, Box 30, Folder 24).

7. Draft book of letters, Library of Congress, Music Division, MacDowell Collection, Box 33.

8. Draft book of letters, Box 33, MacDowell Collection, Library of Congress, Music Division.

9. "MacDowell on 'American' Concerts," *Musical America* 2/20 (May 20, 1899): 5.

❧ **10** ❧

The World's Columbian Exposition of 1893: American Art Music Humiliated

> All Americans who are sincerely concerned for the progress of music in our young land must regret that, in a musical way, more was not done at the Columbian Exposition; that the grandest opportunity this century has yet afforded for evidencing to the world America's present musical status and promise was not fully availed of by the Columbian Exposition powers.
> —Charles Crozat Converse, 1893[1]

> The music at the Chicago Exposition was one of those disgraceful pieces of mismanagement for which America is unfortunately noted. . . . Such a rare opportunity lost through the shilly-shallying and incompetence of tenth-rate busybodies.
> —*The Musical Courier*, 1893[2]

The World's Columbian Exposition, held in Chicago from May to October 1893, has been called the last gasp of the Gilded Age. With its magnificent neoclassic architecture, the famous White City transformed a swamp on the shores of Lake Michigan into a piece of the Old World that was strangely out of place in rough-and-tumble Chicago. Here 21.5 million visitors—second only to the number of visitors to the Paris Exposition of 1889—came to see the splendors of civilization and the progress of nineteenth-century technology.

By rights, this event should have been the crowning glory of the American Composers' Concert movement. Progress was the central theme of the exposition, and the proponents of American music felt that their movement had clearly illustrated American progress in composition. The exposition, they believed, should show the world what American composers were doing and how far they had come toward equaling their European counterparts. The committee for planning concerts was given a large appropriation that should have yielded impressive results, but the outcome could not have been more disappointing. Poor planning, mismanagement, and artistic differences doomed the concerts of art music from the beginning, and the musical section of the exposition proved to be an embarrassment to all concerned. The high hopes of the MTNA and others that the Chicago World's Fair would be the culmination of the movement were sorely disappointed.

Poor planning characterized the event from the beginning. Both New York and Chicago had lobbied for the right to host an exposition commemorating the 400th anniversary of Columbus' arrival in the New World, but by the time Congress finally made a decision on where to hold the exposition, it was too late to make the necessary preparations by 1892. As a result, the dedication ceremonies took place on October 21, 1892, with the official opening of the fair postponed until the following May. Even so, the exposition grounds were not complete on opening day, and visitors during the early weeks of the exposition had to put up with the sights and sounds of ongoing construction work.

As noted in Chapter 7, there was widespread speculation about music at the fair, with no shortage of persons with suggestions. As early as the fall of 1889, before a site had been chosen, E. C. Stanton of the Metropolitan Opera made public his views on music for the fair, which included daily concerts and a supplementary season of opera presented by his company.[3] W. S. B. Mathews devoted an extensive article to suggestions for the exposition in the first issue of his journal *Music* in November 1891.[4] S. G. Pratt, whose grandiose tendencies were heightened by the significance of the occasion, made his vociferous suggestions regarding American music at the July 1890 MTNA convention. In May 1891 he brought out another scheme, this time for a grand choral festival. The plan called for a chorus of 5,000–10,000 voices from all the states of the Union to learn their parts under the guidance of a national director who would bring them all together for the final performances in Chicago during the fair. Pratt's article in *The North American Review* included the following endorsement:

I fully indorse the above plan, and think it might be productive of great good to the cause of music in our country. That a large proportion of the scheme is practical I feel certain; and that excellent results and impressive performances could be obtained with such a mass-chorus properly drilled I am convinced, *provided suitable music is selected.* The appropriateness of inaugurating this work for the Columbian celebration is undoubted, if for no other reason than the general interest which it would awaken in polyphonic music over the whole country; and I hope that the endeavor will be made.

Yours truly,

THEODORE THOMAS[5]

Unknown to most of the musical world, the famous conductor had already been offered the position of director of music at the World's Columbian Exposition and was thinking it over when this article appeared. With Thomas now resident in Chicago, the executive committee of the exposition believed him to be the best choice to plan and direct the music for the fair. He was offered the position in March 1891 and finally accepted on November 18. This unusually long time to make up his mind may have been the result of his experiences as music director for the 1876 Centennial Exhibition in Philadelphia. For the auspicious opening ceremony of that event, he had convinced the directors to commission works from Paine and Buck, the two leading American composers of the time, as well as his musical hero Wagner. The German composer complied with the infamous *Centennial March*, a work whose quality was inversely proportional to the exorbitant fee paid for it.[6] Paine and Buck wrote works that were overshadowed by the attention surrounding Wagner's contribution. The annoyance of the commissions was minor compared with Thomas' losses later in the exhibition, however. The Thomas Orchestra was engaged to perform concerts at an estate several miles from the exhibition grounds. Both the conductor and the concert manager overestimated the interest in these concerts, especially after French composer Jacques Offenbach began a competing series of light concerts in Philadelphia. As a result, Thomas lost large sums of money and saw his library of musical scores impounded by the sheriff and sold at auction. He was urged to declare bankruptcy, but he refused to comply and eventually succeeded in paying off all his debts. This experience should have soured him on exhibitions, but biographer Ezra Schabas notes that although Thomas could not forget the disaster of the Centennial Celebration, his "enthusiasm for all things Chicagoan clouded his judgment."[7] With eighteen months until the opening of the exposition, Thomas had a daunting task that would require all of his skills and the help of some able assistants.

The assistants whom Thomas chose turned out to be anything but able, and in assigning blame for the resulting fiasco, it is difficult to decide how much was due to Thomas' intractability and how much was due to the incompetence of his associates. The conductor chose William L. Tomlins, conductor of the Chicago Apollo Club and known for his work with children's choruses, as his principal assistant. The executive secretary was George H. Wilson, who took the brunt of the criticism for the problems surrounding the music at the exposition. He resigned his Boston positions while still maintaining control of the *Boston Musical Yearbook* and the *Boston Musical Herald* after relocating to Chicago. Thomas, Tomlins, and Wilson were known collectively as the "Bureau of Music," but Thomas was clearly the driving force of this committee. When the first of many scandals involving the bureau was made public in November 1892, *The Musical Courier* went so far as to accuse Thomas of selecting weak men who would not have the knowledge or intelligence to question his actions.[8] The conductor stuck by his chosen committee, and they remained in place for the duration of the exposition.

The late start and even later appropriations meant that the committee had to work quickly to plan the musical program. The exposition was extremely generous, budgeting nearly half a million dollars for performance spaces and musicians' salaries. There were three auditoriums for the musical events: Festival Hall seated 4,500 with space for 2,000 more in the chorus section, Music Hall seated 2,000, and the Recital Hall had seats for 600.[9] Thomas employed his own Chicago Symphony Orchestra, augmented by additional players to 114 members. This group was hired for the entire duration of the fair at the expense of $175,000. What the musical public really wanted to know, however, was what would be performed.

The first official announcement came in March 1892, when the bureau announced the program of the dedication ceremony and gave a preliminary report on the buildings to be constructed.[10] As would often be the case over the next year and a half, the announcement was inaccurate, stating that John Knowles Paine and Edward MacDowell had been commissioned to provide musical works for the October dedication. Paine had, in fact, agreed to provide a work for this event, but MacDowell had turned down the commission that Thomas had offered him. Wilson announced MacDowell's participation prematurely, resulting in embarrassment for the composer and the Bureau of Music.[11] In the end, George Whitefield Chadwick set Harriet Monroe's forgettable "Dedicatory Ode" to music, but not without additional problems from Thomas' subordinates, as we shall soon see.

With the public increasingly impatient for information about the upcoming concerts, Wilson traveled to Europe in March 1892 to invite representative European musicians to participate in the exposition. Thomas wished to make the event truly international, and he hoped that his invitation via Wilson would convince the best of Europe's musicians to attend the fair. Wilson turned out to be a poor emissary, as one musician after another turned down his request. Brahms, Joachim, Rubinstein, Verdi, and others refused to make the long voyage, some more graciously than others.[12] Marc Blumenberg of *The Musical Courier*—admittedly a biased commentator—stated that "Wilson could not speak their language and therefore could not bring his arguments to bear, and besides those who did understand English perhaps did not want to understand Mr. Wilson."[13] The only results of his trip were a probable commitment from Camille Saint-Saëns and a definite commitment from A. C. Mackenzie. Of the latter composer, Blumenberg indignantly stated, "The only musician who has definitely promised to come is Dr. A. C. Mackenzie, of London, a first-class English composer, which means a third-class composer, as England never had any in the first class. He comes in the interest of an English music publishing house with a branch house in New York with whom Secretary Wilson is on the best of footing owing to business transactions."[14] In the end, neither of these musicians actually came to the fair, and the only prominent European composer to do so was Antonín Dvořák, who was living in New York at the time.

Not until after Wilson returned from Europe, on June 30, 1892, did the bureau release a prospectus announcing the musical plans for the exposition. This document detailed the goals of the bureau, gave a general outline of the types of concerts to be given, and solicited the participation of amateur musical societies from around the country. Appended to this announcement was a brief invitation to composers to submit manuscripts for consideration.[15] An announcement of September 28 updated the information given previously with more details on the concerts, including lists of amateur societies that had been invited and works that were in rehearsal. The impressive document mentioned plans for 300 concerts with orchestra along with "several festivals by a chorus of 2,500."[16] The grandiose scale of the concerts was stunning but left some musicians wondering why the schedule had been announced so late.

Even as the plans began to take shape, the problems of coordinating such an unprecedented series of concerts became obvious as Wilson repeatedly bungled small, but important, details. One example involved Chadwick's *Columbian*

Ode. The work was commissioned for the opening ceremonies on October 21, 1892, and published well in advance by Church and Company. When rehearsals began, Tomlins, as choral director, made unauthorized copies of the chorus parts because he did not wish to purchase the more expensive piano/vocal score published by Church. Chadwick wrote an angry letter to Thomas on September 2, blaming the problem on Wilson's "stupidity" and questioning his ability to fill such an important position. He expressed concern over losing his commission fee—which he sarcastically referred to as a "Trinkgeld" (tip)—to the expenses in dispute. He begged Thomas to intervene in resolving the dispute between the World's Fair Commission and his publisher.[17] A letter of September 10 thanked the conductor for brokering a compromise with the publisher. The dispute over the chorus parts only added insult to injury for Chadwick. He and Paine were given $500 apiece for their music, only to find out later that Monroe, a Chicago socialite and amateur poet, had been given $1,000 for her poem.[18]

The dedication ceremony itself was a farce, owing to the fact that 100,000 people crowded into the manufacturer's hall to witness the event. According to Richard Harding Davis in *Harper's Weekly*, this building was the largest in the world, with room enough to enclose all the buildings of the Paris Exposition under its roof. In this setting, without the aid of amplification, the music of Paine and Chadwick was largely irrelevant:

The exercises were conducted in pantomime, and a chorus of several thousand, led by Theodore Thomas, at a distance of a quarter of a mile, broke in on the pantomime at irregular intervals. These interruptions were not serious, as it was only possible at times to know that there was music by watching the leader's baton. Whenever the orator said anything of peculiar interest, the few hundred people immediately about him applauded, and the rest of the audience took this up and cheered and waved handkerchiefs, although they knew as little of what had been said as they did of what was going on at that moment in New York city. The crowd was not as impressive as the crowd in New York city during the late military parade, but the remarkable thing about it was its order. The crowd in New York lined the streets and cross streets, and hung to roofs and balconies, but the crowd in Chicago was either decorously seated or stood in even rows, without shoving or rowdyism of any sort, or occasioning the least accident. Sometimes a thousand or so rose up to see the better, and those behind threw programmes at them and shouted at them to sit down in rhythmic unison, at which the thousand would sink out of sight again, and another group would rise at another point, so that the great field of faces, as broad as Madison Square, was constantly punctured, like the rising and falling in the keyboard of a piano. When anything especially pleased them they would wave their handkerchiefs until the place looked as if snow were falling over it. A majority of the crowd were in the building from nine in the morning until four in the afternoon, and, with the exception of the choruses, had heard nothing of the exercises.[19]

With the dedication ceremony over, officials frantically rushed to complete preparations for the opening in May. Within a short time it became evident that Wilson's ineptitude was more than just carelessness but involved serious mismanagement. The charges involved a conflict of interest in Wilson's dual roles as secretary of the Bureau of Music and editor of an independent music journal. In the fall of 1892, only a few months after his acrimonious war of letters with

The Musical Courier over the Arens tour, Wilson moved his *Boston Musical Herald* to Chicago and renamed it *Musical Herald of the United States*. He had promised readers in the August issue of the former journal that he would maintain his objectivity as editor:

Music at the Exposition will be a principal subject of comment during the next fifteen months or more. The fact that the editor of the HERALD is officially connected with the Bureau of Music of the Exposition will not prevent the fullest discussion in this column of the subject, but it will be the Editor, *not* the Secretary, who speaks. We hope our critics will be fair upon this point. For the present the lips of the Secretary are sealed. The opinions on Exposition music to be expressed in this column will be those of the Editor only.[20]

This lofty goal was lost very quickly with the newly named journal. The November issue of *Musical Herald of the United States* contained illustrations of the music halls under construction at the exposition grounds, which had not been released to any other publication. *The Musical Courier* quickly pointed out that Wilson the editor had an unfair advantage over his competitors because of his connection with the Bureau of Music, adding, "If Mr. Wilson is devoid of the modesty which forbids the man of culture and decency from prostituting his official position for private gain he is unfit for the place assigned him."[21]

As rival journalists dug deeper over the coming weeks, it was discovered that Wilson had sold 7,000 copies of the issue with the illustrations to the exposition to be distributed by the department of publicity and promotion.[22] It was also revealed that he had used a rubber stamp of Tomlins' signature on a circular advertising his new journal, apparently without the consent of the choral director.[23] Blumenberg called for Wilson's resignation in the November 30 issue of *The Musical Courier* under headlines that screamed "Scandal! Grave Charges against Wilson." Though privately dismayed at the secretary's actions, neither Thomas nor Tomlins made a public statement, and the scandal blew over in time to be replaced by another one that involved Thomas directly.

The "Great Piano War," as it came to be known, was a classic example of the Gilded Age's ambivalence between commerce and high ideals.[24] The exposition was intended to display technological progress, but it also served as an unmatched advertising opportunity for American manufacturers. Piano companies were allotted large amounts of space to display their instruments in the Manufacturer's Building. Eastern manufacturers believed that the prime spots had been given to western companies, which led Chickering, Steinway, and sixteen other companies to withdraw from the exposition in early February 1893. Behind the withdrawal was another issue—the eastern firms did not wish to participate in the competition for awards, which they believed was rigged in favor of the western firms.

The exposition's director-general, George R. Davis, tried first to convince the eastern firms to return and then to convince the western firms to allow their eastern rivals to exhibit without competing, but neither side would compromise, even after Davis attempted to break the dissenters' ranks by offering advantages to some firms behind the others' backs. When no agreement was struck, the western firms managed to convince Davis to prohibit performers in exposition concerts from playing on any instrument that was not manufactured by one of the exhibitors.

The first two concerts of Thomas' impressive orchestral series featured Ignacy Paderewski, the famous Polish pianist. Paderewski always played a Steinway, which gave the western firms the opportunity to put Davis' edict to the test. Thomas supported the artist's right to play on the instrument of his choice, which brought down the ire of the Chicago press. Local papers accused the conductor of favoritism because of his long friendship with William Steinway. Davis appointed a special investigating committee, with which Thomas refused to cooperate. Daniel Burnham, designer of the exhibition grounds, had his workers move Paderewski's Steinway to Music Hall under cover of night, and it proved to be too late for Davis to prevent the pianist from playing on the instrument of his choice. The issue was revisited later in the season when Fannie Bloomfield-Zeisler also insisted on playing a Steinway.

During the following weeks, the dispute spread from pianos to the harps used by Thomas' orchestral musicians. Again the press was vicious in its attacks on Thomas, making accusations about Thomas' character and calling for his resignation. Though he weathered these attacks and a May 11 censure from the Federation of Musicians over his use of foreign musicians in the exhibition orchestra, Thomas was shaken by the experience. Schabas sums up the scandal thus:

Certain exposition officials sided with western piano makers and, aided by Chicago's infamous yellow press, viciously attacked Thomas's integrity and provided an open season for Thomas-haters from mid-April until August. Periodicals with long-standing grudges and professional musicians who, at one time or another, had suffered rebuffs or worse from the old warrior, fanned the flames that engulfed Thomas just as he was about to embark on what he had hoped would be one of his greatest achievements. The piano war shattered him like nothing else in his long career, damaged music at the fair, and was a sorry commentary on the ethics of the fair's officials and members of the piano-making industry.[25]

Poor planning, mismanagement, and the scandalous piano war had inhibited the development of the music program from its beginning, but as the fair got under way in May, the music world waited to see if Thomas' high ideals would be fulfilled. The first announcement of June 30, 1892, had articulated two broad goals: "First. To make a complete showing to the world of musical progress in this country in all grades and departments from the lowest to the highest. Second. To bring before the people of the United States a full illustration of music in its highest forms as exemplified by the most enlightened nations of the world." These two ambitious goals were intended to underlie all the concerts of the exposition, and the interpretation of their meaning according to Thomas' views would be what determined the success of the events.

The first goal, of providing a showcase for the musical progress of the United States, might have been interpreted by another leader as an opportunity for American composers. In Thomas' view, this was instead a showcase for American performers. He invited amateur and professional musical organizations from around the country to participate by giving concerts and recitals or by taking part in mass choral events. The list of invitees announced in the press release of September 30 included all of the country's major choral societies, as well as the Boston Symphony Orchestra and New York Philharmonic Society (later replaced by Walter Damrosch's New York Symphony when satisfactory dates could not be found for the Philharmonic). Recitals were also presented by an impressive array of American soloists and chamber groups. Thomas was true to his promise to showcase American musicians "in all grades and departments from the lowest to the highest." There were professionals and amateurs, children and adults, performing a gamut of music from "serious" to "light."

Official recognition of American composers was a different story. The only commissions awarded by the Bureau of Music were the two works by Paine and Chadwick for the dedication ceremonies. Instead, the announcement of June 30, after stressing the importance of participation by as many performers as possible, mentioned composers in a postscript appended after the signatures of the Bureau of Music:

The loyal attitude of the Exposition towards the native composer is shown in the following announcement sent by the Bureau of Music under date of June 30: The Musical Director desires to include in the programs of Exposition concerts representative choral, orchestral and chamber works by native American composers. All scores received by the Bureau of Music before October 15th, 1892, will be submitted to a committee, whose names are shortly to be announced. The favorable recommendation of this committee will be final and insure performance. Both printed and manuscript music may be sent.

This announcement was viewed by American composers as insulting, and the low number of submissions forced the bureau to reiterate its invitation in September and move the deadline to November 15. The *New York Sun* pointed out that all other sections of the exposition offered tangible prizes to exhibitors, but the most an American composer could hope for by submitting his work was to earn the committee's approval and obtain one performance for the piece.[26] Most of the principal composers refused to submit their work to the committee, and Thomas eventually invited Paine, Chadwick, MacDowell, Foote, Bristow, and Strong to name works of their choice to be performed.[27] The original call yielded only thirty-one submissions from twenty-one composers, of which eight were recommended for performance by the committee and three were actually performed. Among the seven composers of those eight works, there was not one composer of the first rank.[28]

The bureau's problems were the result of ignoring the wishes of American composers themselves. On February 22, 1892, a group calling itself "the Columbian Musical Association" had met in the rooms of the Manuscript Society of New York under the leadership of Reginald DeKoven and passed the following resolution:

Resolved, That the Committee on Liberal Arts of the World's Columbian Exposition be respectfully invited to consider the practicability and necessity of officially inviting American composers and musicians to cooperate in the ceremonies and work of the Exposition, and to offer them similar inducements to those which have been offered to workers in other art fields, to stimulate and encourage such cooperation.[29]

The bureau did not respond to this advice, offering no awards and only the two commissions mentioned earlier. Thomas invited scores of performers to participate in the exposition over a year in advance, but his invitations to composers went out only after the degrading submission process failed to yield a representative sample of the country's composers.

Meanwhile, plans for Thomas' second goal were progressing smoothly. When he stated that he would present "a full illustration of music in its highest forms," he had in mind a survey of Western art music that would have been unprecedented at that time had it been completed. With the recording industry still years away, the only way for nineteenth-century musiclovers to hear the music of past eras was through live performance. Thomas' goal was to educate fairgoers by performing all the great masterworks of European music in one six-month period. To fulfill this goal, he expanded his Chicago Symphony Orchestra to 114 players, with the possibility of augmentation to 150 for larger works. He obtained the cooperation of scores of choral societies to present works with choir. Recognizing the enormous expense of his plan and recognizing also that concerts of this quality would not appeal to all audiences, the Bureau of Music adopted admission fees for the concerts of art music while charging nothing for light concerts given by the orchestra and visiting bands. Admission to the symphony concerts was set at one dollar, a figure not out of line with prices at the nation's principal orchestral concerts but quite expensive for fairgoers who had already paid an admission fee at the exhibition gates.

The significance of Thomas' scheme was not lost on commentators. The literary journal *The Dial* drew attention to the scope of the series:

The World's Fair offers at least one exhibit (if such it may be styled) that, in its very nature, permits of no hurried enjoyment, but requires, for its full appreciation, a stay equal in length with the period of the Exposition itself. One may see all the pictures and all the machinery, all the material embodiments of science and the arts, if he choose or be forced to so hasty a procedure, within the space of a week or a month; but he cannot, fortunately, hear all the music without staying all the time. This one of the arts, happier than the others, can make its own conditions, and impose them upon its public; it may be enjoyed only upon its own terms, and demands the attention for which the sister arts can only plead. This point of view must be insisted upon if we are to realize the educational significance of the work planned by the Bureau of Music, or even, perhaps, if we are to justify the great expense at which this feature of the Fair has been provided.[30]

This series of concerts was planned to be the capstone of the career of a man who had devoted his life to educating American audiences in the appreciation of art music. For persons who shared his belief in music as a force for moral improvement, the symphony concerts represented the opportunity of a lifetime. For all others, the high admission price would keep them away. As the concert series began to unfold in May, it became clear not only that Thomas had overestimated the loyalty of his audience but that circumstances had conspired to make his job even more difficult.

Coinciding with the opening of the exposition were several prominent bank failures that touched off a serious financial downturn. The resulting depression would stretch on through the 1890s into one of the worst in U.S. history, but in the early months of the fair, the nation was still unsure of the extent of the damage. Attendance at the exposition was lower than expected, and the concerts with admission fees drew very small crowds. Fairgoers seemed to make their musical decisions on a financial basis, as crowds flocked to the free orchestral and band concerts but stayed away from the expensive symphony concerts. The gross receipts for the first thirty-two admission concerts amounted to $15,135— a tenth of the anticipated income.[31] Thomas' decision to charge for the symphony concerts was increasingly criticized, as even the conductor's staunchest defenders like W. S. B. Mathews admitted that the admission fees may have been a mistake.[32] In addition, the conductor's salary of $2,000 per month and the rental of his library of orchestral scores for $600 per month were widely criticized.

After months of abuse from the press, low attendance at his concerts, and demands for resignation from his superiors, Thomas finally resigned in early August, midway through the fair.[33] The resignation was not unexpected and was seen both as a cost-cutting measure for the fair and also as a repudiation of the conductor's autocratic control of the musical program. His harshest critics, including music journals like *The Musical Courier* and *American Art Journal*, reacted gleefully, while a few commentators expressed regret at his departure. In particular, Mathews chose to defend his record by comparing what he had attempted to do in music with what had been done in other sections of the exposition. He astutely pointed out that many of the other exhibits had been no less expensive but that their expenditures had been made up front, leaving nothing but maintenance costs during the fair. That made the ongoing expense of the orchestra and its conductor seem excessive by comparison.[34] He admired Thomas' devotion to art music and believed that the principal miscalculation by the exposition officials—against Thomas' will, according to Mathews—had been to charge a high admission price for the concerts of art music but make the concerts of popular music free.

The conductor who had made art music of the highest quality central to his planning took a parting shot in his resignation letter by suggesting that "since so large a portion of the bureau's musical scheme has been cut away . . . for the remainder of the Fair music shall not figure as an art at all, but be treated merely on the basis of an amusement."[35] The notion that his departure spelled the end of music as an art at the exposition was greeted with derision by some in the press, but there was a certain amount of truth to what he said. As had been the case at the Paris Exposition, the planners had forgotten that after viewing exhibits all day, weary visitors turn to music for entertainment, not edification. Music of every description, as at Paris, was ubiquitous on the grounds, and fairgoers did not need to pay to hear it or set aside several hours of their time to devote to it.[36] The most successful musical groups of the Chicago Fair were not the world-class recitalists or stellar orchestra but the bands that played at outdoor bandstands throughout the fairgrounds. By the same token, the most lasting contributions to American culture to come from the 1893 fair were not the symphony concerts or the neo-classical architecture but a new ride known as the Ferris wheel and an erotic dance nicknamed the hootchie-kootchie. Historians of popular music point to the eclectic mix of band music and other popular styles during the six-month fair as the probable origin of ragtime, a genre of music that would change American music and the debate over high and low culture in the decades ahead. Art music did not completely disappear from the exposition after Thomas' departure, but there was a noticeable shift toward lighter music in the remaining months of the fair.

Ironically, the attendance at the exposition jumped substantially in early August and remained strong until its closing in October. With the prospect of losing three months of steady employment, the orchestra reorganized under the leadership of concertmaster Max Bendix. The previously announced concert series was abandoned, and in its place was a series of less daunting programs, which nonetheless "will not present the spectacle of encouraging only that style of art that has as its chief result the propagation of the humble but highly nutritious popcorn."[37] The new orchestral series suited the public taste much better, and attendance improved for the duration of the fair.

In the swirl of scandal and the clash of artistic ideals, American art music was virtually forgotten. American Composers' Concerts seem to have been an afterthought, as the entire exposition featured only four by the exposition orchestra and five by other groups. To put this in perspective, there were eight concerts devoted exclusively to Russian music and five concerts featuring only the music of Wagner. This poor showing for U.S. composers was partly due to the cancellation of the second half of the orchestral series, but it was also clearly not a priority for Thomas.

The first of the American concerts took place on the afternoon of May 23 in the unfinished Music Hall. Both Thomas and concertmaster Bendix were ill—Mathews reported that Thomas came off his sickbed to conduct a Wagner festival the previous day but was not well enough to conduct the American concert[38]—forcing assistant conductor Arthur Mees to fill in at the last moment. The result was a ragged performance of three works by Chadwick, Foote, and MacDowell. According to W. Waugh Lauder, Mees butchered Chadwick's Second Symphony, and Foote did little better with his own serenade, with the MacDowell Suite as the only piece that succeeded. The reviewer was impressed, as had been the German critics during Arens' tour a year earlier, with the freshness and imagination of the work. He described it as "more suggestive of an American school of composition than anything I have ever heard. With a single drum tap, a few times repeated, this young American throws a composition at our phlegmatic heads that startles us out of our self-contented critical sleep to find suddenly that we have a real, live orchestral colorist right in our midst."[39] Fortunately for Chadwick and unfortunately for MacDowell, the hall was practically empty—if one reviewer's estimate of an audience of 100 was accurate, the effect in the extremely reverberent 2,000-seat auditorium must have been laughable.[40]

In terms of performance quality, the next American Composers' Concert was a complete contrast. Among the many guest artists to perform at the exposition was the famed Kneisel Quartet of Boston. They performed three concerts in Recital Hall in May, the last of which fell on May 24, the morning after the American concert by the exposition orchestra. The *Chicago Tribune* stated that Chicago audiences had never before heard quartet playing of such refinement, precision, and technical facility. The sense of proportion and musical understanding made their interpretation "exceptional in its artistic worth."[41] The program of the final concert consisted of three works by Boston composers: Arthur Whiting's Sonata for piano and strings in G, op. 17, Chadwick's quintet for piano and strings, and Foote's quartet for piano and strings in C major. Again, the beauties of this performance were wasted—the official report stated that the three concerts by the Kneisel Quartet brought in a total of eighty-three dollars.[42]

During the first full week of July, the fair hosted "musical congresses," in which various organizations held meetings consisting primarily of scholarly papers. According to Mathews, the division of the week was as follows: American College of Music, one day; Music Teachers' National Association, two days; Illinois Music Teachers' Association, two days; and the Woman's Musical Congress, three days. He faulted the program committee for failing to attract any major names to the presentations and bemoaned the dry and unproductive sessions, stating that, "a vast amount of talk was had, and magnificent advertising, which will have an effect upon the public; but of real productive influence upon the progress of the department there was comparatively little."[43] Among the topics discussed was Native American music; the exposition was later remembered as a watershed event in the recognition and scholarly study of this repertoire.

In conjunction with the musical congresses, the exposition orchestra performed two American Composers' Concerts, on July 6 and 7, designed to attract the members of the MTNA and other interested parties who would be in attendance during the week. This was intelligent programming, particularly since the admission fee was fifty cents rather than the usual one dollar. The concerts drew well compared to previous offerings, as the *Chicago Tribune* reported that during the first concert, "the music hall was quite full below and moderately populous in the gallery."[44] The repertoire of the two concerts was curiously arranged, though, as Thomas put pieces by Van der Stucken, Chadwick, Foote, Paine, and MacDowell on the first program, leaving Adolph M. Foerster, Harry Rowe Shelley, Henry Schoenefeld, Ethelbert Nevin, Helen Hood, Frederic Grant Gleason, and Arthur Bird for the second day. Reviewers could not fail to notice that the conductor had used the "first string" on July 6 while sending in the benchwarmers on July 7.[45] The second string was also done a disservice when, as happened repeatedly during the fair, the concert was delayed an hour with no advance warning.

On August 4, after Thomas had written his letter of resignation but before it had been accepted or announced, he and his orchestra finally played a program featuring works that had been submitted in response to the call for scores issued on June 30, 1892. The program consisted of the overture *Witichis*, op. 10, by Margaret Ruthven Lang, the *Suite Creole* by John A. Broekhoven, the Mendelssohn Violin Concerto played by American soloist Maud Powell, and a *Concert Overture* by Hermann Wetzler. The program was noteworthy for the introduction of a major orchestral work by a promising female composer, but it was a disappointing reminder that America's most prominent composers had ignored the Bureau of Music's submission process. The reviewer for *American Art Journal* stated that it was the largest crowd that he had seen yet in Music Hall and praised Powell's playing of the Mendelssohn. He credited Lang's work with "originality and earnestness of purpose" as well as "considerable continuity and sustained power." He went on to state that the orchestration showed lack of experience but pointed out that even Brahms had similar problems with some of his orchestrations. This review was unusual in that the critic treated an orchestral composition by a woman seriously, without any comments reflecting gender bias.[46]

The same reviewer had harsh words for Broekhoven's suite, which had been performed previously at the 1886 MTNA convention in Boston. The work used African American themes in a manner that would become widely accepted under the influence of Dvořák just a few years later but was still difficult for some listeners to accept:

The so-called "Suite Creole" by Mr. Broeckhoven [sic], of Cincinnati, should have no place upon the program of a serious concert. The themes are trite and too frequently repeated, and the orchestration is bizarre. The suite seemed to me to represent negro jollification rather than Creole character. The grotesque humor and suppressed pathos of slave life are sufficiently characteristic to form the burden of songs and symphonies; but I for one do not like to be dragged into the midst of a semi-heathenish barbecue and pelted with melon rinds.[47]

The following week it was made public that Thomas had resigned. Mathews stated that the resignation of Thomas and the cancellation of the concerts of art music "cut off the greater and finer part of the plans of the musical director, the American composer especially coming in for the lion's share of the misfortune, for nearly all the greater American works had been slated for performance during the last two months of the Fair, when it was hoped that the attendance would reach its maximum."[48] But Thomas had not been overly conscientious about programming American compositions to date, and not all critics shared Mathews' disappointment. *American Art Journal* actually took the opposite view, stating that "American composers will no longer be submitted to the outrage of hearing their music butchered while the members of Mr. Thomas' very expensive orchestra laugh and make merry over the indignity."[49] No matter which view one took, Thomas' withdrawal from the exposition meant that there would be no more American orchestral concerts. It did not mean, however, that there would be no more interesting concerts of American music.

On August 14 and 15 the Old Stoughton Musical Society gave two performances in Music Hall. This group, founded in Stoughton, Massachusetts, in 1786, performed early American vocal music in eighteenth-century costumes. The program featured music by William Billings, Daniel Read, and other members of the "First New England School" as well as a few selections from the early nineteenth century.[50] This concert was an anomaly during the era of American Composers' Concerts, when the latest works by living composers formed the bulk of the repertoire. This historical performance was a refreshing change, but as with all performances purporting to have historical authenticity, it was subjected to a different type of criticism: "The singing of the society is plain, direct and effective, and though they aim at the 'good old style,' I have a belief that these ladies and gentlemen would have been regarded with a good deal of suspicion had they lived in the time of William Billings and sung as excellently as they did yesterday."[51]

A very different concert of American music was heard on August 25, which was designated "Colored Americans' Day" at the fair. It was pointed out by contemporary critics and later historians that in keeping with the fair's agenda of progress, persons of color were treated as inferior to the more highly developed European peoples. Though there was a Dahomean village on the grounds that portrayed the life of "savages" in Africa, there was no exhibit showing the accomplishments of African Americans since the Civil War. Frederick Douglass and Ida B. Wells were two contemporaries who decried the fair's portrayal of African Americans, writing a pamphlet titled *The Reason Why the Colored American Is Not in the World's Columbian Exposition.*[52] Wells chose to boycott Colored Americans' Day, while Douglass agreed to give a speech in the afternoon. True to their fears, vendors were on hand with 2,500 watermelons, and hecklers attempted to disrupt Douglass' speech. Under the duress of the moment, the aged orator set aside his prepared text and gave a fiery one-hour speech decrying white America's treatment of persons of color.[53] After the speech, there was a concert by African American performers. Though the concert took place in Festival Hall, it was one of the many performances not officially sponsored by the Bureau of Music. It featured excerpts from the opera *Uncle Tom's Cabin* by Will Marion Cook, a performance by violinist Joseph Douglass (grandson of Frederick), plantation songs sung by the Jubilee Singers, and a reading entitled "Colored Americans" by Paul Lawrence Dunbar. Other performers included Sissieretta Jones, known as "the black Patti," and Harry T. Burleigh.

After the demise of the exposition orchestra, the organ and chamber music concerts represented the most significant remnant of the Bureau of Music's program of art music, with the long parade of prominent American organists remaining an impressive feature of the exposition after Thomas' departure. Many of these organists included one or two American works on their programs, but two of the organists focused their recitals on American composers. On October 9 Frank Taft played a program consisting of three works by Dudley Buck and three works by himself as well as French composer Alexandre Guilmant's Fantaisie on "Home, Sweet Home." The only program expressly announced as an American Composers' Concert was Harrison Wild's on September 20. The concert inspired one of the most humorous commentaries on music at the fair, as Emil Liebling turned the light of sarcasm on the ineptitude of the Bureau of Music. He reported in an article for *The Musical Courier*, later reprinted in *Music*, that the bureau invited artists to perform without giving them a time of day until the very last moment. He said that the Festival Hall was situated so that "the engineers of the intramural trains which pass every minute perform a solo on the whistle whenever they pass the hall, and thus lend an unexpected variety of effect, in which I am pained to say the organ does not always come out on top." After the concert, Liebling reported that the guards shouted immediately to the audience, "Out, out—get out, quick!" Some idea of the treatment of artists at the fair may be gained from the following:

As to the management of Mr. Wild's recital by the Bureau of Music, it left nothing to be desired, although it introduced several features of decided novelty in its treatment of the artist. It is not often that the performer enjoys the privilege of paying for the attendance at his own concert, but Mr. Wild not only paid his admission to the Fair on that day, but also had to patronize the public washrooms, as the dressing rooms at Festival Hall had with rare foresight been kept securely locked. The claim that other organists had all the tickets furnished them which they desired I reject as a base insinuation and a reflection on the Bureau, which I know would not be guilty of invidious favoritism. Well, Mr. Wild can console himself with the thought that his recital was worth every cent he paid.[54]

In a final touch of irony, S. G. Pratt, who had been so active in proposing plans for American concerts at the fair, finally got his chance to participate when he presented a concert of works by Chicago composers on October 28, two days before the closing of the exposition.

Ten days before the conclusion of the fair, Wilson hastily released a statement defending the Bureau of Music's programming of American music.[55] In it he detailed the selection process for American works and listed the American music that had been performed. This bit of spin control was obviously designed to counter the negative impression that the bureau had left regarding American composers. American music had been an afterthought at every stage of the exposition, and Wilson finally seems to have realized this when he presented his apologia to the press.

The statement was too little and too late to offset the feeling that the exposition had been a monumental wasted opportunity. In typical fashion, *The Musical Courier* decried the exposition in colorful terms: "The music at the Chicago Exposition was one of those disgraceful pieces of mismanagement for which America is unfortunately noted. . . . Such a rare opportunity lost through the shilly-shallying and incompetence of tenth-rate busybodies. As it stands now the music section of the great Columbian Exposition of 1893 will ever be a byword of reproach and something to flout and jeer."[56] A more thoughtful observer, Charles Crozat Converse (1832–1918), lamented the fact that the planners of the Chicago fair had not learned from the mistakes of the Centennial Celebration of 1876. A veteran of the American Composers' Concert movement and one of the country's longest-lived composers, Converse summed up the shortcomings of the Bureau of Music succinctly:

All Americans who are sincerely concerned for the progress of music in our young land must regret that, in a musical way, more was not done at the Columbian Exposition; that the grandest opportunity this century has yet afforded for evidencing to the world America's present musical status and promise was not fully availed of by the Columbian Exposition powers—those having in their hands the programming of the Exposition details, in this and other regards. These powers seemed to lack, in the execution of their grand trust, the courage of their convictions as to its importance and prospective success, as well as that of the supremely significant, momentous occasion with the fitting celebration of which they had been intrusted by the American nation.[57]

In fairness to Theodore Thomas and his associates, the failure of American art music at the World's Columbian Exposition was not entirely their fault. The poor planning, mismanagement, and refusal to compromise their ideas were responsible for many of the problems. Less than a decade earlier, though, the MTNA had managed to mount phenomenally successful American Composers'

Concerts despite a quantity of naive bumbling and purposeful mismanagement. By 1893 the movement for American concerts had run its course, and even the best planning in the world would not have attracted audiences to hear more of the same. The movement was essentially over, but numerically, there were still many concerts to be performed. The last gasp of the movement would have the longest life, as composers themselves formed organizations to present their music and had a strong interest in keeping them going despite public apathy. Thus it was that the movement stretched on into the twentieth century, despite the humiliation of the World's Columbian Exposition.

NOTES

1. Ch. Crozat Converse, "After the Exposition," *AAJ* 62/4 (November 11, 1893): 73.

2. "1893," *MC* 27/26 (December 27, 1893): 9.

3. "American Music at the Fair," *The Musical Visitor* 18/11 (November 1889): 287.

4. W.S.B.M., "Music in the Columbian Fair," *Music* 1/1 (November 1891): 39–53; 1/2 (December 1891): 165–73.

5. S. G. Pratt, "A National Chorus," *The North American Review* 152/414 (May 1891): 635–37; reprinted in "Mr. Pratt's World's Fair Scheme," *Chicago Tribune*, May 10, 1891, p. 36.

6. For details of Wagner's scurrilous business dealings in this case, see Ezra Schabas, *Theodore Thomas: America's Conductor and Builder of Orchestras, 1835–1905* (Urbana and Chicago: University of Illinois Press, 1989), pp. 71–73, and Abram Loft, "Richard Wagner, Theodore Thomas, and the American Centennial," *Musical Quarterly* 37/2 (April 1951): 184–202.

7. Schabas, *Theodore Thomas*, 197.

8. "Scandal! Grave Charges against Wilson. His Resignation Should Be Demanded by the Exposition Authorities," *MC* 25/21 (November 30, 1892): 14.

9. "Music at the World's Fair," *The Dial* 14/167 (June 1, 1893): 329–30.

10. *The Musical Messenger* 2/3 (March 1892): 17.

11. Margery Morgan Lowens, "The New York Years of Edward MacDowell" (Ph.D. dissertation, University of Michigan, 1971; UMI 71–23,812), p. 58. See also *MC* 24/10 (March 9, 1892): 5.

12. Schabas, *Theodore Thomas*, 198.

13. "Scandal!," 14.

14. Ibid.

15. This prospectus was printed, among other places, in "World's Columbian Exposition," *BMH* 13/9 (July 1892): 151–52; "Music at the World's Columbian Exposition," *The Musical Messenger* 2/8 (August 1892): 17–18; "World's Fair Music," *The Musical Visitor* 21/8 (August 1892): 207.

16. "Music at the Columbian Exposition," *MC* 25/14 (October 8, 1892): 8–9.

17. Letter, George Whitefield Chadwick to Theodore Thomas, September 2, 1892, Newberry Library, Special Collections.

18. For further information on the music commissioned for the dedication ceremony, see Ann McKinley, "Music for the Dedication Ceremonies of the World's Columbian Exposition in Chicago, 1892," *American Music* 3/1 (Spring 1985): 42–51.

19. Richard Harding Davis, "The Dedication Exercises," *Harper's Weekly* 36/1871 (October 29, 1892): 1038. The first page of this issue (1033) has an illustration of the event from the vantage point of the back of the building.

20. "World's Columbian Exposition," *BMH* 13/10 (August 1892): 161.

21. "A Fair Question," *MC* 25/19 (November 16, 1892): 5.

22. "Scandal!," 13.

23. "Wilson's Exposition," *MC* 25/22 (December 7, 1892): 5.

24. For more complete discussions of this scandal, see Paul Hume and Ruth Hume, "The Great Chicago Piano War," *American Heritage* 21 (1970): 16–21; and Schabas, *Theodore Thomas*, 202–7, which form the basis for the following brief summary.

25. Schabas, *Theodore Thomas*, 202–3.

26. Reprinted in *MC* 25/21 (November 30, 1892): 5–6.

27. Schabas, *Theodore Thomas*, 199.

28. George H. Wilson, "Announcement regarding American Music at the Exposition," *Music* 5/1 (November 1893): 106–7.

29. *The Musical Visitor* 21/4 (April 1892): 100.

30. "Music at the World's Fair," *The Dial*, 329.

31. Schabas, *Theodore Thomas*, 208.

32. W.S.B.M., "Music at the Fair," *Music* 4/3 (July 1893): 311.

33. The entire resignation letter was reprinted in W.S.B.M., "End of Art Music at the Fair," *Music* 4/5 (September 1893): 531–32. See also "Mr. Thomas Resigns," *AAJ* 61/18 (August 12, 1893): 413.

34. W.S.B.M., "End of Art Music," 535.

35. Ibid., 532.

36. "Music at the Fair," *Harper's Weekly* 37/1911 (August 5, 1893): 741–42. This article's description of the musical cacophony in the Midway is reminiscent of Gabriel Baume's description of the Paris Exposition of 1889 as a "musical orgy."

37. "Rare Music in Sight: Return of Exposition Orchestra under Max Bendix," *Chicago Tribune*, August 27, 1893, p. 29.

38. W.S.B.M., "Music at the Fair," *Music* 4/2 (June 1893): 226.

39. W. Waugh Lauder, "Music at the World's Fair: Fourth Columbian Letter, May 27, 1893," *MC* 26/22 (May 31, 1893): 17; Mathews concurred with his praise for MacDowell as an orchestral colorist.

40. Unidentified clipping titled "American Music Failed to Draw—After the Clamor for It Only a Hundred Heard the Thomas Orchestra Play it," Boston Public Library, Allen A. Brown collection, cited in Bill F. Faucett, *George Whitefield Chadwick: His Symphonic Works*, Composers of North America Series, No. 19 (Lanham, MD and London: Scarecrow, 1996), p. 59.

41. "Wealth of Harmony: Music Lovers Enjoy a Week of Pleasure at the World's Fair," *Chicago Sunday Tribune*, May 28, 1893, p. 26.

42. Cited in Schabas, *Theodore Thomas*, 207.

43. W.S.B.M., "The Musical Congresses," *Music* 4/6 (October 1893): 638.

44. "Concert of American Composers," *Chicago Tribune*, July 7, 1893, p. 8.

45. See, for instance, "Concert of Native Compositions: Works Mild in Spirit Presented to the Musical Congress," *Chicago Tribune*, July 8, 1893, p. 3.

46. "Program of American Compositions," *AAJ* 61/18 (August 12, 1893): 413.

47. Ibid.

48. W.S.B.M., "End of Art Music," 532.

49. "Mr. Thomas Resigns," *AAJ* 61/18 (August 12, 1893): 413. This opinion was also expressed by F. X. Arens, who wrote after the first American concert, "I hear of the 'Fearful and Wonderful American Concert' recently conducted by Arthur Mees at Jackson Park Chicago. If fills me with indignation when I read that during the performance of Chadwick's Symphony the members of the orchestra chatted and giggled and altogether had a sweet time of it. When will such shameful occurences be an impossibility in this country. Surely not as long as such men as Thomas frame the

programs of this country." (Undated letter, F. X. Arens to E. A. MacDowell, MacDowell Collection, Library of Congress, Music Division, 2r)

50. For a thorough account of this group's performance, see "Report of President Sanford Waters Billings of the Concerts Given by the Old Stoughton Musical Society and Musical Society in Stoughton at the World's Fair, Chicago, August 14 and 15, 1893," in *The Old Stoughton Musical Society: An Historical and Informative Record of the Oldest Choral Society in America*, ed. Lemuel Standish, (Stoughton, MA: Old Stoughton Musical Society, 1928), pp. 71–87.

51. "Columbian Exposition Music," *AAJ* 61/19 (August 19, 1893): 437.

52. Douglass' introduction to this pamphlet is reprinted in *Frederic Douglass: Selected Speeches and Writings*, ed. Philip S. Foner (Chicago: Lawrence Hill, 1999), pp. 740–46.

53. William S. McFeeley, *Frederick Douglass* (New York and London: Norton, 1991), pp. 367–71.   See also John E. Findling, *Chicago's Great World's Fairs* (Manchester and New York: Manchester University Press, 1994), pp. 27–28.

54. Emil Liebling, "Some Reflections on Harrison M. Wild's Organ Recital at the World's Fair," *MC* 27/13 (September 27, 1893):   10;   reprinted in *Music* 5/3 (January 1894):   259–64.

55. George H. Wilson, "American Music at the Exposition," *AAJ* 62/3 (November 4, 1893):   53;   Wilson, "Announcement Regarding American Music at the Exposition," *Music* 5/1 (November 1893):   106–7.

56. "1893," *MC* 27/26 (December 27, 1893):   9.

57. Converse, "After the Exposition," 73.

❧ 11 ❧

Manuscript Societies and the Ghettoization of New Music

Any such society is bound to give abundant prey for complaint. Musicians are apt to be babies; wantonly sensitive, wantonly jealous, and wantonly undignified. There are few pettinesses that such a body will be above. A combined effort to sink personal quarrels and work shoulder to shoulder for a great national end will always find the line broken by certain pouting boobies; boobies with gray hair, boobies of great personal ability, and yet despicable, little-souled boobies, whose one hunger in this world is the world's attention to their particular voicings of their particular moods.

—Rupert Hughes, 1896[1]

A tsunami characteristically arrives in several waves of varying heights. In the 1960 tsunami originating in Chile, the first wave of only three feet reached Hilo shortly after midnight. A second wave measured nine feet, while the third wave was a towering wall of water with a maximum height of thirty-five feet. So, too, was the American Composers' Concert movement, which enjoyed an initial surge of popularity culminating in the 1887–1888 concert season, followed by a lull in 1889 and 1890, a second wave of concerts in the early 1890s, and a third wave in the late 1890s. The last two waves, which produced the most concerts, came after the movement had lost its novelty with the public.

The American Composers' Concert movement was instigated and carried on by conductors and educational organizations that wished to support and promote American composers. This altruistic impetus lasted throughout the 1880s, but as the MTNA discovered in the early 1890s, the public and the promoting organizations had limited patience for the movement. In order to be self-sustaining, the movement took a different direction after 1890, as the most important promoters of all-American concerts became the composers themselves. Societies for the performance of manuscript compositions sprang up in Boston, New York, Philadelphia, and Chicago. With the strong motivation of self-preservation and a ready supply of new works, these organizations carried the movement well into the twentieth century. The direct involvement of composers had benefits for all concerned, but it created an unforeseen set of problems that would come to a head in the Manuscript Society of New York at the turn of the century.

The first of these societies had the shortest life span and left the least documentation. The Manuscript Club of Boston was founded by Isabella Stewart Gardner specifically to promote the music of local composers. The concerts were held in her home and do not seem to have been reviewed by the press. In addition to prominent Boston composers like Foote, MacDowell, and Horatio Parker, the programs featured works by Clara Kathleen Rogers and Margaret Ruthven Lang. The Lang scrapbooks in the Boston Public Library contain programs for performances on January 19, 1888, and February 28, 1889; a third was reported to have taken place on March 26, 1889.[2]

Also in 1889 a small group of musicians hatched the idea for a similar society in New York. This group eventually grew to include many well-known composers and reached national prominence in the 1890s through its public performances of new compositions. The story of this organization forms an important final chapter to the American Composers' Concert movement.

The sources of information on the Manuscript Society of New York have come to light in stages, causing a handicap for the authors of previous studies of the group. The first important retrospective of the organization was part of a 1932 article by Sumner Salter (1856–1944). This composer, organist, and teacher was active in the organization throughout the 1890s and drew on his personal recollections and the numerous newspaper and journal articles published at the time. He stated that "in some unaccountable manner all of its official records and accumulations, including the library of autograph manuscript compositions contributed by members, have disappeared," forcing him "to obtain from various sources regarded as authentic the material of this account of the society's history and doings."[3] Margery Morgan Lowens included a detailed history of MacDowell's role in the organization's history in her 1971 dissertation, using MacDowell's letters and a volume of programs of private meetings and miscellaneous publications housed in the New York Public Library (NYPL) as primary source material.[4] Since that time, additional materials have been added to the collection at NYPL, including complete programs of the public performances, two volumes of minutes covering the years 1896–1912, treasurer's reports from the years 1904–1918, membership rolls from 1902 to 1918, and a book of letters and financial records from 1903 to 1918. The work of Lowens and Salter provides the foundation for this chapter, but the additional materials make it possible to fill some of the unavoidable gaps in their discussions.

The society had its origin in a social occasion, when Addison F. Andrews (1857–1924), a musical jack-of-all-trades who was active in journalism, arts management, and other aspects of New York musical life, hosted an informal gathering of friends in his apartment on August 27, 1889. The music performed was primarily composed by those present, which suggested the idea of a manuscript society that would re-create the congenial experience on a regular basis.[5] A formal organizational meeting was held in October 1889 at the home of Laura Sedgwick Collins, and a Constitution and By-Laws were adopted in January 1890. The group held monthly meetings from October 1889 through May 1890 with the principal goal of performing each other's compositions in friendly surroundings. All but two of the meetings were held at the studio of Gerrit Smith, who had been elected president. Salter recalled that by the end of this preliminary season,

The membership had steadily increased and included most of the leading composers of New York. Credit for the rapid and substantial growth of the organization was largely due to the indefatigable efforts of the President, Gerrit Smith, whose genial personality, executive ability, high aims and generous provision of a domicile for the society were prime factors in establishing it on a secure foundation.[6]

The compositions featured in the programs of the first season's monthly meetings were limited by the setting to chamber music, both instrumental and vocal. Encouraged by their successes, the composers decided to augment the next season's monthly private meetings with three public concerts on December 10, 1890, February 4, 1891, and April 15, 1891. The first and third of these were with orchestra. The enormous expense of such concerts was defrayed, in part, by the gift of free use of Chickering Hall.[7]

The inaugural concert on December 10, 1890, was greeted with interest by the musical press. Extensive reviews in the *Times* (Henderson), *Tribune* (Krehbiel), *Herald*, *American Art Journal*, and *The Musical Courier* hailed the concert as an auspicious event. Krehbiel pointed out that the organization was not only a corrective to long-standing neglect of American composers but also "the flowering and fruit" of the efforts of the MTNA and Van der Stucken.[8] Henderson noted the significance of bypassing the intermediary of the conductor: "To present a work in manuscript to a conductor and have him say that it has not sufficient merit to warrant its production is by no means satisfactory to the composer. But if he can get it performed and the public and the critics decide against it, that ought to end the matter. On the other hand, if the public decides in favor of the work, the composer can smile and be happy."[9] Henderson, an amateur composer himself, was a member of the society and took advantage of the opportunity to present an unpretentious *Valse Lente* on the third concert of the first season, on April 15, 1891. Given his remarks about the first concert, he must have been gratified by James G. Huneker's admonition to "Give us some more, Master Henderson!"[10]

This first concert consisted of nine unpublished works, all by members of the society. In addition to familiar names like Chadwick, Foote, Pratt, Van der Stucken, and Horatio Parker were lesser-known composers: I. V. Flagler, Homer N. Bartlett, E. C. Phelps, and Harry Rowe Shelley. The printed program, as would be the case for all but two of the future concerts of the organization, featured a manuscript incipit of each piece, written and signed in the composer's distinctive handwriting. Each composer conducted his own work, which detracted from the effectiveness of the performances. *The Musical Courier* pointed out the similarity to the MTNA's problems with composers who could not conduct, noting that when Van der Stucken took the baton to lead the final number of the Manuscript Society program, Chadwick's overture *The Miller's Daughter*, "the orchestra awoke to the fact that they must play, and play they did accordingly."[11]

The novel feature of presenting an evening of untried works was an idea that was recognized as innovative but flawed. The *American Art Journal* was more direct than most in pointing this out:

While the American movement is a needful and worthy one that has met with every possible encouragement at our hands, it cannot be said that the musical results of the concert under review were as gratifying as could have been expected. Whether the programme committee were not permitted to be as rigid as they should have been in excluding mediocre works, whether the authors have not sent in their best efforts, or whether internal jealousies or dissension have been at work it is hard to tell, but we are safe in saying that nearly every name represented upon the programme has written compositions far superior to those given upon this occasion, or they would never have won the reputation some of them now enjoy.[12]

This reviewer turned out to be prophetic in identifying the problems that would eventually sabotage the organization. The stipulation that works for performance be limited to unpublished compositions by members of the society was fine for private gatherings when the members enjoyed food, fellowship, and friendly interchange; presenting these same works to the New York public put the enterprise in an entirely different light. The final program of the first public season contained information about the organization, including a statement of purpose that would be used throughout the organization's history: "Its object, as in the past will be to advance the interests of American Musical Composition, and to promote social intercourse and friendly feeling among its members."[13] This "object" actually consisted of two objectives that would in time become contradictory. Like the MTNA before it, the Manuscript Society of New York would discover that promoting American music with the highest standard of excellence is not always compatible with social intercourse and friendly feeling.

The success of the first season of public concerts (1890–1891) inspired the group to take bold steps to advance its aims.[14] The society was renamed the Manuscript Club, with club rooms to be rented for the following year to promote informal interchange between the members. This innovation turned out to be an expensive one, as neither the club rooms nor the new name was retained beyond the following season. Dues were assessed on a sliding scale dependent on the level of participation:

Composers	$5.00/year resident,	10.00 nonresident
Professional musicians	10.00 resident,	15.00 nonresident
Amateurs	15.00 resident,	25.00 nonresident

There was no initiation fee for composers, but resident professional musicians were charged an initiation fee of ten dollars, and amateurs were charged twenty dollars, while non-resident amateurs paid an initiation fee of ten dollars.[15] When one considers the MTNA's annual dues of two dollars, these fees seem exorbitant, and indeed there would be pressure in future years to reduce them. At the same time, the composers in the group took steps to make admission standards stiffer, requiring the submission of a sample of polyphonic writing as part of the application process. Salter recalled that this engendered a lengthy discussion on the extent of contrapuntal skill to be required for admission, with the membership finally agreeing to accept a short sample of counterpoint rather than an entire polyphonic composition.[16]

When the novelty of the first season was past, it became clear that the press would no longer ignore shoddy performances and mediocre compositions. The *New York Times* pointed out the principal flaws of the society's public concerts after the final concert of the 1890–1891 season. The author of this article, presumably Henderson, echoed Apthorp's sentiments in Boston by lamenting the intellectual energy required to listen to an entire evening of new works, particularly when the concert consisted of a long list of shorter works rather than a few longer ones. He summed up his feelings thus: "One of the chief delights of musical entertainments is the performance of that with which we are acquainted, thus affording us the pleasures of recognition and memory. At all novelty concerts this is denied us, and we must be in a state of mental alertness all the time. It is wearying, and it produces on the hearer the effect of having heard altogether too much."[17] The columnist went on to decry the practice of allowing each composer to conduct his own work, estimating that nine-tenths of those who conducted did not even know how to beat time. Disaster was averted in one piece in the last concert only by the fact that the orchestra wisely ignored the "remarkable gyrations of the conductor's baton."[18] The reviewer's recommendation was to hire a single conductor for all the pieces or at least use the services of one of the experienced conductors who already belonged to the society.

Other reviewers were equally blunt in the next several years. *The Musical Courier*, in particular, did not mince words, describing the December 9, 1891, program as "mediocre, dull, and uninteresting,"[19] the March 25, 1892, concert as "startlingly dull,"[20] and the works of the April 30, 1892, program as "impotent drivelings."[21] The *American Art Journal* attempted to put the best face on things by noting that "there were fewer weak points in this [March 25, 1892] program than in some of the preceding concerts," adding that "it is only too gratifying to note the progress that each of these concerts testifies to. The composers gain experience as they note the defects that a public performance of their work reveals and the music committees become more expert in judging and selecting the compositions that will best stand the test of being brought before a critical audience."[22] The same journal passed an indictment on the whole enterprise, though, by stating of the first concert of the third season that, "it is hardly necessary to add that our American composers are very poorly represented upon a program like the foregoing, and that the Manuscript Society should make an effort to procure the works of some of our first-class writers if it expects to succeed."[23] By the third season it was clear that the two recurring problems cited by reviewers throughout the early 1890s, inconsistent conducting and a paucity of really fine music, were serious impediments to the success of the public concerts.

The first of these problems was addressed in the fourth season (1893–1894), when the organization drew on the services of Walter Damrosch and his New York Symphony for the first and third public concerts and the Beethoven String Quartet for the second concert. The "Gotham Gossip" columnist for *The Musical Courier* noted that the season's first concert was the best that the organization had given, adding:

This was mainly due to the fine work of the New York Symphony Orchestra, under the direction of Walter Damrosch, who has been a member of the society for several years. Heretofore scrub orchestras have been employed, and each composer attempted to conduct his own work, whether he knew how to wield the baton or not. Under the new arrangement the ambitious works of talented young American composers were performed with a considerable degree of perfection.[24]

The arrangement with this orchestra would seem to have been ideal, but, for some reason, Damrosch did not conduct another concert after the 1893–1894 season. In the following season, Anton Seidl conducted, followed by Adolph Neuendorff in 1895–1896, Silas G. Pratt for a season, and Seidl again in 1897–1898. This revolving door of conductors, coupled with a limited number of rehearsals owing to budget difficulties, kept the orchestral concerts from ever attaining a high degree of perfection.

Meanwhile, the society continued to grow during the mid-1890s, attracting ever more composers and performers eager to participate in the monthly private meetings and the occasional public concerts. The membership rolls swelled to 674 by 1895, allowing the society again to rent club rooms for private meetings and the use of members.[25] The membership lists, published in the program of the last public concert of each season, included many of the country's best-known composers of art music, including Dudley Buck, George F. Bristow, Reginald De Koven, Victor Herbert, John Knowles Paine, John Philip Sousa, and several hundred others. Among the professional members were such luminaries as Anton Seidl, Theodore Thomas, Adelina Patti, and Lillian Nordica.[26] In addition to New York composers, the society counted numerous out-of-town musicians among its members, including Mrs. H.H.A. Beach of Boston, Frederick Grant Gleason of Chicago, and Edgar Stillman Kelley of San Francisco.

Though the Manuscript Society of New York was the most prominent organization of its type, the 1890s saw the establishment of several similar organizations that did not last long, as well as two sister organizations that each enjoyed a long history. In all cases they were designed to aid composers in securing performances of their works, and most of them were organized and run by composers themselves.

The American Composers' Choral Association (ACCA) was founded in New York in 1890 to perform the choral works of American composers. Conductor Emilio Agramonte was born in Cuba in 1844 and moved to New York in 1869. He was well established as a choral conductor by the 1880s, and like many of his contemporaries he performed occasional American concerts.[27] The ACCA was an effort to organize these concerts on a systematic basis. The initial concert was presented on November 24, 1890, followed by two subsequent concerts in that season and two the following season. The organization was unsuccessful financially, as *The Musical Courier* reported that the third concert of the first season brought in only six dollars at the box office and that Agramonte had to pay deficits of nearly $10,000 during the two seasons.[28]   In its third season, the ACCA merged with the Manuscript Society of New York.

The Manuscript Society of Philadelphia was founded in 1892 by William Wallace Gilchrist, continuing its activities until 1936.[29] Like the Manuscript Society of New York, this group held regular private meetings for members but only occasional public concerts. A distinctive feature of the group was the tradition of presenting an annual concert of sacred music in one of Philadelphia's churches in addition to a May concert in a concert hall.

Chicago was always supportive of its local composers, and the list of concerts in Appendix 1 shows numerous concerts devoted to Chicago composers in the early years of the movement. It was also home to two organizations for American concerts in the 1890s, both of which were organized under the leadership of Frederic Grant Gleason (1848–1903). This organist and composer, a native of Connecticut, studied there with Dudley Buck and later at the Leipzig Conservatory. He moved to Chicago in 1884, where he played a central role in that city's musical life until his death. He served as music critic for the *Chicago Tribune* from 1884 to 1889, which allowed him to expound his strong opinions on American music. An 1891 article in the *American Art Journal* outlined his optimistic views on the future of American music, which were decidedly cosmopolitan:

A great deal has been said concerning a new and distinctively American school of music—as though that was of the very highest importance—that we should be able to point out in the writing of our native musicians peculiarities which distinguish their work from that produced by natives of any other country. To my mind, this is a matter of little or no importance, at least at present. It may be said of an American school of composition that, like the Kingdom of Heaven, it "cometh not with observation."

It is not at all necessary that the American composer should consciously strive to write in a style which should be characterized as "American" in the sense of differing from the recognized peculiarities to be found in the works of writers belonging to other nationalities. It will be quite sufficient for the present if he possesses ideas, with the scholarship required to express them in accordance with the best standards of existing models—that is, with the technical knowledge required to place what he has to say in the best possible light before his hearers, regardless of whether the work possesses a distinctively national character or suggests what a well-schooled German or other composer might be presumed to do with the same thoughts. As there has not yet been developed an American school of composition, and there is no style of writing to which the name American can be properly applied by way of distinction, there are no standards to be offered other than those of good taste, and the question of the formation of an American school may safely, as it must be necessarily, left to the future.[30]

The American Music Society was founded in the fall of 1891, with Gleason as president. The group gave biweekly concerts for at least two full seasons, resulting in a long list of performances. Gleason's scrapbook in the Newberry Library of Chicago begins with ten blank pages numbered lightly in pencil and then has programs pasted in for the rest of the organization's history. The earliest extant program is for a concert on January 28, 1892, and the last is for a performance on June 28, 1893. Programs 13 through 34 were numbered by the printer. Of the twenty-four concerts for which programs are extant, four used a small orchestra, and the rest were for a variety of chamber combinations. Chicago composers figured prominently.

The Manuscript Society of Chicago was founded in 1896, also under the leadership of Gleason, and lasted until 1920. The organizational structure was taken directly from the Manuscript Society of New York, and these groups had numerous members in common, who occasionally exercised the option to present works to more than one group. Not as active as the New York and Philadelphia societies, the Chicago group went into hibernation on at least one occasion.[31] As we will see shortly, the Chicago and Philadelphia societies sought to establish a formal agreement for exchanging works in 1899, only to be stymied by the New York society.

Back in New York, the 1895–1896 season was the Manuscript Society of New York's most active in terms of public events. On August 27, 1895, the group presented a special day of performances by the Sousa band at Manhattan Beach. The band played two concerts of compositions by society members, consisting primarily of marches and lighter works for band. John Philip Sousa, who had recently joined the society, featured two of his own compositions, a symphonic poem and a suite, in these concerts. He would remain a member of the group for five years. On November 1 and 2 the society opened its rooms to the public for an exhibition of autograph musical manuscripts and letters. In addition to contributions from about 130 members were rare manuscripts of famous European composers on loan for this event.[32] Many of the members' compositions came from the society's permanent library, assembled by requiring each active member to donate a representative musical composition in manuscript. Salter alludes briefly to "the most unfortunate disappearance of this collection of autograph manuscripts" but does not state when or how the works vanished.[33] In addition to these two events, the society presented four public concerts rather than the customary three during the 1895–1896 season, a reflection of the large jump in membership the previous year. This season also saw the establishment of a new tradition of hosting receptions for visiting musicians—the first three to be so honored were Antoinette Sterling, Émile Sauret, and Theodore Thomas. In the following season, the society began publishing a *Bulletin* to publicize its activities.[34]

This flurry of activity masked a continuing dearth of top-quality material for performance at the public concerts. Despite a sizable membership that included many of America's prominent composers, the goal of assembling an entire evening of really interesting manuscript compositions remained elusive. Henderson put a negative stamp on the final concert of the year with his comments on the inadequacies of most of the society's members:

The most discouraging revelation of the Manuscript Society concerts is not the lack of invention on the part of composers, but their deficiency in the higher essentials of musicianship. The majority of them have not a firm grip on the formal materials of their art. They are woefully deficient in mastery of form. It may fairly be doubted whether most of them could construct an overture or the first movement of a symphony if the thematic ideas were provided for them. . . . Some of the American composers whose works are produced by the Manuscript Society do not understand the first principles of scoring, and when to that ignorance is added, as is too often the case, a want of familiarity with counterpoint, and sometimes with fundamental harmony, too, the results are depressing. It seems to me that our American composers have got to take their art a great deal more seriously and devote much more study to it than they have been doing if they expect to achieve anything. The success of men like Chadwick, MacDowell, Strong, and Parker is due quite as much to the certainty with which they handle their materials as to the intrinsic value of the materials themselves.[35]

Henderson may have been unduly harsh in his generalizations, but he touched a sore point, for Chadwick, Strong, and Parker were former members who were no longer part of the society at this time; MacDowell, a resident of Boston, had never been a member. Clearly, the organization was not attracting the first rank of American composers, despite its numerical growth.

From December 1896, it is possible to follow the progress of the organization through minutes of the directors' meetings and annual membership meetings. These records reveal an organization that struggled internally despite the facade of success accompanying the tremendous growth of the previous two seasons. Among the many administrative details covered in the minutes of the 1896–1897 seasons are two new names that would prove to be crucial to the development of the society. The minutes of December 4, 1896, include the sentence, "President Smith read an agreeable letter from Mr. MacDowell expressing cordial and friendly interest in the purposes of the Manuscript Society."[36] The minutes of May 27, 1897, list F. X. Arens as a new member in the "active" (composer) category. Both men had recently moved to New York, and it was characteristic of their personalities that Arens immediately became a dues-paying member, while MacDowell sent out a feeler without committing himself.

At the annual meeting of the society on May 10, 1897, the membership committee reported twenty-four new members, 147 resignations, and twenty-eight members who were dropped for nonpayment of dues, for a total membership of 490.[37] The alarming decline in membership led to the engagement of a canvasser in 1898, who earned 25 percent for each life membership and 15 percent for other memberships.[38] The following year saw the engagement of a debt collector who was to be paid a 20 percent commission on outstanding membership dues that he managed to collect. At the same time the group was forced to give up the services of one Mrs. Steinle, who had been serving as stenographer of the society.[39]

The rash of resignations led to an almost comical series of machinations to retain members, as reflected in the following excerpts from the minutes: "Dressler, seconded by Pratt, moved that W. J. Henderson be re-instated as member of the Society—without dues" (December 3, 1897). "Motion was duly made that Mr. Walter Damrosch be officially notified that his resignation cannot be accepted until his dues are paid" (May 6, 1898).[40] Evidently, it was considered more important to curry the favor of the music critic of the *New York Times* than the conductor of the New York Symphony.

The fundamental problem for the organization remained the lack of a major composer who could bring stature to the organization and raise the level of the repertoire at public concerts. To this end, the directors voted on January 7, 1898, to form a committee consisting of the president, the first vice president, and the chairman of the executive committee "to call upon Mr. Edward MacDowell, and ask if they may present his name for membership."[41] This committee was authorized to add additional members at its own discretion a month later and made a report to the directors—which for some unexplained reason was merely noted but not described in the minutes—at the meeting on March 3. Two months later, on May 6, 1898, the motion was made and carried "that the Nominating Committee be directed to offer Mr. MacDowell the nomination of Presidency of the Society upon an official ticket, with a Board of Directors selected by himself, in accordance with the constitution."[42]

The willingness of the directors to essentially turn the society over to MacDowell is curious, for although the Columbia University professor was America's most famous composer at the time, he had also been the most vocal opponent of American Composers' Concerts since the early 1890s. His views were so well publicized that it is hard to believe that no one on the Board of Directors knew about his opposition to exactly the sort of performances that they had been presenting since their inception. Either they were led by his cordial letter of 1896 to believe that he had changed his views, or else they were so desperate for strong leadership that they were willing to take a risk. Whatever their thinking, MacDowell must have turned them down unequivocally, for three days later, at the general membership meeting on May 9, the society elected Reginald De Koven as president with no mention of a MacDowell ticket. Within days of his election, on May 13, De Koven wrote to MacDowell urging him to join the society, and through his persistent efforts over the next year MacDowell was eventually convinced to join. As Lowens succinctly expressed it, "By 1899, he had succeeded in talking himself out of a job."[43]

While in the process of convincing MacDowell to join, De Koven used his year in office to institute a series of innovations designed to address the problem of inadequate repertoire. His proposals consisted of three relaxations of the formerly stringent rules on public concerts. First, he proposed allowing the repetition of works from past seasons, which would ease the pressure to find new works for every program. Second, he recommended the performance of works by honorary foreign members of the society. Third and most controversial was his proposal to solicit the works of "American composers of acknowledged merit and position" who were not members of the society.[44] Predictably, this suggestion resulted in protests from members who felt that their chances of public performance would be diminished by such a policy. The minutes report two separate petitions with a total of twenty-three signatures protesting this new policy.

Meanwhile, at their November 4 meeting, the Board of Directors discussed a letter from Arens offering his services as orchestral conductor of the society. His application was accompanied by glowing press reports from his European tour seven years earlier and by a number of suggestions on the society's policies. He favored the incorporation of more choral music on the programs and the establishment of a permanent chorus to support this endeavor. He also advocated increasing the number of orchestral rehearsals before a public concert to three, even if this required a corresponding reduction in the number of public concerts given each year. His proposal was discussed extensively, with Pratt the only strong opponent to Arens' ideas. The proposal was tabled, but in the ensuing week, Pratt resigned his position on the board as well as the music committee. On November 11 the board voted to accept Pratt's resignation from the board, to give Arens a chance to conduct the first concert in December, and to appoint Arens to the music committee and the Board of Directors.[45]

The first public concert of the season, on December 22, 1898, put into practice one of De Koven's solutions to the perennial repertoire problem, as all but one of the compositions on the program were works that had been performed in concerts of previous seasons. The program of works by Foote, Kelley, Gerrit Smith, Eduardo Marzo, Bruno Oscar Klein, Victor Harris, and C. B. Hawley was fairly well received, but one is tempted to ask if these were really the best compositions introduced in the organization's nine-year history. *The Musical Courier* was supportive of the composers and the conductor, noting, however, that inclement weather had limited the size of the audience.[46] J. Remington Fairlamb, chair of the Public Meeting Committee, elaborated further on the effect of the diminished attendance at this concert when he made his report at the annual meeting of the society on May 15, 1899:

Owing to various reasons, the attendance at first concert (one of the best the Soc'y has given) was rather limited. Mr. Arens, as Conductor received enthusiastic commendation. His work worthy of exceptional praise. After this first concert the funds of the Society did not permit another orchestral concert. It was decided therefore to give but one more concert and that to be a chamber music concert.[47]

Whether the depletion of funds was caused by the low attendance, by the extra orchestral rehearsals, or by more resignations of dues-paying members is difficult to ascertain, but it is clear that the society was in desperate straits financially. The second and final concert of the season on April 11, 1899, included five chamber works by members of the society and one composition by Giuseppe Martucci, an honorary member from Italy. (This was only the second time that an honorary member's work had been performed—the program on February 9, 1898, had included a work by C. Villiers Stanford of England.) The program of this concert listed Arens as "Director of Music," though there were no orchestral numbers performed.

With the society in imminent danger of extinction, the Board of Directors was amenable to radical change, and thus MacDowell finally joined the society. At the May 1 board meeting, the composer "made an extremely interesting address, in reference to the amendments, which will be presented for consideration at the Annual Meeting, on May 15th."[48] MacDowell was elected an active member of the society at this board meeting, though he was apparently still undecided as to the extent of his involvement. A week later, on May 8, a special board meeting was held, and the minutes record that he finally came down from the fence: "Various members of the Board exchanged views with Mr. MacDowell, who was present, regarding the future of the Society, and unanimously advocating his acceptance of first place on the ticket to be presented for election, at the Annual Meeting, on the 15th inst. Mr. MacDowell finally decided to accept the nomination."[49]

In a turbulent annual meeting on May 15, MacDowell was elected president and brought with him a host of changes. The constitution and bylaws were essentially rewritten to reflect the new president's goals for the society, and the name was changed to the Society of American Musicians and Composers over the protests of some of the longtime members.[50] MacDowell's plan, as explained in a prospectus released on September 30, 1899, was to broaden the work of the society in emulation of the Allgemeine Deutsche Musikverein of Germany and the Société des Compositeurs Français of France. The first organization must have been especially close to MacDowell's heart, as it was at a meeting of that society in Zurich in 1882 that the twenty-one-year-old American had received his first big break with the performance of his *Erste moderne Suite*, op. 10. In keeping with the liberal policies of that group, MacDowell proposed to broaden the repertoire of the New York society:

The Society of American Musicians and Composers has been organized to succeed the Manuscript Society of New York, and to continue its work of fostering the interest of American composers on a more liberal plan than was possible under the policy of the latter organization. . . . Any member of the Society may present works for production by the Society, which will receive due consideration by the Committee in charge. The widest liberality will also be used in the selection of works for production by the Society and musicians will be afforded an opportunity of hearing their compositions performed in other lands. It will not be an essential condition hereafter that a composition submitted for performance shall be in manuscript, and the Society will be at perfect liberty to present any composition which will add to the value of the programmes, or which it will profit American musicians to hear.[51]

Depending on one's views of the gravity of the issues at stake, the actions of MacDowell and the directors of the Manuscript Society may be characterized as either a Greek tragedy or a comedy of errors. Both parties knew that MacDowell was not right for the presidency of an organization whose fundamental aims he despised. He had repeatedly turned down the overtures of De Koven and others before reluctantly capitulating. Ultimately, though, it seems that the board was willing to allow MacDowell complete freedom in reshaping the society in exchange for the prestige that they felt sure he would bestow on their efforts. Significantly, both *Musical America* and *The Musical Courier* featured his name twice in the issue following his May 15 election: once in reference to the changes in the Manuscript Society and more prominently in articles discussing his recent statements to the president of the Federated Music Clubs regarding his aversion to all-American concerts.[52]

As the year progressed, it became evident that MacDowell was not as committed to the Society as its members had a right to expect. He was absent from three board meetings shortly after his election as president (May 22, June 12, and October 6), and when he was present, his highly individualistic ideas precluded the sort of collaborative efforts needed to bring the society back to prominence. His independence is illustrated by a series of events that resulted in a significant missed opportunity for the group.

At the same May 1 board meeting when MacDowell presented his slate of amendments, a letter was read from the Manuscript Society of Philadelphia, proposing a conference of all Manuscript Societies on June 19 for the purpose of discussing the possibility of a national organization. The board voted to respond that owing to the radical changes under way in their organization, they needed to defer a decision until a later date. After MacDowell's election, the Manuscript Society of Philadelphia renewed its invitation, prompting the board to send J. Remington Fairlamb as a delegate to the June 19 meeting in Philadelphia. Fairlamb reported on the conference in MacDowell's absence at the October 6 board meeting and finally, with the president in attendance at a special board meeting on October 16, presented a resolution that had been drawn up and signed by the delegates of the three societies in June:

Philadelphia June 19th, 1899
The undersigned delegates from the Society of American Musicians & Composers of NY City; the Chicago Manuscript Society, & the Manuscript Music Society of Philadelphia, hereby agree to recommend to their respective societies the adoption of the following agreement:
The undersigned Societies, founded for the encouragement of musical composition agree, on the basis of interchange, to give to the compositions of each society, representation upon the programmes of each of the other societies subject to the following conditions:
First—The composition must have been performed by the society sending them
Second—They must be specially recommended by the appropriate committee of the society sending them
Third—The performance of compositions sent by one society is naturally to be subject to the approval of the examining committee of the receiving society.
It is recommended by the undersigned delegates that each Society send to each of the other Societies a list of works available for such interchange.
It is further recommended that each of the Societies interested shall appoint a representative to constitute a permanent committee which shall be empowered to make a final agreement carrying the above-mentioned object into effect.
(signed) J. Remington Fairlamb
P. C. Lutkin
Philip H. Goepp

The proposal was tabled at that meeting, and it was not until the board meeting on November 10 that the issue was finally decided. Fairlamb reported that the membership of the Philadelphia society had adopted the proposal and that Philip H. Goepp, secretary of that organization, had written to urge the New York Society to do likewise. At this point MacDowell moved—significantly, the motion was seconded by Fairlamb—that the society respond in this manner:

That this Society entertains the most hearty sympathy toward the purposes outlined in the Philadelphia agreement, but it feels that it is in a position where those purposes can be carried out without any such formal agreement, & it hopes that the other societies represented in the Phila agreement will entertain a feeling of reciprocal interest in this organization & will be willing to interchange compositions without the formality of a signed agreement, especially as the recent changes in the policy and management of this Society were under consideration before the present proposition was laid before it.[53]

As the monthly private meetings got under way in the fall, it became evident that MacDowell was determined to institute radical change in the organization that he had renamed. The first private meeting on November 13 included works by seven Americans as well as Hummel and Handel. The December 12 program featured works by six Americans, of whom two were not members of the society. The meeting on January 3, 1900, containing eleven works by European composers and none by Americans, proved to be the last straw in MacDowell's short, but eventful, presidency.[54]

A directors' meeting had been scheduled for the next day, January 4, but as there was not a quorum present, the meeting became a regular board meeting. In the midst of this meeting a letter arrived from MacDowell resigning the presidency of the organization unless the entire Board of Directors resigned. After due discussion, action was postponed owing to the lack of quorum, but another meeting was scheduled for the following evening, with Edward Baxter Felton agreeing to visit MacDowell in the meantime.[55] The next day, both Louis R. Dressler and the faithful Arens resigned in accordance with MacDowell's wishes. At the January 5 meeting of the directors,

Mr. Felton reported the results of his call upon Mr. MacDowell who, he said, was definitely decided in his resignation & could not change his decision unless the Board of Directors were reorganized according to his views. He (MacDowell) did not wish to be personal in his action, but wished certain members appointed on a Board, & some present members removed. He felt that there was a great lack of organization in the Society, & wished such a body of Directors as could be held responsible for specific duties. He wished the manuscript idea entirely eliminated.[56]

That evening the minutes record that the various directors aired their views for and against MacDowell's proposal. Edgar Stillman Kelley (now resident in New York) and Robert Jaffray supported MacDowell; Fairlamb and Eduardo Marzo opposed him; John B. Burdett praised the president's high ideals but advised against hasty action; and Carl Valentine Lachmund recommended a compromise involving the appointment of persons known to be favored by MacDowell to the recently vacant positions on the board. In the end, the directors adopted the following remarkable resolution to be conveyed to MacDowell:

We, the undersigned, members of the Board of Directors, present at the Regular Meeting held this evening, have learned with regret that the President feels that it is impossible under present conditions to carry on the work of the Society on the lines desired by him. We believe that the President is under an entire misapprehension in regard to the attitude of the Board in this respect. We desire, however, that there shall be no obstacle to the progress of the Society in carrying on its work, and in order to provide a means for effecting any changes (if such changes should be desired) we hereby tender our resignations as Directors to take effect when our successors shall have been elected.

We further request the President to call a special meeting of the Society in accordance with Article VIII Section 7 of the constitution for the purpose of electing Directors.

We further request the Secretary to send a copy of this minute to all Directors not present at this meeting with the suggestion that they intimate to the President their readiness to join in this action.

Rob Jaffray Jr. Chairman pro tem.
Lucien G. Chaffin, Secy pro tem.
John B. Burdett
J. Remington Fairlamb.
Edwin Baxter Felton
Edgar Stillman Kelley
Carl V. Lachmund
E. Marzo[57]

Again the directors proved that they were willing to go to practically any lengths to retain MacDowell's participation.

The desired special meeting of the society was held on February 2, 1900, at which time MacDowell made a statement to the membership—summarized in the minutes—and withdrew to allow them to discuss his requests. In addition to reiterating his goals for the society, he raised the possibility that he could induce "certain wealthy gentlemen" to contribute an endowment of about $10,000 that would cover the costs of future orchestral concerts and eventually make it possible to have a clubhouse. In order to carry out his plans, he proposed that the members "should empower him to appoint, himself, a new Board of Directors whom he believed would aid him in carrying out his plans."[58]

The details of the following discussion are not included in the minutes, but the meeting ended with a unanimous resolution to the effect that the society declined to accept MacDowell's resignation but that it "finds itself incompetent to take the action suggested by him with regard to a new Board of Directors, and therefore requests the present Board to continue in office temporarily for the purpose of effecting itself such changes as will be agreeable to the President."[59] This response was necessitated by the stipulation in the constitution that board members be elected by the society rather than appointed, but it served only to delay the inevitable. MacDowell's resignation was tabled at the March 7 board meeting, not mentioned at the April 6 board meeting, and finally accepted at the annual meeting on May 21. The members voted at the same meeting to revert to the original name of the society and elected Frank Damrosch as their new president.

After all the change and uncertainty of the past year, the members must have been relieved to find such a competent and well-known musician to lead the society. At the June 12 board meeting, Damrosch announced dates for two public concerts and six private meetings. In an effort to rebuild the society, the board also approved a motion by Marzo to allow any former members to be reinstated upon payment of the year's dues, without an initiation fee. The season opened with private meetings on December 3, 1900, and January 15, 1901.

On January 19, 1901, the Manuscript Society of New York gave what turned out to be its final public concert. The orchestra of fifty-five players was conducted by Damrosch, and the program was the only one in the organization's history (except for the program of the summer concert in Manhattan Beach in 1895) that did not feature the familiar manuscript incipits and signatures of the composers. The evening began with Chadwick's *Melpomene*, a standard American work that had been in print for years. Featured also was a piano concerto by Moritz Moszkowski of Berlin, along with smaller works by Paul Miersch, Hermann Wetzler, and Charles Becker. The concert ended with Henry

Hadley's concert overture *In Bohemia*. Of the six composers featured, only Chadwick was listed in the program as a member of the society. Whether because of the unseasonably cold weather on that date or because of lack of interest, the *New York Times* did not review the concert or even mention it in the list of concerts the following day. *The Musical Courier* gave it two short paragraphs.[60]

At the board meeting on January 22, three days after the concert, Damrosch expressed his displeasure. He stated that it would be impractical to give the full complement of private meetings, because of the "trivial and uninteresting" repertoire that had been submitted. He recommended writing to prominent composers to solicit submissions, presenting "quality, rather than quantity," and urged the board to "take a higher stand on this matter, than it has in the past."[61] The Board of Directors consequently canceled the private meeting scheduled for February 12. The private meeting on March 12 was held as originally planned, but at the following board meeting on March 25 it was announced that there were insufficient funds remaining in the treasury to proceed with the second public concert of the year.

The problems of the society finally came out in the open at a special meeting called by the president on April 22, 1901. According to an article in the *New York Times*, the meeting was attended by only twenty of the society's members. Damrosch was credited with recommending the dissolution of the society, giving the following statement as his rationale:

When the society was first formed, it was expected that it would bring forth compositions of a very high order from its members. It was to give six private concerts of manuscript music by its members and one or two public concerts every year. Since I was elected President last May I found that it was very hard to get the proper material for concerts from the members. We received a great deal of music of a lighter kind, but very little suitable for the concerts. When we did give a concert the greater number of the members were conspicuous by their absence.[62]

Damrosch's remarks reflect the divergence of his goals for the society from those of most of the members. The minutes detail the ensuing debate over the mission of the group, with many members opposed to Damrosch's views as they had been to MacDowell's. Damrosch summed up with this suggestion, as quoted in the minutes:

President Damrosch suggested that two courses were open for the Society to choose. First: to carry out rigidly the plan of high ideals, and, united in a good cause, manage somehow to get some good out of it. Second: not to make this a Society with broad, artistic aims, but a social club. Make it really a nice social club of musicians but do not mix the drinks. I do not believe in the possibility of a compromise.[63]

With this frank statement, Damrosch succeeded in identifying the society's fundamental problem, a flaw that had never been clearly articulated since its inception. The stated objectives of the organization had always been two: "to advance the interests of American Musical Composition, and to promote social intercourse and friendly feeling among its members." Nearly all of the society's problems over the years may be traced to the incompatibility of those two objectives. If too rigorous a standard was held up, then most of the members would not be able to participate; if all members were allowed to participate equally, then the musical quality was understandably mediocre. Damrosch made it clear where he stood, and a committee was appointed to consider his suggestions in the two weeks remaining before the annual meeting on May 6.

The committee of four, consisting of Burdett, Fairlamb, Smith Newell Penfield, and Amy Fay, presented a list of nine recommendations at the annual meeting. Penfield and Burdett had been officers since the early 1890s, Fairlamb had played a crucial role in the events of recent years, and Fay was a relative newcomer to the group who was also the only noncomposer on the committee. Their proposals addressed the concerns by emphasizing the private meetings as the crucial element of the Manuscript Society's mission:

1st. The Manuscript Society to continue its existence, and artistic work.
2nd. Six private meetings to be held as in past years, once a month, commencing in November.
3rd. The musical performances to be confined to the compositions of members, active or honorary.
4th. All active members to be urged to submit their compositions to the music committee, with assurance that they will receive kind consideration.
5th. The social element to be given prominence, and arrangements made for light refreshments.
6th. Receptions to be tendered to distinguished artists from time to time.
7th. Attendance at the Private Meetings to be confined to members; but any member desiring to bring a friend, may, in application, receive a complimentary ticket.
8th. If considered advisable by the Directors, a concert with orchestra to be given near the close of the season.
9th. The rooms of the Society to be placed at the disposition of the members, one evening a week, for informal social and musical purposes.[64]

In the discussion that followed, the membership endorsed these recommendations with only minor changes. At that point, Frank Damrosch cordially tendered his resignation and wished the society well, after which Burdett was elected president. With this action, the Manuscript Society of New York relinquished its goal of promoting American music in public and became a social club.

The minutes become scanty over the next few years, although the programs of private meetings indicate that the group maintained an active schedule through 1912. Arens was elected president in 1908, serving until 1916.[65] He presided over a declining organization, as the membership lists grew smaller each year until it folded during World War I. The treasurer's records show thirty-six dues-paying members for 1915/1916, including Eleanor Everest Freer, Margaret Ruthven Lang, Victor Herbert, Louis Lombard, and Charles Wakefield Cadman. Nineteen members were listed the following year, while the final entry, for 1917/1918, lists twelve members who paid five dollars each in dues. Among those who stayed to the bitter end was Victor Herbert, the famous composer of operettas.

If the foregoing discussion gives the impression that the Manuscript Society of New York was an organization that started with few goals and ended with few achievements, the list of works in Appendix 4 should prove otherwise. Over the course of ten seasons of public concerts, the group presented the works of over 100 different composers, many with full orchestra and professional conductors. If a similar list were compiled for the private meetings, it would show hundreds more composers. The most impressive achievement, then, is the sheer number of works performed. That few of these works went on to become well known was a disappointment to the organizers and critics but was inevitable given the restrictive guidelines for inclusion.

A closer look at the list shows a wide variety of persons. Particularly noteworthy is the strong representation of women composers. While only about 10 percent of the composers featured in public concerts were women, this was a favorable average when compared with the programs of major symphony orchestras at this time.[66] The private meetings included even more women, with at least two programs devoted exclusively to female composers, on December 18, 1895, and November 20, 1901. At its height, the organization included numerous women in both active and supporting roles. The membership roster included with the December 3, 1896, concert lists fourteen women as active members (composers), 102 women as professional members, and seventy-seven women as associate members. The list of honorary members included one woman, Cécile Chaminade. Though women were notably absent from the executive committees over the years, Laura Sedgwick Collins was instrumental in the early organizational history of the group, while Amy Fay and others played crucial roles in later years.

What set the New York Manuscript Society and its sister organizations in Chicago and Philadelphia apart from any other group at this time was the fact that the organization was run by the composers themselves. Despite the weaknesses in conducting and inconsistency of repertoire, the society made its most significant contributions when it was strictly in the control of like-minded composers. These persons had a natural desire to see the enterprise flourish, and before they became complacent in the late 1890s, they contributed many compositions for performance. If few of them were famous or wrote timeless music, that is only to be expected. It stands to reason that a healthy musical culture needs not only a few superstars but also a thriving substratum of *Kleinmeister*. For the minor masters of America, the decade of the 1890s was a Golden Age thanks to the opportunities provided by the New York Manuscript Society, which extended the American Composers' Concert movement to the turn of the twentieth century.

NOTES

1. Rupert Hughes, "Music in America: XV. The Manuscript Society and its President," *Godey's Magazine* 133 (July 1896): 81.

2. These programs are also reprinted in Morris Carter, *Isabella Stewart Gardner and Fenway Court* (Boston and New York: Houghton Mifflin, 1925), pp. 112–14. Rogers implies in her memoirs that there were additional concerts during the first season, but gives no specific information: Clara Kathleen Rogers, *The Story of Two Lives: Home, Friends, and Travels* (privately printed by Plimpton Press, 1932), p. 188. The March 26, 1889, concert, including works by Foote, Beck, Buck, and Arthur Whiting, was reported in "Home News," *MC* 18/14 (April 3, 1889): 266.

3. Sumner Salter, "Early Encouragements to American Composers," *The Musical Quarterly* 18/1 (January 1932): 84.

4. Margery Morgan Lowens, "The New York Years of Edward MacDowell" (Ph.D. dissertation, University of Michigan, 1971; UMI No. 71–23,812), pp. 180–94.

5. Salter, "Early Encouragements," 85.

6. Ibid., 87.

7. Ibid.

8. "The Manuscript Society," *New York Daily Tribune*, December 12, 1890, p. 7.

9. "The Manuscript Society," *NYT*, December 11, 1890, p. 4.

10. "The Raconteur," *MC* 22/16 (April 22, 1891): 389.

11. "The Manuscript Society," *MC* 21/25 (December 17, 1890): 622.

12. "The Manuscript Society Presents American Composers," *AAJ* 56/9 (December 13, 1890): 132.

13. "Programme: Third Public Meeting, Chickering Hall, Wednesday, April 15th, 1891," n.p.

14. The group was organized in the 1889/1890 season for the purpose of holding private meetings. The concert programs and other subsequent literature list 1890/1891 as the first season, however.

15. "The Manuscript Club: A New Society and an Interesting Concert," *Freund's Music and Drama* 15/25 (April 18, 1891): 3.

16. Salter, "Early Encouragements," 93. This issue continued to occupy the membership in future years, as reflected in an article from 1894: Nicholas Douty, "Should the Fugue and the Sonata Form Be the Requirements for Admission to the Composer's Class of a Manuscript Society?" *Music* 7/2 (December 1894): 124–28.

17. "Live Musical Topics," *NYT*, April 19, 1891, p. 12.

18. Ibid.

19. "The Manuscript Society Concert," *MC* 23/25 (December 16, 1891): 715.

20. "The Manuscript Society Concert," *MC* 24/13 (March 30, 1892): 8.

21. "The Manuscript Society," *MC* 24/18 (May 4, 1892): 8.

22. "Manuscript Society's Second Concert," *AAJ* 28/25 (April 2, 1892): 544.

23. "Manuscript Society's Second Concert," *AAJ* 60/10 (December 17, 1892): 222.

24. "Gotham Gossip," *MC* 27/24 (December 13, 1893): 13.

25. Salter, "Early Encouragements," 95.

26. "The Manuscript Society," *NYT*, April 17, 1896, p. 4.

27. His efforts do not seem to have been well publicized. Salter mentions a series of six American concerts in New York in 1885, and he wrote a letter to MacDowell requesting repertoire for a concert on May 3, 1889, but this researcher has been unable to locate programs or reviews for these concerts.

28. Editorial note, *MC* 22/17 (April 29, 1891): 411; and "Emilio Agramonte," *MC* 25/24 (December 21, 1892): 32.

29. For detailed information on this organization, see Martha Furman Schleifer, "The Manuscript Music Society," Chapter 6 of *William Wallace Gilchrist (1846–1916): A Moving Force in the Musical Life of Philadelphia*, Composers of North America, No. 1 (Metuchen, NJ, and London: Scarecrow, 1985), pp. 44–50; Philip H. Goepp, "Philadelphia Manuscript Society," *MC* national edition (December 20–27, 1899): n.p.; and the clipping file on the society at the Free Library of Philadelphia.

30. Frederic Grant Gleason, "American Composers," *American Art Journal* 57/25 (October 3, 1891): 398–99.

31. The organization's structure and constitution are discussed in M'I.B., "The Manuscript Club," *The Daily Inter Ocean*, July 3, 1896, p. 7. In June 1900 the Chicago correspondent to *MC* reported, "I have been requested to state the intentions of

the Manuscript Society. On good authority I am informed that the fount of inspiration has become dry, and that it (the society) is laid up for repairs." Florence French, "Chicago," *MC* 48/23 (June 6, 1900): 27.

32. A copy of the catalog of this exhibit may be found in the Library of Congress, Music Division: "Catalogue of Manuscripts, Letters, Portraits, Autographs, etc. Exhibited in the Rooms of the Manuscript Society, 17 E. 22nd St., N.Y., on Nov. 1st and 2d, 1895."

33. Salter, "Early Encouragements," 96.

34. Minutes of the February 5, 1897 meeting indicate that 1,750 copies of the *Bulletin* were ordered, a number approximately three times the membership of the society. Minutes, vol. 1, p. 15.

35. W.J.H., "Music," *NYT*, April 19, 1896, p. 11.

36. Minutes, vol. 1, p. 5.

37. Ibid., vol. 1, pp. 43, 45.

38. Ibid., vol. 1, p.109.

39. Ibid., vol. 1, p. 143.

40. Ibid., vol. 1, pp. 69, 93.

41. Ibid., vol. 1, p. 73.

42. Ibid., vol. 1, p. 93.

43. Lowens, 183.

44. Minutes, vol. 1, p. 120.

45. Ibid., vol. 1, pp. 116–18.

46. "Manuscript Society Concert," *MC* 37/26 (December 28, 1898): 41.

47. Minutes, vol. 1, p. 158.

48. Ibid., vol. 1, 151.

49. Ibid., vol. 1, 155.

50. The meeting and the changes were made public in "Manuscript Society Changes," *NYT*, May 21, 1899, p. 17.

51. Quoted in Salter, "Early Encouragements," 103 and Lowens, "The New York Years," 185.

52. "MacDowell on 'American' Concerts" and "Manuscript Society Election," *Musical America* 2/20 (May 20, 1899): 5, 9; "Manuscript Society Changes" and "Mr. MacDowell's Words," *MC* 38/20 (May 24, 1899): 18, 21.

53. The entire foregoing story may be traced in the minutes, vol. 1, pp. 150–86.

54. These numbers are cited in Lowens, 186–87.

55. Minutes, vol. 1, p. 195.

56. Ibid., vol. 1, p. 197.

57. Ibid., vol. 1, pp. 199–200.

58. Ibid., vol. 1, pp. 202–3.

59. Ibid., vol. 1, p. 203.

60. "Manuscript Society Concert," *MC* 42/4 (January 23, 1901): 33.

61. Minutes, vol. 1, p. 245.

62. "Manuscript Society Meets," *NYT*, April 23, 1901, p. 9.

63. Minutes, vol. 2, p. 26.

64. Ibid., vol. 2, pp. 29–30.

65. Letter of resignation from F. X. Arens to F. W. Riesberg, secretary, November 8, 1916, unpaginated book of letters and accounts, New York Public Library, Music Division.

66. The Boston Symphony Orchestra, for instance, performed five works by three women during its first thirty-three seasons from 1881/1882 to 1913/1914. M. A. DeWolfe Howe, *The Boston Symphony Orchestra: An Historical Sketch* (Boston and New York: Houghton Mifflin, 1914).

⚭ 12 ⚭

Postlude: Dvořák and New Directions in American Art Music

The coming of Dr. Antonín Dvořák under the auspices of the National conservatory has, too, been a tremendously significant event in the musical history of America, and one that is fraught with the greatest meanings for our musical future. He is a world renowned composer, his activities are unabated, and with his art enthusiasms the blossoming of new ideals in this land of the free may bring forth the most happy results. As a teacher he is doing noble work already, and his example is proving a great stimulus to the ambitious young American composer.

And that reminds us that the unhappy American composer, who from being contemptuously pilloried, gorged with praise, and lately stupefied with indifference, is at last coming to a realizing sense of his position. He now knows that he must stand on his own legs, metaphorically, and must throw away those adventitious crutches, "American composers' concerts," "Yankee Doodle programs," &c. E. A. MacDowell's (he is certainly an American and certainly a composer to be proud of) views on the subject were sound from the outset—a composer of music first and foremost, then an American.

To be sure those whose patriotism is paramount to their talents will disagree with this view of the question. Well, let them bubble with patriotic pride, and the earnest American composer compose music.

—*The Musical Courier*, retrospective of the year 1892[1]

The Musical Courier's juxtaposition of the end of the American Composers' Concert movement and the beginning of Dvořák's tenure at the National Conservatory is more than merely symbolic; for those who had been debating the future of American art music for nearly a decade, it was a paradigm shift that would influence the direction of American music for decades.

The Czech composer came to New York at the invitation of Jeannette Meyer Thurber, one of the most remarkable music patrons of the era. In a country with no government subsidies for the arts, wealthy patrons exercise a disproportionate influence. The irony of this situation in late nineteenth-century America was that this apparently democratic lack of subsidy led to the creation of such decidedly elitist institutions as the Metropolitan Opera. America's musical institutions—and to some extent its musical tastes as well—were shaped by wealthy music lovers like Henry Lee Higginson, Andrew Carnegie, and Thurber. Unique among Gilded Age patrons of music, Thurber exhibited a life-long dedication not only to art music but to American art music.[2]

Born in Delhi, New York, in 1850, Jeannette Meyer studied at the Paris Conservatory as a teenager and married the wealthy businessman Francis Beattie Thurber in 1869. Beginning in the 1870s, she initiated a long series of projects allowing her to use her wealth to enhance musical life in the United States. In 1878 she assembled a group of backers to support the careers of young American singers, the beginning of a lifelong commitment to American performers.[3] She began to attract significant attention in the early 1880s, when her support of Theodore Thomas' children's concerts (1883), cross-country tour (1884), and New York Wagner Festival (1884) earned her the admiration of some and the scorn of others.

In 1885, amid the excitement of the new American Composers' Concert movement, Thurber established the American Opera Company, a group dedicated to performing opera in English using only American singers. The goal was not only to promote opera in vernacular translations but to provide encouragement to American composers who might wish to compose operas in their native language. The democratic notion of opera for the people was enthusiastically supported by those who believed that the Metropolitan Opera was too exclusive and too reliant on the talents of foreign performers and composers. Thomas agreed to serve as music director of this fledgling group while retaining his position as conductor of the New York Philharmonic. The first season opened on January 4, 1886, with a performance of Hermann Goetz's *Taming of the Shrew*. Over the next three months, the group toured the east, with performances in New York, Boston, Philadelphia, Washington, Baltimore, and eventually St. Louis. By the end of the first season the company was deeply in debt, and Thurber's financial partners pulled out.

Unwilling to let her dream die, Thurber reorganized the company under a new name, the National Opera Company, and embarked on a second season. By this time the financial problems of the organization were national news, as singers sued for back salary, manager Charles Locke was arrested, and blame was shifted from one participant to another. The second season took the company all the way to San Francisco, but the debts proved too great to sustain the operation, which was eventually stranded in Buffalo. Thomas suffered serious financial losses through his association with the company, and his reputation was also impugned by the press. The company was a financial failure but a qualified artistic success.[4]

Despite the failure of the company, it demonstrated clearly that Thurber had radical ideas about art music in America. The American Opera Company, had it succeeded, would have been a counterpoise to the Metropolitan Opera, which has been the dominant model for operatic production in the United States ever since. Thurber believed in opera in the vernacular, a concept that has ensured the continuing popularity of opera in European countries like Germany and Italy but has never caught on at the most prestigious opera houses in the English-speaking world. The eventual goal of performing opera in English was to cultivate a repertoire of operas by American composers, a goal that was not achieved in the two troubled seasons of the company's existence. She also believed in the principle of the repertory company, which aims for an ensemble of flexible and uniformly strong singers rather than productions dominated by a few over-paid stars. The star system was already firmly established in nineteenth-century America and has been a feature of American art music ever since. Finally, she believed in using American singers, who would ideally be trained in their home country. This brings us to the only facet of the American Opera Company that was not a failure and the source of Thurber's triumph in the following decade.

As an adjunct to the opera company, Thurber established a conservatory that began instruction in the fall of 1885. The original name of the conservatory was the American School of Opera, and the appointment of French opera singer Jacques Bouhy as its first director confirmed the operatic focus of the school. In the shuffle surrounding the transition from the American Opera Company to the National Opera Company in 1886, the school was renamed the National Conservatory and made independent of the opera company. Over the next few years, the curriculum was broadened to transform the school from an operatic training institute to a comprehensive conservatory. Located in New York, the school grew rapidly during its first five seasons, as Thurber hired the best faculty that she could find and advertised "aggressively." News releases and paid advertisements were sent to papers around the country in an effort to attract a truly national student body.[5] Among the persons whom she hoped to hire for the faculty was Edward MacDowell, whose mother was an administrative assistant at the conservatory. He received a telegram in Wiesbaden on March 7, 1888, offering him a position in harmony and composition.[6] He turned down the offer but moved to Boston later that year. He may later have regretted his decision to refuse Thurber's generous offer, for his letters from the early 1890s reflect a certain amount of resentment over the high salary and enormous attention showered on Dvořák.[7]

In order to enhance the stature of the school, Thurber took the bold step of applying for a congressional subsidy for the institution in 1888. The Paris Conservatory and many of Germany's conservatories were state-supported, and she believed that her school was the logical candidate for similar support. In her request to Congress she noted, "America has, so far, done nothing in a National way either to promote the musical education of its people or to develop any musical genius they possess, and . . . in this, she stands alone among the civilized nations of the world."[8] The timing of her proposal turned out to be its downfall. Although the government had a substantial budget surplus at that time, the 1888 presidential election revolved around the issue of tariffs and trade protectionism. Had it been funded, the subsidy would have amounted to protection of one institution over its rivals, and Congress predictably chose not to approve such a precedent during a volatile political season. Her proposal for $200,000 per year was turned down, despite general support for her aims.

Undaunted, Thurber changed her strategy by sponsoring an American Composers' Concert in Washington, D.C., on March 26, 1890. The program, arranged by Frank Van der Stucken, contained most of the works that he had conducted at the Paris Exposition the previous summer. It was attended by many congressmen and other socialites and was favorably reviewed in local and national papers.[9] The concert was advertised as the first of a series in cities throughout the country that would culminate with a "grand American composers' festival" in Omaha, Nebraska, on November 27, 28, and 29,[10] but there is no evidence that the projected festival ever took place. The choice of an all-American concert in the nation's capital was a brilliant one, for it evoked inevitable associations between a "school of composers" in the broad nationalistic sense and her own school. The reviewer for the *Washington Star* wrote:

Mrs. Jeannette M. Thurber has added another to her many services to our native musical art by arranging this series of American concerts, of which last evening's was the initial one. Such a series could not fail vastly to increase the honor in which our prophets in music are held in their own country, for it would show to the music lovers of the United States that we have a school of composers with something to say and the ability to say it in noble and befitting musical utterance, a school animated by lofty aims and sincere purposes, equipped abundantly in knowledge and technical means and best of all urged on by a real creative impulse.[11]

The ulterior motive behind this concert was to support her renewed efforts to win congressional support. A bill introduced in December included a clause empowering the conservatory to "found, establish and maintain a national conservatory of music within the District of Columbia."[12] The bill was approved in March 1891, making the National Conservatory the only school of music ever granted a congressional charter, though the charter did not include any financial subsidy. The Washington branch of the conservatory was never established, but the prestige of the congressional charter set the stage for a period of enviable successes for the New York school. She continued to lobby for federal funding as late as 1939 over the protests of other private conservatories, which objected to the prospect of becoming preparatory schools for a national conservatory after the pattern of the French conservatory system.[13]

With the blessing of the U.S. Congress, Thurber expanded the school in the 1890s, scoring a major coup with the acquisition of Dvořák as director from 1892 to 1895. The guiding principles of the institution were egalitarian: she insisted on equal opportunities for talented students regardless of race, gender, or physical disability. The school was especially noteworthy for providing training for a group of talented African American students, including Harry T. Burleigh, Will Marion Cook, and Maurice Arnold Strothotte. Her initial proposal to Congress outlined a plan whereby exceptionally talented students who could not afford tuition would be admitted free of charge, with the stipulation that "students are bound, on the completion of their studies, to assist in carrying on the National Educational work of the Conservatory, by contributing, for a specified time in each case, one-fourth of all monies earned professionally by them over and above the sum of one thousand dollars per annum."[14]

The significance of Dvořák's three years in America has been recognized for over a century, and recent scholarly work has clarified many questions about his activities, his thinking, and his influence on American music.[15]   This study adds nothing new to the extensive documentary evidence or the excellent analyses of his role in American life, but it would not be complete without placing his contribution in the context of the American Composers' Concert movement. More often than not, scholars have focused on what Dvořák *began* in America; the foregoing chapters should make it clear that he *ended* something significant as well.

From the beginning, the American Composers' Concert movement had been remarkably accepting of a broad spectrum of American music. The guiding precept of its founders had been that the best way to encourage American composers was to increase their opportunities for performance and publication. With the proper encouragement, the argument went, American composers would produce more and better works, eventually coalescing into a recognizable school of composition. With time, this school of composition not only would become established in concert halls but would produce a composer of real genius to rival the great composers of the European tradition. The promotion of American music was designed to allow composers to do what they do best—be creative—and the inclusion of such diverse works as Chadwick's *Melpomene* and Schoenefeld's *Marcio Fantastico* on the same program is a reflection of the catholicity of taste that prevailed.   Henry Krehbiel articulated the goals of the movement most succinctly in his review of the first public meeting of the Manuscript Society of New York:

Now that the ball is rolling, its progress may be watched with composure and a patience like that of Job himself. Those who believe that America will some day produce a school of composers worthy of her greatness in other respects, are not impatient for that consummation. They can afford to study such manifestations as that supplied by the Manuscript Society at its first public meeting in Chickering Hall on Wednesday night with equanimity, conscious that, though the genius who is to become the exemplar and inspiration of the new school may disclose himself today or tomorrow, yet he will come in the fullness of time.[16]

As it turned out, neither Krehbiel nor his contemporaries had the patience of Job, and they did indeed become impatient.   Rather than remaining true to the original scheme—providing performance opportunities and waiting patiently for the composers to develop naturally—critics increasingly began to question the direction that the composers were taking. Krehbiel, in particular, became uneasy with the cosmopolitan style of the most prominent American composers, believing that American art music was not sufficiently distinctive from that of Europe to warrant its identification as a school.   He began his own studies of Native American and African American music and found himself captivated by what he discovered.

European critics, lacking familiarity with the breadth of American culture, were even less reticent to speak their minds, as we discovered in the responses to the 1889 concert in Paris and the Arens tours of 1891 and 1892.   Their views took the form of imperatives regarding what American composers should do. Despite the recognition by isolated critics that the United States was an unusually cosmopolitan culture, the majority of European commentators expressed the view that Americans should turn to the folk musics of Native and African

Americans for their inspiration. Dvořák was exposed to these ideas before he left Europe, which helps to account for the firmness of his convictions on the subject of American music and the speed with which he reached his conclusions. By making his famous pronouncement, after less than a year in the United States, that the future of American music lay in the folk music of these two disfranchised groups, he was transplanting European views of nationalism to the United States. At the end of his three-year stay, with greater exposure to American culture, he tempered his views, but by then his earlier opinions had been widely accepted.

The significance of Dvořák's pronouncement on American music lay not so much in the materials that he chose to espouse. Rather, it lay in his endorsement of the growing view that there were stylistic imperatives that American composers needed to follow. The authority with which he spoke gave his views a credibility that effectively undermined any remnants of the American Composers' Concert movement. From that time forward, it was no longer acceptable merely to give composers a blank check to write as they chose, but instead it became fashionable to tell composers how their music should sound. Whether this was an advance over the previous practice is debatable. In any case, it would be over half a century before Virgil Thomson could state, "The way to write American music is simple. All you have to do is to be an American and then write any kind of music you wish."[17]

The shift in the critical debate brought about by Dvořák's views moved the emphasis from conceptual Americanism—a pro-American stance that supports the efforts of American composers and performing groups—to compositional Americanism—the desire for musical or programmatic elements that are identifiably American.[18] This view dominated discussions of American art music for decades after his departure, leading composers to experiment especially with "Indianist" music and music on African American themes.[19] The 1920s saw the rise of art music that incorporated elements of jazz, and by the 1930s, American composers like Copland and Harris were still searching for a style of art music that would have an identifiable American sound. In the sense that their music defines the essence of Americanism in music for so many listeners, they are the true heirs to Dvořák's view of American music.

After a tsunami passes, the ocean level returns to normal, but it leaves its mark behind in the form of changes to the land that it has devastated. The tsunami that struck Hilo on May 22, 1960, carried twenty-two-ton boulders as far as 600 feet inland and bent parking meters to the ground, yet when the waters receded, there was no trace of the force that had actually caused the damage.[20] Similarly, the American Composers' Concert movement vanished so completely that it had been forgotten by the late 1890s. When the MTNA presented its all-American concerts at the 1899 convention in Cincinnati, the advance publicity hailed the idea as something new.[21] In 1906 Krehbiel wrote a retrospective article for the *New York Tribune* to inform the current generation that they were not the first to promote American music actively.[22] Sumner Salter's *Musical Quarterly* article of 1932 was yet another attempt to remind a later generation that their efforts on behalf of American music were not the first.[23]

Despite this collective amnesia, the American Composers' Concert movement did leave behind a changed musical landscape. Composers still complained with good reason that their major orchestral works found few champions among the predominantly European conductors of America's leading orchestras. But particularly in the recital hall, American music was much more widely heard than before the movement. Solo recitalists like William H. Sherwood took MacDowell's admonition to heart by including an "American group" in their mixed recitals. He had been one of the champions of the American movement in the 1880s, and it will be remembered that he not only performed concertos on many high-profile orchestral concerts but also performed a number of solo recitals consisting exclusively of American works. Whether because of the criticism leveled at him by Apthorp after his 1887 recitals, because of the fading popularity of such concerts, or for other reasons, he stopped giving all-American concerts well before the movement was over. But his programs from the 1890s until his death in 1911 show that he included a set of American works in nearly every recital. This practice was also common among vocal soloists, and the era witnessed a blossoming of art song composition. Composers like MacDowell and Amy Beach found that their art songs and piano compositions became very popular at home and well known abroad, even as their larger works failed to find a place in the standard repertoire.

The notion of conceptual Americanism, despite its rejection by Dvořák and the American public in the 1890s, left a profound influence on American music. Perhaps the American desire for progress, coupled with a tendency to forget the past, allows the idea to be revived again and again. Individual performers are still drawn to all-American concerts, and the twentieth century saw numerous revivals of organized efforts to promote American music. The American Music Society (1910), the American Music Guild (1922–1924), Howard Hanson's series of American Composers' Concerts at the Eastman School of Music (1925–1971), The American Composers' Alliance (founded 1938), and the American Music Center (founded 1940) all presented American concerts in virtually the same format as their predecessors from the Gilded Age. The century also witnessed new ways to promote American music: the Society for the Preservation of American Music and New World Records specialized in recordings of American music, while the Sonneck Society—now known as the Society for American Music—is dedicated to the scholarly study of all branches of American music. Each of these twentieth-century examples of conceptual Americanism can trace its roots to the American Composers' Concert movement, an idea that was born of idealism and killed by excess but that left a lasting mark on American culture.

NOTES

1. "1892. A Retrospective Glance," *MC* 25/25 (December 28, 1892): 8.
2. Thurber's life work has been documented extensively by Emanuel Rubin. See especially "Jeannette Meyers [*sic*] Thurber and the National Conservatory of Music," *American Music* 8/3 (Fall 1990): 294–325; and "Jeannette Meyer Thurber (1850–1946): Music for a Democracy," in *Cultivating Music in America: Women Patrons and Activists since 1860*, ed. Ralph P. Locke and Cyrilla Barr (Berkeley, Los Angeles, and London: University of California Press, 1997), pp. 134–63.
3. Rubin, "Jeannette Meyer Thurber (1850–1946)," 139.

4. For detailed discussions of the history of this organization, see "From Boastful Dream to Catastrophe," in Ezra Schabas, *Theodore Thomas* (Urbana and Chicago: University of Illinois Press, 1989), pp. 147–67; and Rubin, "Jeannette Meyer Thurber (1850–1946)," 134–63.

5. Rubin, "Jeannette Meyer Thurber (1850–1946)," 150.

6. Margery Morgan Lowens, "The New York Years of Edward MacDowell" (Ph.D. dissertation, University of Michigan, 1971; UMI 71–23,812), pp. 39–40.

7. Alan H. Levy, *Edward MacDowell: An American Master* (Lanham, MD and London: Scarecrow, 1998), p. 109.

8. Quoted in Rubin, "Jeannette Meyer Thurber (1850–1946)," 150.

9. A list of dignitaries who attended the after-concert reception was published in "Society News and Chat," (Washington) *Sunday Herald*, March 30, 1890, p. 3.

10. "A Real Event in Music: The American Composers' Concert at Lincoln Hall Last Night," *Washington Post*, March 27, 1890, p. 2.

11. "American Music: The Signal Success of the First Concert of Promising Series," *Evening Star*, March 27, 1890, p. 8.

12. Quoted in Rubin, "Jeannette Meyer Thurber (1850–1946)," 151.

13. Ibid., 156–58.

14. Quoted in Ibid., 149.

15. See especially the numerous fine essays in *Dvořák in America: 1892–1895*, ed. John C. Tibbetts (Portland, OR: Amadeus Press, 1993).

16. [Henry E. Krehbiel], "The Manuscript Society," *New York Daily Tribune*, December 12, 1890, p. 7.

17. Virgil Thomson, "On Being American," *New York Herald Tribune*, January 25, 1948, sec. 5 p. 5. This famous essay has been quoted and reprinted ever since its initial publication, including a complete reprint in Virgil Thomson, *A Virgil Thomson Reader* (Boston: Houghton Mifflin, 1981), pp. 304–6.

18. These terms were introduced in Barbara A. Zuck, *A History of Musical Americanism* (Ann Arbor, MI: UMI Research Press, 1980).

19. The profound influence of Dvořák's ideas on subsequent generations of American composers is detailed in Adrienne Fried Block, "Dvořák's Long American Reach," in Tibbetts, *Dvořák in America*, 157–81.

20. Walter C. Dudley and Min Lee, *Tsunami!*, 2nd edition (Honolulu: University of Hawai'i Press, 1998), pp. 166–67.

21. "Never before in the history of the M.T.N.A. has the American composer been placed before his fellow musicians in such an advantageous position. Usually but very few American works are performed at the national meetings, but on this occasion the American composer will reign supreme." "M.T.N.A. Cincinnati, June 21 to 23, 1899: A Word about the Programs," *MC*, national edition (May 10–17, 1899): n.p.

22. H.E.K., "On the Performance of American Compositions," *New York Daily Tribune*, April 15, 1906, sec. V, p. 4.

23. Sumner Salter, "Early Encouragements to American Composers," *The Musical Quarterly* 18/1 (January 1932): 76-105.

∽ **Appendix 1** ∽

Selected American Composers' Concerts, 1881–1901

The American Composers' Concert movement resulted in hundreds of concerts in the United States and Europe. The list on the following pages is not comprehensive but rather chronicles the concerts presented by organizations devoted to American concerts and other concerts that were reported in the national press. With a few exceptions, the concerts included the works of several American composers rather than just one composer.

Abbreviations:

ACCA=American Composers' Choral Association
IMTA=Illinois Music Teachers' Association
MMS=Manuscript Music Society (Philadelphia)
MSC=Manuscript Society of Chicago
MSNY=Manuscript Society of New York
MTA=Music Teachers' Association
MTNA=Music Teachers' National Association
NYMTA=New York Music Teachers' Association
OMTA=Ohio Music Teachers' Association
cham=chamber
chor=choral
misc=miscellaneous
orch=orchestral
org=organ
p=piano
v=vocal solo
vln=violin solo

Appendix 1 continued

Date	City (Hall/Event)	Organization/Series/(medium)	Conductor/solo recitalist
3/27/81	Chicago	"Chicago Composers' Night" (orch)	Adolph Liesegang, conductor
5/30/81	Boston	Wellesley College of Music	William Sherwood, pianist; Beethoven Quartette
8/2/82	Chicago		Theodore Thomas, conductor
7/3/84	Cleveland	MTNA (misc)	Calixa Lavallée, pianist
8/5/84	Chicago Summer Night Concerts	"Chicago Composers' Night" (orch)	Liesegang
1/8/85	Chicago, Hershey Music Hall	"Chicago Song Composers" (1st) (v)	C. Jay Smith, conductor
1/23/85	London, Prince's Hall	(v)	Louis Melbourne
2/5/85	Chicago, Hershey Music Hall	"Chicago Song Composers" (2nd) (v)	C. Jay Smith
3/10/85	London, Prince's Hall	(v)	Melbourne
3/10/85	Boston, Union Hall	(p)	Lavallée, pianist (1st)
3/31/85	New York, Steinway Hall	Novelty Concerts (orch)	Frank Van der Stucken
4/29 & 5/4/85	Boston, Music Hall	Apollo Club (Boston Composers) (orch/chor)	B. J. Lang, conductor
5/5/85	Boston	(p)	Lavallée (2nd)
6/17/85	Boston, Music Hall	Music Hall Popular Concerts (orch)	Adolph Neuendorff, conductor
7/2/85	New York, Academy of Music	MTNA (misc)	Melbourne
2/15/86	New York, Chickering Hall	American Concert (misc)	Lavallée (4th)
2/26/86	Boston, Miller Hall	(p)	Lillian E. Stoddard
3/15/86	Northwestern Conservatory of Music	(v)	Lavallée (5th)
4/28/86	Boston, Miller Hall	(p)	Carlyle Petersilea, pianist
5/1/86	Boston, Union Hall	(misc)	Emil Liebling, pianist
5/14/86	Chicago, Kimball Hall	(p)	
6/30/86	Boston, Tremont Temple	MTNA (misc)	
7/1/86	Boston, Tremont Temple	MTNA (chor/orch)	
7/2/86	Boston, Tremont Temple	MTNA (orch)	
9/9/86	New York, Central Park Garden	American Composers' Night (orch)	Adolph Neuendorff
3/22/87	Rochester, NY	(p)	Lavallée

Date	Location	Event/Venue	Performer/Conductor
3/23/87	Detroit, MI	(p)	Lavallée
5/18/87	San Francisco, Odd Fellows' Hall	Loring Club (chor)	David W. Loring, conductor
6/30/87	Columbus	OMTA (Ohio Composers' Concert) (misc)	
7/1/87	Chicago, Central Music Hall	IMTA (Illinois Composers' Concert) (misc)	
7/5/87	Indianapolis	MTNA (chor/orch)	Van der Stucken
7/6/87	Indianapolis	MTNA (chor/orch)	Van der Stucken
7/8/87	Indianapolis	MTNA (p/v)	
11/8/87	Boston	(p)	William Sherwood, pianist
11/15/87	Boston	(p)	Sherwood
11/15/87	New York, Chickering Hall	(chor/orch)	Van der Stucken
11/17/87	New York, Chickering Hall	(chor/orch)	Van der Stucken
11/18/87	Claverack, NY	Claverack College Conservatory (misc)	Charles W. Landon
11/19/87	New York, Chickering Hall	(misc)	Van der Stucken
11/22/87	New York, Chickering Hall	(cham/v)	Van der Stucken
11/24/87	New York, Chickering Hall	(chor/orch)	Van der Stucken
11/29/87	Pittsburgh Female College	(misc)	
1/17/88	Boston,	Miss Plumer's Rooms, Hotel Pelham (cham)	Theodor Salmon, conductor
1/19/88	Boston, Isabella Stewart Gardner Mansion	Manuscript Club	Giuseppe Campanari, et al.
2/16/88	Chicago, Central Music Hall	"Historical Sketch of American Music" (chor)	Frederic Root, conductor
3/16/88	Cincinnati, Odeon	Composers' Night	
ca. 3/88	Pittsburgh Club Theatre	(see *AAJ* 48/22 [March 10, 1888]: 327)	
4/4/88	Chicago, Madison Street Theatre	Gottschalk night	Louis Staab and students
4/18/88	Detroit Conservatory	(p/v)	
4/19/88	Cleveland	American Composers' Night	
ca. 4/88	Cleveland	Detroit Philharmonic Club	(see *MC* 16/18 [May 2, 1888]: 308)
4/12/88	Cincinnati	Apollo Club (chor)	B.W. Foley, conductor
4/24/88	Pittsburgh	(p/v)	Sherwood, pianist
4/27/88	Chicago, Kimball Hall	Emil Liebling, et al. (cham)	
5/1–3/88		Iowa MTA (Iowa Composers' Concert)	
5/9/88	Detroit Conservatory of Music	American Composers' Series: Edward MacDowell	Edward MacDowell
5/21/88	Detroit	Detroit Philharmonic Club (misc)	J. de Zielinski, director

Appendix 1 continued

87/88 season	Dayton, OH	W. L. Blumenschein piano studio (p) (vln/v)	student recital
6/7/88	Cleveland	OMTA (Ohio Composers' Concert) (misc)	George Lehman
6/28/88	Columbus, OH	MTNA (chor/orch)	Thomas
7/4/88	Chicago	MTNA (chor/orch)	Thomas
7/5/88	Chicago	MTNA (chor/orch)	Thomas
7/6/88	Chicago	(band/v)	
8/20/88	Point of Pines, MA		J. Thomas Baldwin, music director
8/30/88	Brighton Beach, New York	American Composers' Night (orch)	Anton Seidl, conductor
Fall 1888	Montclair, NJ	(see *AAJ* 50/13 [October 13, 1888]: 203) (p)	Clara Thoms, pianist
2/89	Buffalo, NY, Chapter House		Frederic W. Riesberg, pianist
2/28/89	Boston, Gardner Mansion	Manuscript Club	
3/26/89	Boston, Gardner Mansion	Manuscript Club	
4/11/89	Chicago, Methodist Church Block	American Conservatory of Music	
4/22/89	Detroit Conservatory of Music	American Composers' Series: Arthur Foote (cham)	
5/7–9/89	Mt. Pleasant, IA	Iowa MTA (Iowa Composers' Concert) (misc)	
6/3/89	Minneapolis	Gounod Club	Charles H. Morse, conductor
6/26/89	Peoria	IMTA (misc)	Illinois Composers' Concert
6/27/89 (*a.m.*)	Cleveland, Case Hall	OMTA (Ohio Composers' Concert) (misc)	
6/27/89 (*p.m.*)	Cleveland, Case Hall	OMTA (American Composers' Concert) (p)	Lavallée, pianist
7/4/89	Philadelphia, Academy of Music	MTNA "Grand Concert of American and Miscellaneous Works" (only one American composer)	
7/5/89	Philadelphia, Academy of Music	MTNA (chor/orch)	Van der Stucken
7/12/89	Paris, Exposition Universelle	Exposition Orchestra (orch)	
7/30/89	Chicago, Exposition Building	Summer Night Concerts (orch)	Thomas
2/90	New York	(org)	William C. Carl
2/18/90	Chicago, Weber Hall	American Conservatory of Music (misc)	
3/26/90	Washington, DC, Lincoln Hall	National Conservatory of Music (orch)	Van der Stucken

Date	Location	Ensemble/Work	Conductor/Performer
3/26/90	Boston	(cham)	Arthur Whiting and the Kneisel Quartet
7/1/90	Detroit	MTNA (misc)	various artists
7/2/90	Detroit	MTNA (orch)	Thomas
7/3/90	Detroit	MTNA (cham)	various chamber artists
7/3/90	Detroit	MTNA (orch)	Thomas
7/4/90	Detroit	MTNA (orch)	Thomas
11/24/90	New York	ACCA (chor)	Emilio Agramonte, conductor
12/10/90	New York, Chickering Hall	MSNY (orch)	
1/29/91	New York, Chickering Hall	Orpheus Club (chor/orch)	Arthur Mees, conductor
2/4/91	New York, Chickering Hall	MSNY (cham/v)	
2/12/91	New York	ACCA (chor)	
2/16/91	Orange, NJ	Mendelssohn Union (chor)	Mees
2/26/91	Albany, New York	Schubert Club (chor)	Mees
3/2/91	Brooklyn Academy	(orch)	Mortimer Wiske, conductor
4/6/91	Berlin Konzerthaus	Meyder Orchestra (orch)	F. X. Arens, conductor
4/10/91	New York, Metropolitan Opera House	*New York Tribune* (orch)	Walter Damrosch, conductor
4/11/91	Dresden Gewerbehaus	Trenkler Orchestra (orch)	Arens
4/14/91	Utica, NY	Utica Conservatory of Music	student composers' recital
4/15/91	New York, Chickering Hall	MSNY (orch/v)	
4/18/91	Hamburg Konzerthaus	Laube Orchestra (orch)	Arens
4/20/91	Chicago, Chickering Hall	American Conservatory of Music (misc)	
4/25/91	New York	ACCA (chor)	
4/29/91	San Francisco	Loring Club (chor)	Loring
5/2/91	New York, Madison Square Garden	"Allegory of the War in Song" (chor/orch)	S. G. Pratt, conductor
7/1/91	Jacksonville, IL	IMTA (misc)	Illinois Composers' Concert
7/5/91	Sondershausen Loh Concerts	Hofkapelle (orch)	Arens
9/24/91	Worcester, MA	Worcester Festival (chor/orch)	Carl Zerrahn, conductor
ca. 9/91	Warsaw, NY	(p)	Clara E. Thoms, pianist
12/9/91	New York, Chickering Hall	MSNY (orch/v)	
1/14/92	New York, Chickering Hall	ACCA (chor)	
1/28/92	Chicago, Mason & Hamlin Hall	American Music Society	Agramonte

Date	Venue	Event	Conductor
1/30/92	Berlin Konzerthaus	Meyder Orchestra (orch)	Arens
2/11/92	Chicago, Mason & Hamlin Hall	American Music Society	
2/25/92	Chicago, Mason & Hamlin Hall	American Music Society, 13th meeting	
3/10/92	Chicago, Mason & Hamlin Hall	American Music Society, 14th meeting	
3/19/92	Dresden Gewerbehaus	Trenkler Orchestra (orch)	Arens
3/23/92	Weimar Tivoli	Hofkapelle (orch)	Arens
3/24/92	Chicago, Mason & Hamlin Hall	American Music Society, 15th meeting	
3/25/92	New York, Chickering Hall	MSNY (cham/v)	
4/7/92	Chicago, Mason & Hamlin Hall	American Music Society, 16th meeting	
4/8/92	Chicago Orchestral Association	(orch)	Thomas
4/9/92	Leipzig Altes Gewandhaus	134th Regimental Orchestra (orch)	Arens
4/19/92	Chicago, Chickering Hall	American Conservatory of Music (cham/v)	
4/21/92	Chicago, Mason & Hamlin Hall	American Music Society, 17th meeting	
4/27/92	New York, First Presbyterian Church	(org)	William C. Carl, organist
4/27/92	Chicago, Athenaeum Hall	National College of Music with the Orpheus Club	
4/28/92	New York, Chickering Hall	ACCA (chor)	Agramonte
4/30/92	New York, Chickering Hall	MSNY (orch)	
5/5/92	Chicago, Mason & Hamlin Hall	American Music Society, 18th meeting	
5/26/92	Chicago, Mason & Hamlin Hall	American Music Society, 19th meeting	
6/10/92	Chicago, Mason & Hamlin Hall	American Music Society, 20th meeting	
6/14/92	New York, Lenox Lyceum	Popular Summer Night Concerts (orch)	Neuendorff
6/28–30/92	Quincy, IL	IMTA (Illinois Composers' Concert) (misc)	
7/5/92	Vienna Exposition	Exposition Orchestra (orch)	Arens
7/6/92	Cleveland	MTNA (cham/v)	
7/7/92	Cleveland	MTNA (cham/v)	
7/8/92	Cleveland	MTNA (cham/v)	
12/9/92	Lincoln, NE	Lincoln Oratorio Society (chor)	Mrs. P. V. M. Raymond
12/13/92	New York, Chickering Hall	MSNY (orch/v)	
12/16/92	Chicago, Mason & Hamlin Hall	American Music Society, 21st meeting	

Date	Venue	Event	Conductor/Notes
12/28/92	Reading, PA	Pennsylvania MTA (chor/orch)	
1/5/93	Chicago, Mason & Hamlin Hall	American Music Society, 22nd meeting	
1/19/93	Chicago, Mason & Hamlin Hall	American Music Society, 23rd meeting	
2/2/93	Chicago, Mason & Hamlin Hall	American Music Society, 24th meeting	
2/8/93	New York, Chickering Hall	MSNY (cham/v)	
2/17/93	Chicago, Mason & Hamlin Hall	American Music Society, 25th meeting	
3/2/93	Chicago, Mason & Hamlin Hall	American Music Society, 26th meeting	
3/16/93	Chicago, Mason & Hamlin Hall	American Music Society, 27th meeting	
3/23/93	Leavenworth, KS	Lotus Glee Club of Boston (chor/v)	
3/30/93	Chicago, Mason & Hamlin Hall	American Music Society, 28th meeting	
3/30/93	New York, Madison Square Garden	National Conservatory of Music (orch)	Seidl, conductor
4/13/93	Chicago, Mason & Hamlin Hall	American Music Society, 29th meeting	
4/25/93	Chicago, Chickering Hall	American Conservatory of Music (misc)	
4/27/93	Chicago, Mason & Hamlin Hall	American Music Society, 30th meeting	
5/8/93	New York	National Conservatory of Music	Dvořák's composition students
5/?/93	Mansfield, OH	Mansfield May Festival, American Day	W. H. Pontius, conductor
5/5/93	New York, Chickering Hall	MSNY & ACCA (orch/chor)	
5/11/93	Chicago, Mason & Hamlin Hall	American Music Society, 31st meeting	
5/17/93	Philadelphia	Manuscript Music Society (MMS)	
5/23/93	Chicago, Columbian Exposition	Exposition Orchestra (orch)	Mees
5/24/93	Chicago, Columbian Exposition	Kneisel Quartet (cham)	
5/25/93	Chicago, Mason & Hamlin Hall	American Music Society, 32nd meeting	
6/8/93	Chicago, Mason & Hamlin Hall	American Music Society, 33rd meeting	
6/28/93	Chicago, Mason & Hamlin Hall	American Music Society, 34th meeting	
7/6/93	Chicago, Columbian Exposition	Exposition Orchestra (orch)	Thomas
7/7/93	Chicago, Columbian Exposition	Exposition Orchestra (orch)	Thomas
8/4/93	Chicago, Columbian Exposition	Exposition Orchestra (orch)	Thomas
8/14 & 15/93	Chicago, Columbian Exposition	Old Stoughton (MA) Musical Society (chor)	Leander Soule, conductor
8/25/93	Chicago, Columbian Exposition	Colored Americans' Day Concert (misc)	
Summer 93?	Antwerp	Royal Society	Van der Stucken
9/20/93	Chicago, Columbian Exposition	(org)	Harrison Wild, organist

179

Appendix 1 continued

Date	Location	Event	Performers
10/9/93	Chicago, Columbian Exposition	(org)	Frank Taft, organist
10/28/93	Chicago, Columbian Exposition	concert of Chicago Composers	S. G. Pratt, conductor
12/12/93	New York, Chickering Hall	MSNY (orch)	Walter Damrosch
2/13/94	New York, Chickering Hall	MSNY (cham)	Beethoven Quartet
3/14/94	New York, Chickering Hall	MSNY (orch)	Walter Damrosch
5/16/94	Philadelphia	MMS	
6/1/94	Minneapolis	Ladies' Thursday Musicale Club (misc)	
6/27/94	Ottawa, IL	IMTA (Illinois Composers' concert)	
6/28/94	Buffalo, NY	NYMTA (cham)	A. Foote, Anne Wilson, Dora Becker
7/4/94	Antwerp Exposition	(chor/orch)	Pratt
12/12/94	New York, Chickering Hall	MSNY (orch)	Seidl, conductor
1/29/95	New York, Chickering Hall	MSNY (cham)	Beethoven Quartet
3/20/95	Philadelphia, Church of the New Jerusalem	MMS	
5/2/95	New York, Chickering Hall	MSNY (orch)	Seidl
5/14/95	Philadelphia, Academy of Music	MMS	
5/27/95	New York, South Church	200th free recital (manuscript comps) (org)	Gerrit Smith, organist
6/24/95	Chicago, Auditorium Recital Hall	Chicago Conservatory of Music	Frederic Grant Gleason's composition students
6/26/95	Bloomington, IL	IMTA	Illinois Composers' Concert
8/27/95	Manhattan Beach	MSNY (band)	John Philip Sousa, conductor
10/24/95	New York, Chickering Hall	MSNY (orch)	Neuendorff
12/5/95	New York, Chickering Hall	MSNY (cham)	Dannreuther Quartet
2/13/96	New York, Chickering Hall	MSNY (orch/v)	
2/23/96	Milwaukee	MSNY (orch/v)	
4/16/96	New York, Chickering Hall	MSNY (orch/v)	
4/22/96	Philadelphia, Church of the New Jerusalem	MMS	
6/3/96	Chicago, Kent Theater	"Illustrated Address on American Music"	Gleason
7/4/96	Chicago Coliseum	Two George Root Memorial Concerts	

Date	Location	Organization	Notes
11/29/96	Chicago, Unity Church	Organ concert of works by MSC members (org)	Harrison M. Wild, organist
12/1/96	New York, Mendelssohn Glee Club Hall	Aguilar Free Library Book Fund (misc)	
12/3/96	New York, Chickering Hall	MSNY (orch/v)	Pratt
12/10/96	Chicago, Summy's Recital Hall	MSC	
1/21/97	Chicago, Masonic Hall	The Klio Association	
2/9/97	New York, Mendelssohn Glee Club Hall	(misc)	Kate Percy Douglass, vocalist
2/11/97	New York, Chickering Hall	MSNY (orch/v)	Pratt
3/17/97	Chicago, Summy's Recital Hall	MSC	
3/20/97	New York, Mendelssohn Glee Club Hall		Douglass
3/22/97	Chicago, Steinway Hall	Amateur Musical Club (in honor of MSC)	
3/24/97	Philadelphia, Swedenborgian Church	MMS	
4/5/97	Chicago, Steinway Hall	Amateur Musical Club	Chicago women composers
4/22/97	New York, Chickering Hall	MSNY (orch/v)	Pratt
4/23/97	New York, Mendelssohn Glee Club Hall		Douglass
5/13/97	Philadelphia, Musical Fund Hall		
10/28/97	Chicago, Handel Hall Parlors	MMS	
11/5/97	Fort Wayne, IN	MSC	
12/9/97	Chicago, Handel Hall Parlors	Morning Musical Club	
12/15/97	New York, Chickering Hall	MSC	Seidl
1/21/98	Chicago, Steinway Hall	MSNY (orch)	Seidl
2/9/98	New York, Chickering Hall	MSC	Seidl
2/28/98	Chicago, Steinway Hall	MSNY (orch)	Chicago composers
3/3/98	Chicago, Handel Hall Parlors	Amateur Musical Club	
3/23/98	Philadelphia, Church of the New Jerusalem	MSC	
4/11/98	New York, Carnegie Hall	MMS	Seidl
4/21/98	Chicago, Steinway Hall	MSNY (orch/chor)	
5/9/98	Chicago, Kimball Hall	MSC	Ragna Linné
5/16/98	Philadelphia, Witherspoon Auditorium	Song Recital of American Composers (v)	
6/29/98	Chicago, Handel Hall	MMS	
12/1/98	Chicago, Fine Arts Building	IMTA/MSC	
12/3/98	Pittsburgh, Adolph M. Foerster studio	MSC	Julia Gibansky, pianist
		(p, v)	Amanda Vierheller, soprano

Date	Location	Organization/Event	Performer
12/22/98	New York, Chickering Hall	MSNY (orch)	Arens
1/5/99	Chicago, Fine Arts Building	MSC	Mrs. T. Carl Whitmer
1/26/99	Harrisburg, PA,	Pine Street Presbyterian Church (org)	
3/2/99	Chicago, Fine Arts Building	MSC	
3/22/99	Boston?	Lecture-Recital on American Composers (p, v)	Mr. and Mrs. Frank Lynes
3/29/99	Minneapolis, Plymouth Church	Ladies' Thursday Musicale Club	Minneapolis composers' concert
4/6/99	Chicago, Fine Arts Building	MSC	
4/8/99	Chicago	American Conservatory of Music	Adolf Weidig's composition students
4/11/99	New York, Chickering Hall	MSNY (misc)	Walter Keller, organist
6/21/99	Cincinnati, Odeon	MTNA (org)	various chamber artists
6/21/99	Cincinnati, Odeon	MTNA (cham)	Van der Stucken, conductor
6/21/99	Cincinnati, Music Hall	MTNA (orch)	Lillian Arkell Rixford
6/22/99	Cincinnati, Music Hall	MTNA (org)	various chamber artists
6/22/99	Cincinnati	MTNA (cham)	Van der Stucken, conductor
6/22/99	Cincinnati, Music Hall	MTNA (orch)	Charles Galloway, organist
6/23/99	Cincinnati, Music Hall	MTNA (org)	Van der Stucken, conductor
6/23/99	Cincinnati, Music Hall	MTNA (orch)	Adolf Weidig's composition students
5/5/00	Chicago, Kimball Hall	American Conservatory of Music	
4/7/00	New York, "Old First" Presbyterian Church	Gamut Club (chor)	W. W. Gilchrist, conductor
5/9/00	Philadelphia	Mendelssohn Club (chor)	Frank Damrosch, conductor
1/19/01	New York, Mendelssohn Hall	MSNY (orch)	

⤬ **Appendix 2** ⤬

Frank Van der Stucken's American Festival, November 1887

On the following pages are the programs of the five concerts presented by Frank Van der Stucken in Chickering Hall, New York, in November 1887. Following each program is a list of reviews of the concert arranged in chronological order according to publication date.

First American Concert
Tuesday, November 15, 1887, Chickering Hall, 8 *p.m.*

"Spring" Symphony   Paine

Air for baritone from *The Tale of the Viking*   George E. Whiting
                     Carl E. Dufft, baritone

Rhapsody for pianoforte and orchestra   Henry Holden Huss
                     Henry Holden Huss, piano

Pastoral for soprano solo, chorus, and orchestra   L. A. Russell
                     Ella Earle, soprano
            Schubert Vocal Society of Newark, NJ
                 conducted by the composer

Symphonic Poem: *Hamlet*   E. A. MacDowell

Dance of the Egyptian Maidens   Harry Rowe Shelley

REVIEWS

"First American Concert." *New York Tribune*, November 16, 1887, p. 4.

"Music by Americans." *NYT*, November 16, 1887, p. 5.

"Mr. Van der Stucken's American Concerts." *New York Sun*, November 16, 1887, p. 2.

"Mr. Van der Stucken's Concert," *New York World*, November 16, 1887, p. 2.

"Van der Stucken's Concert." *New York Evening Post*, November 16, 1887, p. 6.

"First Night with American Composers." *AAJ* 48/5 (November 19, 1887): 68.

"Chickering Hall. The First American Concert." *Freund's Music and Drama* 9/3 (November 19, 1887): 4.

"Van der Stucken-Koncert." *N. Y. Figaro* 7/47 (November 20, 1887): 4.

"The American Concerts." *MC* 15/21 (November 23, 1887): 339.

Krehbiel, Henry E. *Review of the New York Musical Season, 1887/88* (New York and London: Novello, Ewer, & Co.), pp. 29–30.

Second American Concert
Thursday, November 17, 1887, Chickering Hall, 8 *p.m.*

In the Mountains	Arthur Foote
Pianoforte Concerto in D minor Arthur Whiting, pianoforte	Arthur Whiting
Arioso from *Montezuma* Corinne Moore-Lawson	Frederic Grant Gleason
"Scherzo" from Symphony in A	Arthur Bird
Rêverie for strings	Silas G. Pratt
Royal Gaelic March	Edgar S. Kelley
Cantata: *The Voyage of Columbus* H. S. Brown, Stuart Colville, J. T. Drill, H. F. Reddall, soloists Apollo Club of Brooklyn conducted by the composer	Dudley Buck

REVIEWS

"American Composers' Works." *New York Herald*, November 18, 1887, p. 4.
"The American Concerts." *NYT*, November 18, 1887, p. 4.
"Second 'American' Concert." *New York Sun*, November 18, 1887, p. 3.
"Second American Concert." *New York Tribune*, November 18, 1887, p. 4.
"Yesterday's Concerts." *New York Evening Post*, November 18, 1887, p. 5.
"The American Concerts." *MC* 15/21 (November 23, 1887): 339.
"Second American Concert." *AAJ* 48/6 (November 26, 1887): 84.

Third American Concert
Saturday, November 19, 1887, Chickering Hall

Triumphal March	Dudley Buck
Fugue in A minor	Eugene Thayer

Frank G. Dossert, organist

"Moonlight"	Frank Van der Stucken
"Early Love"	

Marie Gramm, vocalist

Scherzo	William Mason
Loreley	Edward B. Perry
Medea	William H. Sherwood

William H. Sherwood, pianist

Madrigal: "Fair Daffodils"	Samuel P. Warren

Choir of St. Stephen's Church

Scherzo	Edgar S. Kelley
Tarantelle	Edmund S. Mattoon

Edgar S. Kelley and William H. Sherwood, pianists

"Sweet Wind that Blows"	G. W. Chadwick
"She Loves Me"	

Frederick Jameson, vocalist

Mazourka	F. Dewey
Gavotte	Wilson G. Smith
Polonaise	William H. Dayas

William H. Sherwood, pianist

Festival Magnificat	W. W. Gilchrist

St. Stephen's Choir

REVIEWS

"The American Concerts." *NYT*, November 20, 1887, p. 2.
"Another 'American' Concert." *New York Sun*, November 20, 1887, p. 2.
"Third American Concert." *New York Herald*, November 20, 1887, p. 11.
"Third American Concert." *New York Tribune*, November 20, 1887, p. 4.
"The American Concerts." *MC* 15/21 (November 23, 1887): 339.
"Third American Concert." *AAJ* 48/6 (November 26, 1887): 85.

Fourth American Concert
Tuesday, November 22, 1887, Chickering Hall

String Quartet in D major   G. W. Chadwick
      G. Dannreuther, E. Thiele, O. Schill, Adolf Hartdegen

"Love Song"   Willard Burr
"I Saw Thee Weep"   Hermann Rietzel
               Effie Stewart, vocalist

Sonata for pianoforte and violin   John Knowles Paine
          G. Dannreuther, violinist
        William H. Sherwood, pianist

"When I Dream of Thee"   Edgar H. Sherwood
"Milkmaid's Song"   Arthur Foote
               Effie Stewart, vocalist

Sextet in D minor   Johann Beck
      the quartet, J. Lendner, and C. Hemman

REVIEWS

"American Chamber Music." *New York Tribune*, November 23, 1887, p. 4.
"The American Concerts." *NYT*, November 23, p. 5.
"Fourth American Concert." *AAJ* 48/6 (November 26, 1887): 85.
"The American Concerts." *MC* 15/22 (November 30, 1887): 355.
Krehbiel, *Review 1887/88*, 36–37.

Fifth American Concert
Thursday, November 24, 1887, Chickering Hall

First Symphony in F major   G. Templeton Strong
"In the Afternoon"
Adagio: "In the Gloaming"
Allegro: "At Midnight—the Wild Hunt"
Allegro Molto: "In the Morn"

Cantata: *King Trojan*   H. W. Parker
Henrietta Beebe Lawton, Charlotte Walker, Hattie J. Clapper,
Max Heinrich, Frederick Jameson, and J. Allen Preisch, soloists

"Carnival" from Suite in F   Ernest Guiraud

REVIEWS

"Chickering Hall," *NYT*, November 25, 1887, p. 4.
"End of the American Series." *New York Sun*, November 25, 1887, p. 2.
"The Last American Concert." *New York Herald*, November 25, 1887, p. 10.
"The Last American Concert." *New York Tribune*, November 25, 1887, p. 5.
"The American Concerts." *Freund's Music and Drama* 9/4 (November 26, 1887): 5.
"Closing Concert of the American Composers' Series." *AAJ* 48/7 (November 26, 1887): 100.
"Die Amerikanischen Koncerte." *N.Y. Figaro* 7/47 (November 27, 1887): 4.
"The American Concerts." *MC* 15/22 (November 30, 1887): 355.
"News of the Month." *Etude* 5/12 (December 1887): 185.
Krehbiel, *Review 1887/88*, pp. 40–41.

⚭ Appendix 3 ⚭

Programs and Reviews of American Composers' Concerts in Europe

On the following pages are programs of the concerts presented by Frank Van der Stucken at the Exposition universelle in Paris in 1889 and by Franz Xavier Arens in Germany and Austria in 1891–1892. Following each program is a list of reviews of the concert arranged in chronological order according to publication date. Reviews of the Arens concerts also include bibliographic sigla that are used in the citation of these reviews in Chapter 8. Each siglum consists of a letter denoted the city and a number denoting the order of publication. For cities in which Arens presented two concerts, the sigla continue sequentially from the first concert to the second (i.e. B9 is the last review of the 1891 concert in Berlin, and B10 is the first review of the 1892 concert).

Paris, Trocadéro, July 12, 1889 (Van der Stucken)

Overture, *In the Mountains*, op. 14 — Arthur Foote

Second Piano Concerto in D minor, op. 23 — Edward MacDowell
Edward MacDowell, piano

"In Bygone Days" — George Whitefield Chadwick
"Milkmaid's Song" — Foote
"Where the Lindens Bloom" — Dudley Buck
Emma Sylvania, soprano

Orchestral suite, *La Tempête*, op. 8 — Frank Van der Stucken

intermission

Dramatic overture, *Melpomene* — Chadwick

Romanze et polonaise for violin and orchestra — Henry Holden Huss
Willis Nowell, violin

Prelude to *Oedipus Tyrannus*, op. 35 — John Knowles Paine

Carnival scene, op. 5 — Arthur Bird

"Moonlight" — Van der Stucken
"Ojala" — Margaret Ruthven Lang
"Early Love" — Van der Stucken
Maude Starvetta, mezzo-soprano

Festival overture on *The Star-Spangled Banner* — Buck

REVIEWS

"American Music: Audition at the Trocadéro of Works by United States Composers." *The New York Herald* (Paris edition), July 13, 1889, p. 1.

Jean de la Tour. "L'Exposition: Chronique du Champs de Mars." *Le Petit Journal*, July 14, 1889, p. 1.

Landely, A. "Concert américain." *L'Art musical* 28/13 (July 15, 1889): 100.

Fracasse [Stoullig, Edmond]. "Courrier des théâtres." *Le National*, July 15–16, 1889, p. 3.

Weber, Johannès. "Critique musicale." *Le Temps*, July 15–16, 1889, supplement, p. 1.

Wilder, Victor. "La Musique américaine au Trocadéro." *Gil Blas*, July 16, 1889, p. 3.

Darcours, Charles [Réty]. "Note de musique: À l'Exposition." *Le Figaro*, July 17, 1889, p. 6; reprinted as "La Musique à l'Exposition." *La Revue théâtrale illustrée* 21/15 (1889): 3; translated as "Van der Stucken in Paris." *American Musician* 14/5 (August 3, 1889): 7.

Balleyguier, Delphin. "La musique à l'Exposition: Concert américain." *Le Progrès artistique* 12/582 (July 20, 1889): 1.

Blois, Andre. "Concert américain." *Art et Critique* 1/8 (July 20, 1889): 121.

Boisard, A[uguste]. "Chronique musicale." *Le Monde illustré* 33/1686 (July 20, 1889): 43.

Flamen. "La Musique à l'Exposition." *La Musique des familles (Musique populaire)* 8/405 (July 20, 1889): 314.

Tiersot, Julien. "Promenades musicales à l'Exposition." *Le Ménestrel* 55/29 (July 21, 1889): 227-29; reprinted in *Musiques pittoresques: Promenades musicales a l'Exposition de 1889*. Paris: Librairie Fischbacher, 1889, p. 55.

Torchet, Julien. "Concert de musique américaine au Trocadéro." *Le Monde artiste* 29/29 (July 21, 1889): 449-50.

L. K. "American Music in Paris." *New York Times*, July 28, 1889, p. 9.

Duvernoy, Alphonse. "Revue musicale." *La République française*, July 29, 1889, p. 3.

Jullien, Adolphe. "Revue musicale." *Le Moniteur universel*, July 29, 1889, p. 818.

Brument-Colleville. "Le Concert américain au Trocadéro." *Le Monde musical* 1/6 (July 30, 1889): 7-8.

Floersheim, Otto. "The American Concert at the Trocadero, Paris." *The Musical Courier* 19/5 (July 31, 1889): 107-08.

Bruneau, Alfred. "Musique." *La Revue indépendente* 12/34 (August 1889): 203–11.

Gallet, Louis. "Chronique du théatre: Musique." *La Nouvelle Revue* 11/59 (August 15, 1889): 821.

Berlin Konzerthaus (Meyder Orchestra)
April 6, 1891 (Arens)

Macbeth	Edgar Stillman Kelley
Marsch	

Scène orientale and Intermezzo	Arthur Bird

Sinfonische Fantasie	Franz Xavier Arens

In den Bergen (In the Mountains)	Arthur Foote

Rêverie pastorale	Carl Busch

Am Bach
Ein Sommerabend im Walde
Rundtanz

Romeo and Juliet Suite	Otis Bardwell Boise

Ballscene
Balkonscene

Serenade for string orchestra, op. 12	Victor Herbert

3. Intermezzo
4. Polonaise

Musik zu Shakespeare's "Sturm"	Frank Van der Stucken

REVIEWS

B1   n. "Im Konzerthause." *Königlich priviligirte Berlinische [Vossische] Zeitung* 160 (April 7, 1891, evening edition): 3.

B2   L. B. "Musik." *National-Zeitung* 44/212 (April 7, 1891, evening edition): 1.

B3   Blanck, Wilhelm. "Konzert." *Berliner Fremdenblatt* 81 (April 8, 1891): 2.

B4   "Im Konzerthause." *Berliner Tageblatt* 20/175 (April 8, 1891): 2:2.

B5   "Musik." *Der Reichsbote* 19/81 (April 8, 1891): 2:2.

B6   Homann, Karl. "Theater und Musik." *Tägliche Rundschau* 81 (April 8, 1891): 323-24.

B7   *Berliner Morgen-Zeitung und Tägliches Familienblatt* 3/82 (April 9, 1891): 3.

B8   Horwitz, B. *Neue Berliner Musik-Zeitung* 45/15 (April 9, 1891): 136.

B9   Lessmann, Otto. "Aus dem Konzertsaal." *Allgemeine Musik-Zeitung* 18/15 (April 10, 1891): 195.

Dresden Gewerbehaus (Trenkler Orchestra)
April 11, 1891 (Arens)

In the Mountains	Foote
Symphonic Scherzo	Johann Beck
Serenade, op. 12	Herbert

Liebesscene
Canzonetta
Finale

Romeo and Juliet Suite	Boise

Ballscene

Symphonische Fantasie "Aus meines Lebens Frühlingszeit"	Arens
Rêverie Pastoral	Busch

Am Bach
Ein Sommerabend im Walde
Rundtanz

Musik zu Shakespeare's "Sturm"	Van der Stucken

Tanz der Nymphen
Tanz der Schnitter
Chase infernale

REVIEWS

D1   v. "Konzert." *Dresdner Journal* 83 (April 13, 1891): 569.
D2   Starcke, Hermann. "Kunst und Wissenschaft." *Dresdner Nachrichten* (April 13, 1891): 2.
D3   F. G. "Konzert der Gewerbehauskapelle." *Dresdner Anzeiger* (April 14, 1891): 23.
D4   "Vermischtes." *Neue Zeitschrift für Musik* 16 (April 22, 1891): 187 [reprint of *Dresdner Nachrichten* advance notice of the concert, with verb tenses altered to make it sound like a review].
D5   *Neue Zeitschrift für Musik* 20 (May 20, 1891): 234 [reprint of F. G.].

Hamburg, Konzerthaus Ludwig (Laube Orchestra)
April 18, 1891 (Arens)

"Balkon-scene" from Romeo and Juliet Suite   Boise

Symphonische Fantasie "Aus meines Lebens Frühlingszeit"   Arens

Romanze and Polonaise   Henry Holden Huss
               Concertmaster Piening, violin soloist

Ouverture to *Die Schmetterlinge*   Carl Kölling
               conducted by the composer

Symphonic Scherzo   Beck

Prelude to *Otho Visconti*   Frederick Grant Gleason

Serenade, op. 12   Herbert

Musik zu Shakespeare's "Sturm"   Van der Stucken

REVIEW

H1   "Theater, Kunst und Wissenschaft." *Hamburgischer Correspondent*
        275 (April 20, 1891, evening edition): 2.

Sondershausen Loh Concerts (Court Orchestra)
July 5, 1891 (Arens)

Fest-Ouverture   Boise

Serenade für Streichorchester   Herbert

Carneval-Scene   Bird

Symphonische Fantasie "Aus meines Lebens Frühlingszeit"   Arens

Rêverie pastorale   Busch

Musik zu Shakespeare's "Sturm"   Van der Stucken

REVIEW

S1   "Sondershausen." *Regierungs- und Nachrichtenblatt für das Fürsten-*
        tum Schwarzburg-Sondershausen 81 (July 7, 1891), 322.

Berlin Konzerthaus (Meyder Orchestra)
January 30, 1892 (Arens)

Dramatische Ouverture "Melpomene"	George W. Chadwick
"If Thou Wert with Me"	Reginald De Koven
"Herbstgefühl"	Ethelbert Nevin
"Raft Song"	Nevin

William Osborne Goodrich, baritone
Anna Gray, piano

Symphonie, op. 34: "Im Frühling"	John Knowles Paine
Suite für grosses Orchester, op. 42	Edward A. MacDowell
"Thou'rt like a Flower"	Wilson G. Smith
"Sendung" [Mission]	Arens

William Osborne Goodrich, baritone
Anna Gray, piano

Fest-Ouverture	Boise

REVIEWS

B10   H. E. [Heinrich Ehrlich].   "Amerikanisches Komponisten-Konzert."
       Berliner Tageblatt 21/57 (February 1, 1892, evening edition): 2-3.
       See also corrections in 21/59 (February 2, 1892), 3.

B11   Blanck, Wilhelm. "Konzert." *Berliner Fremdenblatt* 27 (February 2,
       1892): 2:2-3.

B12   tz. "Konzerte." *Berliner Volks-Zeitung* 40/27 (February 2, 1892): 1.

B13   n. *Königlich priviligirte Berlinische [Vossische] Zeitung* 53 (February
       2, 1892): 5.

B14   L. B. "Kunst, Wissenschaft und Literatur." *National-Zeitung* 45/69
       (February 2, 1892, morning edition): 2:3.

B15   "Berliner Nachrichten." *Signale für die musikalische Welt* 50/11
       (February 1892): 168.

B16   Roth, Philipp. "Berlin letter: The American Composers' Concert
       (Berlin, January 31, 1892)." *Musical Courier* 24/7 (February 17,
       1892), 9.

B17   "Ein amerikanischer Komponistenabend in Berlin." *N. Y. Figaro* 12/8
       (February 20, 1892): 14.

Dresden Gewerbehaus (Trenkler Orchestra)
March 19, 1892 (Arens)

Prelude to *Otho Visconti*   Gleason

Serenade for String Orchestra   Chadwick
          I. Allegro Grazioso
          IV. Finale

Symphonie, Op. 34 "Im Frühling"   Paine
          I. Winters Abschied
          II. Eine Maiennacht-Phantasie
          IV. Die Herrlichkeit der Natur

  Dramatische Ouverture "Melpomene"   Chadwick

Suite charactéristique, op. 15   Henry Schoenefeld
          a. Tempo di Menuetto
          b. Marcio-Fantastico

Suite für grosses Orchester, op. 42   MacDowell
          In einem verwunschenem Walde
          Lied der Hirtin
          Waldgeister

REVIEWS

D6   N. F. "Konzert." *Dresdner Anzeiger* 162/81 (March 21, 1892): 4.
D7   v. "Konzerte." *Dresdner Journal* 66 (March 21, 1892): 470.
D8   "Kunst und Wissenschaft." *Dresdner Nachrichten* 37/81 (March 21, 1892): 2.
D9   "Dresden, den 19. März. 'American Composers' Concert'." *Leipziger Musikzeitung* 2/4 (April 1, 1892): 28.
D10   Ingman, A. "Dresden Letter (Dresden, March 20, 1892)." *Musical Courier* 24/15 (April 13, 1892), 8.
D11   *English and American Register*, cited in *American Art Journal* 59/5 (May 14, 1892): 145 [no extant copies known].

Weimar, Tivoli (Court Orchestra), March 23, 1892 (Arens)

Suite für Streichorchester		Foote
	Gavotte	
Ouverture "Melpomene"		Chadwick
Liebesscene		Herbert
Suite charactéristique, op. 15		Schoenefeld
	Marsch	
Symphonie, op. 34 "Im Frühling"		Paine
	Scherzo	
	Allegro giocoso (Finale)	
	intermission	
Ouverture		Arens
Ägyptischer Tanz, op. 42		Harry Rowe Shelley
Suite für grosses Orchester, op. 42		MacDowell
	In einem verwunschenen Walde	
	Hirtenlied	
	Waldgeister	

REVIEWS

W1   r. "Kunst und Wissenschaft." *Deutschland* 44/100 (March 27, 1892): 3:1.

W2   w. "Konzerte." *Weimarische Zeitung* 76 (March 30, 1892): 1.

W3   G[ottschalg, Alexander Wilhelm].   "Offener Brief an unsern 'neuweltlichen' Redakteur Herrn Leo Kofler in New-York." *Der Chorgesang* 7/15 (May 1, 1892): 342-43.

W4   Gottschalg, A. W.   "American Composers' Concert at Weimar." *English and American Register*;   reprint *American Art Journal* 59/8 (June 4, 1892): 211.

Leipzig Altes Gewandhaus (134th Regimental Orchestra) April 9, 1892 (Arens)

Prelude to *Otho Visconti*   Gleason

Symphonie, op. 34 "Im Frühling" Paine
        Winters Abschied—Erwachen der Natur
        Mainacht-Fantasie

Rêverie pastorale, op. 15   Busch
        Am Bach
        Rundtanz

Symphonische Fantasie "Aus meines Lebens Frühlingszeit"   Arens

Dramatische Ouverture "Melpomene"   Chadwick

Suite, op. 25   Foote
        Gavotte

Serenade, op. 12   Herbert
        Liebesscene

Suite charactéristique   Schoenefeld
        Marcia fantastica

Suite für grosses Orchester, op. 42   MacDowell
        In einem verwunschenen Walde
        Lied der Hirtin
        Waldgeister

REVIEWS

L1   Vogel, Bernhard. "American Composers' Concert am 9. April 1892." *Leipziger Nachrichten* 32/102 (April 11, 1892): 2.

L2   *Leipziger Zeitung* (11 Apr 1892), cited in *The Musical Courier* 25/6 (August 10, 1892): 8 [no extant copies known].

L3   Pfohl, F[erdinand]. "Concert im Alten Gewandhaus." *Leipziger Tageblatt und Anzeiger* 187 (April 12, 1892): 2541.

L4   *Anglo-American* [Berlin], (17 Apr 1892), cited in *The Musical Courier* 25/6 (August 10, 1892): 8 [no extant copies known].

L5   Schucht, J. "Concertaufführungen in Leipzig." *Neue Zeitschrift für Musik* 88/16 (20 Apr 1892): 184.

L6   o. "Leipzig." *Musikalisches Wochenblatt* 23/17 (April 21, 1892): 216.

L7   Simon, Paul. "Amerikanische Componisten in Leipzig." *Neue Zeitschrift für Musik* 88/17 (April 27, 1892): 191.

L8   Vogel, Bernhard. "Leipzig." *Neue Musikzeitung* 13/10 (1892): 115.

L9   [Michaelis, Alfred]. "Leipzig, d. 9. April: American Composers' Concert." *Leipziger Musikzeitung* 2/5 (May 1, 1892): 37.

L10   Calculus. "Leipzig." *Der Chorgesang* 7/16 (May 15, 1892): 374-75.

L11   "Letter from Leipzig." *Monthly Musical Record* (June 1, 1892): 127.

L12   Simon, Dr. Paul. "American Composers' Concert." *Leipziger General-Anzeiger*, April 12, 1892, 1039-40.

Vienna Musical and Theatrical Exhibition (Exhibition Orchestra), July 5, 1892 (Arens)

Prelude to Act II of *Vlasda*, op. 9   Van der Stucken

Symphonie, op. 34 "Im Frühling"   Paine
          Abschied des Winters--Erwachen der Natur
          Mainachts-Phantasie

Suite, op. 42   MacDowell
          In einem verwunschenen Wald
          Gesang der Hirtin
          Waldgeister

Overture, "Melpomene"   Chadwick

Carnival Scene, op. 5   Bird

Three movements for string orchestra
          Gavotte   Foote
          Love Scene   Herbert
          "Marcia Fantastica"   Schoenefeld

Symphonische Fantasia, op. 12   Arens

REVIEWS

V1   h-m. [Theodor Helm]. "Amerikanische Componisten in Wien." *Deutsche Zeitung* [Vienna] 7370 (July 6, 1892, morning edition): 6.

V2   "Amerikanische Componisten in der Tonhalle." *Illustriertes Wiener Extrablatt* 21/186 (July 6, 1892): 4.

V3   rbt. [Bricht Balduin]. "Internationale Musik- und Theater-Ausstellung." *Oesterreichische Volks-Zeitung* 38/186 (July 6, 1892): 3.

V4   r. h. [Robert Hirschfeld]. "Concert." *Die Presse* [Vienna] 45/186 (July 6, 1892), 9; 45/189 (July 9, 1892): 1-2.

V5   "Internationale Musik- und Theater-Ausstellung." *Wiener Fremdenblatt* 46/186 (July 6, 1892, evening edition): 2.

V6   R. Hr. [Richard Heuberger]. "Von der Ausstellung: Amerikanische Komponisten." *Wiener Tagblatt* 42/186 (July 6, 1892), 5; 42/187 (July 7, 1892): 4.

V7   G. Ar. "Amerikanisches Concert." *Neue Freie Presse* 10,010 (July 7, 1892, morning edition): 7.

V8   dr. h. p. [Hans Paumgartner]. "Aufführung von Werken amerikanischer Componisten." *Wiener Zeitung* 154 (July 7, 1892): 2-3.

V9   K. Anders [Albert Kauders]. "American Composers' Concert." *Wiener Allgemeine Zeitung* 4272 (July 8, 1892): 7.

V10 E. "American Composers Concert." *Deutsche Kunst und Musikzeitung* 19/20 (July 10, 1892): 184-185.

V11 a. *Wiener Extrapost* 11/547 (11 July 1892): 6.

V12 "Amerikanisches Konzert." *Neues Wiener Tagblatt* 26/191 (July 11, 1892): 3.

V13 h. w. "Musik- und Theater-Ausstellung." *Wiener Sonn- und Montags-Zeitung* 30/28 (July 11, 1892): 5.

V14 Graf, Max. "Amerikanische Componisten." *Musikalische Rundschau* 7/19 (July 15, 1892): 161-62.

V15 H. P. [Hans Puchstein]. "Ausstellungsconcerte." *Deutsches Volksblatt* [Vienna] 4/1272 (July 19, 1892, morning edition): 1-2.

V16 Stolzing, Josef. "Concerte in der Tonhalle." *Ostdeutsche Rundschau* 3/30 (July 24, 1892): 6.

V17 Dietz, Max. "Ausstellungskonzerte." *Allgemeine Kunst-Chronik* 16/14 (July 1892): 367.

V18 F. W. [Felix von Wartenegg]. "Musik-Ausstellungs-Concerte." *Neue Zeitschrift für Musik* 35 (August 31, 1892): 396-97.

V19 Helm, Theodor, ed. "Die Wiener Musik- und Theaterausstellung." In *Fromme's musikalische Welt: Notiz-Kalender für das Jahr 1893*. 18. Jahrgang. Vienna: Carl Fromme, 1893. P. 42.

☙ Appendix 4 ☙

Repertoire Performed at Public Meetings of the Manuscript Society of New York, 1890–1901

Ambrose, Paul	"The Madrigal," four-part song (12/5/1895)
Andrews, Addison F.	"The Phantom Gondolier," male chorus (3/14/1894)
Arens, F. X.	Symphonic Fantaisie, "Life's Springtide," op. 12 (2/9/1898)
Aronson, Rudolph	*Oriental Dance* and *Polish Mazurka* (8/27/1895) *Pickaninny*, serenade for orchestra (12/3/1896)
Bartlett, Homer N.	"Thus Saith the Lord—The Finger of God," Recitativo and Aria (12/10/1890) "Ballade" and "Caprice de Concert" for piano (2/8/1893) "Khamsin," dramatic aria for tenor and orchestra (3/14/1894) "Caprice Espagnol" (8/27/1895) "Rêverie poetique" and "Etude de concert" for piano (12/5/1895) Violin Concerto, op. 109 (4/22/1897) Toccata for organ (4/11/1899)
Bassford, William K.	"Farewell My Own," selection from an opera (2/13/1896)

Beach, Mrs. H.H.A.   "Chanson d'Amour," song (2/8/1893)
                         Bal masque for orchestra (12/12/1893)
                         "Villanelle: Across the World I Speak to Thee,"
                             (1/29/1895)
                         "Ecstasy," song (8/27/1895)
                         Festival Jubilate Deo, op. 17 for grand chorus and
                             orchestra (4/11/1898)

Beck, Johann H.   Sextette for Strings (2/4/1891)

Becker, Charles   *Scenes from Luxemburg*: (1/19/1901)
                             "Promenade"
                             "Woodland's Whisperings"
                             "Dancing on the Green"

Becker, Gustav L.   *Festival March* for orchestra (4/22/1897)

Biedermann, E. J.   "Cradle Song" (5/5/1893)

Bird, Arthur   Two Episodes for orchestra: "Scène orientale" and
                             "Intermezzo e trio" (2/9/1898)

Brandeis, Frederick   Duo for tenor and bass with orchestral
                             accompaniment (4/30/1892)
                         "The Old Guitar" and "An Answer," songs
                             (2/8/1893)
                         Trio in G for piano, violin, and cello (1/29/1895)
                         "Fly not thus my Brow of Snow," song (4/22/1897)

Brewer, John Hyatt   "The Russian Lover," song (2/4/1891)
                         "Romanza" and "Danse Rustique" from sextet for
                             strings and flute (5/5/1893)

Bristow, George F.   *Jibbenainosay*, tone poem (12/12/1894)
                         The Great Republic, overture (8/27/1895)
                         Seventh Regiment March (8/27/1895)
                         Choral Symphony, "Niagara" (4/11/1898)

Broekhoven, John A.   *Suite Creole* (4/15/1891)

Brounoff, Platon   *The Angel*, cantata (2/13/1896)
                         Russia, festival overture (12/15/1897)

Busch, Carl   Prologue to *The Passing of Arthur*, op. 25
                             (4/11/1898)

Camp, John S.   "There is a River," song (5/2/1895)

Carri, Ferdinand	Cavatina for violin, piano, and organ (2/8/1893)
Catenhusen, E.	String Quartet in G, op. 31 (1/29/1895)
Cauffman, Frank G.	*Salambô*, symphonic poem in two parts (part one only) (4/16/1896)
Chadwick, G. W.	*The Miller's Daughter*, overture, preceded by the song (12/10/1890) *Melpomene*, dramatic overture (1/19/1901)
Chapman, William R.	"This Would I Do," song (2/11/1897) "Silence and the Sea," part song (2/11/1897)
Claasen, Arthur	*Hohenfriedberg*, symphonic poem (12/13/1892)
Cole, Rossetter G.	Three movements from Sonata in D for violin and piano (1/29/1895)
Collins, Laura Sedgwick	"Ave Maria" for male quartet (3/25/1892) "A Farewell," "Be Like that Bird," and "Shadowtown," songs (5/2/1895)
Converse, Charles Crozat	*The Annunciation*, overture (12/12/1893)
Coombs, C. Whitney	"Serenade" for tenor, violin, cello, and piano (12/12/1893) "Ave Maria" for soprano solo (4/16/1896)
Coon, Oscar	"Theme and Variations" from String Quartet (12/5/1895)
Cutter, Benjamin F.	Piano trio in A minor, op. 24 (2/18/1894)
Damrosch, Walter	"To Sleep" (Tennyson), song (4/15/1891)
DeKoven, Reginald	Nocturne in A minor for violin and piano (3/25/1892) *Moorish Serenade* for baritone and orchestra (12/12/1893)
D'Ernesti, Titus	"Finale: Exaltation" from Symphony (4/15/1891) Suite for orchestra (12/13/1892)
Dossert, Frank G.	"Desire" and "Chimes," songs (12/9/1891) "Gloria" and "Benedictus" from *Messe solenelle* (4/30/1892) Introduction and Andante Religioso for piano, organ, violin, and cello (2/18/1894)

Dressler, Louis R.   "Fly, Little Song" and "Drink to Me Only with
                              Thine Eyes," songs (12/3/1896)

Dunkley, Ferdinand   "In the Mountains" and "The Village Wake" from
                              Rustic Suite for orchestra (3/14/1894)

Edwards, Julian   Overture to the opera *Elfinella* (12/12/1894)
                              Prelude, *King Réne's* [*sic*] *Daughter* (8/27/1895)

Fairlamb, J. Remington   "The Little Blue Pigeon," song (4/16/1896)

Feininger, Karl   String quartet, op. 30 (3/25/1892)
                              Meeres-Weben (Stimmungsbild) (5/2/1895)
                              Uriel Acosta, overture (2/11/1897)

Felton, Edward Baxter   "The Hostess' Daughter," descriptive dramatic ballad
                              (4/11/1899)

Flagler, I. V.   Concert Piece for Organ (12/10/1890)

Florio, Caryl   String quartet no. 2 in F major (12/5/1895)

Foerster, Adolph M.   Festival March for orchestra (12/9/1891)
                              "Hero and Leander," op. 44, aria (12/15/1897)

Foote, Arthur   "Bugle song" for male quartet (2/8/1893)
                              String Quartet in G minor, op. 4 (5/5/1893)
                              Francesca da Rimini, overture (3/14/1894)
                              Song without words (8/27/1895)
                              Suite in D minor, op. 36, for grand orchestra
                              (4/22/1897 & 12/22/1898)

Franko, Sam   Polonaise for violin solo and orchestra (4/30/1892)

Gärtner, Louis A. von   Piano concerto in F minor (5/2/1895)

Gaynor, Jessie L.   "Spring Song," "Fireflies," and "The Riddle,"
                              songs (4/22/1897)

Gilbert, Henry F.   *Two Negro Idyls*: "Legend" and "Episode" for
                              orchestra (12/3/1896)

Gilchrist, W. W.   Rondo from Suite for piano and orchestra (12/9/1891)
                              Piano quintet in C minor (2/18/1894)
                              Symphony in C, no. 1 (2/11/1897)

Gilder, John Francis   *Tarantelle fantastique* for band (8/27/1895)

Gleason, Frederick Grant *Praise Song* for orchestra (4/30/1892)
March—Processional of the Holy Grail (5/2/1895)
Edris, symphonic poem (12/3/1896)

Gloetzner, Anton *Christ is Risen*, sonata in C minor for organ
(4/22/1897)

Gori, Americo "Kling, Klang," song (4/15/1891)
"Evening Bells" for mixed chorus (4/30/1892)

Hadley, Henry K. *Hector and Andromache*, overture (3/14/1894)
Ballet Suite No. 2 (10/24/1895)
Symphony in F (12/15/1897)
In Bohemia, concert overture (1/19/1901)

Harris, Victor "A Night-Song" and "Entreaty," songs (12/9/1891)
"We Said Farewell" and "Madrigal," songs
(12/13/1892)
"Go, Hold White Roses to Thy Cheek," part song
(3/14/1894 & 12/22/1898)
"A Melody," "Butterflies and Buttercups," and "I
Know not if Moonlight," (12/12/1894)
"Madrigal," "Music, when Soft Voices Die," and
"In Springtime," (8/27/1895)

Hawley, C. B. "Spring Song" and "Marguerite," quartets (2/4/1891)
"Because I Love You, Dear," song (8/27/1895)
"Kate," four-part song (12/5/1895 & 12/22/1898)
"Bugle Song," male quartet (2/8/1893)

Henderson, William J. *Valse lente* for string orchestra (4/15/1891)

Herbert, Victor "Legende" and "Mazourka" for cello and piano
(5/5/1893)
"Ah, Cupid" and "Badinage" (8/27/1895)

Herman, Reinhold L. Overture to *The Bride of Messina* (4/30/1892)
Sonata in D minor, op. 42, for violin and piano
(2/8/1893)
Three movements from *Egyptian Suite* (5/2/1895)
Scenes from the romantic opera *Vineta* (2/11/1897)

Hood, Helen "To a Butterfly" and "A Cottager to her Infant,"
songs (10/24/1895)

Hopkins, Harry Patterson *Death's Dance*, overture (2/9/1898)

Howson, Frank A.   "Amontillado, Vintage 1826," song for baritone and
                              orchestra (12/9/1891)
                          Sampson, sinfonia (12/13/1892)
                          "Amontillado" with euphonium obligato (8/27/1895)
                          An Enemy to the King, fantasia for orchestra
                              (4/22/1897)

Huss, Henry Holden   Scherzo and Romance for cello and piano
                              (12/10/1890)
                          Nuptial March (4/15/1891)
                          Trio in D minor for piano, violin, and cello
                              (3/25/1892)
                          "Minuet," "Etude Romantique," and "Polonaise" for
                              piano (5/5/1893)
                          "Home they brought her warrior dead," song
                              (12/12/1894)

Kelley, Edgar S.   "Chinese Fantasie" from *Aladdin* (4/15/1891)
                          Aladdin, a Chinese suite for orchestra (2/13/1896 &
                              12/22/1898)
                          Gulliver, His Voyage to Lilliput, a symphony
                              (4/16/1896)

Klein, Bruno Oscar   *Concertstück* for piano and orchestra (4/15/1891 &
                              12/22/1898)
                          "Ingeborg's Lament" and "Lead Kindly Light" for
                              soprano and orchestra (12/13/1892)

Kroeger, E. R.   *Sardanapalus*, symphonic overture (12/15/1897)

Lachmund, Carl V.   Tarantella for orchestra (12/12/1894)

Lambert, Alexander   Romanza for cello and piano (2/4/1891)

Lang, Margarent Ruthven   "Hjarlis," ballad (2/18/1894)
                          "Sappho's Prayer to Aphrodite," vocal (10/24/1895)

La Villa, Paolo   "In the Forest," duet (1/29/1895)

Lent, Ernest   *Spinning-Song* for string orchestra (12/9/1891)
                          Rhapsodie Erotique, op. 23 for string orchestra, harp,
                              and horn (12/15/1897)

Levett, D. M.   Pastorale for string orchestra (4/15/1891)
                          Columbus, op. 27, symphonic poem (12/12/1893 &
                              8/27/1895)
                          Harlequinade, morceau characteristique for grand
                              orchestra (2/11/1897)

Lewing, Adele   "Scherzo," "Romanza," and "Characterstück" for
                         piano (4/11/1899)

Lindsley, H. W.   *Galop militaire* (8/27/1895)

Lombard, Louis   "Pastorale" from the operetta *Juliet* (4/30/1892)

Longacre, Lindsay B.   "Poet and Water-Lily" and "Soft, Soft Wind," songs
                         (1/29/1895)

Lucas, Clarence   Larghetto for violin solo and orchestra (12/9/1891)

McCollin, E. G.   "Hymen Late his Love-Knots Selling," part song
                         (5/5/1893)

Manney, Charles Fonteyn "O Mond, erlösch dein goldnes Licht," "Sweetheart,
                         Sigh no more," "A Ditty," songs (2/9/1898)

Martucci, Giuseppe   Piano Quintet, op. 45 (4/11/1899)

Marzo, Eduardo   "Sunrise," op. 36 (12/12/1893 & 12/22/1898)

Miersch, Paul Theodor   *Concertstück* for violin and orchestra (3/14/1894)
                         Indian Rhapsody for orchestra (12/3/1896)
                         Elegy for string orchestra (1/19/1901)

Miller, Russell King   *Fantaisie* for violin and piano (2/8/1893)

Mosenthal, Joseph   "Songs are Sung in My Mind" and "A Faded Rose,"
                         songs (12/9/1891)

Moszkowski, Moritz   Piano Concerto in E, op. 59 (1/19/1901)

Muehlert, Max   "The Shepherd" and "Vespers" from Orchestral suite
                         (12/12/1893)
                         The Crusaders, legend (10/24/1895)

Müller, Carl C.   Scena for tenor from Tennyson's *Maud* (4/15/1891)
                         "Andante tranquillo" and "Scherzo" from
                         Symphony, op. 30 (12/12/1894)
                         Nathan the Wise, overture (4/22/1897)
                         String Quartet, op. 63 (4/11/1899)

Mulligan, William Edward "Thou'rt Like Unto a Flower," song (4/15/1891)

Murio-Celli, Adelina   "True Heart of Mine," song (5/5/1893)
                         "The Bells of Love," romance (1/29/1895)

Neidlinger, W. H.   "Ave Maria" for soprano with cello obligato
                                   (3/25/1892)

Nevin, Arthur   *Lorna Doone*, op. 10, orchestral suite (4/11/1898)

Nevin, Ethelbert   "Wedding Music" (string quartet): allegro
                                   (2/4/1891)
                               "Rappelle-Toi," song (12/12/1893)

Nicholl, H. W.   Grand march from *Elsie; or, the Golden Legend*
                                   (4/30/1892)

Page, N. Clifford   *The Village Fête*, petite suite in B flat for orchestra
                                   (4/16/1896)

Paine, John Knowles   *As you like it*, overture (12/3/1896)

Park, Edna Rosalind   "A Song," "A Memory," "Love's Rapture," songs
                                   (4/11/1899)

Parker, Horatio W.   Overture, *Count Robert de Paris* (12/10/1890)
                               "Andante lento" and "Scherzo" from String quartet
                                   in F major (2/18/1894)
                               Suite in A major, op. 35 (2/8/1893)

Penfield, Smith N.   "In Our Boat" for mixed chorus (4/30/1892)
                               "Beyond" for alto solo with orchestral
                                   accompaniment (3/14/1894)
                               "Summer Reverie" (8/27/1895)
                               Dream Pictures, soprano and orchestra (2/11/1897)

Phelps, E. C.   Orchestral Scene, "Meditation at Mount Vernon"
                                   (12/10/1890)
                               March, *La Fête* (8/27/1895)
                               Tone poem, *Columbus* (10/24/1895)

Pizzi, Emilio   "Gavotte poudrée" and "scherzo" for string quintet
                                   (3/25/1892)
                               "Andante cantabile" and "Allegro moderato" from
                                   Second String Quartet (5/5/1893)

Pratt, Silas G.   Serenade for String Orchestra (12/10/1890)
                               The Tempest, symphonic suite (4/30/1892 &
                                   10/24/1895)

Roeder, Martin   "Souvenir de Venise," song (5/5/1893)
                               "Ballet music" and "Pilgrim March" from the opera
                                   Vera (3/14/1894)

Ruttenber, Charles B.	"The Owl," part song (4/15/1891)
Salter, Sumner	"Homeward," part song for mixed voices (2/4/1891) "Eventide" and "Lesbia Hath a Beaming Eye," duets for alto and tenor (12/13/1892) "O Mellow Moonlight" and "Let My Voice Ring Out" for male quartet (1/29/1895)
Sawyer, Frank E.	"Love Song," "To Sylvia," and "Serenade" (from *Ben Hur*), songs (5/5/1893) "Ma Belle Amie" and "Le Printemps," songs (2/18/1894)
Scharwenka, Xaver	Selections from the opera *Mataswintha* (2/13/1896)
Schnecker, P. A.	"The Shepherdess," song (12/12/1894) "Bedouin Love Song," song (8/27/1895) "Excelsior" for baritone solo (2/11/1897)
Schoenefeld, Henry	*Suite caracteristique* for small orchestra (4/30/1892) *In the Sunny South*, overture (12/3/1896)
Shelley, Harry Rowe	"Thou Knowest Not," song (12/10/1890)
Shepperd, Frank N.	"Still Like Dew at Evening Falling," "To Julia," and "Quick! We Have but a Second," part songs for male voices (3/25/1892)
Smith, C. Wenham	*Gavotte moderne* for orchestra (4/16/1896)
Smith, Gerrit	Selections from *25 Little Songs* (2/4/1891) "A Carriage to Ride in" "Little Children Asleep" "The Toyman of Nuremberg" "The Barley Brownie" "Rain Song" "It is the Voice of my Beloved," Recitative and Air (5/2/1895) "The Night has a Thousand Eyes," "Slumber Song," "There's Nae Lark," (12/22/1898)
Sousa, John Philip	*The Chariot Race*, symphonic poem (8/27/1895) *Fall of Pompeii*, suite (8/27/1895) "In the House of Burbo and Stratinice" "Nydia" "Destruction" *Nymphalin* and *The Coquette* for orchestra (2/11/1897)

Spencer, Fanny M.	"Awake my love" and "When I know that thou art near me," songs (4/30/1892) "Awake," "The Daisy," and "I Love Thee," songs (5/5/1893)
Stanford, C. Villiers	Prelude to *Oedipus Rex* of Sophocles (2/9/1898)
Sternberg, Constantin	Trio in C minor for piano, violin, and cello (2/4/1891)
Van der Stucken, Frank	"Thou'rt like unto a flower," "Pastorale," and "Maiden with the Lips so Rosy," male quartets (12/10/1890)
Venth, Carl	Dedication for violin and piano (2/4/1891) "Minuet," "Gavotte," and "Tambourine" from Suite for Horn, Harp, and string orchestra (12/9/1891) *Prelude* and *Norsk* for orchestra (12/13/1892) Quintet for piano and string quartet (12/5/1895)
Walter, Carl	Scherzo for two pianos (2/4/1891)
Weidig, Adolf	*Sappho of Grillparcer*, overture (2/9/1898)
Wetzler, Hermann Hans	*Engels Konzert*, tone poem (1/19/1901)
Wood, Mary Knight	"Ashes of Roses," "Don't Cry," and "Autumn," songs (3/25/1892) "Love Blows into the Heart," "Afterward," and "Thy Name," songs (4/16/1896)
Woodman, R. Huntington	Serenade for violin, flute, horn, Liszt organ, and piano (4/15/1891) "In the Gray of Easter Even," song (3/25/1892)
Zech, Frederick, Jr.	Concert overture for orchestra (12/9/1891)
Zielinski, Jaroslaw de	"Prelude" and "March" from *Cleopatra*, suite for orchestra (12/9/1891) "Barcarolle" and "Orgie" from *Cleopatra*, suite for orchestra (12/12/1894)

Bibliography

Abbate, Carolyn. "*Tristan* in the Composition of *Pelléas*." *Nineteenth-Century Music* 5 (1981): 117–41.

Adams, Mrs. Crosby. "American Composition in 1877." *Music* 19/4 (February 1901): 432–33.

"Amerikanische Musik und Sänger." *N.Y. Figaro* 10/27 (July 5, 1890): 8.

Arnold, Matthew. "Civilization in the United States." *Nineteenth Century* 23 (April 1888): 481–96.

Badger, Reid. *The Great American Fair: The World's Columbian Exposition and American Culture*. Chicago: Nelson Hall, 1979.

Beckerman, Michael. "Henry Krehbiel, Antonín Dvořák, and the Symphony 'From the New World.'" *Notes* 49/2 (December 1992): 447–73.

Benedictus, M. *Les musiques bizarres à l'Exposition*. Paris: Hartmann, 1889.

Bio-Bibliographical Index of Musicians in the United States of America since Colonial Times. 2nd edition. Washington, DC: Music Section, Pan American Union, 1956.

Biographie universelle des musiciens et bibliographie générale de la musique. 2nd edition. Ed. François-Joseph Fétis. Paris, 1873–1880; reprint Brussels: Culture et Civilisation, 1963.

Blackstone, Sarah J. *Buckskins, Bullets, and Business: A History of Buffalo Bill's Wild West*. Westport, CT: Greenwood, 1986.

Boime, Albert. "The Chocolate Venus, 'Tainted' Pork, the Wine Blight, and the Tariff: Franco-American Stew at the Fair." In *Paris 1889: American Artists at the Universal Exposition*, by Annette Blaugrund. Philadelphia: Pennsylvania Academy of the Fine Arts, 1989.

Bomberger, E. Douglas, ed. *Brainard's Biographies of American Musicians*. Westport, CT, and London: Greenwood Press, 1999.

———. "The German Musical Training of American Students." Ph.D. dissertation, University of Maryland, 1991. UMI 92–25,789.

———. "When American Music Was King of MTNA." *American Music Teacher* 49/3 (December 1999/January 2000): 32–37; 49/4 (February/March 2000): 23–29.

Bonds, Mark Evan. *After Beethoven: Imperatives of Originality in the Symphony*. Cambridge and London: Harvard University Press, 1996.

Brody, Elaine. *Paris: The Musical Kaleidoscope, 1870–1925*. New York: George Braziller, 1987.

Brooks, Van Wyck. "'Highbrow' and 'Lowbrow.'" From *America's Coming of Age* (1915). Reprinted in *Three Essays on America*. New York: E. P. Dutton, 1934, pp. 15–35.

Broyles, Michael. *"Music of the Highest Class": Elitism and Populism in Antebellum Boston*. New Haven, CT: Yale University Press, 1992.

Burr, Willard, Jr. *A Catalogue of American Music, Comprising Carefully Selected Lists of the Best Vocal and Piano-Forte Compositions by American Composers, Giving Key, Grade, Compass and Price*. Philadelphia: Theodore Presser, 1888.

"Calixa Lavallée." *The Musical Courier* 22/4 (January 28, 1891): 75–76.

Carter, Morris. *Isabella Stewart Gardner and Fenway Court*. Boston and New York: Houghton Mifflin, 1925.

Chmaj, Betty E. "Fry versus Dwight: American Music's Debate over Nationality." *American Music* 3/1 (Spring 1985): 63–84.

Cipolla, Wilma Reid. *A Catalog of the Works of Arthur Foote, 1853–1937*. Bibliographies in American Music, No. 6. Detroit: Information Coordinators, 1980.

Crawford, Richard. "Edward MacDowell: Musical Nationalism and an American Tone Poet." *Journal of the American Musicological Society* 44/3 (Fall 1996): 528–60.

Dahlhaus, Carl. *Nineteenth-Century Music*. Trans. J. Bradford Robinson. Wiesbaden, 1980; English edition Berkeley, Los Angeles, and London: University of California Press, 1989.

Dudley, Walter C., and Min Lee. *Tsunami!* 2nd edition. Honolulu: University of Hawai'i Press, 1998.

Dvořák in America: 1892–1895. Ed. John C. Tibbetts. Portland, OR: Amadeus Press, 1993.

Ehrlich, Heinrich. *Modernes Musikleben*. Berlin: Allgemeiner Verein für deutsche Literatur, 1895.

Elson, Louis C. *The History of American Music*. New York and London: Macmillan, 1904; 2nd edition, 1915; revised edition by Arthur Elson, 1925.

Faucett, Bill F. *George Whitefield Chadwick: A Bio-Bibliography*. Bio-Bibliographies in Music, No. 66. Westport, CT, and London: Greenwood, 1998.

———. *George Whitefield Chadwick: His Symphonic Works*. Composers of North America, No. 19. Lanham, MD, and London: Scarecrow, 1995.

"Faut-il haïr l'Amérique?" *Passages* 82 (April 1997): 8–22.

Feldman, Ann E. "Being Heard: Women Composers and Patrons at the 1893 World's Columbian Exposition." *Notes* 47/1 (September 1990): 7–20.

Findling, John E. *Chicago's Great World's Fairs*. Manchester and New York: Manchester University Press, 1994.

Floersheim, Otto. "An American Composers' Society." *The Musical Courier* 7/24 (December 12, 1883): 343.

"The Foreign Craze." *The Musical Courier* 7/26 (December 26, 1883): 375.

Frederick Douglass: Selected Speeches and Writings. Ed. Philip S. Foner. Chicago: Lawrence Hill, 1999.

Furnas, J. C. *The Americans: A Social History of the United States, 1587–1914*. Toronto: Longmans, 1969.

Garraty, John A., and Mark C. Carnes, eds. *American National Biography.* New York and Oxford: Oxford University Press, 1999.

Gatzke, Hans W. *Germany and the United States: A "Special Relationship"?* Cambridge: Harvard University Press, 1980.

Gleason, Frederic Grant. "American Composers." *American Art Journal* 57/25 (October 3, 1891): 398–400.

Goubault, Christian. *La Critique musicale dans la presse française de 1870 à 1914.* Geneva and Paris: Slatkine, 1984.

Grant, Mark N. *Maestros of the Pen: A History of Classical Music Criticism in America.* Boston: Northeastern University Press, 1998.

Greene, Gary A. *Henry Holden Huss: An American Composer's Life.* Composers of North America, No. 13. Metuchen, NJ, and London: Scarecrow, 1995.

Hervey, Arthur. *Alfred Bruneau.* London: John Lane, 1907.

Higham, John. "The Reorientation of American Culture in the 1890's." In *Writing American History: Essays on Modern Scholarship.* Bloomington and London: Indiana University Press, 1970.

Hipsher, Edward Ellsworth. *American Opera and Its Composers.* Philadelphia, 1927; reprint New York: Da Capo, 1978.

Hitchcock, H. Wiley, and Stanley Sadie, eds. *The New Grove Dictionary of American Music.* New York and London: Macmillan, 1986.

Hitchcock, H. Wiley. *Music in the United States: A Historical Introduction.* 3rd edition. Englewood Cliffs, NJ: Prentice-Hall, 1988.

Hoogenboom, Ari, and Olive Hoogenboom, eds. *The Gilded Age.* Englewood Cliffs, NJ: Prentice-Hall, 1967.

Howe, M. A. DeWolfe. *The Boston Symphony Orchestra: An Historical Sketch.* Boston and New York: Houghton Mifflin, 1914.

Hughes, Rupert. *American Composers.* Revised edition. Boston: Page, 1914.

———. "Music in America: XV. The Manuscript Society and its President." *Godey's Magazine* 133 (July 1896): 80–86.

Hume, Paul, and Ruth Hume. "The Great Chicago Piano War." *American Heritage* 21 (1970): 16–21.

Johnson, Allen, and Dumas Malone. *Dictionary of American Biography.* 20 vols. New York: Scribner's Sons, 1927–1995.

Johnson, H. Earle. *First Performances in America to 1900: Works with Orchestra.* Bibliographies in American Music, No. 4. Detroit: College Music Society, 1979.

Jones, F. O., ed. *A Handbook of American Music and Musicians.* Canaseraga, NY, 1886; reprint New York: Da Capo, 1971.

Kearns, William K. *Horatio Parker, 1863–1919: His Life, Music, and Ideas.* Composers of North America, No. 6. Metuchen, NJ, and London: Scarecrow, 1990.

[Krehbiel, Henry E.] "American Composers." *New York Daily Tribune,* June 17, 1888, p. 4.

———. "How to Listen to Wagner's Music: A Suggestion." *Harper's New Monthly* 80/478 (March 1890): 530–36.

———. "The Manuscript Society." *New York Daily Tribune,* December 12, 1890, p. 7.

———. "On the Performance of American Compositions." *New York Daily Tribune,* April 15, 1906, sec. V, p. 4.

———. *Review of the New York Musical Season,* 5 vols. New York and London: Novello, Ewer, 1885/1886–1889/1890.

Krum, Herbert J. "Americanism Musically." *Music* 6/5 (September 1894): 544–47.

Krummel, D. W. et al. *Resources of American Music History: A Directory of Source Materials from Colonial Times to World War II*. Urbana: University of Illinois Press, 1981.

Lahee, Henry Charles. *Annals of Music in America*. Boston, 1922; reprint Freeport, NY: Books for Libraries, 1970.

Lavallée, Calixa. "The Future of Music in America." *The Folio* 30/1 (July 1886): 13.

Lavedan, Henri. "Adieux à Buffalo. " *La Revue illustrée* 8/95 (November 15, 1889): 319–20.

Lawrence, Vera Brodsky. *Strong on Music: The New York Music Scene in the Days of George Templeton Strong*. 3 vols. New York: Oxford University Press, 1988; Chicago and London: The University of Chicago Press, 1995–1999.

Levine, Bruce. *The Spirit of 1848: German Immigrants, Labor Conflict, and the Coming of the Civil War*. Urbana and Chicago: University of Illinois Press, 1992.

Levine, Lawrence W. *Highbrow/ Lowbrow: The Emergence of Cultural Hierarchy in America*. Cambridge: Harvard University Press, 1988.

Levy, Alan H. *Edward MacDowell: An American Master*. Lanham, MD, and London: Scarecrow, 1998.

———. *Musical Nationalism: American Composers' Search for Identity*. Westport, CT, and London: Greenwood, 1983.

Loft, Abram. "Richard Wagner, Theodore Thomas, and the American Centennial." *Musical Quarterly* 37/2 (April 1951): 184–202.

Loring, William C., Jr. *An American Romantic-Realist Abroad: Templeton Strong and His Music*. Composers of North America, No. 4. Lanham, MD, and London: Scarecrow, 1996.

Lowens, Margery Morgan. "The New York Years of Edward MacDowell." Ph.D. dissertation, University of Michigan, 1971. UMI 71–23,812.

Luebke, Frederick C. *Germans in the New World: Essays in the History of Immigration*. Urbana and Chicago: University of Illinois Press, 1990.

Marschalck, Peter. *Deutsche Überseewanderung im 19. Jahrhundert: Ein Beitrag zur soziologischen Theorie der Bevölkerung*. Stuttgart: Ernst Klett, 1973.

Mathews, W. S. B. "The Case of the American Composer." *The Musical Record* (January 1893): 12.

———. "End of Art Music at the Fair." *Music* 4/5 (September 1893): 531–40.

———, ed. *A Hundred Years of Music in America: An Account of Musical Effort in America*. Chicago, 1889; reprint New York: AMS, 1970.

———. "The Musical Congresses." *Music* 4/6 (October 1893): 633–38.

———. "Musical Journalism and Journalists." *Music* 2/3 (July 1892): 232–42; 2/4 (August 1892): 331–45.

Mazzola, Sandy R. "Bands and Orchestras at the World's Columbian Exposition." *American Music* 4/4 (Winter 1986): 407–24.

McColl, Sandra. *Music Criticism in Vienna, 1896–1897: Critically Moving Forms*. Oxford: Clarendon Press, 1996.

McFeeley, William S. *Frederick Douglass*. New York and London: Norton, 1991.

McKinley, Ann. "Music for the Dedication Ceremonies of the World's Columbian Exposition in Chicago, 1892." *American Music* 3/1 (Spring 1985): 42–51.

McLoughlin, William C. *Revivals, Awakenings, and Reform: An Essay on Religion and Social Change in America, 1607–1977*. Chicago and London: University of Chicago Press, 1978.

McPherson, Bruce, and James Klein. *Measure by Measure: A History of New England Conservatory from 1867*. Boston: New England Conservatory, 1995.

Mermet, Émile. *Annuaire de la presse française*. Paris: Mermet, 1889.

Montaignier, Jean-Paul. "Julien Tiersot: Ethnomusicologie à l'Exposition Universelle de 1889." *International Review of the Aesthetics and Sociology of Music* 21/1 (June 1990): 91–100.

Moore, Homer. "How Can American Music Be Developed?" *Music* 1/4 (February 1892): 321–35.

Moos, Jean. "The National Element in Musical Art." *Music* 3/1 (November 1892): 35–44.

———. "The Origin and Growth of National Music." *Music* 1/6 (April 1892): 531–43.

Mussulman, Joseph A. *Music in the Cultured Generation: A Social History of Music in America, 1870–1900.* Evanston, IL: Northwestern University Press, 1971.

Myles, Douglas. *The Great Waves.* New York: McGraw-Hill, 1985.

The National Cyclopaedia of American Biography. 64 vols. New York: James T. White, 1891–1984.

Noel, Édouard and Edmond Stoullig. *Les Annales du théatre et de la musique.* Paris: Charpentier, annual from 1875 to 1916.

Odell, George C. D. *Annals of the New York Stage.* 15 vols. New York: Columbia University Press, 1927–1949.

Osburn, Mary Hubbell. *Ohio Composers and Musical Authors.* Columbus, OH: F. J. Heer, 1942.

Otis, Philo Adams. *The Chicago Symphony Orchestra: Its Organization, Growth, and Development, 1891–1924.* Chicago: Clayton F. Summy, 1924.

Pararas-Carayaunis, George, ed. *Tsunami Glossary: A Glossary of Terms and Acronyms Used in the Tsunami Literature.* Intergovernmental Oceanographic Commission Technical Series, No. 37. Paris: UNESCO, 1991.

Penfield, S[mith] N[ewell]. "The American Composer." *American Art Journal* 63/4 (May 5, 1894): 65-67.

Peoples' [sic] Symphony Concerts: The Story of One of New York's Unique Institutions, 1900–1970. N.p.

Perkins, H. S. *Historical Handbook of the Music Teachers' National Association, 1876–1893.* N.p., [1893].

Pisani, Michael V. "'I'm an Indian Too': Creating Native American Identities in Nineteenth- and Early Twentieth-Century Music." In *The Exotic in Western Music.* Ed. Jonathan Bellman. Boston: Northeastern University Press, 1998, pp. 218-57.

———. "The Indian Music Debate and 'American' Music in the Progressive Era." *College Music Symposium* 37 (1997): 73–93.

Pratt, Waldo Selden, ed. *American Supplement to Grove's Dictionary of Music.* 2nd edition. New York: Macmillan, 1920.

———. *The New Encyclopedia of Music and Musicians.* revised edition. New York: Macmillan, 1929.

Reitano, Joanne. *The Tariff Question in the Gilded Age: The Great Debate of 1888.* University Park: Pennsylvania State University Press, 1994.

Riemann, Hugo. *Riemann Musik-Lexikon.* 12th edition. Ed. Wilibald Gurlitt. Mainz: Schott, 1959–1975.

Riis, Jacob A. *How the Other Half Lives: Studies among the Tenements of New York.* New York: Charles Scribner's Sons, 1890.

Rogers, Clara Kathleen. *The Story of Two Lives: Home, Friends, and Travels.* N.p.: Plimpton Press, 1932.

Rubin, Emanuel. "Jeannette Meyer Thurber (1850–1946): Music for a Democracy." In *Cultivating Music in America: Women Patrons and Activists since 1860*. Ed. Ralph P. Locke and Cyrilla Barr. Berkeley, Los Angeles, and London: University of California Press, 1997, pp. 134–63.

———. Jeannette Meyers [*sic*] Thurber and the National Conservatory of Music." *American Music* 8/3 (Fall 1990): 294–325.

Sadie, Stanley, ed. *The New Grove Dictionary of Music and Musicians*. New York and London: Macmillan, 1980.

———. *The New Grove Dictionary of Opera*. New York and London: Macmillan, 1992.

Saerchinger, César, ed. *International Who's Who in Music and Musical Gazetteer*. New York: Current Literature, 1918.

Saffle, Michael, ed. *Music and Culture in America, 1861–1918*. Essays in American Life, vol. 2. New York and London: Garland, 1998.

Salter, Sumner. "Early Encouragements to American Composers." *The Musical Quarterly* 18/1 (January 1932): 76–105.

———. "The Music Teachers' National Association in Its Early Relation to American Composers." In *Proceedings of the M.T.N.A., Washington, D.C., December 27, 28, 29, 30, 1932*. Ed. Karl W. Gehrkens. Oberlin: MTNA, 1933, pp. 9–34.

Schabas, Ezra. *Theodore Thomas: America's Conductor and Builder of Orchestras, 1835–1905*. Urbana and Chicago: University of Illinois Press, 1989.

Schleifer, Martha Furman. *William Wallace Gilchrist (1846–1916): A Moving Force in the Musical Life of Philadelphia*. Composers of North America, No. 1. Metuchen, NJ, and London: Scarecrow, 1985.

Schmidt, John C. *The Life and Works of John Knowles Paine*. Ann Arbor, MI: UMI Research Press, 1980.

Slonimsky, Nicholas, ed. *Baker's Biographical Dictionary of Musicians*. New York: G. Schirmer, 1940, 1958, 1965, 1992.

Smith, Wilson G. "American Composition." *The Etude* 5/10 (October 1887): 141–42.

———. "American Compositions in the Class and Concert Room." *The Etude* 6/8 (August 1888): 129.

Sonneck, Oscar G. "National Tone-Speech versus Volapük—Which?" trans. Theodore Baker, in *Suum Cuique: Essays in Music*. New York, 1916; reprint Freeport, NY: Books for Libraries Press, 1969.

Standish, Lemuel, ed. *The Old Stoughton Musical Society: An Historical and Informative Record of the Oldest Choral Society in America*. Stoughton, MA: Old Stoughton Musical Society, 1928.

Tawa, Nicholas E. *Arthur Foote: A Musician in the Frame of Time and Place*. Composers of North America, No. 22. Lanham, MD, and London: Scarecrow, 1997.

———. *The Coming of Age of American Art Music: New England's Classical Romanticists*. Contributions to the Study of Music and Dance, No. 22. Westport, CT, and London: Greenwood Press, 1991.

Theodore Thomas: A Musical Autobiography. 2 vols. Ed. George P. Upton. Chicago: McClurg, 1905; abridged reprint New York: Da Capo, 1964.

Thomson, Virgil. *A Virgil Thomson Reader*. Boston: Houghton Mifflin, 1981.

Tibbetts, John C. "The Missing Title Page: Dvořák and the American National Song." In *Music and Culture in America, 1861–1918*. Ed. Michael Saffle. Essays in American Music, vol. 2. New York and London: Garland, 1998. Pp. 343–65.

Tiersot, Julien. *Musiques pittoresques: promenades musicales à l'Exposition de 1889*. Paris: Fischbacher, 1889.

Tischler, Barbara L. *An American Music: The Search for an American Musical Identity*. New York: Oxford Univrsity Press, 1986.

Ulrich, Homer. *A Centennial History of the Music Teachers National Association*. Cincinnati: Music Teachers National Association, 1976.

Upton, William Treat. *Art-Song in America: A Study in the Development of American Music*. Boston and New York: Oliver Ditson, 1930.

Van Cleve, John S. "Americanism in Musical Art." *Music* 15/2 (December 1898): 123–33.

Weichlein, William J. *A Check-list of American Music Periodicals, 1850–1900*. Detroit: Information Coordinators, 1970.

Weimann, Jeanne Madeline. *The Fair Women*. Chicago: Academy Chicago, 1981.

Weld, Arthur. "A Contribution to the Discussion of 'Americanism' in Music." *Music* 5/6 (April 1894): 633–40.

Yellin, Victor Fell. *Chadwick: Yankee Composer*. Washington, DC, and London: Smithsonian Institution Press, 1990.

Zuck, Barbara A. *A History of Musical Americanism*. Ann Arbor, MI: UMI Research Press, 1980.

Index

Chaminade, Cécile, 162.
Chapman, William R. Works:
"Silence and the Sea," 205;
"This Would I Do," 205.
Chicago Conservatory of Music, 180.
Chicago Evening Post, 92.
Chicago Manuscript Society. *See*
Manuscript Society of Chicago.
Chicago Symphony Orchestra, 129,
133, 135, 137, 138, 139, 140.
Chicago Tribune, 137, 138, 151.
Chicago World's Fair. *See* World's
Columbian Exposition of 1893.
Chickering Hall, 30, 35, 40, 147, 169.
Chickering Piano Company, 132.
Chopin, Frederic, 17. Work: Piano
Concerto in F minor, 76.
Der Chorgesang, 93.
Church and Company, 131.
Church of the Holy Trinity,
Brooklyn, 4.
Cincinnati Gazette, 23–24.
Cincinnati May Festivals: 1880, 68;
1882, 68.
Civil War, 2, 4, 140.
Claasen, Arthur. Work: *Hohenfried-
berg*, 205.
Clarke, Hugh A., 76.
Claverack College Conservatory,
175.
Cleveland, Grover, xv.
Cleveland Gesangverein, 89.
Cleveland Philharmonic Society, 89.
coddling of children as a metaphor for
support of American composers,
18, 25, 26, 65, 71.
Cody, "Buffalo Bill," 57–62.
Cole, Rossetter G. Work: Sonata in
D for violin and piano, 205.
Collins, Laura Sedgwick, 147, 162.
Works: "Ave Maria," 205; "Be
Like that Bird," 205; "A Fare-
well," 205; "Shadowtown,"
205.
Columbian Musical Association,
134.
Columbus, Christopher, 128.
composers as conductors of their own
works, 14, 137, 147–48, 149,
150.
Concerthaus Ludwig, Hamburg, 90.
Congress of the United States, xv, 66,
103, 128, 167–68.

Conservatoire national, Paris, 12, 50,
53, 63n.38, 122, 166, 168.
conservatories, 68, 116n.10, 167–68.
Converse, Charles Crozat, 127, 141.
Work: *The Annunciation*, 205.
Cook, Will Marion, 168. Work:
Uncle Tom's Cabin, 140.
Coombs, C. Whitney. Works: "Ave
Maria," 205; "Serenade," 205.
Coon, Oscar. Work: String quartet,
205.
Cooper, James Fenimore, 58.
Copland, Aaron, 170.
copyright law, 5, 11, 12.
cosmopolitan style, 4, 5, 13, 25, 35,
48, 54, 57, 61, 82, 93, 103–4,
105, 108, 110, 114, 115, 151,
169–170.
cowboys, 57–60.
Cranz, August, 104.
Crystal Palace, London, 90.
Cutler, H. S., 76.
Cutter, Benjamin, 97. Work: Piano
trio in A minor, op. 24, 205.

Dahlhaus, Carl, 56, 105.
Damrosch, Frank, 159–61, 182.
Damrosch, Leopold, 30.
Damrosch, Walter, 26, 66, 150, 153,
177, 180. Work: "To Sleep,"
205.
Dana, William H., 75.
Danbé, Jules, 49.
Dannreuther Quartet, 180.
Darcours, Charles, 49, 50, 51, 54.
Davis, George R., 132–33.
Davis, Richard Harding, 131.
Dayas, William H., 34. Work:
Polonaise, 186.
Debussy, Claude, 46, 57, 109–10,
120n.80.
DeKoven, Reginald, 119n.66, 134,
150, 154, 155, 156. Works: "If
Thou Wert With Me," 195;
Moorish Serenade, 205; Noc-
turne in A minor for violin and
piano, 205.
Delibes, Leo, 48.
D'Ernesti, Titus. Works: Suite for
orchestra, 205; Symphony, 205.
Detroit Conservatory of Music, 67,
72n.6, 175, 176.
Detroit Philharmonic Club, 175.

About the Author

E. DOUGLAS BOMBERGER is an Associate Professor of Music at the University of Hawaii at Manoa. The author of many journal articles, he is the editor of *Brainard's Biographies of American Musicians* (Greenwood, 1999).